NERO

A NOVEL

NERO

VINCENT CRONIN

STACEY
INTERNATIONAL

NERO

Stacey International
128 Kensington Church Street
London W8 4BH
Tel: +44(0)20 7221 7166; Fax: +44(0)20 7792 9288
Email: marketing@stacey-international.co.uk
www.stacey-international.co.uk

ISBN: 978 1906768 14 0

edited by Allegra Mostyn-Owen

Printed in Great Britain by CPI Anthony Rowe

CIP Data: A catalogue record for this book
is available from the British Library

FOR CHANTAL

Also by Vincent Cronin

The Golden Honeycomb: A Sicilian Quest (1954)
The Wise Man from the West: Matteo Ricci and his Mission to China (1955)
The Last Migration (1957)
A Pearl to India: The Life of Roberto de Nobili (1959)
The Letter After Z (1960)
A Calendar of Saints (1963)
The Companion Guide to Paris (1963)
Louis XIV (1964)
Four Women in Pursuit of an Ideal (1965) (also published as *The Romantic Way*, 1966)
The Florentine Renaissance (1967)
Mary Portrayed (1968)
The Flowering of the Renaissance (1969)
Napoleon (1971) (also published as *Napoleon Bonaparte: An Intimate Biography*, 1972)
The Horizon Concise History of Italy (1972) (also published as *A Concise History of Italy*, 1973)
Louis and Antoinette (1974)
Catherine, Empress of All the Russias (1978)
The View from Planet Earth: Man Looks at the Cosmos (1981)
Paris on the Eve, 1900-1914 (1989)
The Renaissance (1992)
Paris: City of Light, 1919-1939 (1994)
Chile Rediscovered (2009)

Contents

Foreword

Bronze statues of gods hauled up from deep water, floor mosaics of Roman ladies exercising with dumb-bells, a legionary's letter to his wife hidden in a cleft of Hadrian's Wall – such finds remind us of the part played by chance in our knowledge of the past.

Prominent Romans esteemed literature and added to it with zest. Augustus's autobiography, Tiberius's poems, his brother Germanicus's plays, Claudius's history of the Etruscans – these are a few of the lost writings we should like to have. Firsthand biographies were written, of which only the life of Agricola, governor of Britain, has been preserved thanks possibly to its author's original style rather than his subject.

Seneca stands out among those Romans about whom we would welcome a firsthand biography, for he was arguably the most original thinker and reformer of imperial Rome. The survival of Seneca's writings through the course of the Middle Ages is due to his association with St Paul. That Seneca and St Paul became friends is a tradition dating to the third century AD: their collected correspondence was revered by early authorities though it was later dismissed as fake.

The main facts of Seneca's life are too scanty to form the basis for a factual biography. We know that he was born near the Spanish town of Cordoba (ancient Corduba) probably about 1 AD and that he studied law and philosophy in Rome. After service in Egypt, he was elected to the Senate where he opposed the monarchical pretensions of Caligula, then of Claudius. His marriage to a girl from Gaul was particularly close but did not preclude a romantic attachment to one of Claudius's cousins, for which he was exiled. On his return, he became tutor to the boy later known as Nero, and eventually Nero's chief adviser, winning respect as a philosopher who dared to apply his principles in public life. After refusing to join a conspiracy against Nero, he died in the year 65.

From his extensive writings, we know much about Seneca's character, his moral, political and religious beliefs, and his tastes such as his fondness for swimming and for tables of fine workmanship. All this is valuable but it is tantalizing, indeed unsatisfying. We do not have the connections between his private character and his public achievements and so, ever since his death, Seneca, for all his fame, has remained a puzzling figure. I decided to set the man squarely in the period that shaped him and which he helped to shape by presenting a memoir written by a contemporary with access to Seneca's private papers. The setting would be factual, the main events strictly truthful, but the complexity of Seneca's character would have to be shown in episodes not documented in our sources. So Mela's Memoir of Seneca as I conceive it is largely a work of imagination but of imagination in the service of a true-to-life portrait.

Seneca's life was closely linked with Nero's. As his tutor, he helped shape Nero's character and, when Nero became *princeps*, he was his closest friend and adviser. So much do we learn from the two historians of the period whose work chance has saved, Tacitus and Suetonius. Both esteem Seneca, but they depict Nero as serial killer, arsonist and sexually perverted libertine. The anomaly has long puzzled students. There seems to be something fundamentally incredible at play, as though Prospero had wandered into Shakespeare's *Richard III* as the king's closest adviser.

The puzzle can be explained, I think, if we bear in mind that neither Tacitus nor Suetonius knew Nero and they wrote some thirty years after his death. Both were senators at a time when senatorial rights were under threat. Now towards the end of his short life, Nero made an unwise move which cost him the Senate's hatred. After his death, he became the subject of eulogies from the populace and vituperation from senators and their friends. By drawing exclusively on the latter and adding the stock in trade of Roman calumny – gratuitous carnage and carnal perversion – Tacitus and, to a larger degree, Suetonius, created a bogeyman to warn off any ruler minded to infringe senatorial rights.

If we probe beneath the political message, we discover something of more permanent interest: a series of personal and domestic dramas, of agonising dilemmas that have counterparts in our own day. Amidst these shadows, we discern a living, credible Nero, one who accords with Seneca's writings, which are our only *contemporary* evidence for Nero's principate. This view accords with Trajan's considered opinion that, in five years, Nero did more for Rome than any of his predecessors.

When Paul of Tarsus arrived in Rome to have his appeal case heard by Nero, it is likely that Seneca, as Nero's advisor and a student of religion, would have wished to meet him, and that Paul would have welcomed such a meeting. The tradition that Paul and Seneca became friends is attested in the same period as the tradition that Paul's place of martyrdom was Rome so it deserves to be taken seriously, the more so since Tertullian, writing in the early years of the third century, describes Seneca as '*saepe noster*' – in many ways, one of us.

When Nero was vilified posthumously, Seneca too came in for blame. This would have harmed the whole Seneca clan; it would have been especially painful to Mela, Seneca's younger brother and confidant. It would have been natural for Mela to write and publish the truth about his brother as an act of justice and as the best way of protecting the family name. He was in a position to furnish an intimate portrait and to point up character with dialogue as in theatre, a style already current in Petronius's *Satyricon*. The book that follows is the Memoir I believe Mela might have written.

Vincent Cronin

PART ONE

The Making of Nero

M y setting, my stage and, in part, my subject is Rome. Forget all
you've read and walk with me east from the loop of the Tiber,
make your way into one of the streets winding up the Aventine and,
at the second belvedere, pause for a while. What do you see? Public
buildings in ochre limestone, russet brick houses set in gardens
alongside wattle and daub homes in a tangle of narrow streets:
surprising disorder from people who claim to love order. This medley
sweeps down, along, then up the next hill, the Palatine. And from
there to the next hill. Undulating in three visible dimensions: there
you have Rome.

I'm not forgetting our shops and services. You'd like a six ounce
gold filigree necklace for your wife? Custom-made in a week. A yacht
with a bathroom to each cabin? Launched and ready to cruise in six
months. And for those so inclined, there are sensual pleasures to gratify
the most sophisticated or depraved. A throbbing city, strident, greedy,
brazen but not without humanness, for here no one is destitute. A
city, some would claim, containing everything worth having in life,
her name to be spoken with the reverence Hindus accord to *Om*.

Claudius recently ordered a count of Rome's inhabitants, and the
total when announced startled, amazed and even alarmed. Within its
nine miles of walls were one million inhabitants, to be precise one
million two hundred and thirty. A thousand thousands, surely not
possible, must be some mistake, yet census rolls were there for
anyone to check.

Always glad of a hard nut to crack, our Philosophical Society
debated the implications of a figure with no known precedent. Some

averred that more producers and more buyers added up to more prosperity and so should be welcomed. And quantity should not be viewed as the enemy of quality; in fact it was one of the conditions of improved quality.

Others argued that so large a number must strain to breaking point the supply of free grain; it must reduce the free scope of each citizen, and the city itself to a termite mound.

In the seventh year of Claudius's principate, one of those who had taken a lead in such discussions – but that was some years back – could be seen walking in the direction of the Palatine. He was robustly built, held himself straight and took long strides. His features were regular, unusual only in that the brows swept away from the top of the nose in pronounced parabolas, setting off lively hazel eyes and lending the face authority. Hence his sobriquet, 'Arches'. Thick and curly dark brown hair hinted at a Spanish origin. Looks and bearing were those of someone assured, probably highly placed. Any spy – there might well have been one watching – would have been puzzled by his threadbare gown and still more by his behaviour. The man paused to survey the view behind him or to stare at the façade of a new building; he ran his hand fondly first along a balustrade, then along the withers of one of the many pack donkeys. He showed no interest in souvenir vendors and was evidently not a tourist.

Halfway up the hill, he halted by a food stall and judiciously sniffed the steam rising from a bubbling pan. He asked for a bread and jam fritter, put a hand in his pocket, fumbled for some moments, then apologetically cancelled his order.

'Come without my purse.'

Continuing up the hill, he halted at a flagstone incised with a circle close to the temple of Cybele and from there, fixed his eye on the temple pediment. There he waited until the sun and the tip of the pediment converged: in midsummer this happens at noon. He then walked smartly to a nearby medium-sized brick house flanked by a decorated stone portico.

A flight of ten steps led up to the entrance, where a janitor slid open a panel on his wooden shelter, asked the visitor's name, consulted a list, then came out to look him over. Moments later, he placed both hands under the visitor's armpits and began to slide them slowly down his sides. The other stepped back sharply.

'Frisking you. Standard.'

'Since when?'

The janitor sniggered. 'Where have you been? Years now we've done body search.'

He continued until on the lower right thigh he felt a ridge-like excrescence.

'Aha!'

The visitor cut him short. No weapon, but instead the scar of a battle wound crudely patched up.

The janitor, disappointed, passed him as 'clean' and he was allowed to pass into an anteroom where a clerk in the service of the Secretary for Petitions eyed his shabby dress with distaste.

The visitor gave his name. 'I'm to see Caesar at noon.'

The clerk consulted a paper. 'Not on the list.'

The tone of the visitor's voice hardened. 'Then put me there.'

The clerk shook his head. 'Wednesday... Caesar works all day at his book.'

'I got a personal summons this morning. For noon.'

The clerk sighed annoyance and reached for a file. 'Here we are. It's Caesar's wife you're to see... Better hurry.' He got up quickly. 'Follow me.'

They arrived at Agrippina's private office, a small, sparsely furnished room lit by a north-facing window. A high oak reading desk with a slanting top, a bench against one wall, a niche framing the finely moulded head of a forceful looking man. The floor tiles glistened with sage water, evidently used to clear the room of impurities rather than the fragrant lavender or rose petal essence usual for a lady's apartment.

As the clerk left, the visitor seated himself heavily on the bench. He had landed that morning after two days of storm at sea, sleepless and sick. Exhaustion drooped his eyes, reducing his vision; his head throbbed, his limbs ached and the smell of sage acted on him as a depressant.

He had no idea why he had been summoned. Claudius the public figure he knew, but the lady who had recently become his fourth wife he had never met. As a direct descendant of Augustus, through Augustus's daughter Julia, and as the eldest and favourite child of the popular general Germanicus – who had died young on active service – her very name possessed a double aura of distinction.

A door in the panelling opened quietly and a lady came in. Slightly taller than average, she held her head high on a strong neck, her glossy black hair drawn back from her brow.

The visitor stood up and was inspected. 'So you are Lucius Annaeus Seneca.'

Rome has many good-looking women: what set this one apart was her voice – clear, firm, enunciating each syllable distinctly. Some say that, during her years of adversity, she earned pin money giving elocution lessons to foreign diplomats, and it may well be so.

Stepping up to her lectern desk and selecting a key from the ring on her belt, she lifted the top and took out neatly clipped papers. Lucius remained standing.

'A responsible job has become vacant.' Her voice, thought Lucius, is like lettering on marble. 'I am interviewing candidates, of whom you are one.'

Of all the possible reasons for his summons, this struck my brother as the most improbable. His career was finished, he no longer counted; who would want to employ him? Before he had time to ask, Agrippina said he would learn the nature of the job in due course.

'Your public career I have at hand.' She tapped the file. 'Speak to me of your family, your boyhood. It's detail I want.'

His early years were precious to Lucius, spoken of rarely even to friends. And just when he needed to feel his way back to Rome, the last thing he wanted was to revive long-ago Spain.

He began with the family house. It stood near Corduba, high on the hills, bold against the horizon, built from the local fawn stone, surrounded by olive groves in quincunxes. 'Father belonged to the equestrian order, physically very strong, all muscle, demanding of himself and others. He retired early from practising law and single-handedly enlarged the house, carting the stone himself, mixing the cement and laying the roof-tiles. He was known as the 'wheelbarrow knight'.

'At fifty he married a girl of twenty from a ship-owning family in Gades. She had been highly educated. Her house had its own small theatre where she and her brothers acted little plays of their making, and she had her own flower garden. She was not practical but she was friendly. She took to people easily and liked gentle intelligent conversation. The last person in the world to run a remote country house on a small budget to father's exacting standards. She would go to buy cabbage and apples, become absorbed in the market-woman's latest doings and return without the apples. Suddenly there would be no salt in the house, no flour, no eggs. Thunder turned the unboiled milk, and this caused father to thunder. He was constantly scolding her and she, just as constantly, complained that he was hard on her, impossibly hard, on and on. Visitors would exchange looks but this was their way of expressing a deep attachment, as other couples exchange endearments.'

Lucius saw that Agrippina was taking notes with one hand, the other tapping her desk. Practical hands, the nails cut short. What were they noting? This was Caesar's house, one imprudent word could be used against him. He felt, or thought he felt, the breathlessness of incipient asthma. Stay calm, he ordered, keep control.

'There were three of you; no girls.' Her glance told him to particularize and he began to do so nervously, jerkily.

'The eldest, Novatus: athletic, a leader, the kind who enjoys helping lame ducks. He contended with father. I came next, at ease in that position; but always trying to keep up with Novatus. Last came Mela, small, bright, acquisitive. He'd lend us money for cakes at high interest.

'Father treated us firmly but fairly. No favouritism. For our midmorning apple, he had mother cut each apple in half and mix up the halves before handing them to us.

'He taught self-reliance. We asked for a skittle-alley such as other boys had. "Fine, I'll provide the planks and you can lay them." Which we did.'

'And lessons?'

'A retired schoolmaster came to the house. Cautious, painstaking, a good sort. Composition, history, geography, maths. Novatus liked to hear about battles and the generals who won them. Mela was clever with numbers, he'd solve sums in his head the instant they were chalked on the board. Lessons that posed a puzzle were what interested me. I'd ask why we count in tens and not in sevens like the Iberians, why poets praise horses and look down on the more useful donkey. Doubtless very tiresome. Teacher called Novatus "Master Who Won?" Mela "Master How Much?" and me "Master Why?"

'And after lessons came a different kind of competing. Novatus would lead the three of us against neighbouring teams for cross country, long jump, javelin, swimming. "We have to win!" Novatus would say; that was his way in everything, and most of the time we did win.'

Agrippina looked up from her notes. Her expression in repose is agreeable, thought Lucius, but she doesn't let me see what she's feeling.

'Before settling in Corduba, your father made his name here in the law courts. When Augustus of sacred memory divided government between the Senate and himself as *princeps*, your father sold up and left... Why?'

At last, the dangerous question. Lucius answered warily. 'He considered the title of *princeps* hadn't been properly defined and Augustus's authority would grow to overshadow the Senate's. He took the view that Rome had had her day and that republicanism would survive in provincial towns like Corduba.'

'Yet you returned here for your higher education... Your mother's doing?'

Lucius nodded. 'Father had written half of a valuable text book about Forms of Pleading. Sight of the unfinished manuscript continually irked him. Mother worked on that, persuaded him that a limited stay in Rome would allow him to catch up on new procedures, complete his book and publish it. Then we could go home.'

'So the five of you returned here.'

'To a rented top floor flat.' Then, smiling, 'Mela and I spent our first day racing up and down stairs. We'd never seen a staircase.'

There was no answering smile.

'Secondary school, law school – and after that?'

'Service in Egypt. Then I stood for the Senate and got in.'

'Thanks to the influence of your maternal aunt Sestilia, widow of the Prefect of Egypt.'

Lucius felt surprise that she should know this and pique at being put down.

'In the House, you urged Senate and *princeps* to end their long struggle to be first in the State, to forget past injuries and recriminations. Government, you suggested, should take the two-horse chariot as a model: Senate and *princeps* in pair. You became the Senate's champion against any infringement by the *princeps*. Then one day you went too far... How long were you abroad?'

Was she trying to belittle him again? 'I believe you know.'

'Seven years.'

'Less sixty-eight days.'

'Precision,' she murmured. 'That is good.'

Moistening her lips with the tip of her tongue, she met his eyes and held them. 'I have an only child – Domitius – nine years old; I was married very young. He's gifted and by virtue of his descent – through me – destined for a prominent role. In the past, boys of his rank have been taught by a freedman. For Domitius, with his father no longer alive, I envisage a different class of man and one with political experience. I am offering you for a trial period the position of tutor to my son.'

Had the last sentence come from anyone else, Lucius would have thought he'd misheard, but there could be no mistaking Agrippina's clear diction. So this was the job: he was to tell me later that no proposal had ever caused him such surprise and that he who never stammered found himself fumbling his reply. He was a lawyer, not a schoolmaster, had no child of his own, no qualifications as a teacher, no experience of the classroom...

She interrupted. 'In your last two years... abroad you ran a school for fishermen's sons.'

Lucius explained that he had taught them the rudiments of Latin, reading and writing, quite different from what her son would require.

'Let me be the judge of that.' Stiff, severe.

'But your husband?' It was Claudius who had brought him to trial before his peers and demanded a punitive sentence.

'Domitius is *my* son. *I* decide. Consider my offer with care. Should you prove satisfactory, it might be possible for you to recover your seat in the House and your property. I say "might". You will wish to consult you wife. Remind me of her name... Yes, Paula. Discuss it with her. At noon tomorrow I shall expect your answer.'

She gathered her papers and nodded towards the door to signify that the interview was over.

Agrippina was correct in assuming that Lucius would consult his wife, for her offer would affect her too and adversity had made their marriage a byword for closeness. Yet the mere idea of such a marriage had at first seemed unthinkable. Differences of age, background, fortune and interests, and disapproval by all the Senecas, not least me, precluded it.

That they met at all was one chance in a thousand. Lucius was a rising young senator when the consuls chose him to go to southern Gaul, where bandits had been attacking and looting properties belonging to Roman citizens. He was to report and arrange compensation, an important job for a man of thirty-four and, when he and his staff arrived in Orange, he was invited to parties and made a fuss of. With Novatus better at sport and me at lessons, as a boy Lucius had had no occasion to become conceited but now his new-found status rather turned his head.

From Orange one afternoon he rode to an estate in Veziers consisting of a solid stone house within a walled courtyard, a well-kept farm and an extensive apricot orchard. It belonged to an army officer serving on the Rhine and it was his wife, Marcia, who came out to meet him. Slightly built and slim, she walked stiffly as though with rheumatism. When he stated his mission, she laid a hand trustingly on his arm. 'Why did they do it? We've never harmed anyone. If my husband had been here they'd never have dared.'

Lucius had dealt with several such ladies, shaken and angry yet still savouring the drama. He encouraged her to describe what had happened.

'There were four of them, on horses, with swords. They burned down that courtyard tower, our cattle barn and the river bridge. As a precaution, we'd buried our silver, which is what they were after. They tied up my daughter – brutes! – shut her in a hayloft and said they'd abscond with her unless the silver was produced. She managed to sever the cords on her hands by rubbing against a wall and ran to our neighbours. Next morning, men from the village drove the wretches off with pitchforks and pointed stakes... But they took six valuable ceramic figures.'

Lucius assured her he would itemise all losses and she would receive compensation.

'Also a lovely cleft pole for holding up my laundry. They threw it onto the flames. Why? Why?' This in particular seemed to distress her for she closed her eyes and shook her head. 'Without it I can't hang out my laundry.' Lucius told her he would try to find a replacement.

Marcia showed him to a whitewashed guest room, its furniture plain but solid, its linen scented with lavender. From there, he joined his hostess for supper under a vine pergola.

Marcia's daughter Paula had prepared the meal. She had an oval face with plump rosy cheeks in marked contrast to the pallor of Roman girls. Her slim nose rose slightly at the bridge, she had lively hazel eyes and light brown hair parted at the side and held back by a ribbon-band. She was then aged sixteen and still wore a childish look.

Paula laid a shawl unobtrusively round her mother's shoulders – the evening had turned cool – and as she counted feverfew drops into her mother's glass, Lucius noticed the red burn marks on her wrists. He expressed concern and asked her if she had been very frightened.

She answered shyly. 'At first, yes. Then a gust of wind slammed the hayloft door with a bang and their leader jumped, dropping his sword. He picked it up scowling and started to slash the air – like this – trying to show me how fierce he was. I saw he was just as frightened as me!' She smiled to herself. 'After that it was easy.'

Lucius thought it time to impress. 'Claims are considered alphabetically. Veziers being low on the list, compensation would normally take a full year, but if one happens to know the right persons and make the right noises...' He glanced meaningfully at Marcia, who looked confused and it was Paula who said, 'I think we should wait our turn.'

'As you wish.'

Lucius described his tour, how he had found the *Commentaries* of Julius Caesar, tyrant though he was, a useful guide to Gaul and its troublesome tribes. 'No myth, no eulogy, no purple passages, just hard fact. That's the direction of the future.'

Marcia asked whether there was to be no more poetry.

'Lots, I hope. But separate from factual history. A friend of mine has written a perceptive essay on the subject. Lucilius – you won't have heard of him.'

'Oh but I have.' Marcia's troubled face brightened. 'When we lived in Rome, I went to his lectures. Much above me of course... His slim white hands shaped each phrase like a potter.'

'That's the fellow,' said Lucius, pleasurably surprised that this countrywoman should have literary interests.

Supper culminated in raspberries with soured cream. Lucius enquired where they managed to find ripe berries out of season, to which Paula innocently replied, 'If one happens to know the right bush and make the right noises.'

'Paula!' exclaimed her mother with mild reproof.

Next morning, up early, Lucius asked to see the damaged bridge. Paula said she would take him there but she had work to do first. Unaccustomed to being made to wait, Lucius felt annoyed.

Work consisted of setting up ladders in the apricot orchard and gathering the ripe fruit. Paula was helped by two village girls with whom she chatted and laughed to make their hard task less tedious. Lucius watched from his window, the girls calling to each other in the branches like birds, the fruit orange-pink in the morning sun. Basket after basket was filled, and Lucius came down to help lift them onto an oxcart. Only then could he and Paula head for the river.

Gently flowing clear water purled over boulders between poplars and willows. Lucius spoke of the brown Tiber with its ceaseless traffic of barges. 'How calm it is here! At the centre of things one seldom pauses, seldom gets time to reflect.'

In the shadow of the river bank he pointed out a trout. Paula said her brother fished the river when on leave: he too was in the army.

They arrived at what remained of the bridge. Tie-truss beams of ash and poplar blackened and charred hung askew. Lucius took measurements, made a sketch and itemised the damage.

Paula was needed in the house and Lucius went on alone to examine the remains of the cattle barn and courtyard tower, returning to pack his saddle bags and strap them to his horse. Mother and daughter joined him. Still wishing to impress, Lucius spoke of his exacting schedule, the difficulty of distinguishing valid from fabricated claims, the need to win co-operation from local officials. That evening he would be dining with the provincial governor.

He wished them goodbye. 'One of my secretaries will be in touch.'

Paula played the innocent. 'You have several?'

'One for claims, one for correspondence.'

'I thought you'd need half a dozen at least, at the centre of things.'

Lucius bridled, then saw the flash of fun in her eyes.

'You won't forget my laundry pole?' Marcia inquired anxiously.

'Mother! Lucius Annaeus is a very busy man.'

Back in Orange, Lucius wrote to his aunt Sestilia, who had ambitions for him and entertained on his behalf. 'I expected Provence to be arid and dull. But here the countryside is fertile and wooded. Slim willows and poplar; patches of bugloss. And the light! Compared to ours it's like honey-cake to bread.' He described the apricot-picking, Marcia's concern for her laundry pole.

Sestilia's answer arrived by return. 'Young men don't usually expatiate about landscape. Lucius, I believe you're falling in love. If so, it simply won't do. Were you to belong to one of the oldest families in Rome, you might permit yourself a Gaulish girl from the back of beyond. But should you, a new man, marry a provincial, you might as well say goodbye to political advancement... If you wish to rise higher than that laundry line, return at once.'

The letter caused Lucius to reflect. Until now he had envisaged a conventional marriage, but he couldn't get out of his mind the spirited girl with the teasing laugh who declined to be impressed by rank. He found her twice as alive as most girls he knew, yet half as self-conscious. Attentive to her mother out of affection, not duty. He decided to revisit Veziers.

Lucius had been able to allocate funds without favouritism and he found workmen trying to rebuild the partly burned tower. He brought a strong ash pole with a cleft top for Marcia. 'You remembered!' Her pleasure lasted several minutes and he sensed he had made an ally.

Her maid had the day off and Lucius found Paula preparing a midday meal. She was about to fetch parsley for a sauce and he accompanied her along a sanded path to a trim rectangular plot enclosed by clipped box hedging. 'Thyme, fennel, rosemary...' she pointed out her herbs. A wooden peg with its name stood by each specimen.

'Now what's the matter with you?' She bent over a clump of basil. 'You were watered yesterday and you've got plenty of light, just settle down and be good.' She turned to Lucius, 'You can buy basil in Veziers but it's more fun, don't you think, to find it wild and make it your own... Here are the curative plants. Camomile, feverfew...'

'You know them all, yet you label them?'

'To make things clear... and tidy.'

'You're naturally tidy?'

She laughed. '*Un*tidy... but trying to improve.'

After the midday meal, Marcia went to her room for a siesta and Lucius decided to speak. He began by saying he liked country life just as she clearly did but Rome was where one could be useful and, in politics, entertaining counted for a great deal. 'My Aunt Sestilia does that for me and very well indeed. But ideally it should be one's wife.'

He paused before continuing. 'It's plain you love this house and you're very close to your parents. Could you bear to live away from them?'

'*Far* away?'

'In Rome, say... I have a pleasant apartment but it's always in a mess. Things get mislaid, then lost. I'd like to see it as tidy as your herb garden.'

He saw that he'd put his suggestion clumsily but she chose not to tease him about it, saying simply that they had known each other a very short time.

He agreed. She would wish to reflect. He would write to her. Perhaps she would write to him.

'Care of your correspondence secretary?'

He returned her smile. 'Did you know you're extremely disrespectful?'

'You must learn that from the start.'

It was time for him to leave. Marcia reappeared. He said goodbye and then rode off, encouraged by Paula's 'from the start' and determined to see her again.

Back in Rome, Lucius ran into opposition from Novatus, head of the family since father's death. He had married a consul's daughter and made much of the fact that Paula would bring only a small dowry. No useful connections and doubtless many a cousin cadging favours. I was also against it on the grounds that a country girl would never adapt to the ultra-conventional world of Roman society and would soon be pining for home. But Lucius, who had run for the Senate against father's wishes, again stood out against family. To mother he wrote: 'She is a better person than me. Much better, and if she consented to marry me, some of her goodness might rub off on your son.' I think Lucius sensed he had become too pleased with himself by far and saw the remedy in this teasing adolescent.

Four months later, this impossible marriage took place. Here is the contract:

In accordance with the Julian Law that the purpose of marriage is the procreation of children, Paolinus Pomponius has given in marriage as house-mistress his maiden daughter Paula, whom L. Annaeus Seneca is marrying, and has pledged to him as dowry in gold jewellery a very long earring and necklaces weighing one and a half ounces, and a variety of silver weighing seven staters; and in clothing eight sleeveless tunics and a light cloak; a little flask, a bronze Venus, a mirror and a clothing chest; two oil flasks, fifty-one small boxes, an easy chair, a perfume box, a basket; and her father's servant Heraida, with her tunic and mantle.

Heraida, I should add, was to join Paula only in the second year of marriage.

Paula began to keep house. Brought up to be thrifty and by temperament venturesome, she made for markets on the city outskirts where food was fresher and cheaper. But she possessed almost no sense of direction and kept getting lost, arriving back late and exhausted. Lucius teased her: 'When you think you should turn left, turn right, and vice versa.' For each sortie he drew her a plan. Nothing helped and twice Lucius had to call on a watchman to find her and bring her home.

More serious; Paula, unused to our damp chilly winters, began to contract feverish colds. Refusing to pamper herself, she would continue her usual routine; the cold would get worse, Lucius's doctor would call and insist on her taking to her bed.

Lucius at first was solicitous. He declined invitations, kept her company in the evening and sometimes read to her. But as the winter progressed, he became impatient and one evening decided to attend what promised to be an amusing party.

Shortly before eight he took a bath, put on his best tunic and gown, gave his hair a final brush. He kissed Paula on the brow, rather coolly.

'Where are you going?'

'To Decimus Maximus's.' Even, factual.

'Alone?'

'You obviously aren't well enough to go.'

'No.'

'I told you not to wear a cotton dress. Cotton isn't for March. I said it twice.'

He crossed to the door and paused there. He still felt firm, but did not want to be unkind. Paula had propped her head on one hand, her cheeks were very flushed.

'You go out just as though you weren't married.'

'Many husbands go to parties alone.'

'True... but our marriage was going to be special. We would go through life hand in hand. It was you who said it. And now you go out alone.'

'You're not so ill you cannot be left.'

'No, I am not very ill.'

'Well then.'

'But I shall miss you.'

Her voice was soft though it might reasonably have been a little stiff. The softness of it fell round his shoulders like a lanyard. But he determined to shake free. He needed to get out, away from the coughing and camphorated oil.

'This promises to be an important dinner. Useful contacts. After all, one has an obligation to one's career.'

He left without kissing her. He was determined to have a good time and treated himself to a litter.

Decimus had spared no expense: there were two man-servants in the hall, one to take his cloak, another to hang it. Decimus received him warmly and conversation soon turned to foreign travel. Lucius described a trip to Upper Egypt, monkeys swinging from the palms, a javelin attack by Nubians. Perhaps he exaggerated but, he told himself, within pardonable limits.

After dinner, acrobats performed double backward somersaults and he pictured Paula, limbs aching, barely able to move. Perhaps he should leave. He considered the idea carefully, felt himself frowning. It would be quite unreasonable to leave so soon, rude to Decimus. In order to settle the matter he drank a glass of strong myrtle liqueur and joined in a complicated argument about how best to control arena crowds.

He returned home late, hoping to find Paula asleep. But she was still awake, the bedside lamp casting a glow on her flushed cheeks.

25

She looked at him with feverish eyes, scanning deep behind his forced smile. It was a loving look, but the love was tinged with disappointment, and also with pleading.

He stopped between the door and the bed. 'You look at me as though I'd done something wrong.'

'Have you?'

'What is wrong in going to a party?'

'It is not for me to say.'

'Anyone would think I'd been unfaithful.'

'We were going to be faithful in small things too... weren't we?'

Just that. He tried to hold back, but her look drew him towards her. He knelt and laid his head on the quilted counterpane. Paula had made it; it was neatly done but she had asked more than once whether it looked too home-made. The curtains too. Rome must be frightening sometimes and she needed assurance, tonight more than usual, and what had he done? Slipped away. Slimily. Slimily, no other word. He said to himself, 'By all the gods, Lucius, you're a real twister.'

Paula laid a hot hand lightly on his brow, stroked the edge of his hairline. He felt tears coming and said brokenly, 'I'm sorry. So very very sorry.'

Her face softened into something deeper and stronger than tenderness, a kind of enfolding love that held both past and present, and she drew his head to the soft place between shoulder and breast. The peace, the happiness – in waves! He sensed too a solemnity, as on New Year's Eve. Before he had wanted Paula to be happy, but had not wanted to be troubled making her happy. He had gone on being a bachelor. From tonight, he thought, our marriage will really start.

With the warmth of spring things improved. Guided by Lucius, Paula began to entertain his friends and those he hoped to make his friends. She showed a gift for bringing out the best in others and sidetracking bores without hurting them. As she grew more experienced, she drew conversation away from the intricacies of politics and so evolved a new kind of dinner party, where conversation reached out to a variety of subjects and different views could illuminate without dividing.

These years were a time of stress for Lucius, who was in and out of the Senate. Paula, I have to admit, responded well, supporting him in danger and providing him with the calm he needed for clear thinking. Then came the day when he made his fatal mistake; his peers in the Senate pronounced him guilty of *lèse-majesté*; he sailed for Corsica and his house was sequestered.

Paula leased a tiny apartment in a run-down district and managed to support herself, but only just, by embroidering cushions and coverlets. Two and a half thousand days and nights later, Lucius arrived there penniless from the docks to find a lady who was neither the wife he had left nor wholly a stranger. Like two ships trying to draw alongside in high waves, they veered and yawed and, before there was time to surmount shyness and adjust mistaken preconceptions, an orderly had arrived with the summons to Caesar's House.

From there, two hours later, Lucius now hurried back to his wife, her hair gathered up instead of in the loose curls he had always known, against a background of furniture he did not recognize. Knowing he was famished, she had prepared a late breakfast of oat cakes and milk sweetened with honey and cinnamon. Before asking for his news, she made him sit down to eat.

Lucius summarized his interview with Agrippina succinctly and asked Paula for her views. As was her way, she saw the situation in terms of people. First, Agrippina. Proud of her dashing father and like him strong-minded; her morals – said to be above reproach. But as Augustus's great-granddaughter, could she be sincere in saying she favoured a strong independent Senate? She had married Claudius against the advice of his powerful Secretary of State Narcissus – no friend to the Senate and in charge of Claudius's son Britannicus by his previous wife. Could Agrippina's offer be a ploy: insecure in her new position, might she wish to have a senator to teach her son in the hope of winning support for herself? On the other hand it would surely be unnatural for a mother to subordinate her son's upbringing to political advantage.

'Then Claudius,' she continued. 'Now grown very forgetful he may not recognize you and if he does, won't exactly welcome the man who tried to cut him down to size.

'And Domitius. His father, a not specially gifted governor of Sicily, died of dropsy when Domitius was only four, with all that that implies, and Claudius has little time for the boy, preferring his own son Britannicus.'

Lucius listened attentively. 'So the job's too risky and you think I shouldn't take it?'

'I've guessed at the risks, but only so you know what you'd be in for.'

Lucius thought aloud. In one way, this was a dream post, allowing him to train a boy who would one day wield great influence. But how would it look to his friends? 'Lucius, they will say, has bought his way out of prison by putting his gifts such as they are at the service of a would-be autocrat. He's reneging on his Stoic principles, deserting fellow-senators in the Cato Club, sleeping with the enemy...

'And it would involve a radical change of style. From speaking my mind and taking the lead, I'd have to become circumspect, hold myself in, obey orders from a man who has no reason to like me. Another thing. Drumming dates and irregular verbs into the head of a small boy day after day, what time will there be for Maltha?'

Maltha is a cement prepared from fresh lime, lumps of which are soaked in wine, then pounded with hogs' lard and figs. It is the most tenacious of all cements. Lucius and Paula used the word in a private sense for the invisible cement of civic cohesion which binds a million people together, many of different ethnic groups, each bent on his own interests and advantages, yet managing to live peaceably. It was Lucius's ambition to define civic cohesion and thereby provide a shield against the bloodshed that had long plagued Rome, but so far he had arrived at no satisfactory definition.

Paula: 'Couldn't you live with all that if you knew you were doing a job of lasting value?'

Lucius did not answer, for he was aware of another more daunting obstacle. He had brought Paula seven years of sadness, was uncertain whether he still had her love. If he took the job, instead of making up for lost time by being with her, he would be absent most of the day, she would worry for his safety. She too would surely be suspect to her friends, most of whom belonged to senatorial families. Instead of having helped her by returning, he would be making things worse for her. He didn't see how he could bring himself to do that.

These fears he put to her. Paula admitted that they were justified, but immediately met them. 'I was given to you not just to share your bed and table like a concubine but to be a true partner in your joys and sorrows and ventures... And now you're beside me again, I can make do with fewer or no friends.'

Her words sent Lucius's pulse pounding with elation, relief, admiration. This was the Paula he knew. She hadn't changed. And he hadn't lost her love. All the same he felt he couldn't accept what she offered, and told her so.

Paula was not to be dissuaded. 'You're still living under the dark shadow of Corsica. You can't bring yourself to admit that our life's beginning anew. *Therefore*,' she smilingly emphasized a favourite word of his, 'let's put the soufflé in the oven, as we used to say, and for half an hour forget about it.'

She went to a cupboard in a corner of the room, took out a ludo board, counter and dice and began to set them up on the table.

Lucius gave her a puzzled look. 'At a time like this!'

'We'll think about the dice and who's winning. Left in peace, our selves will slowly merge.'

Lucius shrugged doubtful acceptance and they seated themselves on either side of the board. As they threw dice to see who would start, Lucius thought aloud: 'One thing puzzles me. Agrippina had never seen me in her life and as far as Rome is concerned I might as well be dead. How did she come to consider me for the post?'

Paula lowered her eyes and after a moment raised them to his, just a shade apprehensive. Lucius understood, said nothing, only shook his head a couple of times, smiling to himself, and made the first move of the game.

Two mornings later Lucius stood in a day-room of Caesar's House, waiting to meet his pupil. At Agrippina's call, a boy came running in. He had a chubby face, curly fair hair, pale blue eyes, a small freckled nose, and a firm rounded chin.

Casting a wary look at Lucius, he went to his mother, who put her arm round his shoulders and smoothed a curl away from his brow.

'Your new tutor. What do you say?'

The boy looked Lucius over. 'Any good at wrestling?'

'Three times champion of Corsica.'

'Funny man.' The small nose wrinkled.

'And you?'

'Beat anyone my weight.'

'Domitius performs well at all sports,' purred Agrippina, at which the boy turned a couple of cart wheels, rubbed his palms together, then placed them challengingly on his hips, legs apart.

The previous day, when Lucius accepted the post, Agrippina had informed him of school hours, and what subjects she wished her son to be taught. 'I intend him to be a soldier, like his grandfather,' and her eyes had rested reverently on the wall-niche bust.

They walked along a passage, Agrippina unlocking two doors on the way with keys from her belt and locking them again behind her, and arrived in a room furnished with desks and a lectern, where she introduced Domitius's three classmates, all of patrician families, though Lucius had asked for boys from mixed backgrounds. She then left by another door.

Lucius assigned desks: Domitius in front by the window; next to him Curtius, tall, pale and quiet-looking; behind them Fulvius who had already pulled three or four faces found by the others to be wildly funny, and Gnaeus, puny but reportedly clever.

Lucius said they would begin the day with geography. What did they know about the land of the Pharaohs? The Pyramids – yes, and the obelisk in the Campus Martius. Mummies. The Nile. In the menagerie, the boys had seen a crocodile. They came bigger than that, said Lucius. Sailing up the Nile, he'd seen a boy swimmer attacked by a ten-foot croc.

'Please sir, did you measure it?' asked Domitius, with a wink at Curtius.

'About ten foot. We drove it off with oars but not before it had crunched off a boy's right hand.'

As Lucius described Augustus's conquest of Egypt and how, since then, the *princeps* made himself responsible for bringing Egyptian wheat to feed Rome, Domitius began to look bored. He said he had the sun in his eyes; could he change places with Mad Dog, meaning Fulvius. Lucius agreed and the boys switched. Domitius then complained of a fug and asked for the window to be opened. This done, at a nod from Domitius, Gnaeus began to cough. As the coughing continued, Mad Dog made panting noises while, with studied solicitude, Domitius explained that Gnaeus was in a draught, and he had weak lungs. Soon the boys were arguing noisily for and against the open window.

Lucius told Gnaeus to leave the room and return when he'd stopped coughing, then asked for two hundred words on Egypt.

When Domitius brought up his paper, Lucius looked in dismay at the messy scrawl, with some lines sloping up the page, others down. A five-year-old could have done better. He told Domitius he must learn the importance of order.

'Order's for sissies.'

No. The word came from a line of soldiers drawn up for battle. If the line wasn't orderly they wouldn't win. So order wasn't just for sissies.

Then his handwriting: r's looked like p's, he hadn't closed the loops of his o's and q's.

Domitius defended his writing. It had character – his last tutor said so – and he wasn't going to change it.

'You hope to become a cavalry officer, right? You're in the field and need reinforcements. You write a message to your general. But he can't read your scrawl. Help doesn't arrive…Well?'

Domitius scowled. 'I'd have sent my adjutant,' at which the class tittered.

Lessons continued, Domitius orchestrating stock disruptive practices: humming, yawning, rattling desk tops, passing notes, throwing darts. While checking excesses, Lucius declined to be drawn. He believed that Curtius and Gnaeus, keen to learn, would soon damp down their friend.

At noon the boys broke for play in the courtyard. Here Domitius became a different person. Relaxed and bouncing, he took the lead in organizing tag, then a ball game, performing well and obviously enjoying himself.

In the afternoon arithmetic passed off without protest, but history brought further defiance, Domitius writing only half the required number of words on Hannibal, 'because I have nothing more to say.'

So ended Lucius's first day as tutor to Agrippina's son. As he closed up the classroom, he reflected that previous teachers had probably let the boy get slack, but that could be remedied.

Next morning Lucius arrived to find Domitius with a cork and leather helmet, quartered red and white, tilted on the back of his head. Bobbing up and down, he waved a stylus as though it were a whip. 'Coming up on the far right, he's chasing the favourite. Passed him. Up to the line. Wins by a nose.' He flung up a hand while the others cheered.

Lucius made them settle down and told Domitius to remove the helmet.

'My helmet.'

'But not for indoors.'

'My helmet, my house.'

'My classroom. Pass me the helmet.'

'Brings him good luck, sir,' said Gneaus. 'Can't work well without his helmet.'

Sulkily Domitius removed the helmet and flipped it across the room. Lucius caught it, put it on his lectern and began the day's teaching.

The helmet was more than a disruptive prop, it symbolized the boys' passion for chariot racing. They idolized top charioteers and knew by heart their long lists of victories; they recited the highlights of recent races, evoking daring feats of overtaking and mastering of panicky horses.

To this zest for physical prowess they gave expression in their once-a-week workout in the central gym. After turns on the vaulting horse and parallel bars, Domitius joined an older friend, Marcus Otho, for a wrestling lesson. Stripped to the waist, muscular torsos and slim legs gleaming with oil, the boys listened attentively as their trainer indicated the muscles and pressure points involved in an exacting new hold.

Lucius watched Domitius perform the hold. Otho lunged with his right hand; Domitius seized the exposed right arm at wrist and biceps, pulled smartly, causing Otho to lose balance and somersault onto the matting, then jumped astride the prostrate body, rocking it to one side, then to the other and finally flipped him over onto his back, pinning his shoulder blades to the matting for a count of eight.

When the boys had mastered the hold, they faced up to each other in combat. Though Otho was bigger and heavier, Domitius won two of the three contests. If he can master balance and timing to this degree, he should be able to order his thoughts and handle a pen legibly, Lucius mused.

But as they moved into the third week, it did not happen that way. Aware of his physical prowess, Domitius believed he had no need of academic accomplishments. In fact, from his answers to Lucius's reproofs it seemed that he divided the world into real people, those who won races or athletic events or made useful things (for he admired artisans and liked to hang around their workshops), and the rest who lived at one remove from reality: the drones and sissies.

To 'unreal' subjects such as grammar, Domitius paid little attention and scored badly in the tests that followed. But he was by no means stupid and sharp enough to amuse his classmates with an exact imitation of Lucius dropping the r in certain words – a Spanish habit.

Sensing deliberate resistance, Lucius decided to read out marks at the end of each day. Domitius consistently came last and, as he lost face with his friends, Lucius offered him a chance to pull up by dictating six lines of the *Aeneid* which Domitius had already studied, to be reproduced without mistake.

Domitius, who always hurried, was the first to bring up his copy. He had misspelled words with which he was perfectly familiar, other words had been crossed through or written over so as to render them illegible. As Lucius went through it, he noticed Domitius's defiant look, as though hoping for a clash.

Very well, then. Dismissing the others, Lucius told Domitius to copy twenty lines without fault in a neat hand.

'You'll stay at your desk till you've finished.'

'Can't do that.'

'Why not?'

Darkly, 'You'll see.'

The others fled out, leaving Lucius at his lectern and Domitius humped over a copy of the *Aeneid*.

Presently a manservant came in with a message from Agrippina: this was the afternoon when Domitius joined his mother in the aviary and he should go there without delay. With Lucius's grudging permission, Domitius made a self-satisfied exit.

Lucius decided he must have a serious talk with Agrippina, in fact there was no time to lose. He closed the classroom, left by the outside door and re-entered the house by the front. By now he was familiar with its layout and went directly to the balustrade looking onto a small courtyard enclosed with netting. Here stood two figures whom Lucius could watch unobserved.

Agrippina had a hen minah perched on her wrist and was stroking its rare all-white plumage; facing her, Domitius clasped a black male minah to his shoulder. The birds were speaking, exchanging stylized amorous endearments, their high-pitched voices and occasional mispronunciations adding a touch of comedy.

The performance was evidently still in rehearsal for the birds were made to go through their lines again, and weak points corrected. Then the whole was repeated once more, evidently satisfactorily, for the birds were rewarded with candied fruit.

Other minahs were summoned by name from their perches. Two engaged in a mock argument, snapping and jabbing with their beaks. A third had been trained to make a short speech in a voice uncannily like Agrippina's: fourth, on the wing, plucked a cherry from her lips. All this set off ripples of happy laughter.

As Lucius watched, the scene took on an idyllic quality. Mother and son in an enclosed world of their own, at ease with each other, playing out their affection through the birds they had trained together. It was good to see, yet in one respect disturbing. Domitius, he thought, must see me as an interloper.

Mother and son left the aviary, Agrippina locking the door behind her. While Domitius hurried away for his weekly bath, Agrippina's eye fell on Lucius and, before he could explain his presence, she spoke. She had been surprised, extremely surprised, that Lucius should have kept her son in after class.

Lucius described the boy's resistance to correcting certain bad habits and said a mild punishment had been necessary, such as was usual in schools.

'Domitius is not a "usual" boy. He is spirited and has a full programme. I do not want him to be kept in again.'

Lucius was unprepared for so curt a rebuff and some moments passed before he could reorder his prepared approach. 'I can impart knowledge,' he said, 'and techniques for clear thinking and expression, but for these to "take", a boy must have a certain respect for what his teacher imparts, as for his parents and the gods. *Pietas*. But *pietas* is a value, and a value, I'm sure you'd agree, cannot be proved on the blackboard, it has to be imbibed at home.' Lucius then suggested that Agrippina might wish to help him by reminding Domitius of that aspect of *pietas*.

Agrippina's expression did not change but her neck tendons stiffened and, for the first time since he had known her, Lucius sensed she was angry. 'That would be quite the wrong approach. Domitius and I are very close. He wishes to please me. That is ample incentive for good academic work. It is for you to win my son's respect, and I have no intention of doing that for you. When you have won it, he will heed you. But he is not the sort of boy to be browbeaten... And now I have an appointment.'

Lucius thought Domitius's cavalier attitude to knowledge that didn't interest him might derive from closeness to his mother. If he could somehow show this attitude to be impoverishing, it might remove one hurdle at least between master and pupil.

Once a week Lucius took the boys out of doors and centred his lesson on a sight, such as Romulus's reed-and-wattle hut. For their next outing he chose a walk round Ostia, telling them to keep their eyes open so that they could later write about what they'd seen.

After touring the port and town, the boys opened their packed lunches. Instead of the others' bread, cheese and sausage, Domitius had been provided with breast of duck, diced vegetables in a rich sauce and honey cakes. He insisted on sharing these equally with the others and seemed to take pleasure in doing so: a small incident that Lucius saw as a hopeful sign.

Next day the boys read their essays out aloud, beginning with Curtius. He described the look of the town and its chief buildings: a temple of Neptune decorated with foliage for a coming festival, a new market under construction, a barracks from whence a squad was being marched to duty at the customs. Being the son of a soldier, he was able to identify the squad from their uniforms. He also described prisoners, legs manacled, awaiting shipment overseas.

Fulvius followed. He concentrated on shops in the town and market stalls, what they sold and at what price. He enumerated the many types of fish: tunny, octopus, squid, crab, shrimp. He also described oddities: a busker playing a tibia and drum simultaneously, a fire-swallower and a fat man on a thin donkey, both wearing straw hats.

Gnaeus, who came of a naval family, concerned himself with the port: the way it was organized and administered, the names and provenance of ships berthed, the nature of their cargoes.

Domitius also wrote about the port but from a different angle: the new lighthouse under construction, the different cranes and winches used for loading and unloading freight, and how each worked. He described in detail an iron-beaked naval trireme and identified gulls and other sea birds swooping on scraps discharged from fishing boats.

Lucius then asked the class, 'If I handed your essays to someone who didn't know you, what would he think?'

'That we'd been on different walks,' said Curtius.

'Exactly. Now Domitius, let's take your essay and Fulvius's. Were you aware of the fish market?'

'Yes, but not of the kinds of fish or the prices.'

'Do you think Fulvius saw these or made them up?'

Domitius laughed. 'He's a mad dog but not a liar.'

'The same would hold of Curtius's essay and Gnaeus's. Each of you noticed only what happens to interest you – and this may blind you to important things. Ostia lives by its fish market. So if you had to describe the town to a foreigner, would you draw on your firsthand knowledge or on that plus the knowledge of the class?'

Domitius's answer came grudgingly. 'The second'.

'By combining your view with the observations of the class you get what's called a synoptic view. More complete and no less real than your private view. Still more complete when it draws on knowledge from the past. The synoptic view plays an important part in holding a city together. We'll talk about that another day.'

Continuing to try to widen Domitius's range of acceptance, Lucius turned from the set textbook, Livy, to a more recent work of history.

Agrippina seemed greatly to admire her father – his bust was the one ornament in her office – and Lucius decided to draw on Germanicus's *Memoirs.*

From his victories in the field Lucius passed to the general's literary work – he had translated Greek plays and written poetry. He described how as a student he had watched Germanicus ride in triumph through the streets of Rome, chained prisoners behind his chariot, and noted his extremely ornate dress, which had won him the sobriquet of 'The Peacock'.

Domitius listened with more attention than usual so it came as a shock when he brought up the précis of the lesson, in parts illegible. Yet the boy's expression showed that this time he wasn't trying to provoke. 'If you continue to write what no one can read,' said Lucius, annoyed, 'it's because you've something to hide. Domitius – what are you hiding?'

This brought a spurt of fury. Face contorted, fists clenched, eyes fierce, the boy hissed out a defence. What would he have to hide? Nothing. Not a thing. It was horrible to suggest he had secrets. Was Lucius a teacher – or a spy?

Lucius sensed that his inkling had been correct but that to pursue it now would be harmful. Returning the paper, he said quietly that Domitius should try harder next time.

The following afternoon, answering a summons to her office, Lucius found Agrippina without her usual agreeable expression. Coldly she told him that his history lesson had been unsatisfactory. By dwelling on her father's occasional literary efforts he had given the impression that Germanicus was a dilettante, whereas he had been a soldier through and through.

Here she paused and Lucius thought angrily that she must have heard this from Domitius.

Why, she continued, had Lucius thought fit to speak of her father's taste for ornate and expensive clothing?

'Boys like heroes to have a foible or two. It brings them closer.'

'The sobriquet you chose to cite came from the gutter and you should not have mentioned it. Germanicus was a great man, whom

Domitius must hold up as a model... I feel sure you understand and there will be no repetition of this unfortunate episode.'

Lucius bowed and left, nettled at being told what and what not to teach in words so precisely enunciated they gave the impression of being incontrovertible. As he walked down a passage leading to the hall he met Domitius in sleeveless tunic and shorts, heading for the gym. Lucius stopped him. 'You've been tale-telling to your mother.'

The boy thrust forward his chin. No. He didn't tell tales.

'You do. You want trouble for me with your mother; so you sneak.'

'Don't sneak. Don't, don't.'

'You make it worse by lying.'

'Not lying.'

'I think you are.'

The boy's face turned white. Wrinkling his nose and grimacing, he poked out his tongue; then, backing off, he lowered his head and ran at Lucius, butting him full in the stomach with his forehead and knocking him backwards onto the tiled floor. Then he ran off.

A few mornings later, Domitius failed to show up in class. There had been a late party for Claudius's birthday and Lucius thought he might have overslept. He went to the boy's room: bed empty, drawers left open, clothes trailing on the floor beside muddy boots. A maid had begun to tidy. She said Domitius had gone to wash and, as she stripped the coverlet from the bed, Lucius saw a damp patch in the centre of the undersheet.

This was enemy territory but Lucius happened to have an ally. In one of his first lawsuits, he had taken immense pains to win damages for a small farmer in respect of a cargo of pigs lost at sea. The farmer had come to Lucius's chambers with a gift of two squealing piglets, causing amusement in the Forum, and his gratitude extended to his niece, the maid now tidying Domitius's room.

Lucius asked whether Domitius often wetted his bed. Yes, she said, ever since he has stopped sleeping with his mother; that would be about two years ago, when he was seven.

She had more to tell. Domitius spent almost an hour every early evening with his mother before she went to supper with Claudius.

She often heard laughter. What did they talk about? Mainly about Domitius's lessons. Agrippina insisted on hearing what had happened, every little detail – in order to train his memory, she said.

So maybe Domitius hadn't sneaked. That was good news, though annoying to have accused him mistakenly. As for the bedwetting, it posed troubling questions. What was the boy nervous about? Perhaps the fact that, while he loved his mother, he felt uneasy about the strength and demands of her love for him. And being 'sissy', bedwetting had to be kept secret, adding to his nervousness.

Lucius had been invited to dinner by Agrippina so that he could see Domitius at ease in his home. He arrived before his hostess in the main reception room to find a boy sitting in an alcove, ensconced in a book. When Lucius introduced himself the boy got up politely. This was Britannicus, Claudius's son by his previous wife, three years younger than Domitius but tall for his age. He had a very pale face, long thin nose, short-sighted eyes, and was said to be delicate and clever, evidently too clever to brush his hair.

'I hear you like chess.' The boy nodded pleasantly but, when Lucius suggested they might have a game one day, he said he only played with his father.

They were joined by the boy's tutor, Sosibius. A former slave of Greek origin, he had been charged by Secretary of State Narcissus with turning Britannicus into a prodigy of learning while not overtaxing his body, a trying task that had left Sosibius with shifty eyes, greying hair and needling manner.

'Still having trouble with your dissident pupil?' Sosibius enquired. Lucius chose to ignore the sarcasm. They were settling down, he said evenly, as Domitius came running in to inform his half-brother excitedly that Scythian acrobats were performing on the Aventine: amazing double handsprings. He suggested the two of them go there after dinner. Britannicus looked keen until Sosibius reminded him he was just getting over a cold and the Aventine district was 'insalubrious'.

A tall figure shuffled in looking at the floor, as though absorbed by his thoughts. Since Lucius had last seen him, Claudius had put on weight, especially round the jowls, but at fifty-eight remained a handsome man with big regular features and a full head of white hair.

As a child he had been shy and clumsy. He had never known his father and was considered a muff by his mother and aunts. He stammered and could not sit a horse. But he was studious and as a young man instead of holding public office devoted himself to palaeoroman epigraphy.

When his nephew, *princeps* Gaius, alienated the Senate by demanding the honours due to a god and fell to an assassin's dagger, many senators sought a return to rule by two annually elected consuls, but Caesar's family and associates, as well as the Praetorian Guard speaking for the people of Rome, preferred to retain the principate. In the turmoil following Gaius's murder, Claudius was found hiding in a cupboard and, in the absence of any obvious candidate, hauled off trembling to the Praetorians' camp and there hailed as the new Caesar.

He was unsuited to the job. He stooped, meandered in his speech and dreaded public appearances. But a sense of duty had carried him on.

Claudius crossed the room to embrace Britannicus, then acknowledged Domitius's greeting with a distant nod before turning to Agrippina, who introduced Lucius. He showed no sign of recognizing the man he'd condemned to exile, simply repeating the name Annaeus questioningly and turning to his wife for help. He then gave Lucius a long bleak look. 'You have a pupil who is all brawn and no brain. One sees it in his squat neck.'

They moved to the dining room, Lucius being placed beside Domitius at one table, Britannicus and Sosibius at another, while Claudius reclined on a couch, Agrippina seating herself beside him.

'How was I, my dear?' Claudius had been reviewing the guard.

'You held yourself pretty steady. But your speech dragged.'

'I referred to you twice as Augusta.'

'That is my title.'

'Augusta...' He spoke the name twice slowly, almost sensuously. 'Such overtones!'

He touched her hand and she responded with a kindly glance. 'I sometimes think I interest you as much as one of your ancient inscriptions.'

He seemed to take this seriously and paused before replying. 'Some inscriptions, my dear, have resonance possessed by no living person.'

His taster was sampling a dish of asparagus in a rich cream sauce. Mindful of Gaius's fate, Claudius even had food for his household delivered in locked boxes. The taster having declared the food safe, a manservant served Claudius with a ladleful of asparagus; then, prompted by impatient gestures, he added two more.

Without waiting for his wife, Claudius thrust a handful into his mouth, chewed with gusto and even as he swallowed, followed with a second, then a third, as though fearful of the food being taken from him.

The next dish, partridge pie garnished with mushrooms, he attacked at the same speed, pausing only to declare that the mushrooms were the food of the gods and admonishing Lucius for not having taken any.

Lucius had a healthy appetite himself and liked seeing people enjoy their food, but he had never encountered anything like Claudius's performance. Guzzling on such a scale must indicate a desperate need for reassurance, he thought.

Agrippina was unobtrusively controlling the service, plying Claudius with small talk and keeping an eye on the boys. Noting Domitius's empty plate, she told the servant to give him the last piece of pie, whereupon Britannicus too demanded more. Agrippina pointed out that rich sauces made him sick, so he appealed to his father. 'Good food cannot hurt him,' Claudius said. 'And he needs building up.' Britannicus was given the pie and Lucius saw Agrippina's neck stiffen.

The meal finished, they returned to the living room, where Domitius was handed a bowl of sweets by his mother to pass round. As he offered them to Claudius, he asked permission to play him a new tune on his reed whistle. Claudius took a handful of sweets and said dully that he would listen some other time as he had promised Britannicus a game of chess. Domitius turned away looking hurt and Lucius felt a twinge of sympathy.

The chessmen were set up. Lucius, invited to watch, noted the almost boyish pleasure Claudius took in the game. If his son made an unwise move, he would pounce. 'Moron of morons!' But when one of his own pieces was taken, he would laugh delightedly and ruffle the boy's hair. 'Cunning little rogue!'

Between moves, he spoke to Lucius as to a fellow scholar. Of all subjects, the one he preferred was history. While today was flux, the past remained fixed, solid, reassuring. Lucius suggested that our view of the past was continually being modified by the find of an amphora here, an inscription there.

'Only as regards detail... I go out as little as possible, crowds make me nervous. When I return to my study there are my Etruscans, just as I left them... With the past you know where you are.'

Again Lucius was aware of paradox. This head of State tormented by marrow-deep insecurity – pathetic in a way, cruel in another, for it was that which had led to their fatal confrontation.

The majesty of Rome had long been held sacrosanct, any violation of it counting as treason. This principle had been extended by Augustus to his own person, as head of State. When Claudius became *princeps*, knowing that his then wife was being unfaithful and fearful that she might be subverted in order to overthrow him, he had extended the law to all members of his family.

This Lucius had denounced as unrepublican, Pharaonic, a threat to civic liberty. A complication occurred when Paula had to leave Rome for several months and Lucius, lonely and under stress, formed a romantic attachment with Claudius's niece Julia. Though warned by friends of his danger, he decided to continue the liaison as a means of challenging the law. An informer denounced him and he was tried by the Senate sitting as a court. He had prepared a very powerful and convincing speech to defend his action but Claudius, overstepping his authority, refused to let him deliver it, with the result that he had been declared guilty by the Senate and sentenced to indefinite exile.

Claudius had evidently forgotten this or believed he had acted correctly, for he went on chatting good-humouredly to Lucius, watched from the far side of the room by Domitius. His doctor said he ate too much but with a wife who devised such delicious menus how could a man do otherwise? 'When I go into town I take two bodyguards. One to protect me from assailants, one to protect me from myself, from slipping into a cake shop and spoiling my appetite for dinner.'

Presently he called over Agrippina to complain of pain in his stomach: evidently a familiar occurrence for she left the room and quickly returned with a glass of water and a phial. Pouring its contents into the water, she passed it to Claudius, who drank in sips, pulling a face, then handed the empty glass back with a grateful look. Profiting from the distraction, Britannicus took his father's queen and won the game.

Apparently delighted by his son's astuteness, Claudius rose from his seat. Lucius saw that he was expected to leave, and crossed the room accompanied by Agrippina. At the door she turned to face him. 'Now you have seen what you need to know. Here in his home I will look after Domitius's... future. I count on you to do as much in the classroom.'

'Domitius's future' the pause that preceded the second word and the emphasis she gave it – what could she be getting at? Like everything else, Agrippina kept her emotions under lock and key.

As he walked home, Lucius brought together his thoughts about Domitius. A boy with no father, scorned by his stepfather, denied friendship with his half-brother by the powerful Secretaries opposed to his mother and therefore to him, in a divided household rent by tensions. It followed that Domitius depended on his mother not only for affection today but for a fairer place tomorrow in his own home. Under such pressure, dependent so largely on a woman, no boy could feel secure, and any friendly overture by a newcomer must appear to him as a threat in disguise.

Lucius called on me one evening. Generally he keeps trouble to himself; not that he's insensitive but he controls it, and it's in allusion to that solidity and the marked curve of his brows that he's known to his friends as Arches. A jar of our favourite Salernum beside us on my apartment balcony and Lucius began to talk. We've always been close and when he does unburden, it's usually to me. A banker's views seldom provide a solution but sometimes they clarify.

Domitius had observed Lucius chatting amiably at length to Claudius at the family dinner and concluded that his tutor was not just a tiresome interloper but an ally of the stepfather who had eyes only for Britannicus and daily made Domitius feel small. Someone dangerous, secretly working against him. His attitude had changed from non-cooperation to near-insolent obstruction. If Lucius asked a difficult question, for example, Domitius would have the whole class protrude their upper teeth and wriggle their noses in allusion to Spain's large rabbit population.

'That's how things stand,' Lucius concluded sombrely. But I knew there was more. My brother received no payment, since Agrippina considered his job a privilege, and to make ends meet he had to work late at demanding testamentary cases, a field where he excelled. As a result, the social life for which he and Paula were known, had come to a halt.

'Even if you managed to win this boy's respect,' I said, 'would it be worth it? A nervous little bed-wetter with no father and a possessive mother in whose eyes he can do no wrong...'

Lucius raised a pained hand. 'You don't need to spell it out, Mela.'

But I went to the end. 'A family quarrel is never pretty: in Caesar's House, it could turn very ugly indeed. If I were you, I'd cut my losses before getting further embroiled.'

Lucuis gave a faint laugh. 'Profit and loss. You're right of course according to the account ledgers. The reasonable decision, and I'm tempted to take it. But something holds me back. Something that happened when I was a few years older than Domitius. I was too ashamed of it even to tell you.'

Lucius poured himself more wine and ran fingers back and forth through his thick hair, as though pondering how to begin.

'I was in my second year at law school. I had social ambitions and joined a select dining club, members paying in turn for a weekly dinner. I enjoyed convivial evenings with smart new friends but soon found I was heavily overspending my small allowance. In order to pay club dues I took work three nights a week unloading barges on the Tiber wharf. In time the strain told. I dozed off in class, essays got low marks and the school director warned me that, unless my work improved, I'd be expelled. The solution was obvious but I could not bring myself to resign from the club and lose face.'

After a specially enjoyable evening, during which the diners had returned late, arms linked, singing drinking songs, Lucius was wakened by the school bedmaker, Aelius, a cheery middle-aged fellow with a wizened ear, popular with the students. Aelius drew aside the curtains, predicted fine weather and began to pick up Lucius's clothes from the floor while humming a tune of the day.

Lucius was hung over and, in a spasm of fury, he threw back his bedclothes, ran at Aelius and hit him hard near his wizened ear. 'Shut up, you fool, shut up!' Aelius gave him a terrified look, whereupon Lucius hit him a second time, then a third, before the man ran out.

As boys we had learned to treat domestics fairly, and Lucius had kept to this better than me. As he lay on his bed reliving the scene, he realised that he had done something not only outrageous but quite against the grain of his character. 'Why on earth have I struck a man I've always liked?' he asked himself. 'Am I going mad?' And he recalled how one of our great-aunts, advanced in years, would of an evening recite Ovid to a clump of poplars, convinced that poetry gave them pleasure.

Father was back in Corduba, Novatus at cavalry school. In need of advice and for lack of anything better, he went to the Street of Philosophers. Who to choose? The skeletal fellow with skewers through his cheeks who claimed pain did not exist, the man opposite who affirmed that the secret of the universe lay in the number Six, they and a dozen others boasted of instant solutions. But Lucius distrusted grand claims. He stalked the street until by chance he passed a doorway where a subaltern of the Fifth Legion was taking leave of an older man with effusive thanks, at which the other clicked his tongue self-deprecatingly. 'You did the acting. I was just your prompter.'

Over the door in small letters was written 'ATTALUS A STOIC'. Lucius did not know what a Stoic was, but he liked the man's manner and went in. Attalus was then aged fifty: slightly built, with sloping shoulders, not tall but with a very fine small head: salient blue-grey eyes, aquiline nose, lips that lifted at the corners, a small chin ending in a dewlap. As a young man in the wine trade, his ship had been boarded by Mauretanian pirates and male passengers made prisoners for ransom. Attalus was chained and set to row on a galley, while his family tried to raise the ransom. After three months, the pirates cut off one of his fingers and sent it to his family as a warning.

Attalus's fellow oarsman was a North African: though not specially muscular, for long periods he took the whole weight of their oar while Attalus rested. That way, he survived eight months until the ransom arrived and he was released, having lost a third of his weight. Since the African did not understand a word of Latin, Attalus had been unable to thank him.

The experience changed his life. He became more reflective and asked himself about the link between men that causes a complete stranger to behave altruistically. He began to attend lectures on natural philosophy and eventually found a teacher who gave him satisfactory answers to the questions which perplexed him. After completing his course and coming into a small legacy, he decided to repay his debt by trying to take the weight of their oars from others who might be flagging.

In reply to Lucius's enquiries, Attalus said that he did offer advice about personal problems and left clients to decide on a fee according to their means. He then listened to Lucius as he explained why he had come, and questioned him at length about his background, tastes and ambitions.

At the end of all this, Lucius put the question, 'Why did I repeatedly hit someone I like who'd done me no harm?'

Attalus replied quietly, 'You didn't hit him... It was yourself you hit. Your better self. The contented person you used to be and felt you were no longer capable of being. You saw him in your chirpy bedmaker and, angry at having got yourself into an impossible situation, vented that anger on him.'

What were they going to do about it? Again Attalus had an answer. Lucius should sleep on the floor – on a mat – and refrain from eating meat.

Lucius didn't see how that could help but agreed to try it for a month.

Here Lucius broke off to look pensively over the rooftops at the sinking sun. I guessed his mood was bittersweet, poured him more wine and urged him to continue.

'As you can guess, when I was next at a Club dinner and declined the meat dish, I seemed to be distancing myself from the rest of the Club and they asked me to leave, something I could never have brought myself to do. My finances mended, I gave up my night job, my marks improved.

'But my tutor, who ate with the students, noticed me not touching the meat served up in the canteen which was usually pork because it's cheaper. Now a Jew had recently persuaded a Roman lady to contribute towards restoring the Temple, then pocketed her money and disappeared, whereupon Tiberius had put a ban on Jewish proselytising and on Romans converting. My tutor accused me of infringing this ban.

'I denied the charge but refused to prove my good faith by eating meat. He warned me that even to appear to be breaking the law would damage my chances of success at the bar. I clung to the precept that had already got me out of a bad mess, but finally agreed to go with my tutor to see Attalus.

'Attalus explained there was no magic link between a meat-free diet and a disciplined life. He asked what my favourite foods were and I said oysters and mushrooms. "Give them up," he said, "resume eating meat and continue to sleep on a mat."

'I followed that advice and I assure you, without it, I'd never have passed my exams.'

Here he stopped. After a pause, he smiled self-deprecatingly and awaited my reaction. 'Because you were rescued from a mess you feel an obligation to rescue Domitius?'

'Anyone would.'

'And if you do get him to listen, will you teach him to sleep on a mat?'

'I'll try to take him out of himself, show Rome's need for sound men at the top.'

This he said with marked earnestness. On anything touching Rome, you felt that Lucius *cared*. Cared desperately for the city to be well governed, because that would ensure the wellbeing of every component part.

Was that approach wise, I asked, and cited my elder boy Lucan, brought up to respect the gods, put family before self, imitate Cato who never accepted a sweetener. 'And the result? On his seventeenth birthday he went shopping "to find himself", sampled the swamis, Cynics and half a dozen charlatans and ended by declaring himself an anarchist. Last month he and his group were arrested for urinating on the statue of Chastity... I have opened my eyes. My younger boy is learning to read, write, handle figures. No models, no imperatives. Let the young imbibe morals from society, say I, or they'll end up misfits. They don't want to be told their purpose in life; they'll choose that for themselves.'

Lucius disagreed. Domitius didn't have a father to measure things against. He was confused, and in order to move from confusion to coherence he needed one or more public spirited models personifying sound values.

We had arrived at this impasse before. 'What *are* sound values? What were father's? Farming, thrift, saving, keeping things in the family. Thirty years on, we value bricks and mortar, borrow at low interest, risk investment overseas, partnership with bankers. Apply father's values today and you'd go broke. The same holds all the way down the line. You were brought up to admire flowing, rounded periods, to copy long passages of Cicero. Look at the speeches you've delivered in the House: crisp, concise, some say over-concise. Almost the opposite of Cicero. Not because the Senate has more business to get through than in Cicero's day.'

Lucius objected that, without Cicero, he wouldn't have a style at all, then turned back to what weighed on him. He said he would stick at his job, try to show that he wasn't taking sides in the family quarrel and work to get a fair hearing.

The evening had turned chilly. We drank the last of the wine and went in. Whether it was the wine or the fact of having been able to confide, Lucius left looking less harassed than when he'd arrived.

A few days after our talk, Lucius had an unexpected break. Curtius, a studious boy, enjoyed learning, while Gnaeus, cleverest of the four, knew that he couldn't count on family influence and must do well in his coming-of-age exams if he was to get into the navy. So when Domitius interrupted or tried to ridicule what Lucius said, these two told him to shut up and let the lesson proceed, while Mad Dog, who had acted a claque, realized the wind had turned and now kept quiet.

As the months passed and Domitius grew taller and stronger, he made quite a name by his feats in the gymnasium. While this gave him a certain assurance that compensated for his poor performance in class, it increased his scorn for mere book learning. In response, Lucius launched a trial lesson that wouldn't rely on books.

'Today we'll talk about Rome. You look bored, because you think you know Rome backwards. Let's see if you do. Suppose you want to convey the essentials to a country cousin who's never been here. You might start with maps.' He hung up a street plan on the board. 'That would show him the general layout. Now this.' He hung up one more schematic. 'A tourist's map. Temple of Jupiter, Field of Mars, Theatre of Marcellus and dozens more. He'd have an idea of grandeur... Here's a third. Can you guess what it is?' The boys couldn't. 'The quaestor's plan of the water supply, mostly underground. Why is water important for Rome?'

'For drinking, washing...' said Gnaeus.

'And just as important, for fighting a fire. See the hydrants clearly marked.'

Lucius produced other maps, one for street lighting, one showing all the twenty-four food markets, another stations for men of the watch.

'Suppose you showed all these to your country cousin? "There you have Rome. Now you know." What would he say?'

'You've told us nothing about the people who live there.'

'So you produce voters' lists: Larius, baker, such and such a street, Nevis, copyist, Bootsellers' Row. Columns of names, occupations and addresses. Then your country cousin would want to hear about their intentions... Suppose we compare a city to a public gymnasium. All sorts of people go there. They're strangers to one another but they have a common purpose. Domitius, can you tell us what it is?'

'To get fit and, whatever their sport, to win.'

'Exactly. I believe people choose to live in a city because there they meet competition. Which makes them perform better than if left to themselves.

'But competition brings tension. One million people crowded together, each with his ambitions and fears, each struggling to get ahead of the rest, yet somehow they don't fragment. So what holds Rome together?... Gnaeus?'

'Buying and selling.'

'Commerce. That does play a part. But surely it also intensifies struggle.'

'Having a good time,' said Mad Dog. 'Watching animal fights and racing.'

Lucius pointed out that chariot-races often ended in fist-fights between supporters of the Reds and Greens.

'Rat-catchers then,' continued Mad Dog. 'Without rat-catchers Rome would starve.'

'Domitius, let's hear from you.'

'I say it's the *princeps*. The money in our pockets bears his head and he's head of the army.'

Curtius, the soldier's son, disagreed. The army was hundreds of miles from Rome, only two thousand in the Praetorian Guard were on hand, and not allowed within the walls.

Domitius stuck to his view. Rome had begun as an armed camp, and fear of the army still kept people quiet. Lucius guessed he was repeating what his mother had taught him, and thought it prudent not to argue the point. Instead he spoke of a pamphlet by the King of Bithynia's ambassador after a long posting in Rome. This man had been struck by the low crime rate. Plenty of shouting and verbal disputes in the street, but violence, murder and arson were almost unknown. He attributed that to conscientious policing by the watch.

'At law school we had to write an essay on the ambassador's pamphlet. I went to the captain of the watch to look at the crime figures. The ambassador had got them right but the captain maintained he'd drawn the wrong conclusion. In all Rome, he said, we have two hundred watchmen, only half of them on duty at any one time. That makes seven per district. How can seven watchmen keep an eye on all the rows, quarrels, brawls, feuds of 80,000 people? Impossible. "Like other Mediterranean people," he said, "Romans flare up, but one thing makes them different. Instead of pulling out a knife, they go to law. Why? Because in the courts they know they'll get a fair deal."

'So, back to our first question. What holds Rome together?'

'The law,' said Curtius. 'But that's according to you.'

'Meaning, because I happen to be a lawyer. Good point. So let's go up to the Capitol, where you'll see some of those laws and you'll judge for yourselves.'

Five minutes' walk brought them to the Capitol, the temple of Jupiter in the form of a square, 200 feet on each side, approached by a flight of a hundred steps, the gates bronze, ceiling and tiles gilt. An annexe at the north corner served as a repository of the law, rows of bronze tablets clamped to one wall.

Lucius began with some of the oldest and most elementary, in archaic script. This one laid down that two plough-widths must be left clear at the edge of every field. Why? To allow for a footpath. This one prohibited incestuous marriages, for they would weaken the stock. A third safeguarded truth-telling in courts of law: anyone guilty of perjury would be punished by being hurled to death from the Tarpeian Rock, a few yards from the Temple.

He described more recent laws: the procedure and tax for freeing a slave; the right of citizens abroad to appeal to the Senate if they considered their governor remiss or unfair: a veteran's right to land at the end of his engagement. All were there for everyone to see and obey.

Curtius tilted an eye. 'Except the *princeps*?'

'Including him. The *princeps* governs the city of Rome and frontier provinces: the rest, the Senate governs. The *princeps* is also ex officio a member of the Senate and so can vote in lawmaking. That dual role gives him much authority, but doesn't entitle him to break the law.'

Gnaeus asked to see the law on treason. Lucius produced and explained it. Treason was a capital offence against the safety of Rome or the safety of the head of state. In the latter case, the *princeps* might try the offender privately, with power of life and death.

Gnaeus and Curtius exchanged dark glances, Domitus turned away, Mad Dog flopped his head to one side, up and down, as though his neck had been severed.

But this was a subject Agrippina would not wish explored. 'Now we'll see where the laws are made,' said Lucius, leading the way through bronze doors into the Temple of Jupiter Best and Greatest, its vast marble floor segmented by shafts of light from apertures high up. Along each side stood benches, some of them occupied by senators. At the far end, beside a golden statue of the goddess of Victory, stood the senior consul, regulating a debate in progress. For Lucius, who had last spoken from its floor on the day before his exile, it was a moving moment.

'Who can tell me why senators do their business here in a temple?' No one replying, Mad Dog smiled brightly. 'Plenty of room and keeps out the rain.'

'But why in the temple of Jupiter?... Because he keeps order in the sky and favoured us Romans in war and peace, even sending down his eagle to designate the right person for high office. So senators have chosen to place themselves under his watchful eye and begin each session by invoking his guidance.'

Lucius explained the subject being debated: how to reduce fatal accidents at sea. Some were calling for tighter inspection of ships, some for a proper school for training seamen, some for restricting voyages during winter months.

'How will they agree? They won't. Remember your Ostia walk, each of you adding to a synoptic whole. The same will happen here. Then they'll be able to vote knowledgeably and if a majority favour the bill, it becomes law.'

Curtius had a question. The Senate here, and five hundred yards away, the *princeps*. Legislature and executive, each with its duties and rights. But suppose one started to impose on the other?

'Then you get real trouble. Who can tell me why?'

'No one above them,' Gnaeus suggested. 'No higher authority to decide who's right.'

'Exactly. So it's important to try to forestall any infringement.' Carried away by the aura of the hall, Lucius remembered happier days. 'For seventeen years I worked here with my friends in the Cato Club, and more than once I think I can claim to have acted in time.'

Through all this, Domitius had been looking restless and now red-faced, he erupted. 'It was Caesar who acted. All *you* did was talk, talk, talk. Lawyer's boring jargon. And look how you've ended up.'

The boy's contempt for him – or was it anger at hearing views different from his mother's – took Lucius aback. He swallowed hard before replying quietly, 'Insolence won't win you an argument.'

'But it can topple swagger.'

The other boys looked disconcerted, perhaps shocked by Domitius's outburst, perhaps believing it justified. Either way, thought Lucius, the sweep of our lesson's been lost.

In silence they left the solemn hall for the bustle of a crowded street. In the old days, Lucius would slip out for an occasional cake from a nearby confectioner's. He wished to mark the day as special so that at least his point about the importance of law would be remembered and now he bought cakes for them all. Domitius however refused his, saying he wasn't hungry.

That evening was not a happy one in Lucius's apartment. Paula guessed what was wrong but was hoping Lucius would tell her. Lucius stuck to his rule – part pride, part unselfishness – of not burdening her with his professional troubles, if you could so dignify a schoolboy's cheek.

Heavy rain had fallen the day before, causing a stain to form where the ceiling met the top of a dormer window. The repair man had promised to come, but hadn't: it was raining again, the stain growing larger and darker by the hour, like a graph of their pinched circumstances and present unease.

When tense or troubled, Lucius had a curious habit of winding himself in one of the living room curtains. One turn, two, three, slowly, until the curtain was wrapped tight round his body, then he would let himself unwind, quite fast. After a pause he would repeat the performance. He maintained it was a valuable exercise, easing tension and clarifying his thoughts.

If this calmed Lucius, it set Paula's nerves on edge. She felt sure he would end by pulling down the curtain rail. Finally she could bear to watch no longer and sought calm in a no less curious way. Removing her slippers, she picked away with her fingers at the thickened skin on the soles of her feet. This habit grated on Lucius's nerves, invariably eliciting the same exchange. The skin was there to protect her soles, she was doing permanent damage to her feet and Paula's riposte: not at all, it was dead skin and had to be sloughed off, like a snake's.

I had witnessed this situation more than once: at first it had struck me as funny; now I regard it as a useful safety valve.

Unlike Lucius, Paula was never easy with silence, and it was she who eventually spoke. 'When are you going to tell me what's wrong?'

Her tone had an accusing note and, half-way through his curtain twist, Lucius replied defensively, 'Nothing's wrong. A problem needs to be solved, that's all. And I intend to solve it.'

'Without pulling down the ceiling I hope.' Then, more conciliatory. 'Perhaps I could help ... if you can bring yourself to confide in your wife.'

Lucius hesitated. Almost the last thing he wanted was to display his situation in all its pettiness and confess that it had thrown him. On the other hand, aware that Paula was on edge, even less did he want a domestic row.

Unwinding, he sat down beside her and told her the essentials, how he now had the class listening, the others receptive but not Domitius, who treated everything Lucius taught as suspect, so that his lessons were producing just the opposite of the intended effect.

'You say Agrippina has turned Domitius against you. But why should she want to? She needs her son to be well educated and chose you from a long list of candidates to impart it. She may disagree with some of your views, but that's her privilege as your employer.'

'Then how to explain his hostility? It's not normal in a healthy young boy.' Paula suggested that Lucius was looking at it from a grown-up's perspective and overcomplicating. 'See it from a boy's point of view. Who does he esteem? Who are his models?'

'Charioteers, I suppose. Wrestlers, anyone good at sport.'

'Does he know how to swim?'

Lucius said probably not, since it was not a usual part of patrician upbringing.

'That is something you could teach him.'

As a boy, Lucius had been taught to swim by Novatus in the Baetis River, and it was the one sport he did better than his brother. He swam every summer at Baiae and, however cold the weather, celebrated New Year by taking a plunge in the Tiber.

Lucius said he doubted whether Agrippina, conservative as she was, would permit her son to swim, but Paula clung to her scheme, urging Lucius to find some way of getting Agrippina's approval and by bedtime had persuaded him to try.

City-born Romans are not at ease with water and have never produced seafarers comparable to Spaniards. Water to them means shipwrecks, drowning and no known grave. However, after being shown a passage in her father's *Memoirs* where he describes swimming the Meuse by night to launch a surprise attack, Agrippina had granted permission and ten days later, on a warm afternoon, tutor and pupil stripped beside a pool of the Tiber up river from Rome, Lucius to his running shorts, Domitius to his wrestler's jockstrap.

Lucius tied an inflated goatskin under the boy's armpits, to which was attached a looped cord, and gave him a hand down the bank into shallow water, noticing that his teeth were chattering from fear. Taking a stout bamboo pole, he pushed the end of it through the protruding loop of the cord so that he could give Domitius additional buoyancy.

The lesson began. Domitius still in his depth let himself float but instead of making the arm movements he'd been taught and taking deep regular breaths, he splashed, spluttered, floundered and shouted for help. Lucius quickly drew him back with the pole, explained again what he should do and they tried again.

It proved a slow business. Domitius kept fighting the water as though it were a wrestling opponent and after repeated duckings climbed up on the bank to rest, obviously viewing the whole undertaking as a waste of time and energy.

Lucius decided he needed encouragement. Diving from the bank, he swam the thirty yards' width of the river overarm and returned underwater, surfacing just once.

Lucius flopped on the bank in the shade of an alder, breathing heavily, supporting his head on his bent arms. He awaited some snide remark – 'Didn't you bring us a fish?' – but instead felt a boy's hand on his flexed left biceps; the hand pressed, gripped tight then withdrew.

Lucius had his father's deep chest, indispensable for a public orator but when the atmospheric pressure dropped he had to fight off catarrh and breathlessness. He had a muscular upper body and Domitius was doubtless impressed by his firm biceps, given the respectful tone of his voice and for the first time a question that showed interest in Lucius as a person.

'Who taught you to scud like an otter?'

Lucius described how he and Novatus used to race against neighbouring boys and practise for it all year. 'Competition – remember?... Nothing to stop you doing the same.'

Domitius showed a willingness to learn. Slowly he overcame his fear of drowning and succeeded in swimming overarm passably well. What came next? Lucius showed him backstroke, somersaults, twist dives.

On their way to and from the river Domitius would enquire about life in Corduba and wanted to hear exactly how olive oil was made.

One day Lucius brought a small melon to share and brought out a knife from his gown. A single blade folded out by turning a ring on the silver casing. Domitius asked to examine it, praised the workmanship and enquired about its origin.

Lucius said the knife had been Cicero's. While trying to make peace between Senate and the military, he had been decapitated and, when his effects were sold, it had been bought by Lucius's father, who had bequeathed it to his son.

'Who decapitated him?'

'Augustus and Mark Anthony. They had his tongue and hands nailed to the rostra for all Rome to mock... But such things are best forgotten.'

'Then why do you carry the knife?'

'To remind me of what he tried to achieve.'

As their outings continued and Domitius was patiently taught new skills, his attitude to Lucius grew less hostile. With a boy's strange logic he seemed to have reasoned that, since Lucius performed so well in the water, what he said in class might be worth listening to and since Lucius took such trouble to help him in the river, it would only be fair for him to take trouble at his desk. Nothing of this happened quickly. But the river had become a visible, tangible link, the vocabulary of swimming terms a shared language and Lucius began to tackle his original goal: the serious education of a youth who would one day be influential.

A large secluded pond fringed with reeds in the Gardens of Marcellus, north of the city wall, sustaining an abundance of insects, tadpoles, frogs, fish, duck and other birds served for nature studies. After a third afternoon of observing, Lucius asked for views of the pond and its creatures.

Domitius answered first with an excited report on a heron. He'd watched the wide-winged bird circle, choosing its moment to drop among the reeds. There it defecated on its legs, turning them shiny white, and stepped into the water. Waited there patiently, shifting its legs very slightly to make them glisten. A big perch noticed and, mistaking the legs for the scales of a fish, swam close. One quick thrust of its pointed beak and off it flew with the fish. The heron, he concluded, was certainly lord of the pond.

'Why,' asked Lucius, 'are you always looking for a winner?'

The question seemed to surprise Domitius. 'There has to be a winner. In a race, a contest, a game. Everywhere.'

'Let's look more closely at your heron. After catching his perch, he at once flies off. He knows he's been observed by his enemy the fox, and he won't return that day. Perhaps not for several days. Because of his fear he fishes only now and then. This keeps the perch from overpopulating but doesn't eliminate them.

'So the heron can't be called lord of the pond. But nor can the fox, because he has an enemy too – man: in this case the warden in charge of the gardens.'

While Domitius looked for an answer, the others spoke and Lucius summed up their views.

'One of you likens the pond to a rich man's swimming pool, delicious food on floating tables. The School of Cynics would agree. They argue that man is an animal, animals don't work, don't build houses, don't wear clothes, therefore man should do none of those things. But you who've studied logic will spot the flaw. Remember our catch syllogism: mouse is a syllable; a syllable doesn't eat cheese; therefore a mouse doesn't eat cheese.

'Gnaeus, you view the pond as a prison. Epicurus thought much like that. He said that everything, including each one of us, even our thoughts, are composed of tiny material particles – he called them atoms each hooked to other atoms, and these move in predestined patterns. So in everything we think or do, we're prisoners of the hooked atoms. The gods we believe exist are only god-shaped atoms in our brain. Since we can't break or alter the atoms' movements, the best Epicureans can do is enjoy the good things of life with like-minded friends.'

'Pluck each day like a fruit,' said Curtius, airing his knowledge of Horace.

But hooks worried the others. Grappling hooks on naval triremes and hooks for lifting quarried marble – these they knew – and on a smaller scale hooks they fished with and hooks on ladies' earrings. But hooks in nature stumped them until one cited the spider's ability to suspend a fat body by hooking the tips of two slim legs round a vine shoot. Perhaps tiny atom hooks were after all conceivable.

Lucius returned to Domitius. 'Your battlefield pond produces strange ripples. If man decides he inhabits a world where enmity is the norm, he will be on his guard against his fellows. He'll distrust their opinions. He'll say, I shall decide my own set of values based only on my private experience. I'm to be the measure of all things. That's what the School of Sophists teaches.

'Curtius, your view of an orderly pond, and of the order as immensely complex, balanced on a knife-edge, that was something Zeno the Stoic shared. He went on to ask, how did the order get there? He and his school were unconvinced by Epicurus's chance-linking of atoms and Cicero answered like this: "As well contend that words and verses come from the chance shifting of the 21 letters of the alphabet, and that the poems of Ennius could be produced by shaking together a sufficient quantity of these in a box, then tipping them out on the ground. Chance would hardly produce a single verse."

'Zeno preferred a different explanation of order. The ingredients of life are so numerous, and so many different forms of life are held in balance, with no one kind predominating so as to destroy the others, that it is reasonable to suppose some powerful Mind has been, and still is, at work and that this Mind is beneficent. Zeno gave it the name Pneuma, Greek for Breath of Life or Spirit.'

The class looked puzzled and Curtius asked, 'Has anyone seen Pneuma?'

'No. But we can't see the wind either or hear a dog's high-pitched whistle.'

Here I must explain how Lucius became drawn to Stoic teaching. When he went to pay Attalus and thank him for getting him out of his mess at law school, he thought they were seeing the last of each other, but Attalus encouraged him to speak of Spain. When Lucius mentioned having stayed with his grandmother in Gades, Attalus asked whether he'd watched the tide sweep in three days after a full moon. Lucius said he had and, like everyone else, marvelled at the water's seven-foot rise. Attalus then revealed that he had studied under the famous Panaetius, who believed some regulating force connects the ocean tides and the moon's phases, and if so, it would be reasonable to infer that the same force operated on earth. Attalus said he was giving six evening talks on the subject.

Lucius, who had come to respect Attalus, attended the lectures and there got his first glimpse of Stoic cosmology, which holds that God is not outside our everyday world – up on Mount Olympus or beyond the stars – but continually present here below as a force for order and harmony permeating all living things. The perceptible sign of this is the air we breathe and share with others, and if we choose we can help to extend that order around us, first having made our private life orderly by learning indifference to comfort and discomfort.

'Unlike the Epicurean,' Lucius continued, 'the Stoic has ideas about the State. When men decided to go beyond nature, say to build a city, they can nevertheless learn from nature. They see different species cohabiting, no one of them predominant, they see interdependence, tolerance of precious individuality, complexity arranged in such a way as to safeguard continuity. If they apply those lessons well, they will have a city that coheres.'

Domitius frowned. 'Why do you go on and on about cohesion?'

'Because it matters. The Civil War is just one page in your history book, but for a hundred thousand young Romans it was the last page in their book of life. Rome split apart – though no one believed that could happen. Two camps: Senate and Julius the dictator. When I was your age, my father took me to Muneda, not far from our home, an oval of stone and wooden ramparts where the last remnants of the Senate's army held out for two days against Caesar before succumbing. Caesar had five hundred prisoners decapitated and their heads stuck on poles around the camp. There they remained till they stank and rotted away. Twelve of our clan were among them, brave men all.'

Domitius was growing to adolescence and soon would be entering on his coming-of-age rites. From five foot two inches, when Lucius first saw him, he had grown to five foot eight, from ninety-eight pounds to a hundred and twenty-six. He now had a dimple in his cleft chin, his fair hair had less of a curl and dark fluff was appearing on his upper lip.

He had become a willing pupil. He had made progress in maths and geography but was still poor at handling ideas and developing an argument logically. His essays strung together facts, unconnected by anything save the emotion of the moment. A gift for mimicry which Lucius had noticed in the aviary made him shine when they read through a play in class. His interest in horses and racing had continued, and he now had a horse of his own, a firm-limbed Asturian grey with a fast short pace named Phaeton. To Lucius, he had proudly shown off its snow-white blaze and socks, flat mouth, neck all dash and swagger. As it arched its long plumed tail to defecate, he announced proudly: 'Even its droppings smell sweet.'

Lucius knew that adolescence is a time of confusion. No idea who or what you are; you've done nothing, yet everything's expected of you. And if you don't have a father to measure things against you're even more confused.

Claudius still gave all his attention to Britannicus, who was turning out something of a prodigy, and was never short of a wounding remark for his stepson. As a result Domitius sought reassurance from Lucius and was now beginning to see him in a complementary role to that of his mother, *in loco parentis*. Lucius thought this would help Domitius but felt afraid for himself. Agrippina had recently hinted that she might soon give him back his property and seat in the Senate, and for this he knew he must continue to satisfy her. Already, however, she had blamed him for training her son to respect others' opinions, whereas she wished him to lead and command, and if she now found Domitius sharing with his tutor the affection and trust she wanted only for herself, it might wreck his chances of reinstatement or worse. Lucius thought gloomily, if Domitius is hovering between larva and imago, I'm hovering between employment and disgrace.

One result of Domitius's need for reassurance was that, in the zigzag way of adolescents, he now treated everything Lucius said in class with respect. At first Lucius felt pleased – this after all was what he'd been working for from the start. But only at first.

Matters came to a head when Lucius gave a lesson on why the Greeks made war on Troy. Scholars of the subject had come up with six possible motives. These Lucius described, then asked the class to write about the one they considered most likely. Afterwards Lucius questioned Domitius. 'You say the Greeks besieged Troy to capture its trade. What goods passed through Troy?' 'Furs.' 'Only furs? Surely there must have been other goods.' Domitius agreed but didn't know what. 'If you didn't know, why did you choose that explanation?' 'It was the one you described warmly, as though you considered it correct.'

Shaking his head and repressing a smile, Lucius squeezed the boy's arm and asked him to listen to a true story.

'There are copper mines around Corduba, and our family owns one. Country people consider mining wrong and unnatural: raping mother earth and cheating what is hers. So father rarely spoke of our mine except to warn us boys not to go near it. Out tutor Timotheus added a second caveat. The stars in their regular circling of the heavens embody perfection and, the further away things are from the stars, the more imperfect they become. Under the earth lies only ugliness and uselessness: rot, worms, moles, snakes. Nothing to learn there, so keep away.

'I believed Timotheus, but I was curious to see for myself. Two men worked the mine and one day I persuaded them to take me down. Rickety ladders led to narrow galleries where we had to bend double. These opened up to a more spacious part that was being worked and here the men raised their lamps to the walls.

'I'd seen phosphorescence in the waves at Gades; here in the seams of ore was the same kind of inner light, twisting and turning like a shoal of gleaming fish, on and on into the dark. So the mine wasn't ugly, it had its own kind of beauty. I saw it as a world hidden away but signaling to man with its glistening that here was something useful to us.

'Later I watched the ore being smelted, refined, compounded with tin and hammered into coins in the Corduba mint. Learned about other metals, iron especially, how without it there'd be no tools for farming and we'd still be eating acorns. The point for you is this. Pay attention to what I say in class but, when I express an opinion, think it out for yourself. Will you do that?'

Domitius smiled. 'You want me to become a dissident?' But he nodded affirmatively.

On the morning of his coming-of-age, the family barber came to Domitius's bathroom, sat him on a stool and, watched closely by Agrippina, shaved off the fluff from his cheeks and chin. The shavings he carefully placed in a small ivory box belonging to Agrippina. This she carried to her apartment, to be placed alongside other precious family mementoes.

Next the family tailor arrived, carrying the white gown for which Domitius had been measured up a month earlier. After drawing attention to its fashionable cut, the regularity of its pleats and its neatly stitched seams, he helped Domitius put it on, explaining that he was now under full sail and must navigate accordingly. In a hurry or a stiff wind he must be sure to gather up the lower folds in one hand.

Domitius quickly got the hang of his gown and went down to breakfast. Then family and friends arrived and formed themselves into a procession which escorted Domitius to the Temple of Juventus. Here the senior priest welcomed him and explained the importance of the occasion. Then he invoked the goddess with a sequence of prayers, imploring her to take the son of Augusta Agrippina under her protection during the formative years ahead. While thurifers puffed billows of incense, the priest poured libations at the foot of the goddess's statue.

Then back to Caesar's House, where guests at last got a chance to gossip, comment on the ladies' dresses and, with a show of modesty, proffer the gift each secretly believed would be judged top of the heap.

Two days later, after the last lesson, when Lucius prepared to correct the boys' written work, Domitius stayed behind. Somewhat shyly he said he had something to ask, if Lucius could spare the time: about his birthday or rather the night after his birthday when he couldn't get to sleep. Whereupon he perched himself on the desk opposite Lucius's lectern, swinging his leg, and launched into a breathless account.

'You know what it's like – a birthday. People mean to be kind but aunts and lady cousins go on and on about when you were small. It's drama they go for. How I was feet down in mother's tummy, couldn't come out like that but a very adroit midwife managed to turn me. Then my head's too big and she had to prize me out with forceps. Mother dear hadn't enough milk but luckily there was a country girl with big boobs. Later mother was too busy and engaged a nurse. Eclogue was fat and cuddly, taught me rhymes and songs I still remember. Aged four, I fell ill with spots and fever, the doctors panicked but Eclogue stayed with me day and night and pulled me through. Then we moved to Rome. A bad woman who hated mother put a viper in my nursery. Mother came in to kiss me goodnight, saw the viper slithering up my cot and killed it with the heel of her shoe.' Domitius held up his left wrist where part of the viper's skin was mounted as a bracelet.

He paused for breath looking to see how Lucius was taking it. Lucius nodded encouragingly. 'Do go on.'

'Baby clothes were brought out, and my rattle. It was all well meant but it made me squirm. When everyone had gone and I got to bed, I lay thinking. What was it all about? What did a birthday amount to? Just having that many years inside you. People had said how fortunate I was. And I saw it was true. A strong body, a remarkable mother, ancestors to be proud of, some good friends, my minah birds and my horse. Then I saw that these were only visible things, and I was fortunate in dozens of other ways... Take my body – or yours. You know how much wheat an average man consumes in a year? Fifty bushels.'

'I think you mean measures.'

'Measures then. Some farmer has to plough, sow, harvest and thresh that wheat. And fishermen risk their lives for our tunny and turbot. Not to mention oil, cheese and fruit. Then there's the cook who prepares it and the man who carts off the peelings. It's amazing how many people contribute just to our staying alive.' Shaking his head at the thought, he pushed himself off the desk and began to dab at the floor with the tip of his sandal.

'I thought about the presents I'd had, the congratulations. "Well Done, Domitius." But what have I done well? Nothing. Nil. It's all been done by others, a whole relay team. So why presents? It's other people who've stacked up those fourteen years inside me. You see what I'm getting at.'

Lucius nodded. 'None of us emerges fully formed as Minerva did from Jupiter's head.'

Domitius looked relieved at being taken seriously. 'And now I come to the worrying part. They've done all this for me and I'd like to give something in return. Not just "like to"; it's more of an itch.

But the question is – how? There's so many I'll never meet. And those I do know – what could I actually give?'

Lucius felt a double surprise: that Domitius should have thought so hard about his short past life and then have confided in him. He thought back to the drawn-out battles for correct spelling and grammar, legibility and clear argument, to the boy's flares of temper and sulking, his cold resentment of what Lucius was, of all he stood for. And now in mid-puberty, the age of secrecy, this openness, an unfolding of himself. So sudden! Lucius thought of a setter pup that leaves off frisking and chasing its shadow to stop sharp, with tail, back and head in one straight line, for the first time pointing.

As he tried to understand the mechanics of Domitius's transition, Lucius recalled an event from his own adolescence. Father had taken him and his brothers to sit in on a lawsuit. The plaintiff wished to eject a widow from her wattle-and-daub home because she regularly fed her nine cats after midnight and their caterwauling kept him awake. The widow, burly, red-faced, with a market-woman's loquacity, kept interrupting; how she grew superior endives in her patch of garden to sell to the discerning, how her last husband, a veteran, wounded too – she cited pitiful details – had sworn her never to part from the house he'd bought with his bounty; then, aggressively, she enumerated the virtues of her feline family and how anyone who understood cats knew that after midnight they needed a bowl of titbits. Aware of the magistrate's impatience, father murmured, 'Lost herself the case.'

A trainee lawyer, friend of her cousin, defended the widow, suggesting that the plaintiff had bought up land for an apartment block but needed the widow's plot to round off his scheme. He showed that a doctor's testimony to the plaintiff's wife's insomnia had been issued before the lady moved to Rome.

After questioning both parties, the magistrate found for the widow and Lucius had uttered a jubilant whoop. Justice – against the odds! At that age he had been obsessed – how ridiculous it now seemed – with the goose-flesh texture of the skin on his thighs, not noticeable on the thighs of his friends, which he considered repellent. With the court's verdict, a new-found determination to follow in the steps of the trainee lawyer eclipsed all other thoughts.

As for Domitius, Lucius had no way of knowing what key had turned his lock, but he recalled one incident that might have been the trigger. Walking down the Via Sacra, the class had met head-on the unfortunate half of a creature, no legs and a stump arm, wheeling himself painfully along on a rickety board. While Curtius and Gnaeus looked away and Mad Dog mimed crab-like movements with his hands, Domitius turned to Lucius with a feeling look that said, 'What if you or I were reduced in that way?'

Lucius's satisfaction at Domitius's disclosure was diluted by awareness of how little he could do to shield his sensibilities. He recalled his own pangs from older boys' sneering: 'Lawsuits are rigged in the back room'; 'Justice is blind, yes, but she counts the coins slipped into her hand.' So now Curtius, a militant fan of the Red Charioteers, was urging his classmates to prove their manhood by punching up the Blues and breaking some teeth, while Mad Dog was daring Domitius to get high on mushrooms.

Lucius would have liked to respond with some practicable solution, but all he could offer was scraps: Domitius couldn't expect to repay fourteen years overnight, he must first acquire the necessary skills. Meanwhile, if he got a chance to be helpful no matter to whom or in however small a way, he should take it. A helping hand had a knock-on effect and might eventually reach one of the persons he'd named. And last, Domitius should write the date of his coming-of-age on a card and keep it preciously: it would remind him of generous intentions that might otherwise be forgotten.

Though probably disappointed at not being provided with a complete answer to his quandary, Domitius promised to write the card and keep it in a locked box only he knew about. Then, giving his mentor a friendly look, he went to change into riding clothes and Lucius left his papers uncorrected till morning and hurried to my office to tell me that Domitius had good stuff in him.

Lucius had been invited by Agrippina to dinner with the family. He was to take his class to view a newly unearthed Etruscan site and details of the journey had to be worked out. Agrippina hoped Domitius would later impress Claudius with a description of the site.

Since Lucius had first dined in this room, Britannicus had grown taller but still more delicate. His shoulders sloped and he had the beginnings of a stoop. He took no exercise, for Sosibius believed this tired him, and a studious indoor life had left him with an unhealthy pallor. In his leisure he worked at mathematical puzzles and was said by Sosibius to be five years in advance of his age.

Lucius found Claudius had grown even plumper, face as well as torso and paunch, earning himself the nickname of Pumpkin. He took pride in the son who shared his preference for books rather than people. He continued to do his paper work thoroughly but to appear in public as little as possible and, in the temporary absence abroad of Secretary Narcissus, he had taken to consulting Agrippina about his constant 'dilemmas'. These ranged from how to handle the Tiber boatmen's claim for higher wages to whether his new slippers should be calf or doeskin.

At dinner, Claudius ate copiously of the turbot, complimented his wife on her cheese sauce and not for the first time declared that a civilization should be judged by the inventiveness of its cuisine. The tables were then cleared and bowls of sweets, candies and pastries brought in from which each person could help himself.

Through an open window there began to be heard cymbals, tambourines and ocarinas, growing gradually louder to end with a flourish. Moments later, the door opened to admit a round little man dressed Greek-style in a knee-length gown of pale blue shot-silk trimmed with gold. His complexion was sallow, his eyes bulged, his chin receded and a protruding stomach obliged him to lean backwards as he walked, but so colourful was his dress, so animated his eyes, so expansive the billowing movement of his pudgy hands that one disregarded his looks and saw only a man savouring life.

'Earlier than expected,' the new arrival announced happily, raising his arms high as though to acclaim his safe return. 'A favourable wind plus eagerness to be back in my dear Rome. You heard the music? Friends kindly arranged it to welcome me back and to signal my pleasure at re-entering Caesar's home.'

He bowed as low as his stomach allowed to his master, nodded coolly to Agrippina, then embraced Britannicus, who with a rare smile had risen to greet him. 'You've grown, dear boy. I've a present for you – later.' He extended a hand to Domitius, then more warmly to Sosibius. To Lucius, who named himself, he darted a sharp look.

He turned back to Claudius and with a waggish 'May I?' selected a candied cherry from one of the bowls, popped it into his mouth, then took a second.

Claudius asked for his impressions of Alexandria.

'The stories you've heard about its shops – double, triple them. Silks, brocades, silver, crystal – and jewels! Black pearls, pink diamonds, dark red rubies – I for one couldn't resist.' Laughingly he placed his left hand under his right, pretended to lift it, then let it sag, as though the rings, one and sometimes two on each finger, made it too heavy. By playing up his love of ostentation, Narcissus created the impression that he was a man with nothing to hide or, at worst, was too frivolous to be politically dangerous.

'The harbour entrance has been dredged, new wharves constructed, bigger and better than ours at Ostia. In the last decade traffic's increased by eighty per cent. Think of the port dues!'

'You appear to place Alexandria ahead of Rome,' said Agrippina severely.

Narcissus held her off with an easy smile, 'Conspicuous wealth will never replace solid virtue.'

Lucius thought back in time. Fledgling lawyers wait in the Forum hoping to attract their first client by trying to look worthy of confidence, for example by flaunting an expensive ring. Narcissus had started life by hiring such rings and Lucius had been one of his early customers. The Levantine had then risen to be financial adviser and confidant to Claudius's previous wife Messalina, then Secretary to the great man himself.

Claudius led the company into the garden salon, where he motioned Narcissus to a seat at a table between himself and Britannicus. 'And my friends in the Academy?'

'Eager for news of your latest writing. I took the liberty of organizing a little "occasion": readings from your Etruscan History. Received most favourably.' He lowered his voice. 'What would you think of a Museum in Alexandria for the study of North African history, the prime text to be your seminal book on the Carthaginians?'

'Seminal would you say?'

'An adjective I heard used more than once. Every day a chapter would be read aloud and discussed: every year a colloquium, proceedings to be published there and here.'

Claudius's eyes narrowed. 'Who suggested this?'

'They did. But they needed... guidance, to which your most humble servant pleads... guilty.' He turned down the corners of his mouth in mock penitence, then broke into laughter, his big stomach heaving.

'An architect friend has sketched a possible plan. Twelve-column façade – the solid Doric you like. Circular entrance hall in porphyry, mosaics of Clio holding up one of your books.'

Claudius pressed the Levantine's hand. 'You're a noble soul, Narcissus.'

With the Secretary's entrance, Agrippina's agreeable expression had turned cold and Lucius noticed her neck tautening at this effusion.

'The architect is spending the night with me before continuing to Naples. If you would do me the honour of coming tomorrow morning to my humble villa, the three of us could go over the plans.'

Agrippina crossed to her husband. 'Tomorrow you receive the Parthian ambassadors.' She kept a close eye on foreign affairs.

Claudius frowned; Narcissus rolled his eyes. 'Are there still Parthians alive to send ambassadors? I thought your legions had disposed of them all.' At which Sosibius, standing nearby, laughed obsequiously.

Claudius looked hesitantly at his wife. 'These talks have dragged for weeks. Perhaps one day more...'

'They will feel snubbed and harden their terms,' Agrippina said decisively.

Shifting his gaze from his wife to his Secretary, then back to his wife, Claudius murmured miserably, 'Dilemmas, always dilemmas...'

Narcissus raised his eyes meditatively to the ceiling. 'A few square miles of parched terrain or a museum to promote the study of history – bearing the name of Claudius.'

This last proposal caused the *princeps* to open his mouth in wonder, looking, thought Lucius, like a fish swallowing bait. Presently he announced in a loud voice, 'The ambassadors can wait.' He rapped the table hard to show he meant what he said.

Agrippina frowned and without a word left the room, while at a nod from Claudius Sosibius took Britannicus off for his afternoon rest. This left Claudius seated facing Narcissus, with Lucius and Domitius in an adjoining alcove beginning to work out their timetable, within earshot of the older men.

Claudius spoke first. 'The museum must have a library. Heated.'

'Underfloor heating.'

'We can't build on that scale with copper coins.'

This was one aspect which was receiving attention, said Narcissus cheerfully. He then recalled the death of a wealthy knight, Publius Lucilius. It was customary for a millionaire to make a hefty bequest to the *princeps* and Publius had added the province of Britain to Rome's dominions. But he had failed to make any bequest.

'Ingratitude is distressing – but not an offence.'

'It can be an expression of disapproval. Indeed, of dissidence.' Publius Lucilius had left his property, including priceless statuary by the famous Agasias, to his nephew Caius Lucilius, a self-styled philosopher.

Lucius had been following the conversation and he stiffened on hearing the name of Caius Lucilius. This was the man he had commended to Paula's mother and who had since become a valued friend.

Narcissus's tone turned nasty. 'There's dissidence in that family, take it from me.'

'You've got something on Caius?'

'My people have never actually heard subversive language. But in this case they may not need to. Sometimes a statue can speak for its owner.'

'A statue?' Claudius echoed peevishly. 'You know I dislike mystery.'

'Patience, sire. All will unfold tomorrow. And now, if you permit, it is time for me to regain my modest Penates and begin to unpack.'

The rationale behind the conversation which Lucius had just overheard were as familiar to him as they were to me. Caesar's Secretaries of State are paid servants of foreign, usually lowly birth, handlers of money and manipulators of protocol – all good reasons why knights and senators look down on them as menial.

Early in their respective careers, Narcissus and his fellow Secretaries, Pallas and Polybius, came in for snubs and social exclusion. This fostered a grim determination to win power and respect by making themselves millionaires. What better way of doing so than wresting those millions from the very senators and knights who so despised them? The means lay to hand. Claudius, painfully insecure, trembled at any sign, however slight, of an impending coup such as had overthrown his predecessor. Spies were paid to sniff out any whiff of dissidence. A paid agent watching from a crack in the ceiling cornice would record an imprudent remark made at the dinner table below; the speaker would be charged and tried before Claudius's private tribunal under the law *de maiestate* with a sentence ranging from exile to the axe, while his wealth went to the Secretaries for having successfully brought the case.

As he left Caesar's House and walked homeward, Lucius considered the implications of Narcissus's conversation with Claudius. Lucilius and his wife Cynthia were among the few friends who had remained loyal. Lucilius liked discussing moral philosophy, while Cynthia and Paula did much of their shopping together. Lucius of course knew that the Secretaries preyed on Claudius's weakness to the point where, on spies' evidence, he would pass summary sentence of death in a secret tribunal. But that Lucilius, a bookish apolitical knight, should now be the intended victim seemed to mark a new and more alarming development in atrocity. Lucius returned home: still the same small apartment but lately made more welcoming by Paula, who had redecorated the living room, painting one wall with a trompe l'oeil vine-entwined trellis against a blue sky, so that it seemed less small for the intimate dinners they liked to give 'in the shade of our grape vine'.

As a rule, Lucius did not talk politics at home but that evening he made an exception, telling Paula what he had overheard.

Her women friends meant a great deal to Paula, and Cynthia was a special favourite. She was expecting a third child and wasn't strong. Any shock might cause her to miscarry. Paula said they must do something to help.

Lucius of course agreed. But it wouldn't be easy. He was nearly always tailed, and had been just now on the way home. 'Why,' he asked, 'did Narcissus, normally so secretive, speak in such a way that I overheard? Because he intended me to hear, in the hope of setting me up. If I were to go to Lucilius's house, I'd be seen and the visit reported to Claudius. That would certainly bring about my dismissal, with much more at stake than my reputation and future.'

His experience of Claudius and his two predecessors had convinced Lucius that their acts of cruelty stemmed from deep insecurity in early life. It was probably too late to change Claudius, so hope must rest on the next *princeps*. Britannicus was the heir-apparent but poor health could debar him, in which case the choice might fall on Domitius. Hence the importance of bringing him up to feel confident as well as tolerant.

'Without conceit, I can say my work with Domitius is important. I'm reluctant to put it at risk even to help a friend.'

A bleak silence was broken by Paula. 'Couldn't you warn Lucilius with a written message?' 'Be sure it would be intercepted and used to charge me with meddling in Caesar's affairs.'

Further silence failing to deliver a plan, Lucius crossed to the curtains and began what he termed creative winding, while Paula stretched on the couch and harried the soles of her feet as though they were to blame. From time to time, one would come up with a bright suggestion which, after discussion, proved to be wholly impractical. Their gloom deepened. That evening was one they readily forgot.

Next morning Lucius gave his class an introductory lesson to the Republic's second language, Greek, with a sour taste in his mouth, aware that within the same walls Rome's ruler was being manipulated by a former slave from Greek-speaking Asia Minor. But the afternoon brought compensation. Domitius wished to visit the Street of Blacksmiths and Lucius accompanied him. The boy, who had been there before, entered a specialist forge to watch smiths heating iron red-hot, hammering it into shape on an anvil and fitting the resultant axle into the hubs of chariot wheels. He discussed tension, fracture and breaking-point with the foreman, then swapped stories about recent races. His manner was both friendly and respectful of their skills, and the workmen clearly warmed to him. One more reason, thought Lucius, why he'd do well in high office.

When he returned home, Paula had news for him. She had gone on foot to Lucilius's house on the Esquiline. Lucilius was out but she had talked with Cynthia. It appeared that a dozen statues, part of the inheritance, had been set up in the garden. Cynthia did not know what they represented but she promised to pass on Paula's warning when Lucilius returned. Lucius reacted crossly. 'Why didn't you tell me you were going?'

'You might have been implicated for not stopping me.'

He asked her whether she thought she had been observed. Near Lucilius's house, she had spotted a man hugging the shadows. She stopped and ticked him off. He said he was authorized to keep her under surveillance and inquired as to the nature of her business on the Esquiline. Paula had shown the contents of the basket on her arm: rompers and booties she'd knitted for a friend nearing her term. The man sloped off and she did not see him again.

Lucius emitted a drawn-out groan. It was so like Paula to help a friend without a thought for her own safety. She couldn't be faulted for that, yet he wished she'd stayed at home.

Next day, as darkness was falling, Narcissus's men raided Lucilius's garden in search of a full-length bronze figure worth millions as a work of art. In the eyes of a timid *princeps*, it was damning evidence of treasonable design, for it represented Julius Caesar's assassin, Brutus. They could not find it. Lucilius had sent his Brutus to safety in the hold of a ship bound for Crete.

The following morning, Lucius arrived in class to find Domitius strangely subdued. During the break, the boy stole up to him and whispered unhappily, 'My stepfather's giving you the sack. Sosibius told me.'

Lucius spent the rest of the morning and early afternoon alternately cursing the Pumpkin and searching for a way to stay on. He glimpsed one possibility, but had no reason to think it would work. In any case, he found the prospect distasteful, for it would mean throwing himself on the good graces of a woman whose attitude remained cool and impersonal. He resented the thought of becoming indebted when he had taken pains to preserve his independence.

It took Lucius twenty-four hours to decide to ask Agrippina for an appointment, which she granted the same afternoon, her aloofness serving to rattle him further.

He explained how Paula had gone to Lucilius's wife as a brave act of friendship, without in any way apologizing for it. 'It was imprudent on my part to tell Paula what I had overheard.' He then asked Agrippina to intercede with Claudius for her son's sake.

'It isn't Claudius who wants you dismissed; in fact he quite enjoys talking history with you.' Once again her precise diction made an unlikely statement sound incontrovertible. 'It's Secretary Narcissus, not from any personal animosity but because at every turn he tries to thwart my influence.'

'Then I've troubled you for nothing.'

'As it happens, Narcissus overstepped his authority in raiding a knight's house on false information. I will bring that to my husband's notice. Although he turns the law to his advantage... rest assured you will continue as my son's tutor.

'One other thing. Tell your wife in future to control her impulses – for your sake.'

Lucius made a sign of compliance but had no intention of admonishing Paula. For one thing, he knew that Paula's giving nature was a fountain that couldn't be capped.

Now that her son was of age, Agrippina considered it important to show him off to Romans whose opinion counted. The obvious way would have been for him to accompany his stepfather on the rare occasions he appeared in public but Claudius objected that that would infringe Britannicus's prerogative.

Agrippina looked for another way. While watching Domitius pass his horsemanship test, she was reminded of the traditional Troy Games in which teams of youths from patrician families used to compete in a display of riding to commemorate Aeneas's arrival from Troy. She spoke favourably of the contest to Claudius, adding that it was sad it had been allowed to lapse.

With his antiquarian leanings, Claudius had already revived several half-forgotten ceremonies and rites, and at first showed interest. But soon his mood darkened. While arguing a knotty mathematical problem with Sosibius, Britannicus had grown overexcited, suddenly seeing what he described as a burst of golden lights and had fallen to the floor unconscious. A few days in bed put him right, but he was forbidden to exert himself and obviously couldn't take part in the games.

Agrippina had foreseen this. She suggested that Claudius might allow his son to preside over the games and present the laurel wreath trophies. This would not tire him and would be considered an honour.

There followed customary twists and turns and wavering but, after further prompting, Claudius agreed and Agrippina lost no time in choosing the participants, changing the venue from the traditional Campus Martius to the more fashionable Circus Maximus, and sending personal invitations to four hundred influential citizens.

Curious to watch the boy I had heard so much about, I joined a large crowd in the Circus. At a signal from Britannicus, four teams of eight boys emerged from under Caesar's lodge and rode into the sanded ring, forty yards in diameter. Each team wore distinctive headdresses and coloured bows tied to their horses' tails, identifying them as Trojans, Achaeans, Persians and Egyptians.

In turn, the teams marched and counter-marched single file through latticed arches in the centre of the ring, first at a walk, then at a trot. Next came wheeling to music played by the guards' band, first slow, then gradually faster. Domitius, captaining the Trojans, sat straight, controlling his mount with a strong knee grip and a light touch of the reins, while guiding his team by inclining his head.

In a final display, each rider had to raise himself up to a kneeling position on his horse's hindquarters, make two rounds of the ring, then dive back astride. During this exercise, Domitius's horse bucked but he found his seat and quieted the animal without fluster. This received the applause it deserved.

The Trojans were adjudged the most skilful team and Domitius received from Britannicus a circlet of laurel. After removing one leaf, he presented it with a bow to his mother.

Highly placed guests crowded round to offer their congratulations to Claudius and his wife. 'Only just of age, yet such bearing, such poise! Clearly a born leader!'

Agrippina waited for the news to spread round the city and for Claudius to hear it echoed in the Forum. Choosing a moment of high spirits after flamingo tongues had been served at dinner one evening, she spoke. Claudius had seen how popular his stepson was becoming. That must surely gratify him, yet it could also be a sign of danger. The patrician families had never taken Claudius to heart, saw him as a stopgap, and would welcome any opportunity of replacing him. 'Domitius's clan name of Ahenobarbus is at least as distinguished as yours. What is to prevent them rallying round him – perhaps strengthening the tie by a marriage – and attempting a coup? This is possible, all too possible...'

Her words touched a sore spot. Claudius's pillow-reading was Greek drama; he had often brooded on dethroned kings obliged to beg their bread and shuddered at his own vulnerability. He knew that Agrippina wished him to protect himself by adopting Domitius. But that he did not want to do. He felt secretly jealous of Domitius, of his vibrant health and open manner and because he meant more to Agrippina than her husband. What's more, his dear Britannicus would feel sidestepped.

Keeping these thoughts to himself, Claudius replied that Secretary Narcissus kept the patrician families under close surveillance. Any rumble of discontent and he taught them a lesson. If Domitius were to be adopted, they might well see it as evidence that Claudius knew himself to be insecure and draw encouragement for a coup.

Agrippina had come prepared. The great Augustus, she reminded him, had faced a similar threat in respect of his stepsons, whereupon he adopted them, though he had grandsons of his own, and Tiberius too, though with children of his own, adopted Germanicus. 'You who value precedents have two important ones from the recent past... Take Domitius into your family and so forestall any threat to yourself, while Domitius's future success will add lustre to your principate.'

'Dilemma, dilemma,' sighed Claudius miserably and cut the discussion short by beckoning Britannicus to set up the chessmen.

That evening, he appointed a cadre of three super-spies to cram more dirt into agents' reports on over popular citizens. Lucius noted in his diary: 'Just as wars among mortals are attributed by Homer to domestic quarrels on Mount Olympus, so not a few of Claudius's malicious public acts derive from painful dust-ups at home.'

In the days that followed, Narcissus used flattery and optimism to try to prevent a move that would increase Agrippina's power at the expense of his own. No ruler had so enriched the present with discoveries from the past, no ruler had been more loved by his people. Claudius's situation was rock-firm. Britannicus, now happily recovered from his unfortunate seizure, was shaping up admirably. Why upset the balance in his home by a quite unnecessary change?

Claudius had a habit of shirking decisions by shutting himself in his writing-room and adding another chapter to his Etruscan History. He attempted this now, only to find that the narrative would not flow. Fear of Domitius as a future rival seemed to congeal the ink on his pen and not even his jealousy of the boy could dispel it.

He had promised to have his book ready for the opening of the Museum in Alexandria and, after several days of stagnation, he became seriously alarmed. It was in this mood that he summoned Agrippina and said he was prepared to adopt her son.

Custom required that Domitius should take a new name. Agrippina had already decided that he should take the name of her brother Nero, put to death on a false charge by Tiberius. Claudius agreed.

Domitius didn't see why he should change his name. It was the name his mother had chosen for him and he liked it. Nor did he wish to take as his legal father a man he couldn't respect. Agrippina said it would give him more weight with the people of Rome, at which he grumbled that he didn't need a new name for that.

The adoption went ahead. Drafted in due legal form and approved by the Senate, it took place privately in Caesar's House, from where Domitius emerged as Nero Drusus Caesar. Narcissus and Sosibius masked their pique, but not Britannicus. Next day when Nero, as I must now call him, returned home after class and wished his stepbrother a good day, the other retorted pointedly, 'And to you, Domitius Ahenobarbus!'

Nero could quickly flare up when provoked. He did so now, rushing at Britannicus and throwing him to the ground. He sat on his back, twisted one arm and ordered him to address him by his new name. The other howled. Sosibius ran up, tried unsuccessfully to pull Nero off and shouted for help.

Claudius shuffled up, demanding to know what had happened. As Britannicus explained through his tears, Claudius turned angrily on his stepson. 'Is this how you repay me? Go to your room and stay there the rest of the day.'

Guided by his tutor and Narcissus, Britannicus worked to retain his father's affection, while Nero tried to overcome his mistrust. Rivalry between the two parties intensified.

The day after Lucius had taken him to the Etruscan dig, Nero described to Claudius what he had seen, notably tombstone statuary depicting a man and his wife reclining, as at a feast, both wearing broad smiles. Leaving the room, he returned a moment later holding a small brass lamp on a round base, which he proudly handed to Claudius, saying it was a present.

Claudius turned the lamp slowly in his now arthritic fingers, assessing its shape and decoration. 'See that foliage moulding – typical Etruscan.'

Nero explained that it had been unearthed on the site. 'There appears to be an inscription.' Claudius ran a finger along a line of shallow engraving, then turned to the ever-present Narcissus. 'My sight's not what it was. You spell it out.'

Narcissus plucked from his pocket the jeweller's glass he always carried and, studying the inscription, named the letters one by one. Claudius's face darkened. Taking the lamp and the glass, he peered at the work.

'The letters are Etruscan but they don't make words. Just gibberish.' He rounded angrily on Nero. 'What do you mean, young man, by offering me a fake, and a poor one at that?'

Nero flushed and denied he'd had any intention of deceiving him; he'd bought the lamp in good faith and had only meant to please him.

'You got it from an accredited antiquarian?... I thought not. Picked it up from a hawker. Quite as shameful as wilfully trying to deceive me. You've been well and truly gulled.'

Narcissus shook his head knowingly. 'Won't go far like that. Such a blunder is sure to make the rounds.' And later he made quite sure that it did.

Changes were appearing in Lucius's pupils. Nero's voice dropped, as did Gnaeus's, an incipient much-envied moustache darkened Mad Dog's upper lip. Furtive glances alternated with suppressed giggles and extended visits to the latrine led to surreptitious whispering which would break off when Lucius approached. He caught snatches: who had pubic hair and how thick? Who had seen his sister undressing? Who had had a wet dream?

Perhaps because he had been cuckolded by his previous wives, Claudius insisted on adherence to high standards of sexual morality from his household and entourage. When Agrippina drew his attention to Nero's pubescence, he took special care over the customary paternal talk. He regularly published his thoughts on moral and physical health; he had brought out a memorandum on the dangers to digestion if one did not belch freely at meals, and his advice on sex to Nero he also published. Now, after twenty years, it is almost a period piece and close in substance to the talk father gave us boys when we came of age; it throws light on Lucius as well as on Nero.

> The sexual impulse in man differs from that in animals because it is continuous, therefore intrusive, and because it can be controlled unlike a destructive torrent. Normally the sexual impulse is channelled into marriage for the purpose of procreating and rearing legitimate children in which case it is constructive.

The sexual behaviour of women has been found to be linked to the welfare of the community. If wives are chaste and rear their children with devotion, the earth yields a plentiful harvest. If they are unfaithful or purposely abort, crops fail. That is a well-attested fact for which there are two not necessarily exclusive explanations. Nature is a linked whole, so taint in one part can damage other parts. But also, if Juno goddess of marriage is affronted, it is to be expected that she will persuade Ceres to withhold her usual gifts.

Claudius turned next to virginity, describing it as a valuable state since the virgin, belonging to no one man, can smile on all or, if so drawn, can give undivided attention to worship. Especially estimable were the six Vestals, who served Rome by tending the sacred flame.

Responsible parents with a nubile daughter – Claudius continued – preserve her virginity until marriage, so that she may bring this once-only state to her husband as a gift which both prized. Compare the cornerstone of a dwelling.

A young fellow has a stronger sexual urge than a girl and cannot be expected to control it. What then? He may form a tie with an older woman. But then he will arrive at his marriage day with intimate memories he hasn't shared with his bride. That can work against fidelity. And the importance of fidelity is something we Romans discovered. Even the Olympians don't practise it.

A young man's dilemma is solved by the brothel. There the girls are available to all and no close relationship results. Compare a street food stall with a well-planned dinner at home.

The last part was what mattered to a healthy adolescent preoccupied with his genitals. A house in a back street of the Esquiline, long accredited to the *princeps'* family and marked with a circular bas-relief of two entwined phalluses, received instructions to accommodate Nero twice a month, the bill to go to Claudius. There, one spring evening, accompanied by Gnaeus, who already knew the place, Nero was received by the madam and entrusted to a Circassian girl in her twenties named Melita. He entered her room, the heat of desire chilled by self-doubt: he left it proud of having proved himself a man.

Over the next few months, Lucius observed the steady rise in Nero's satisfaction with himself and life in general. But then it started to tail off and, since this was one subject he could not discuss with his own mother, Nero unburdened himself to Lucius. Melita, he confided, had a delectable body; to Lucius's amusement, he compared her to 'Venus rising from the waves', a painting by Dorotheus in an anteroom of the public baths. She said very sweet things to him and he'd begun to notice that they were always the same things but, when he tried to find out something about her past, she would change the subject. This disappointed him, for he wanted to know as a person this girl with whom he shared such pleasure.

From longer experience, Gnaeus had confided that the brothel girls didn't experience pleasure in the sexual act. No pleasure at all. They just pretended and perhaps this accounted for Melita's secrecy. While Nero continued to visit the back-street house, he admitted to Lucius that he found unsatisfying the whole business of buying a girl's attachment. What he wanted was someone to whom he could give all his affection and from whom he could receive all hers.

At parties, girls of his own age crossed his horizon. Some had the slender white neck which was the focus of sexual desire for Nero's age-group. With one of these young paragons there might be an exchange of glances, an encouraging spark in her eye, even a brief conversation, banal but thrilling. However such girls were closely guarded by mothers or chaperones who were concerned to arrange safe and useful marriages with their own kind, so the conversation led nowhere.

Now that he had tasted the pleasure a woman could give, Nero responded in a new way to his mother's physical presence. She was well-preserved and he could sense her allure. In the company of his peers, he was used to playing down her prominence in his life; now he took occasion to show her off. He felt proud to stand beside her at public ceremonies, while Agrippina seemed to take pleasure in her well-built if also somewhat pimply son; she appreciated the interest he took in her well-cut dresses and her silver jewellery – gold she disdained as parvenu.

So much for young Nero's attitude to women. But now another player was about to make her entrance on the stage. Waiting in the wings was Claudius's daughter by his previous marriage who lived in the ladies' part of Caesar's House. Octavia was a year younger than her brother Britannicus and three years younger than Nero. On the way to his mother's room, Nero had occasionally passed her in the corridor but these encounters were not to her advantage: once she'd appeared in a turban after she'd washed her hair; another time, she'd had a cold and her nose was running. Nero only began to take notice of her one afternoon when he happened to see her playing with a girl friend in the courtyard. She was well made, with wide-set dark eyes, light brown hair worn in a pigtail, pretty as far as an eleven year-old can be, and performing with agility difficult jumps with a skipping rope.

Octavia's education had been entrusted by her father to an elderly cousin in reduced circumstances, who was told to bring the girl up strictly. Claudius did not explain his instructions, but the governess knew that he was especially concerned for his daughter's modesty because of the behaviour of her mother, whose name he never uttered.

The story of Octavia's mother Messalina may be said to have begun on the day there arrived in Rome a lady with the alluringly blonde hair and fair complexion of her Thracian forbears and a high intelligence sharpened in the court of Alexandria. Cleopatra, seventh of that name, had conquered Julius Caesar's heart and been brought to his home to share his bed, from where it was believed – at least by his enemies – that she ruled Rome.

Here was something new in the city of seven hills: an intelligent lady with the advantage of beauty assuming behind-the-scenes power. The example gave Roman women a lead. The ambitious Messalina had married her father's cousin when he was forty-nine. It did not take her long to discover his weaknesses and subservience to his Secretaries. Clearly there was no future here for the new Cleopatra she intended to become.

Flashing her dark eyes and guided by a strong sexual appetite, she set herself to win the hearts – and purses – of prominent citizens displeased with Claudius. She built up a power base, with her lovers seeing her as merely adorably capricious until they were invited to an almost unthinkable ceremony: Messalina's bigamous marriage in public to a young senator, Gaius Silius, at which she revealed her secret purpose. As Caesar's wife, she intended to transfer supreme power from a contemptible, increasingly cruel *princeps* to a more worthy recipient, her new husband.

It was a nightmarish situation for Claudius. He dashed for the Praetorian Camp and hid. For forty-eight hours the city fathers hovered, then saw the whole affair for the fantasy it was. Messalina and Silius paid with their lives, and Octavia grew up in the shadow of their disgrace.

Octavia was taught the usual curriculum deemed suitable for a girl: tales about heroes and moral fables, enough arithmetic to manage household accounts, how to write a polite letter. Her governess felt sorry for the girl with no mother yet never free of her mother's shadow and could not bring herself to be strict. So Octavia dabbled and acquired no one strong interest around which to shape her character.

By grown-up visitors, she was either eyed askance or shown exaggerated consideration. She guessed the motives for each and, in rebellion against them, opted for self-assertion. Arriving purposely late at a girls' party, she would announce loudly: 'Caesar's daughter present!' and wait for the hush.

At the age of eleven, she was allowed into the house proper and sought to get close to her father. She would fetch a footstool for him when he came home tired, and search for whatever object he had mislaid. He for his part felt sorry for the girl, but could seldom think of anything to say to her other than asking about her progress in cross-stitch. Sometimes he would pull her pigtail playfully and tell her she must soon dress her hair and put it in curls. But in her wide-set eyes and the planes of her high cheekbones, he found a resemblance to her mother and this depressed him.

She tried to get close to Britannicus. Frisking around the house, she would steal up behind him and cover his eyes: 'Tell me what you're reading.' When he obliged, she would giggle that she couldn't understand a word and persuade him to play her at spillikins. Though Britannicus would have liked to be friendly, the charm of such games soon palled for them both.

In Nero, the one healthy male in the house, Octavia of course showed interest. But his many outside occupations gave her few openings to speak to him and, when she did, she was disappointed at being patronized banteringly as baby sister.

After he had seen Octavia's performance with her skipping rope, Nero noticed her lithe body and the budding breasts beneath her shift. He began to chat to her and, learning that she liked skittles, suggested a three-game match. They slipped off to the skittle alley on the far side of the courtyard, where Octavia showed herself a proficient player. They agreed on a return match the following day.

This was not lost on Agrippina. When she had arrived as Claudius's new wife, she had offered a friendly hand to Octavia. But although the girl dissociated herself from her mother, she could not bring herself to disown her altogether – for so she saw it – by accepting advances from the woman who had replaced her in the nuptial bed, and Agrippina made no further attempts. Change was called for, since Octavia was potentially an important piece in the domestic power game.

Lucius believed the time had come to introduce Nero to Greek literature as a first step to understanding the Greek achievement. He knew that this to him obvious move would meet with opposition. Greece is an idea whose connotations differ according to class and profession. The educated generally admire Greek art and literature, recognize that our own are inferior and have been encouraged to emulate the Greeks by government from Augustus onwards. At the same time, we look down on the Greeks for having squabbled, city against city, and making themselves easy prey for our legions.

Within that broad context are disparate opinions. Military families link Greek art to sensual pleasure, lack of manliness and hence to political decline. On the other hand, we in commerce, believe that the Greeks are secretly planning a political comeback by turning their creative gifts to manufacturing high quality goods at low prices, and intend soon to capture our markets. We see them not as a spent force but as a threat.

Claudius thought highly of the Greek language, richer in concrete words than Latin, and had lately made two speeches to the Senate in Greek. He also admired the Greek dramatists, whereas Agrippina despised them for writing about fate instead of acting to forfend it, and he would shuffle off alone to sniffle at a Sophocles production.

Lucius therefore carefully planned his approach to Agrippina. He reminded her that a young man of her son's rank was expected to speak Greek elegantly; moreover fluency in the language and apt allusions to Greek texts would show Claudius that Narcissus's sniping at Nero as a mere wrestler and jockey was unjustified.

'What texts are you talking about?' asked Agrippina and, when Lucius suggested starting with Homer's *Odyssey*, she looked horrified. Odysseus was a moonstruck vagabond, easily misled from his stated goal, no model for a future soldier. 'Start with *The Iliad*,' she commanded, then she dismissed him.

Stress was laid in Caesar's House – particularly by Agrippina – on the military origins of the principate, on Caesar's power rather then on an authority freely granted by the populace and shared with the Senate. Now that Nero had come to the stage of imbibing not just facts but values, Lucius faced the challenge of conveying a less one-sided view while still hanging onto his job. *The Iliad* was the last text he would have chosen, for its poetry of unparalleled vigour and beauty glorified military prowess as man's highest ideal.

Lucius's solution was to begin his first lesson by saying that a useful way of approaching *The Iliad* was through the first word of the first line – *menin*, meaning anger. The first word in literature, of great historic and symbolic importance. Why had Homer chosen to begin his epic thus? Because the whole long epic could be seen as a working out of the tragic consequences of a single act of anger – that of Achilles after King Agamemnon confiscates a prize rightfully his, a girl named Briseis.

After sketching the development of the theme of anger, Lucius said they would start with Homer's account of the victory Games organized by Achilles. He read aloud the episode where five war-chariots compete in a close-fought race. Diomedes eventually takes the lead, driving with the whip, swinging his arm back for every lash, and making his horses leap high in the air as they speed on to the finish. 'Showers of dust fell on their drivers all the time, and as the fast pair flew over the ground, the chariot overlaid with gold and tin came spinning after them and scarcely left a tyre-mark on the fine dust behind.'

As he recited, Lucius was surprised to see Nero's eyes brighten, his head nodding in time to the beat of the verse. He showed his pleasure by clapping at the end of the last line. 'I can just hear the swish of those chariot wheels!'

Lucius turned next to the passage where Andromache prepares a bath for her husband Hector, fighting for his life outside the walls. Hoping to capture Nero's interest, he asked him to read it and again had a surprise. Nero caught the flow of the lines and matched his tone with their meaning. In the ensuing discussion, he was the boy who showed most interest, citing words he liked and criticizing with insight. 'Andromache loves Hector. She wouldn't have been fiddling about with bath water, she'd have been up on the battlements, agonizing over every move in the fight.'

By the time of the third lesson on *The Iliad*, Nero was enjoying its sound, rhythm and imagery to a degree Lucius found quite unusual. After class, he would confide his excitement at finding an epithet 'bang on target' and soon was enquiring about other poets – a chance for Lucius to describe the odes of Pindar, which celebrated the successes of Greek rulers in the Olympic and other games. Pindar, he told Nero, had shown that skill and courage in the stadium can be just as heroic as on the battlefield.

Nero borrowed Lucius's copy and read it in his spare time. He warmed to Pindar even more than to Homer to the point where, three months later, he said he would like to try writing Greek verse, a project Lucius encouraged.

For Claudius's sixty-second birthday on the first day of August, Nero turned out a short poem in Greek on a well-worn subject: Dido's lost treasure. A Roman traveller in North Africa is caught in a storm and passes the night in a shepherd's mountain shelter. He dreams that he sees a cave with a narrow peaked entrance between two boulders: he enters and finds it stacked with gold plate, jewels, pearls. With daylight, he explores and eventually finds the cave of his dream. He goes in but it is empty. The shepherd explains that this was indeed the place where Dido hid her treasure from the Romans, but brigands had long since found and removed it. The traveller concludes that so rich a treasure, enclosed in a remote hiding-place, had left an aura perceptible in a dream.

That this muscular and supposedly dim stepson should be writing verse surprised Claudius. Sosibius said he must have had help, a charge denied by Nero and, when he was summoned, by Lucius too. Evidently regretting his suspicion, Claudius leapt to the other extreme: he embraced Nero, saying the poem had given him much pleasure and, by way of making return, treated him to an interminable description of current excavations in Dido's former realm.

Agrippina remained silent throughout these proceedings and called Lucius to her office immediately afterwards. Wearing a stony expression and tapping the arms of her chair for emphasis, she said she was astonished that Lucius should have allowed her son to write verse. He replied that the initiative had come from Nero, who, he believed, had artistic leanings.

'If he has, they do not come from my side, and must at once be rooted out. As for the subject of his poem, I consider it deplorable – an unhealthy make-believe world of no practical use.'

'If you'll allow me, ma'am, the subject does not reflect Nero's predilections. It was just a peg on which to hang his undoubted feel for the Greek language.' He offered her other examples.

Agrippina's usual self-control began to give. 'I'm not going to be drawn into an argument. There will be no more Homer, no more Pindar. In future, your sole text will be Thucydides' *History of the Peloponnesian War*, and all exercises will be in prose.'

Lucius left feeling hard done by. Just as he was beginning to get Greek lessons moving in the direction he thought would most help Nero's development, he had been shown once again that he was only there on sufferance, just another of Agrippina's minah birds, instructed to repeat her words as his.

Agrippina was lending attention to Octavia. The girl had been allowed to get her own way too often, leaving tasks half-done, building no store of knowledge and yet she was opinionated. Still, she had a pleasing natural vivacity and manifested a touching need for affection.

Her favourite occupation was shopping, so Agrippina began by offering to take the girl to a mercer's where she might find a curved long-toothed comb to support her hair at the nape. Having found one that pleased her, the girl haggled about the price and eventually obliged the mercer to climb down. Later, Agrippina suggested that it was not for Caesar's daughter to use her rank thus, even though she received very little pocket money from Claudius. Pleased with her comb, Octavia accepted the criticism in silence and with no sign of pique.

Noting Octavia's admiration for visible signs of wealth, Agrippina invited her to help clean and polish some of her fine silver. She showed the girl how to mix a paste, to spread it well into the relief work and how to bring up a shine with a soft cloth. As they worked,

Octavia spoke of her spotty skin and how she was trying a lotion of camomile flowers. Agrippina suggested that a surer remedy would be fewer fritters and honey cakes between meals. 'Try a plum or half a pear instead.'

As she won the girl's confidence, Agrippina spoke to Nero. Octavia liked him, and didn't have any friends. She might like to join them in the aviary. It would be amusing to have a third person for their games with the minahs. Nero was at first ruffled: the aviary had always been a domain apart, just for him and his mother. But he felt flattered that a girl should like him, especially one who could sometimes win at skittles. And so he agreed.

Lucius was careful not to betray any curiosity about Nero's out-of-class doings. It was no business of his. Agrippina periodically summoned him to monitor his Greek literature lessons and on one such occasion he was asked to wait. He paced up and down on the balustrade overlooking the aviary where he had first heard mother and son laughing as they played with the minahs. This time too he heard happy voices, but there were now three, and one was a girl's.

A novice bird was being taught to repeat a phrase, another was uttering saucy quips, a third imitating an old man's cracked voice. On and on went the chatter and laughter, allowing Lucius plenty of time in which to reflect.

He believed he knew what was in Agrippina's mind and could see the advantage for Nero within his family circle, but he had been brought up to believe that the marriage of first cousins should be avoided, since it could produce mentally retarded children. As after Agrippina's veto on Greek poetry, Lucius saw himself trying to work for Nero's good in situations beyond his control.

For some months, Narcissus had been less in evidence: he had been occupied with an important engineering scheme, draining the Fucine Lake east of Rome. One day he bounced into Claudius's study with his usual exuberance and spread out for him drawings he had just received of the first phase of the Museum. They showed the entrance complete, and the façade ready to be roofed.

Claudius studied them, his pleasure as always assailed by doubt. Now Narcissus presented him with a coin and Claudius was again distracted. Where had he found it?

'In the most apposite place possible – the province you yourself conquered.' A friend in the Surveyor's Office had advised him that the rise and fall of the Thames was about to be measured accurately for the first time, and he had advised Narcissus what the probable figures would be. London's docks were scheduled to be built down-river, and riverside sites in London itself were going cheap. Narcissus quickly snapped up a hundred and twenty acres.

When the measurements were published, they showed that shipping could safely use the city proper and the docks were duly relocated. 'Our profit is funding your Museum and the library.

'Incidentally, the docks will ensure regular supplies of your favourite whitstable oysters. And another noteworthy detail. One of the towns you founded – Chester?... no, Colchester – has put up a small temple to honour your genius.'

Claudius's look of satisfaction was short-lived. 'What bearing has that on my present worries?'

'A great deal, sire. Rome needs to be reminded that your British campaign has enriched us with silver, tin and pearls. What better way than to strike a new coin?'

Claudius pondered the suggestion. 'Commemorative?'

'Anticipatory. The coin would show the head of your son. The conquest of Britain lives and will continue to live in Britannicus.'

'Not bad... Not bad at all.'

'There is more, sire. Your son's health is holding up. No repetition of that puzzling fall. We have every reason to believe...' With a smile and upturned palms he mimed vibrant health. 'So the reverse of the coin should depict a helmeted Mars wearing a cuirass, holding spear and shield.'

Claudius puffed out one cheek, while glancing dubiously at the speaker. Narcissus smiled reassuringly: 'Coinage is for Caesar and his kin what cosmetics are for women.'

To ensure success, Narcissus enlisted the help of his colleagues. Pallas, Secretary of the Treasury, a former slave who claimed descent from the Kings of Arcadia, went personally to the mint to order sufficient quality metal. Polybius, Claudius's Secretary for Petitions, also a former slave of Greek origin, now a multimillionaire, wrote the inscription and commissioned an artist friend to do the lettering and figure. They then jointly put in motion their apparatus for influencing public opinion: proclamations, allusions in the cabarets, hints to bookmakers that Claudius was preparing to designate Britannicus as his heir.

The climax was a spectacle at the Campus Martius. The Guards' band played martial music while captured British basket chariots filed past. Pallas presented a coffer containing the new *denarii* to Claudius, who read a short speech from which Pallas had deleted an antiquarian digression. Britannicus, tall and thin but quite impressive in a military uniform, then received the coffer from his father's hands and distributed the coins one by one to notabilities present.

Agrippina had word of the new coinage but found herself powerless to prevent it against the combined Secretaries. On the day the coins left the mint, she bought up as many as she could afford. But the damage had been done, while the remaining coins assumed rarity value and attracted collectors: this too Narcissus leaked to the gossip-mongers. It was noticed that he rewarded himself with a pair of fine sapphire earrings.

I witnessed the sequel myself when, from my office balcony, I watched the New Year's Day procession of notables make its way down the Via Sacra to the temple to attend the ritual sacrifice of a heifer for the safety of Rome.

Following the Praetorian band came a boy's choir, dignitaries from the provinces, cowled priests and last, the magistrates in office. Here

I could hardly believe what I saw. Walking between the two consuls – an honour usually accorded to triumphal generals – was no other than Secretary Polybius. A step ahead of the consuls walked Claudius, beside him Secretary Pallas and Secretary Narcissus, each preceded by a solemn-faced lector bearing the bundle of birch rods accorded senior magistrates, Pallas's festooned with the insignia of honorary *quaestor*, Narcissus's with the still higher insignia of *praetor*. Pallas's habitual expression of surly arrogance remained unaltered, but Narcissus beamed at the crowd, raising a hand gleaming with rings to acknowledge cheers he took to be for him personally.

I confess I was shocked. Bad enough that the Secretaries feasted on taxpayers' money, bad enough that they pounced on a senator's least imprudence with a charge of treason, bad enough that Pallas had wormed his scabrous brother Felix into the governorship of Judaea; now, with Claudius's approval, they were gratuitously assuming honours hitherto won by years of hard work in the Senate, overstepping the Republic's main structural boundary, that between executive and legislature.

Almost to a man, the senators reacted angrily. Until now they had shown forbearance, but things were going too far. They would show their disapproval of Claudius by blocking any measure within their power. And one such way, as Narcissus had foreseen, lay to hand.

For some time, Agrippina had been drawing Claudius's attention to the fact that Octavia had reached an age suitable for betrothal. The daughter of a *princeps* traditionally marries into a patrician family, but who was to say that such an honour would not turn the bridegroom's head and make him a dangerous rival to his father-in-law? The only safe course was for Claudius to promise his daughter to her cousin Nero. Marriage proper would have to wait until Octavia became nubile.

Claudius remarked that the plan had already occurred to him, but that there existed an insuperable obstacle. Union of first cousins required a dispensation from the Senate. It would be humiliating for him to have to go before that body in their present mood, when many of them wished him dead, and ask them as a favour to allow him to choose a husband for his daughter. What if they refused? Never would he do it.

Lucius came to see me, saying he wanted to talk, to try to straighten things out. He needed to make sense of disturbing events, to set them in a framework where he could see objective truths as operative. Putting it another way, he was looking for certainty to help further action.

While still a law student, Lucius held private talks with Attalus. Like most Stoics, he believed it impossible to lead a virtuous life in the scheming turmoil of politics. Lucius, set on a political career, disagreed. He argued that virtue could only continue to flourish by making Rome safe for virtue.

Zeno had said, 'If I were to be granted wisdom without being able to share it, I would rather not be wise.' Influenced by that apophthegm, Lucius went on to offer his own definition of philosophy at the age of 30. It was not, as most Stoics held, about wisdom informing a virtuous life. It was about practising and instilling sympathy, fellowship and feeling for others – underpinned of course by the Stoic practice of self-discipline and restraining one's wants.

From there, Lucius went on to approach conventional opposites not as incompatibles but as potentially complementary. It led him to see the linking element in human affairs as all-important, hence the recurrence in his writings of words like co-operation, consensus and cohesion. It led him also to resist exclusion, whether by senators or by the *princeps*, hence to his fame – notoriety, others would say – as a political dissident.

I asked Lucius whether recent experiences had given him a clearer understanding of civic cohesion. His was a qualified affirmative. As well as law and law-abidingness, cohesion entailed citizens, especially those in government, respecting the rights of others.

I nodded bleakly. 'Precisely what Claudius does not do.' I then asked whether if Lucius were able to explain to Claudius that his actions were likely to lead to dissension, even a breakdown of government, would he change?

'Too late.' He looked glum. 'His own safety now means more to him than that of the Republic.'

'So what can be done?'

'In the long term, education. In the short term, manoeuvring. Cutting a fire break to contain a fire. And that brings me to Agrippina. Last night, she asked me to go to my old friends in the House, convince them of the desirability of the betrothal and get them to vote a dispensation against consanguineous union.'

'And you'll do it?'

For answer he held up his left hand. On the little finger was a silver ring in which was set a small piece of porphyry cut in the shape of a pyramid. For Stoics, the pyramid is a symbol of constancy.

'Not once have my friends in the Senate seen me work in Caesar's interest against theirs. I'm not going to waver now. And there's a second reason for saying no to Agrippina. Claudius's public honours to his toads were outrageous and the Senate is right to show its disapproval by non-cooperation.'

As he walked away, pondering how to deal with Agrippina's request, Lucius decided to look up the law in question. He turned into the Senate annexe where the archivist produced a copy of the text. Formulated in outdated phraseology, it made clear that the law on consanguinity specifically forbade marriage. It said nothing about betrothal, a mere intention to marry, which therefore in itself could not be accounted an illegal act.

Pleased with his discovery, Lucius reported to Agrippina who for once had the grace to thank him. She then began preparations. She intended the betrothal to be a showpiece worthy of her rank and also a singular occasion that would impress on people's memories the notion that the young couple were to all intents united.

She had the garden drawing-room decorated with cut-out felt images of winged cupids aiming their arrows and fashioned her hair in a becoming new style, softly waved, with one curl falling over each shoulder. She welcomed her guests who included, at Nero's request, Lucius.

With the arrival of Octavia's maternal kin, the Messallas, in large number, Claudius began to look miserable. Patricians who looked down their pendant-like aquiline noses at the parvenu Caesars, very rich because most of the silverwork and jewellery trade was in their hands, they caused Claudius to relive those panic-stricken hours in hiding after Messalina's public bigamy. It did not help that Britannicus stood in a corner looking like a beaten dog.

Agrippina directed guests into a half-circle facing Octavia who wore a chaplet of flowers on her hair next to Nero in a white gown. The couple looked self-conscious as Claudius stepped forward to make his address.

He spoke affectionately of his daughter, referred to Nero as 'my wife's son' – nothing more – then drifted into one of his notorious non-sequiturs about birds of favourable omen. Of these: there were two kinds, birds whose flight was an omen, such as the eagle and osprey, and birds whose cry was an omen. Such were the crow, woodpecker and jackdaw. The cry of the woodpecker and jackdaw were auspicious when coming from the left, and he cited examples. However and this he found most interesting – the opposite held true of the crow. 'If ever you hear a crow cawing from the left,' he warned, 'be sure to take utmost care.'

Lucius watched the Messalla group. At first they listened attentively, trying to look as though they detected a thread of argument but, as he rambled on, their expressions showed boredom and one even put a hand to his cheek and closed his eyes sleepily. At last, Claudius came to the point. Today quite a new bird of favourable omen would arrive from the left. A pause, then a manservant entered carrying a cage. Opening the cage door, he released three minahs. A white one flew to Octavia, perching on her shoulder; a black one to Nero's wrist; another white one to Agrippina's wrist. Little gasps of surprise from the guests were followed by a pause, as the birds were stroked and put at ease.

Nero's bird spoke first a string of pretty compliments to the future bride. Octavia's bird replied with coy courtesies. Each cleverly mimicked the voice of its owner, Agrippina's to express satisfaction at the betrothal. The three birds then clustered on Agrippina's wrist to recite in chorus the lines of a rhymed epithalamium.

The set-piece left everyone looking pleased. As they moved to a table spread with sweetmeats and watched the young couple hand-feed their pets and chat with them, they exchanged nods and smiles: here was something unusual to tell their friends about.

As the last guests said goodbye to a smiling Agrippina, Lucius seized an opportune moment to ask whether she would now restore to him his property and seat in the Senate. Her expression turned cold. 'Spoils are distributed when the battle is over not before.' My brother's muffled expletives may readily be imagined.

Nettled by the attention given to his half-brother, Britannicus veered between over-demonstrative affection for his father, petulant complaints to Sosibius and hints to Narcissus that something should be done before it became too late. Narcissus did not heed the hints.

On Claudius's orders, a tunnel was being bored through the mountain between the Fucine Lake and the river Liris, a major work that would make land available for farming. Narcissus had assumed overall charge but, being busy with more congenial schemes, he rarely visited the site. To his annoyance, the date for the opening had had to be postponed when it was found that the tunnel had not been sunk to the bottom of the lake.

Now all was ready and Narcissus went to Claudius to propose a grandiose show: a banquet near the lake's outlet and an infantry battle between gladiators and pontoons moored in the lake. Claudius agreed that Britannicus should adjudge the battle and, on behalf of his father, order the retaining dyke to be breached.

On the day of the ceremony, Claudius arrived to find spectators massed on the banks of the lake. He wore his purple cloak as commander-in-chief of the army – many considered him overdressed – while Agrippina wore a cape of cloth of gold.

Under the calm guidance of Afranius Burrus, Commander of the Praetorian Guard, Britannicus correctly directed a mock battle in four acts, enlivened by trumpet calls, fierce shouting and alarm cries as retreating soldiers fell off the pontoon, to be rescued from the water by rowboats.

Next, a banquet was served on ground with a good view of the lake's outlet. When the last dishes had been emptied, Claudius and Britannicus climbed to a platform commanding the works. Here Claudius introduced his son: 'Soon to come of age and to take his place at my side.' Britannicus declared the tunnel open. At this, a silver-plated Triton, raised by a rachet-wheel, emerged from the centre of the lake and sounded its horn, the signal for workmen to knock out the thick retaining dyke. Water poured into the tunnel, but the tunnel proved too narrow. With terrifying speed, onrushing pent-up water rose higher and higher to flood the shore nearest the outlet then roar over adjoining ground, close to the platform. Claudius raced to higher ground, shedding his purple cloak on the way. Spectators too fled before the fast-rising flood.

In the carriage returning to Rome, Agrippina acted from strength. Large sums had been poured into a prestige project and to what purpose? The tunnel had collapsed, months of work rendered useless and three people drowned. Claudius could redeem the fiasco only by exposing those to blame. She demanded that the project's accounts be referred to the Audit Office. Still shaken by the memory of that wall of water, Claudius agreed.

Agrippina saw to it that the auditors acted swiftly. They found that large sums had been diverted from engineering work to private accounts. Narcissus was summoned but, pleading ill-health, he obtained leave of absence and went to take the waters in Sinuessa – suffering, quipped some, from dropsy. Agrippina argued that Narcissus's absence was evidence of his guilt, and called for the dismissal of Narcissus's protégé, Sosibius. When Claudius, still reeling from Narcissus's blow, made only feeble objection, she appointed as Britannicus's tutor a tough young man upon whom she could count. Agrippina realized that she could soon lose her ascendancy if Claudius transferred his trust to Polybius or another Secretary. She must act fast.

Senatorial anger with Claudius had spilled over into demand for change. On a moonless night, one hot-headed political idealist climbed into the garden of Caesar's House. Security guards spotted him and after a scuffle overpowered him. Claudius, a heavy sleeper, heard nothing but Agrippina was woken by the shouts. Dressing quickly, she took charge. For half an hour, she questioned the intruder, a well-educated son of a prosperous market-gardener, armed with a butcher's knife. Summoning Guard Commander Burrus, she ordered him to escort the man to the Mamertine prison, then returned to bed and, such was her willpower, at once went back to sleep. So much is public knowledge: what follows comes from my brother's transcript from an entry in Agrippina's diary.

The incident occurred at an opportune moment for Agrippina, who informed her husband at breakfast, 'A discontented intellectual broke in last night who believed he would be doing Rome a service by killing you. I can quote you his very words: "I swore I would thrust my knife through Claudius's scrawny neck."'

Claudius flinched, then passed a hand complacently over his neck. 'Scrawny! Man must be mad.' Pettishly, he coated the last of the oat cakes with honey and told Agrippina to bring him more, a demand she disregarded, asking him what action he intended to take.

'Tighten security.'

'Only you can do that. You know what that assassin told me? He said that if he killed you now, with no heir in sight, the principate would die too and Rome would get back her two-consul executive… *With no heir in sight…* there's your security gap.'

Claudius stopped chewing and sat back looking reflective. 'I carry out my duties. At the lake, the crowd's cheers echoed off the mountain. Why would anyone want to get rid of me?'

'Go to the Mamertine. Hear it from the man's own lips.'

Claudius chortled. 'Really, my dear! What next?'

Agrippina struck a pleasing note. 'Think of those you love, your son, your daughter, not to speak of me. Their safety as well as yours depends on appointing an heir. Now, at once.'

Claudius sighed and ran a hand over his brow. 'Dilemma, dilemma.'

'There *is* no dilemma. There is one reasonable course.'

Claudius lifted a soothing hand. 'Be patient, my dear. I must take advice.'

'From whom? From Narcissus who betrayed your friendship and is even now perhaps plotting a coup? Or others of his gang?'

'At present there is no suitable heir.'

'Nero, is he not eminently suitable?'

'He is not my son. Not flesh of my flesh. We must wait until Britannicus comes of age.'

It was the last thing Agrippina wanted to hear – and spoken so firmly. Yet she had foreseen it. Britannicus's delicate health – three times now without any warning he had fallen to the floor unconscious, the doctors could not discover the cause and also his solitary temperament made him totally unsuited to be head of State. She knew Claudius could be particularly obstinate on this subject: at Britannicus's age, he had suffered from poor health and outgrown it; as his son grew older and stronger, so he would slip easily into a public role.

She had prepared a flanking manoeuvre, a dangerous tactic, to be used only in an emergency. But this, she decided, was an emergency.

'I know you're pleased that I've been much taken with our dear Octavia lately. It has set me reminiscing about her mother. I wonder whether you knew just how morbidly jealous that woman was of my son, so much sturdier than her own little boy. I've never told you this, but she actually tried to kill little Domitius by hiding an adder in a linen basket, then having her maid carry it to the child's nursery after dark. Happily I was able to foil her horrible plan.'

'Why are you telling me this?' asked Claudius angrily. 'She's a part of my life I've chosen to forget.'

'Of course this is painful to you, but I think you should hear. For it shows the sort of woman she was *at the very start* of her marriage.

'In the spring following your nuptials, you travelled to Naples – alone. It was March, to be exact. You were gone fifteen days. During that time your wife made a round of parties, invariably escorted by a notorious playboy – I will mention no names. No, this isn't gossip: I saw the pair of them and heard the comments they provoked. In November, exactly nine months after your absence in Naples, your wife went into labour and gave birth to a boy.'

Claudius turned pale and threw her the pleading look a prostrate gladiator had often turned on him from the arena. Ignoring it, she drove home her point. 'Can you be quite sure that boy is flesh of your flesh?'

Like a pudding tipped out of its mould, the contours of Claudius's face crumbled, leaving only the pain in his eyes; his voice when it came was faint and faltering. What she said was malicious, what she implied was unthinkable. He forbade her to mention the subject again. He rose unsteadily to his feet and shuffled out of the room.

Agrippina had expected to lance a fatal occlusion; instead she came to see that she had desecrated a hallowed place, the shrine of paternal love for a bright intelligence struggling, like a son of Laocoon, with the serpent of ill-health.

When wounded and driven to the wall, a weak character will sometimes take refuge in inaccessibility: so it happened now. Except at meals, Claudius shunned his wife, and Lucius also, to whom he had formerly confided snippets of history.

Evenings he divided between reading the tragedies of Aeschylus and playing chess with his son, interspersing moves with maudlin talk. Heedless of the proximity of Agrippina and Nero, he would dwell on past misfortunes, how he'd had to sacrifice his ambition as an archaeologist to the thankless duties of high office, how a favourite had betrayed him and, above all, how unlucky he had been in his marriages.

'It's my destiny,' he was heard to say, 'first to endure my wives' misdeeds, then to punish them,' the penultimate word hissed venomously.

One evening Claudius reminisced how, aged two, Britannicus had a vocabulary of 40 words, and could recite his times table when he was just three. 'At times I've been harsh with you, should have shown more patience. And lately I took a step that caused you much pain...' Pressing the boy's fingers to his lips, in a voice quavering with emotion, he quoted a line spoken by Achilles in one of the Greek plays he'd been reading: 'The hand that wounded you shall also heal.'

Soon afterwards, to Agrippina's acute alarm, she saw Claudius showing his son the phoenix seal with which a *princeps* validates letters and documents. 'Augustus had it made. One day it will be yours and Rome will have a true-born Caesar.'

Later Claudius called in a distinguished Greek jurist and remained closeted with him for more than an hour. Greeks are notorious for finding loopholes in our laws and it seemed likely that the pair discussed ways of bringing forward by a year Britannicus's assumption of the *toga virilis*, for there followed a visit from Claudius's tailor.

Agrippina watched, listened and manoeuvred. Two of Claudius's long-serving manservants, one in charge of his wardrobe, the other of his bathroom and massage, she dismissed on the grounds that they were slacking, and replaced them with retainers from her Antium estate. Claudius grumbled but could not protest since domestic management is a wife's prerogative.

Further small incidents struck Lucius as odd. He arrived one morning to find that he could not get into the classroom. The door was locked as usual but his key no longer turned the bolt. The janitor explained that Agrippina had had all the locks in the house changed overnight 'for Caesar's better security', and handed Lucius a new key.

Some days later, Claudius complained at table because no sauce had been served with his angler fish. Agrippina explained that Locusta, the cook's countrywoman assistant who prepared all sauces, as well as tisanes and herbal sedatives, had three days' leave to visit her ailing mother. Now Lucius happened to know that Locusta's mother had died many years before.

On a misty mid-October morning, Lucius went to Caesar's House to pick up Nero, due back shortly from an early ride, prior to meeting the other members of the class for an expedition to a model farm. He found Claudius slouched in a cushion chair, shifting position uncomfortably, his round cheeks and waxy complexion more than ever suggestive of a pumpkin. Lucius obeyed his signal to sit by him.

'I rather overdid it last night,' the great man confided unhappily.

Lucius had noticed. He had been invited to the family dinner to talk about Stoic philosophy with Claudius and his literary adviser Polybius. Conversation took a different turn when steamed asparagus served upright in individual silver containers was carried in and hailed by Claudius with outstretched arm: 'We who are about to eat, salute you!'

The dish once tasted, Polybius ventured a remark. 'Archestratus says asparagus is improved by a sauce of cream and raw egg.'

'Then he's an arch-idiot. Oil and vinegar: anything more distorts the flavour. Peasant fare, you think? Nonsense. To achieve the correct balance is art of the highest order. Though we do not acknowledge her, there is certainly a tenth Muse – of cookery.'

The main dish consisted of a brace of wild duck, roasted and served with fly agaric mushrooms – the bright vermilion of their caps which fades in cooking restored with cochineal – interspersed with chunky brown ceps, cut thin and lightly fried with slices of bread and garlic cloves.

Lucius ate only the duck, for he still held to his youthful abstinence from oysters and mushrooms, but Claudius took two helpings of both duck and mushrooms.

Claudius described his pleasure in the meal to Lucius. 'To send food like that back to the kitchen would have been an insult to the gods, which is why I took...' The sentence remained unfinished. Clutching his stomach with both hands, he called to Agrippina, who at once hurried to him. 'I'm not well... Not at all well.'

Kneeling beside him, Agrippina loosened his dress and laid a hand on his brow. As Claudius began to groan and screw up his eyes in pain, she summoned Nero, who had just returned and told him to fetch the duty doctor. Then she ordered Lucius and Polybius to lay the heavy body onto a couch.

Minutes later, Xenophon was drawing back the sick man's eyelids, measuring his pulse and, under its dome of white fat, palpating the stomach. 'To bed,' he commanded. 'Hurry.'

A litter was sent for. Holding back tears, Britannicus clutched at Xenophon's sleeve. Was it serious? A question doctors are taught to ignore. 'I intend,' said the other gravely, 'to induce vomiting.'

Ordering everyone else to remain in their places, Agrippina led the way to Claudius's bedroom, followed by Xenophon, the bearers and their burden.

Lucius believed this to be just another attack of acute indigestion and trained his attention on the behaviour of the others: Nero looked troubled, Britannicus sobbed into the sleeve of his gown and was comforted by his new tutor Arsenus, while Polybius kept muttering, 'What will become of me?'

Presently Agrippina returned. 'Xenophon has successfully used the goose-feather and is now administering an enema.' Her even voice and self-possession raised these humble details to the status of a victory bulletin. 'Arsenus, take Britannicus to his room and give him a sedative. Lucius and Polybius, guards will escort you to your homes. Speak to no one: not a word, you understand. Nero, come with me.'

Of these events, I knew nothing until the following morning, when a tablet was affixed to the gate of Caesar's House stating that the *princeps* had been taken ill and asking for prayers to be said for his swift recovery. An hour later, a second tablet signed by Xenophon declared the patient's pulse to be stronger. Soon afterwards, a troupe of comedians went in: evidently Claudius felt well enough for entertainment. But at nine, a third tablet announced complications, whereupon the House convened and instructed the consuls and college of priests to pray to Jupiter, Juno and Rome for recovery.

Unknown to me or anyone in the city, hours earlier, at two in the morning, behind a door hung with thick double drapes to muffle his screams and locked from the inside, Claudius had drawn his last breath in the presence of his wife only. Agrippina had immediately worked through his papers but found no will. As soon as it grew light, she summoned Burrus, commander of the guard, a man of few words and proven integrity.

'Just before his end, my late husband fixed his eyes on me and said in a clear voice, "I commend my son Nero to the guard, to the Senate and to the people." His exact words.'

Burrus snapped to attention. 'Your son can count on my loyalty.' He then advised her to consult astrologers about the most auspicious moment for Nero to appear before the guard.

Nine hours after the death, shortly before eleven, a herald cloaked in russet mourning announced that the *princeps* was no more, the cause of death according to his doctor was either acute indigestion or a knotting of the small intestine occasioned by persistent worry.

I hurried to Lucius and the details he gave me aroused my suspicions. Fifteen hours between dinner and the onset of pain, so it seemed to me, ruled out indigestion but was compatible with a slow-acting poison. I happen to know about fungi for they are plentiful in the stand of oaks on my country estate. The edible cep has a close relative which is poisonous, the so-called cep of Hades, with red instead of yellow gills and flesh that turns blueish under the knife. The one is easily mistaken for the other.

If ceps of Hades had been served, why had no one else been taken ill? Evidently because they had been served to Claudius alone without first being cleared by his taster. Lucius recalled Agrippina's change of servants and Locusta's curious absence. If Locusta was an expert on aromatic herbs and healing plants, she would also have known about deadly mushrooms.

Our discussion was interrupted by noise coming from the street. We went down to see what the commotion was about and joined a crowd surging towards Caesar's House. There, at noon precisely, the hour chosen as auspicious, a fanfare of trumpets sounded and Nero appeared. He walked slowly down the step to the forecourt where the guard was drawn up in three nervous-looking ranks. Some of the guards exchanged puzzled glances and whispers: 'Where's

Britannicus?' Though none of them knew it, he was still locked in his room, the key to which hung on Agrippina's belt.

Over recent months, Nero's warm manner and straight back on the parade ground had produced a generally favourable impression and now, when the youthful figure halted before Burrus and was hailed by him: 'Nero our commander! Nero Caesar!' his men needed no prompting to roar out the same acclaim.

At the guards' camp outside the walls, this scene was repeated on a larger scale. Claudius had given a donative of 150 gold pieces to every man of the guard: a bad precedent, but dangerous to ignore. On Agrippina's instruction, Nero promised the same sum, adding that the Senate would meet after the funeral in order to enact the people's wishes as expressed by the guard and so invest the *princeps* with his *imperium.*

Back at Caesar's House, the captain of the duty cohort presented himself to enquire what password Nero had chosen for use that evening, a choice believed to throw light on the new incumbent. Without hesitation, Nero replied: 'The best of mothers!'

Next morning, I joined the crowd in front of a myrtle branch pyre in the Campus Martius. The sky was grey, the air chilly. On a high platform opposite, wearing russet mourning, stood the dead man's family. Britannicus's pallor was accentuated by his red swollen eyes.

With a nod, Agrippina signalled for the pyre to be lit. As flames crackled and spread, I fixed my eyes on the shrouded body. This reluctant ruler, plaything of greedy freedmen, had sent a hundred or more prominent Romans ahead of him to Hades. But he had loved his little son and wanted to do the right thing by him. That virtue, rather than his vices, had probably cost him his life.

Lucius joined me. He had long secretly hoped that Nero would become the new ruler of Rome but his pleasure in the event fell short of jubilation. He saw that his services as tutor would no longer be required and he felt the resultant wrench of separation. He regretted not having been granted time – even just one more year to point Nero towards those reforms of which Rome stood in need.

As flames licked at the fat paunch, at the cream sauce curdled inside, the crackling softened to a hiss. In spite of myself, I shuddered and turned my eyes back to the platform, to our *princeps*-designate. According to Lucius, he was a gifted all-rounder but he was nevertheless alarmingly young – not yet 17. Beside him, noting his every move, stood 'the best of mothers'.

PART TWO

Influence and its limits

Senators shed no tears for Claudius but shook their heads doubtfully over his successor. Young, said his well-wishers, therefore modest and malleable. But his uncle Gaius had also been young when he became emperor and, by styling himself a living god, had proved a perpetual nuisance. Nero's tutor, it appeared, had imparted sound ideas about the Senate's role, but how far had they penetrated? And not a few had suspicions about the circumstances of Claudius's death. The house awaited impatiently the new *princeps*'s inaugural speech.

The speech preoccupied Agrippina too. Her son cut a good figure in public but too often lost the thread of what he wanted to say, leaving hearers puzzled and unconvinced. Mindful of Lucius's reputation as an orator, she asked him to help Nero.

Lucius asked for nothing better, and the two met in Claudius's former writing room. Outwardly their roles were reversed, but neither was embarrassed and they got off on their old footing, with Lucius asking Nero how he saw his new office.

'It gives me the chance to make a return for the advantages I've had. I want to work for the people of Rome, labour as hard as the blacksmith in his forge and eventually perhaps win the kind of applause athletes win at the Olympics.' Glancing round the room with a shudder, he continued: 'This is where Claudius held his secret tribunal... I think of that phrase of yours, "Numerous executions discredit a *princeps* as numerous funerals a doctor." I should like never to have to sign a death sentence.'

I went to the visitors' enclosure to hear that speech. Facing 600 of our most eminent and critical men, Nero began shaking but, after the first two sentences, he found his stride. There are some passages I recall.

'My boyhood was unclouded by civil war or family strife, so I bring to my task no hatreds, no desire for vengeance. I will keep personal and State affairs separate. There will be no favouritism, no secret tribunals...

'The Senate will preserve its time-honoured functions and will enact laws with no interference from me. While legal cases from frontier provinces will continue to come under my jurisdiction, appellants from Italy and the senatorial provinces who may have grievances, after first applying to the consuls will have access to our courts.. In the New Year, I shall offer myself as consul and, if elected, will act with my fellow consul as his equal, not as Caesar.'

In tone and content this was so far from Claudius's speeches that senators could hardly believe their ears. But at the end they applauded with unusual warmth, though a few doubters murmured that it was only a programme. The consuls ordered the speech to be inscribed on the *stele* in gilded lettering, doubtless partly in order to remind Nero as he grew older.

Shortly after this happy occasion, Agrippina summoned Lucius and invited him to join Nero's inner Cabinet, responsible for policy-making, the members of which are styled 'Caesar's Friends'. He should bring her his answer next day. This was a step-up, unexpected and flattering, but it came at an awkward moment. Nero no longer requiring a tutor, Lucius and Paula had been making plans to travel: to revisit Veziers and for Paula to see Corduba. They had even worked out their itinerary on Lucius's maps.

On his way home, Lucius stopped at a fashionable confectioner and bought an exorbitantly expensive box of crystallized chestnuts, Paula's favourite. He couldn't quite have said why, except that he had a premonition of difficulties.

The evening was mild and Lucius, always one for the outdoors, suggested they sit out on their balcony with its view west to the setting sun. Installed there, with the open box beside Paula, he told her that he had just seen Agrippina.

'About restoring our house and property?'

'No. But I spoke to her yesterday about that. She promised to attend to it but for the moment had too much urgent business. I could see she meant it.'

Paula did not seem convinced and helped herself to a second sweet. A pause followed filled by hawkers' cries drifting up from the street. Then he told her of Agrippina's offer.

Paula's expression brightened. 'She was pleased with the speech you wrote. And hopes you will write more?'

'Probably.'

'And what else would you do?'

Lucius sketched the work of the Cabinet.

'Who would preside? Nero?'

'When he's older. For now, Agrippina.'

She gave him a mischievous look. 'So you would see a lot of that good-looking lady whose voice you once described as a siren song.'

Lucius smiled. 'Don't worry. She says nothing to me as a man.'

'We shall see... May I ask you something? Is Agrippina Nero's mother, or is Nero Agrippina's son?'

'For now, the latter.'

'So you would be in the Cabinet with Agrippina presiding and only in virtue of your relation to Agrippina's son.'

'Agreed. And, take it at the worst, put there only as a sop to the Senate. Once installed, I believe I can convince Cabinet members that the *princeps*'s strength – safety too -lies in working closely with the Senate.'

'And if she sees you beginning to convince her son of that?' The question answered itself, and Paula went on. 'I'm not suggesting you should turn down the job, only trying to show what it might entail... One thing more. I think you should make Agrippina feel that you like her.'

Lucius considered this for some moments, then steeled himself.

'You know what it would mean for our holiday?'

She met his eyes seriously, uncomplainingly and nodded.

Darkness had fallen. They went in and closed the balcony shutters.

When I heard of the offer to Lucius, I saw it as an honour to him and, by extension, to me as his brother, but I confess I felt alarmed. Lucius had done well in the cut and thrust of the Senate – that was where he belonged – but the upper reaches of government are an arena for heavily armed gladiators. Lucius was a provincial, a 'new man' with no famous forebears or family – I'm thinking about uncles and cousins and brothers-in-law who hold consular rank, command of an army or have millions in gold to lend. Lucius in Cabinet becomes Caesar's Friend for as long as he agrees with Caesar and with Caesar's mother. The moment he chooses to disagree, he becomes Caesar's enemy. And for a man with no power base, I didn't like to picture the consequences.

As it happened, my views weren't sought. By now, Lucius's life had acquired its own momentum and it was this that decided the matter. Not for the first time Paula had come off badly as I saw it. Lucius had trained himself to limit his wants, as Stoic teaching demanded, and could readily choose the less pleasurable of two courses. Often this meant that Paula, whose temperament was by no means Stoic, had to forego pleasures which she held dear.

Cabinet consisted of Nero, Agrippina, Burrus as commander of the Guard, Cornelius as City Prefect and Lucius. They sat around a table in Agrippina's study, with Agrippina at the head. Claudius's Secretaries had been replaced by unpretentious freedmen from Latin-speaking provinces: they were men with clean hands whom she called in as needed. An amanuensis recorded proceedings in shorthand. Much work in Cabinet consists of questioning expert advisers: here I report only the business that led to important decisions.

Agrippina, the only one with top-level experience, began the first meeting by defining procedure and allocating responsibilities. She would decide the agenda, make senior appointments and handle foreign affairs. Nero would look after corn distribution, preside over the court of appeal and allocate funds from his privy purse, which drew income from properties in Egypt and Asia Minor, to new buildings, shows and games. Burrus would liaise with the legions and ensure Nero's safety; Cornelius would keep public order while Lucius would advise on provincial affairs, write Nero's speeches and help him in the appeal court. She turned next to coinage. In view of Nero's youth, the emphasis would be on lineage and continuity. She proposed that the first issue depict two heads – Nero's and her own.

Burrus remarked that this might divide the loyalty that ought to be focused on Nero, but Agrippina insisted that her head and her title Augusta would add weight to her son's authority. She then passed around a sketch: it showed mother and son facing each other, she wearing her hair in a long plait at the back, with a becoming ringlet trailing her ear. Nero liked it, Lucius and the others found no reason to dislike it, and the coin was approved.

Seizing what seemed to be a favourable opportunity, Lucius suggested striking a second coin: it would depict the civic crown of oak leaves as a type-symbol of liberty and the restoration of senatorial authority. Agrippina responded coolly but, when Nero and Burrus said they welcomed the idea, she grudgingly yielded.

During Cabinet meetings, Lucius learned much about the logistics of running Rome: notably the transport of wheat from abroad, the stocking of huge reserves for the winter when all cargo vessels remained in harbour, and the measures taken to protect stocks from rats: all in order to provide every citizen with his daily bread.

While learning, Lucius also kept a close eye on his former pupil as he settled into his new role. Nero found legal and administrative affairs difficult and boring but, as soon as roads, bridges, aqueducts and the like came up for discussion, he showed keen interest and precocious understanding. To his mother, he showed deference though once or twice he openly disagreed with her. He often consulted Lucius after Cabinet and it was a relief to my brother that the gap in status had not made their relationship less cordial.

Nero's betrothal to Octavia had met with popular approval and, as Octavia reached sexual maturity and had her first menstrual period, people expected marriage to follow. The Senate saw no advantage in opposing public opinion and gave the needed dispensation. Though Lucius seldom saw Octavia, he understood that she was much attached to her husband and that Nero was content with his girl-wife.

In Cabinet, Agrippina would herald a grave topic by leaning her elbows on the table and slowly joining the tips of her fingers, thus drawing attention to her fine white hands, of which she took good care. A month into the new principate, she made an issue of recalling how Julius Caesar and Augustus were posthumously declared to have joined the gods and were then known as *Divus*. The reason? Both had extended the frontiers.

When the legions conquered Britain, her late husband had been in command. It followed that he too had now joined the gods, should be termed *Divus* and in due course allocated a star by the Society of Astronomers. Lucius experienced an unpleasant double jolt on hearing her words. To grant such an honour to one whose tergiversations and susceptibility to flattery he had watched at close range would be to drain the word 'divine' of much of its content. And, as a senator, it revolted him to think that reverence should be paid to one who had shed senatorial blood.

Lucius marshalled his arguments, toning them down in deference to Agrippina. He turned to the subject of 'deification', as it was often misleadingly known. Who had brought it to Rome? Julius. When? On his return from Egypt. Why? Because his mistress Cleopatra, mother of his son Caesarian, described herself as a god honoured as such in Egypt. Under her influence and wishing to bolster his claim to be sole ruler in Rome – perhaps, as enemies claimed, to become king – Julius made public a tradition in his family that the Caesars descended from the goddess Venus. More than once, he stated that divine blood flowed in his veins. On Julius's death, the young Octavian had enhanced his prestige by asserting that, by virtue of his many military victories, his stepfather had won the supreme honour of joining the immortals.

Octavian – Augustus as he then became – based his claim on a carving found at the temple of Abu Simbel. Julius's staff had seen the four colossal seated statues of Ramses II and the sunken reliefs enumerating his military victories. They reported that Ramses had been honoured as a god because of those victories.

'As a young man,' said Lucius, 'I visited the temple at Abu Simbel. In the sanctuary I saw those four statues: Ramses seated as their equal beside three Egyptian divinities. But Ramses was there not because of his victories but because of his kingship and the name he had assumed on the day of his enthronement: "the chosen of Re, great in truth and justice." The best way to deal with this notion of a man joining the gods as an equal because of victories in the field was to let it lapse. Not only was it spurious but it also fed all kinds of unrepublican toadying in Greek-speaking lands.

Agrippina's self-control was never more apparent than when meeting opposition. 'What you say interests me, Lucius, but it has no bearing on what the people believe and wish to continue to believe. A public cult of Claudius would add weight to the new government. I propose therefore to build a temple in his honour in the centre of Rome at my expense and to institute a priesthood of which I shall be the first member.'

The proposal was discussed at length, with Nero and Cornelius in favour, Lucius and Burrus opposed. Agrippina's casting vote meant it was adopted. Lucius had of course known from the start that he would have to abide by a majority view. The raising of Claudius to the level of a god was abhorrent to him and his friends in the Senate would assume that he was in agreement unless he resigned. But resignation would scupper for good any influence he might have at the top.

He was about to turn his mind to possible delaying tactics when a message was handed to him in the Forum that Agrippina's recent order for the return to him of his house and all other personal effects had passed through the various relevant departments and that he was now legally entitled to take repossession. This news, so long hoped for in vain, drove everything else from his mind and he hurried to share it with Paula. They kissed, hugged and danced around the apartment like prisoners who have just learnt of their pardon.

Lucius had bought the house because it was close to the airy Gardens of Marcellus: brick-built of medium size, it stood on three sides of a garden patio. Lawyers at that time were not allowed to charge fees, but Lucius had been rewarded by grateful clients with goods in kind and generous legacies, and he had paid cash down.

Lucius and Paula went to view it next morning, picking up the key on the way. They expected to find the place in a poor state and knew it would be empty of the furniture which had to be recovered separately from the State depository. Still, they felt excited and mildly triumphant.

Ivy and roses running wild almost hid the entrance and Lucius had to oil the key in a nearby shop before he could turn it in the rusted lock. Inside, the paint on the walls of the hall had faded, damp patches discoloured the ceiling and the panelling had buckled. The bedrooms, redecorated by Paula just before sequestration, had suffered most for they faced north, and their window frames were green with mould. The garden had reverted to an iron-age tangle of weeds and creepers.

After assessing the visible damage, they locked up the house in silence, Paula close to tears and Lucius angry. On the walk back, Paula announced in broken voice that she would start at once to clear and redecorate. A man she knew would help. They could do it all at very little cost. This was the moment when Lucius felt close to tears. He brooded on a triumph turned to fiasco.

An extreme situation, he finally decided, called for extreme measures whereupon he hurried to the leading firm of interior decorators, Fatta, spoke to the manager and there and then commissioned him to redecorate his house without delay in the then fashionable style. The price quoted was steep; but a reserve of money in my keeping would cover it. On his return, he embraced his wife and informed her that, in a month's time, she'd be receiving friends for a house warming party in her own house.

She smiled sadly. 'Not in a month, Lucius. One day, yes.'

Then Lucius made what he thought was his big announcement, hoping to see her eyes light up. Instead her brows met in a frown and her lips tightened.

'But, Lucius, then it won't be our house, it'll just be one more...'

'The Fattas have a good name, and they lead the fashion.'

'...which next year will look out-of-date.'

Seeing Lucius unconvinced Paula turned to expense. She could do the work for a fraction of the cost; and she'd enjoy it.

'And end by wearing yourself out. Forget the expense. This is my way of showing you my love.'

In normal times, they would have discussed this good-humouredly but the prospect of regaining their old home had keyed up Paula's expectations as well as Lucius's. Their exchanges became sharp and ended with Lucius saying he had given Fatta the commission, that was that, and Paula would see it was all for the best.

They went to bed without speaking and next day, just when they had most reason to be happy, found themselves locked in one of those contests made difficult to resolve by the fact that each is thinking of the other's good.

Here I must speak of Lucius's finances. Stoic philosophers warn that wealth should be avoided because it makes us arrogant, ostentatious and fearful of losing it. By shifting the emphasis of philosophy from individual self-sufficiency to man as a social being bent on promoting fellowship, Seneca adopted a different view. He saw wealth not as harmful in itself but as something to be used to help those in need through no fault of their own.

As a young lawyer, Lucius received no fees. The system has changed since but, in the old days, grateful clients left him an appropriate legacy in their wills. Lucius had already trained himself to live unostentatiously and he asked me to bank his earnings on his behalf. Though I say it myself, I invested it astutely.

Lucius spent only a small part of his income, mainly on Paula; he also helped a number of students and scholars. But the fact that Lucius had a considerable amount of money to his name while writing essays warning of the dangers of wealth to the unwary brought stinging charges of double standards. These criticisms did not ruffle Lucius unduly but they did harm his reputation as a philosopher.

My wife Acilia called on Paula and was distressed to find her pale from sleepless nights. She was a close enough friend for Paula to confide what she had kept to herself out of respect for Lucius's feelings. Acilia has a more than usual capacity for righteous indignation at any hint of oppression. She returned home convinced that Lucius was behaving badly and that this paragon of happy marriages was on the verge of collapse. She said it was my duty to help. I told her I never meddled in my brother's marital life but she got around me, and even provided me with arguments.

When I visited, I found Lucius looking miserable: that afternoon a man from Fatta had brought samples of the colour scheme: Paula had refused to look at them. So I began slowly, recalling his setback in Cabinet and his natural impatience to show the Senate that he was again comfortably rehoused by throwing a lavish party. Hence the commission to Fatta. But was he being honest in claiming to act in Paula's best interests? He viewed a house as four walls where he could write and entertain but, for Paula, it was an expression of herself, more so even than her dress, for it conveyed her affections. I cited the bedroom occupied by her mother when she stayed: how Paula had painted it periwinkle blue, her mother's favourite flower, found ribbon of the same shade to edge the counterpane, and put a blue glass shade on the bedside lamp.

Let's face it, I said, you don't have visual taste, but Paula does and needs to express it, in her own style with her own hands. I might have added but refrained, that Paula's gift for making her home a harmonious whole created a mood propitious to Lucius who, returning there after an unproductive day, could once again believe that solutions were after all perhaps attainable.

Lucius showed no pique at my criticism and listened attentively but unconvinced.

'I refuse to see my wife on hands and knees scraping floorboards.'

'You don't need to. Just delegate the heavy work.'

He gave me a dark look and a pause followed.

'It's simply not reasonable,' he said with finality, screwing up his face as though at a bitter taste.

'So it offends the philosopher in you. Paula's had a bad time of it, and you feel she deserves compensation. But think in terms of her character: Paula is one of the world's givers. If you stop letting her give, you make her unhappy.'

He scowled, continued to enumerate all the disadvantages of delay, more for the sake of form than out of conviction, and I felt fairly sure my last thrust had pierced his armour.

Lucius continued to search for some way to express his disgust at the honours to be accorded Claudius. It was out of the question to make any direct criticisms in Cabinet given Agrippina's commitment to the project. He had regained senatorial rank with the freeing of his property but, in his position as Caesar's Friend, he could not sit in the House nor organize opposition there. He decided to ridicule the plan with a stinging satire.

Lucius's writing procedure was always the same. Convinced that ideas flow best at dawn, he breakfasted early and alone, then went to his desk, where he placed on his head, just above the brow, a circlet of parsley prepared the evening before. Though a Roman through and through, Lucius retained a sentimental attachment to country ways. He slept with the window wide open, took long walks in the countryside and thought seasonally, always beginning a new book in autumn. He believed, as Cordubans do, that the scent of parsley activates the brain. When ideas failed to materialize, he would slip out to the garden, pull up a handful of radishes and nibble these at his desk.

It took him ten days to write the satire. Entitled *Transfiguration of a Pumpkin-head*, the piece depicts an overweight, bewildered Claudius staggering into Heaven and mumbling a request couched in the form of Greek quotations, of which no one at first can make head or tail. Eventually it emerges that Claudius is asking to be made a god. The Olympians take his request seriously until Augustus intervenes. 'This fellow, who seems incapable of shooing a fly, killed men as easily as a dog lifts his leg... You want to make him a god? Who do you expect will worship him? Who will believe in him? If you make gods of such stuff as this, men will stop believing that you can be gods.'

The Olympians are convinced. They tell Mercury to seize Claudius by the neck and haul him off to Hell. Here he is met by a crowd of former associates, whom he greets warmly. 'The world is full of friends! How did you get here?' 'You dare ask how!' replies their leader. 'Who sent us here but you, butcher of every friend you had!'

Claudius is made to stand trial before Aeacus, one of Hell's terrifying Judges. The charge is mass murder. Aeacus declines to hear a defence – just as Claudius used to do on earth. He finds the prisoner guilty and, recalling his fondness for quibbles and chicanery, condemns him to serve in perpetuity as his legal secretary and drudge.

The satire was circulated unsigned, but senators recognized Lucius's inimitable style and got the message. Agrippina almost certainly knew who its author was but said nothing.

Nero's good-natured wrestling partner, Marcus Salvius Otho, now a career officer, had married Poppaea Sabina. She was said to be clever; due to his lack of small talk, he was know as 'Biceps Salvius'. Soon after their first child was born, the young couple gave a party, to which Nero and Octavia consented to go. Lucius, socially in demand as Caesar's Friend, accepted an invitation and I was invited too, having arranged a loan for Otho to buy his house.

Small and not in a fashionable part of the city, the house was decorated inexpensively in an original way, recesses in one long wall holding a turquoise glazed bowl, creamy at the edge, from Parthia, a box encrusted with ivory and pistachio marquetry, a piece of driftwood shaped by the waves into art.

Otho greeted me and, edging his way through a circle of admirers, introduced me to his wife. What struck me most was her pearly petal-smooth complexion, set off by auburn hair with amber glints. She was slim with generous breasts, a little above average height and wore a lemon shot-silk taffeta dress and no jewellery. She had taken the trouble to learn something about me and we exchanged a few words about my schoolboy son before she turned to a new arrival. From the far side of the room, my eyes kept returning to that glowing pearly complexion and I thought, Otho, you're a lucky man.

Poppaea came of good family – a forebear, Poppaeus Sabinus, was a successful general brought up in Naples, where the arts, especially music, are more highly esteemed than in Rome. Most of the guests were her friends – poets, musicians, dancers, actors. The talk turned on art – politics being considered beneath notice and the adjectives I heard most often were 'decorative', 'witty' and 'transporting'.

A young painter drew me into an alcove to show me a fresco of Galatea, hair streaming in the breeze, riding the waves in a shell drawn by dolphins. Poppaea, he said, encouraged young artists, spending rather more than her husband could afford, and had commissioned the painting, for which she had posed. He expounded on his own work in terms of cross-lights and the Golden Section, while Otho hovered round the room, evidently waiting for Nero to appear.

A maid passed a tray of white lemon sorbets in scooped-out halved lemons decorated with sprigs of lemon leaves and a spray of mint. Unlike most hostesses, Poppaea did not concern herself with this side of things and, as soon as the sorbets had been consumed and praised, she formed guests into a circle and introduced the first artist, an Indian girl who performed a curious bent-knee dance, all popping eyes and cracking finger-joints.

Then a grey-haired man with an air of authority sang a ballad in a fine strong baritone voice. He was followed by a Neapolitan girl who rendered what she termed 'an ode without words'. Lucius was standing near me; he is quite unmusical and I heard him comment to his neighbour, 'Isn't she slightly off-key?' The other said, 'Of course. That's what's original.' 'She sounds like a cat.' 'That's her intention,' said the other sternly and moved away.

Accompanied by Octavia, Nero arrived late, a *princeps's* prerogative. Shy with ladies he did not know, he was awkward with

Poppaea and uttered some prepared phrase about how her husband had often spoken of her.

'Not unkindly, I hope?' Her voice was soft and slow.

'He said you do much to help young artists.'

'I love music and painting and theatre. They are the rainbows of life, don't you think?'

Nero considered. 'Our paintings at home are mostly of generals and battles, and the only music I know is the guards' band.'

Poppaea smiled; she hoped the performance to follow would please him. Otho led Nero away to talk double shoulder locks, while Poppaea made Octavia feel at ease.

The baritone again took the floor, carrying a lyre. He was, I learned, Poppaea's music teacher – and when he had tuned all seven strings, Poppaea came forward. He struck the key note and she began her first song. It told of swallows in April, dipping and skimming water, then soaring to welcome spring with loops and bows and arches. She moved very little, just an occasional lift of the head. Her voice, though not strong, had a sweet tone and she used it with every refinement of descant and grace notes.

In her second song, Proculus's lament for Dejanira, she managed to convey Proculus's struggle to control his grief. Everyone in the room now seemed bewitched by her beauty and the expressiveness of her voice. Appreciative comments were heard. One man said, 'She makes sorrow as convincing as joy. That demands considerable art.'

Nero was one of the first to offer congratulations. He asked about her musical beginnings and learned that her mother, a gifted soprano, sang her lullabies. 'Later, if I wanted something special to wear, she made me ask by singing. Only if she thought well of my request did I get what I asked for.'

'Judging by tonight, I suppose you always did.'

She let her eyes rest on his. 'I believe there's only one person in Rome who always gets what he wants…'

Nero replied cautiously with one of Lucius's maxims: 'Like any office-holder the *princeps* can do no more than apply the law.'

She laughed lightly. 'You disappoint me.'

Nero was at a loss for what to say and Poppaea seemed about to turn to another guest. Otho now helped things along. Nero, he informed his wife, liked poetry and sometimes declaimed Homer in the baths. When Poppaea showed interest, he added: 'He even writes the stuff.'

'So you have a good ear?' Nero said he'd never asked himself the question so she invited him to find out. The lyricist was called over and introduced as Arcturus, head of the music academy. He agreed to take Nero to an adjoining room in order to test his ability to render in turn five ascending notes.

Soon after, Arcturus returned to say that Nero possessed the faculty of distinguishing sounds of different pitch and also had the making of a bass voice – but of course it would need training. Nero shuffled gauchely while Poppaea brightened further. The enjoyment she said he had found in their little evening was as nothing to that to be derived from making music oneself. Despite his many engagements, she hoped he would find time to take a trial singing lesson and see how he got on.

Nero looked disconcerted. A *princeps* taking singing lessons! But when Poppaea added that she went to the music academy herself once a week to keep her voice in trim, and perhaps not wishing to appear negative, Nero said he would think about it. With smiles on all sides, Nero rejoined his wife and their litter was summoned.

In Caesar's House, Nero and Octavia were settling in to married life. For Octavia it had not been easy at first. The loss of her father left her vulnerable; it was much worse for her brother. Passed over for the principate, deserted by Narcissus and Sosibius, Britannicus lost all interest in living. After yet another sudden fall, he never regained consciousness. Octavia, aged 15, was left with no family and was solely dependent on Nero. She needed reassurance and found it in her husband's good looks, energy and assiduous love-making, even when allowance was made for his eagerness to father a son.

Nero's duties as *princeps* kept him extremely busy in Cabinet, in the House and at public ceremonies during all of which he was accompanied by his mother. At her instigation, he took a weekly lesson in sword-fighting at close quarters, a preliminary to formal training as a cavalry officer. He also continued his early morning canter on Phaeton.

Octavia reacted to loneliness by calling attention to herself. One day, the buckle on one of her best sandals worked loose and she sent it to a cobbler for repair. A week later, the buckle fell off, this time in the street, and she had to go home in a litter. When Nero returned from a busy session in the House she complained about the cobbler's negligence, which she took as a personal affront.

Agrippina never aired annoyances – she dealt with them herself – so Octavia's grievance came as something new to Nero. He found it rather silly. But he commiserated and offered to buy her new sandals. It was not what she wanted. She asked him to go to the cobbler, give him a dressing-down and make him apologize to her personally for the considerable inconvenience he had caused Caesar's wife.

Nero tried to make her see that she was overreacting but found her determined to stick up for what she said was her prerogative. Lucius related that she was quite a good girl but insecurity made her stubborn.

In the interests of the marriage, Agrippina intended to move out of Caesar's House once she had trained Octavia. She began by taking her to the kitchen to watch the cook prepare a meal. To Octavia's objection that this was 'lowly', she replied, 'Nothing is lowly that adds to your value.' She taught Octavia to keep household accounts and refined her manners. In company she should speak less about her day's shopping and shouldn't cap another woman's clever remark with 'Exactly' or 'Just what I always say'. She should stop pottering about the house barefoot in a negligee. 'A man likes to undress his wife, doesn't want it done for him.'

Agrippina then installed herself in a dower house two streets away, actually larger than Caesar's House, taking her aviary and three personal servants including Locusta. There she received regular visits from the government secretariat and from Nero.

Soon after meeting Poppaea, Nero called at the music school. Arcturus told him he would need to strengthen his lungs so Nero began the practice of lying on the floor with lead plates on his chest which he had to raise and lower without strain by inhaling and exhaling. Other demanding exercises would bring precise control of face muscles and vocal chords. 'Now you understand why first-rate singers are as rare as champion charioteers, and just as popular.'

Poppaea looked in on one lesson, her auburn hair setting off her creamy complexion more dramatically by day than by lamplight. Nero said he welcomed a challenge that was physical as well as artistic, but felt uneasy about what people would say.

Poppaea reassured him. 'A *princeps* by definition goes first. Doesn't follow fashion, creates it. Wouldn't you agree?'

As yet he didn't feel much of a leader but could not help agreeing in response to her warmly encouraging look. He was rewarded with a promise that, once he had mastered the basics, they would try a duet together.

Nero did his exercises and some of his practising at home. Octavia laughed on seeing him bare to the waist with lead weights on his chest but, faced with his dedication, tried to make encouraging comments. When she learned from friends who thought she ought to know that Nero sometimes conversed with Poppaea at the music school, she remained unconcerned: Poppaea was safely married with a child and was no match to Caesar's daughter.

Lucius continued to play an active role in Cabinet. From his experience of municipal life in Corduba and his tour of Gaul, he was able to correct mistaken views about provincial attitudes to the capital. After putting out his satire, he had forgotten about the temple to Claudius; he appreciated Agrippina's qualities – her energy, her attention to detail, her patriotism – and tried to show that he liked her.

One morning, Agrippina arrived looking especially thoughtful and began to speak about the eastern frontier, where Armenia, a tableland backed by the Caucasus, faced the mountainous kingdom of Parthia, stretching far to the east. Pompey had conquered Armenia more than a century earlier, made it a Roman protectorate and installed a king. But Parthia disputed the Roman presence; a sporadic war had lately been fought which ended in a long-standing truce.

Arching her fingertips, Agrippina pronounced: 'The present situation is unsatisfactory. Parthians have no business to be in a Roman protectorate, and a truce, far from being a solution, is tantamount to admission of failure. I intend therefore that our legions should launch all-out war against Parthia and drive their troops back where they belong. I expect to have your approval.'

This marked a radical change of policy, bound to surprise and so it did. But Lucius reacted at a deeper level and, to explain why, I must go back in time to his military service.

He first saw action against German tribesmen in a bloody two-hour battle. One incident he would never forget. A trumpeter from the legion's band had been trapped unarmed. Whipping his instrument from its shoulder clip and gripping it tight in his right hand, mouthpiece forward, he swung it far back, then rammed it hard into the mouth of his assailant as he yelled his predatory war-cry. Down went the brass mouthpiece into the larynx, silencing the vocal chords, down hard into the trachea.

The victim tugged with both hands at the flared bell protruding from his lips but it had lodged firm in the trachea's cartilaginous rings. Twisting, dancing and kicking, he struggled to mitigate his agony, while gasps of fading breath emerged as pathetic peeps from the instrument designed for victory fanfares until at last he slumped to the ground.

The legion made a tactical withdrawal and, on the following day, Lucius crossed the Rhine alone to scout enemy movements. From a wood above the enemy village, he watched the dead being carried home, among them doubtless two who had fallen under his sword. Wives, mothers, daughters, sisters knelt beside the bodies, wailing and shrieking their grief. All night the lamentations continued, while Lucius watched.

Two days later he sustained a javelin wound above the left knee and, while he lay recovering, he pondered on the battle and its aftermath. Why was he killing his fellow men? Not in self-defence for they posed no real threat. Not for loot, poor as they were. For the glory of Rome? But Rome was already radiant with glory.

He had learned from Attalus that, if spirit has ensured the conditions of life, it is reasonable to believe it intends men to safeguard life and pass it on, notably in a city, which strives to keep men united in all their precious diversity. But Stoics had nothing to say about war, and it was Lucius, applying Stoic generalities to his recent experiences, who first drew what he took to be the logical conclusion, putting it like this in a letter to Lucilius:

> We are mad, not only individuals, but nations too. We restrain manslaughter and isolated murders; but what of war and the so-called glory of mass killing? Our greed has no limit, nor our cruelty. When crimes are committed stealthily by individuals they are less harmful, less monstrous; but deeds of cruelty are done every day by command of Senate and popular assembly, and servants of the state are ordered to do what is forbidden to the private citizen. The deeds that would be punished by death if committed in secret are applauded when done openly by soldiers in uniform. Man, the gentlest of animals, is not ashamed to glory in blood-shedding and to wage war when even wild beasts are living together in peace.

Lucius was only too aware how views like his would shock prevailing attitudes. Rome lives by the metaphors of battle and conquest. Her founder Romulus had been fathered by Mars, god of war, and our national epic glorifies Aeneas's feats of slaughter. Privately to confess pacifism would be considered idiosyncratic; to do so in public would be to lose all credibility.

So Lucius had had to work undercover, always a risky business. In class he hadn't said a word against Homer's encomium of war but often pointed out that moral courage in civilian life could be as heroic as courage in the field. He never questioned the need for a large standing army but hinted it would be best employed building roads, bridges, dykes and preventing one tribe massacring another's women and children.

So Lucius listened in bleak consternation to Agrippina's call for war. Rome must either expand or decline. For too long there had been no territorial gains. The legions in the east must inevitably be restive. They had enrolled with the promise of spoils and spoils they must have. For Rome too there would be spoils to be had from the profitable trade between the Caspian and Black Sea.

Agrippina looked around the table for comment. Nero remained silent, as did Cornelius, whose interests seldom extended beyond the city walls, and it was Burrus normally a man of few words, who spoke. The Parthian army's tactics might be crude, but the country was vast, extending from the Euphrates to the Indus. A full-scale war might see Rome sucked into Central Asia with communications stretched beyond breaking point. Even if the Parthians were driven out of Armenia, how would Rome hold that Kingdom, with very few towns and no structured society on which to build.

To this, Agrippina replied curtly that England had been successfully conquered, though the legions had had to cross a thirty-mile sea with all their equipment and supplies. Burrus had no grounds for pessimism.

Lucius spoke next, producing arguments other than his pacifism which would find no echo round the table. He begged leave to doubt that a military victory would strengthen Rome. Why? Because in Armenia many soldiers would lose their lives, leaving children orphaned to grow up disadvantaged, and widows who would otherwise have mothered more sons for Rome. Even if victory resulted, losses on such a grand scale would weaken Rome.

Agrippina said she would take note, then went on to make a second even more startling announcement. 'My son will assume the purple cloak of *imperator*, go out to Armenia and there take command of the legions. This is what the people expect of him.'

Cornelius's face twitched nervously. Surely a new *princeps* should remain prominent in Rome, accustom the populace to seeing him perform his duties. Would it be safe for him to leave so soon?

The reply came pat. His mother, with her title of Augusta and in view of her sharing his *imperium*, would ensure his position at home.

Lucius prickled at the word 'sharing', but it was Burrus who spoke. 'Too young.'

'Pompey went to war at 17, Augustus at 19.'

'Not in Asia.'

'It is age we're talking about, not geography.'

Before Burrus could put in a sharp retort, Lucius spoke his mind. Given the wider implications of these proposals, could they have time to ponder and adjourn at Agrippina's convenience? This won murmurs of approval from the others, including Nero. Agrippina agreed.

Lucius spent the following morning alone with Burrus. The Guards' Commander was a laconic widower who lived with his sister. He was a man of few words with a brusque manner which masked what Lucius discovered to be an unusual and loveable character. As a subaltern in Germany, he had become interested in wolves and at night would lie awake listening to the cries of a pack in the nearby pine forests. In what at first seemed random howling, he came to distinguish individual voices, each with its own pitch and notes. In time, he learned to identify individual wolves by their call, then to imitate those calls and finally to join in their nightly concert and elicit replies. He went on to study wolf habits and concluded that the wolf did not deserve its name as man's natural enemy since every authenticated attack had followed provocation.

One day, Burrus had found a young she-wolf caught by her hind leg in a trap. He freed the animal, took her to his quarters, treated her kindly and managed to tame her. He gave her the name Moren. When she died, he made her thick grey-brown pelt into a coverlet for his camp bed and was said every evening to confide to her the day's doings.

This affection for wolves and for wild life generally led Burrus to question the axiom that barbarians are by definition Rome's natural enemies. He sympathized with – though did not share – Lucius's pacifism.

Lucius began by asking Burrus what he thought of Nero as an army officer.

'Parade soldier, yes; fighting man, no.'

'Lacks aggressivity?'

'Jumpy.'

Lucius nodded but said it was not an evaluation worth sharing with Agrippina as she would never believe it.

What then? Nero probably did not want to go to Armenia, but he would do as she wished. And what of her motives? As Lucius saw them, she wished to exercise alone her undoubted skill in government until Nero became more mature. Of her prime concerns, ambition for Rome and love of her son, he believed the second would always be foremost. Burrus agreed that this was the way to persuade her and slowly they hatched a plan.

When Cabinet next met, Burrus supplied the facts, Lucius the talking. First, terrain. Steep mountains bare of cover, rocky, subject to land slips, impossible for heavy cavalry, so Nero's equestrian expertise would be wasted. Second, Parthian tactics. Surprise raids behind our lines, swooping down on fast ponies to release volleys of well-aimed arrows. Dozens of senior officers had died this way. Third, climate. Severe frost and deep snow on the heights, gale-force desiccating winds that cut to the bone. All the more lethal since Roman bases lay in the hot lowlands of Syria. 'It was there,' Lucius pointed out, 'that fever robbed us of Germanicus, still a young man.'

For once, Agrippina's face registered concern. Did Burrus know Armenia first-hand? No, but his second-in-command had served there, and the details she had heard from Lucius came from him. Any young officer who went to Armenia without being acclimatized and without training in mountain warfare was putting his life at risk for very doubtful territorial gain.

Agrippina esteemed Burrus for his honesty and loyalty and Lucius sensed she was impressed by his warning but took care not to show it. This new data, she said, would receive full consideration; for the moment, a decision would be delayed. A month passed without any order to place the legions on a war footing, and Lucius concluded that one reason for proposing a military campaign was to provide Nero with scope to shine as a soldier.

I next saw Lucius at a family function, looking sad as dockweed or basset's ears. When I asked what troubled him, he glared at me. '"Conquest keeps a city vigorous," so says Agrippina. *There's* the trouble.'

'And you can't argue her out of it?.. Of course not. You dislike river snails; I love them and you'll never make me change.'

'My dear Mela, if values were only tastes, see what follows. One kind of animal cannot breed true with another, so we classify each as different species. Apply this to rational animals – for so we claim to be, at least on our good days. If inborn taste should prevent us breeding true, that is, from producing an agreed truth, you belong to one species, I to another, Novatus to a third and so on. I'm not going to swallow that.'

'You'll continue to argue, sure of convincing? Then why so dejected?'

'It may take months... years.'

'And you have a congenital distaste for waiting!'

He shook his head, but half-smiling, as with someone incorrigible.

Some days later, Agrippina swept into Cabinet looking perturbed and holding in her hand a gossipy newsletter, adept at putting two and two together to make five. From it she read an 'exclusive' item: the *princeps* is often to be seen at a fashionable music school, which happens to be a favourite haunt of the lady with Rome's most dazzling complexion.

She looked hard at her son, who made a dismissive gesture. 'Pigeon droppings!'

'They stain,' snapped his mother. Government wasn't a play park. His position in the State was at best tenuous and dependent in large degree on his marriage.

Nero made a show of nonchalance. Poppaea was just one of a dozen ladies he met in the social round, no more than an acquaintance.

'But two days ago at that music school you and that acquaintance sang duets.'

He threw her a huffy look. 'So you're having me watched.'

Lucius had caught a sense of Nero's feelings for Poppaea the day after her party. 'Everything she does,' he confided, 'just crossing the room or picking up a cushion, becomes a line of verse. She seems to flow. Beside her I feel a complete savage.' Since then a dangerous situation had arisen and when, before Cabinet met, Agrippina asked Lucius to speak out, he had readily agreed.

Nero remained silent and surly. Lucius managed to catch his eye and held it.

'Otho is one of your oldest and closest friends. He's in love with his wife. They've just had a child. Do you want to break up your friend's marriage?... Do you?'

This brought any angry frown. Why such a fuss? Why jump to conclusions?

'It is for you,' said Lucius, 'to decide what the conclusion will be. Now.'

Nero did not reply and Agrippina turned to Burrus, asking his opinion of Otho, who had served under him on the Meuse.

'Sound officer. Lives close to his men. Merits promotion.'

Agrippina nodded approval. 'An important command falls vacant next month. In Lusitania.'

Nero grimaced. 'Tail-end of the world. Can't send Otho there.'

'Why not?'

'His wife loves Rome so much. That's where she belongs.'

'We all love Rome. Which is why we have to make sacrifices on Rome's behalf. I'm sure you're man enough to do what's best for your friend.'

In the silence that followed Nero scowled, sighed, swallowed hard, looked this way and that, cupped his chin in his hands. Eventually he gave a grudging nod.

At a sign from Agrippina, a secretary brought in the requisite order, prepared beforehand. Nero read it, the secretary dripped melted wax beneath the last line and Nero, removing his ring, imprinted the wax with his sphinx seal. As the meeting broke up, Agrippina appeared on the point of showing her approval by giving her son a warm embrace, but seeing how angry he looked, she evidently thought better of it.

Two days passed. Otho packed his trunks, chose his staff and sailed for Lusitania. But, surprise of surprises, his wife did not go with him. She remained in Rome, explaining that her baby had a worrisome cold. But according to wags, it was she whose conjugal love had grown cold.

At the music school, where Nero continued his voice training, Poppaea was not to be seen and he did not dare add to gossip by calling at her house. Then one afternoon she reappeared and confided why she had stayed. She could not bring herself to part from dear friends – old ones and particularly new ones. These words she accompanied with a tender glance.

It awed Nero that this accomplished lady, only four years older than he but with so much more experience of the world, should wish to continue to see him. When she added that she hoped he would find an occasion for presenting her to his mother, he quickly said he would.

Once home, Nero opened a locked room where the precious dresses, mantles and shawls acquired by ladies of the *princeps*'s family since the time of Augustus's wife were stored. Some were of silk, some of brocade, others adorned with gold filigree or semiprecious stones.

One that caught his fancy was a damask gown decorated with coral stars. Removing it from its hanger, he wrote an affectionate accompanying note and told a servant to carry it to his mother's house.

That evening, he called on her, expecting compliments for his obedience and an embrace for his gift. Instead, he was met by an angry outburst and cutting reproaches. All he possessed – property, wealth, political power – had come to him through her doing. Did he imagine he could pay her back with one miserable dress and keep everything else? He protested but to no effect and returned home, puzzled and hurt.

Looking for a way to make things up, Nero decided to celebrate Agrippina's approaching birthday in style at his own expense. On level ground near the stables, he had two earth and stone ramps built ten feet high and 40 yards apart, then bridged the gap between them with two thick ropes, attached at either end to iron stakes. These were stretched tight and parallel, a chariot's width apart.

Here on the afternoon of the birthday, 300 guests assembled. A flourish of trumpets, a roll of drums and a male African elephant lumbered into view, met by little gasps of surprise and a few frightened squeals. Slowly its boy rider coaxed the elephant up the nearest ramp. Prodded by the rider's cane, it eased one heavy padded foot onto the near rope, the other onto the far one, slowly inching forward and then raising its hind legs to balance them in mid-air. Amid gasps from the crowd, the massive beast made its way slowly along the ropes to the far ramp. It ambled down to ground level, where Nero stood waiting with a small leather box. Folding this in its trunk, the elephant crossed to Agrippina, knelt before her and extended its trunk. She took the proffered box, found and pressed a catch. Inside lay a brooch set with a big ruby. She examined it with as much care as a jeweller, then held it up proudly for guests to admire.

When the excitement had subsided, Nero, accompanied by Poppaea, made his way through the crowd and embraced his mother. Then, his hand on her elbow, he drew Poppaea forward and introduced her.

Agrippina drew back a step, recovered and ran her eyes appraisingly over the newcomer.

'You have a pleasing voice I'm told. I hope you'll devote it to our traditional Italian songs, they are unsurpassed. My duties allow me little time, but one day perhaps I will ask you to sing for me. As regards your career, would you like me to give you a word of advice?'

Relieved at not being snubbed, Poppaea breathed an eager yes.

'Each of us has his destiny. Mine and my son's is to keep Rome strong and great, yours to practise and encourage the arts. Each calls for dedication, discipline and single-mindedness. As in a race, let us keep to our respective lanes.'

Arcturus held a summer party for associates and pupils, conceived and organized by Poppaea, which I heard about afterwards from one of the guests. It took place in Arcturus's garden on rising ground outside the walls. Nero drove himself there and was welcomed by Poppaea resplendent in mauve. She had much to attend to but would seek him out later.

Supper in an open tent. Game, pastries and aspics supplied by a caterer depicted the Great Bear, Orion's Belt, the Lion. Around a crescent-moon cake clustered seven smaller cakes! The Pleiades were all delineated by tiny candles. Among artistic people for whom rank counts, little Nero could mix as a plain citizen and he joined in their talk about horoscopes and the music of the spheres.

Guests moved on to a glade at the top of the garden where leather cushions had been laid out. The cleverer pointed out constellations by their correct names, while the less clever marvelled at the way the southernmost stars merged with the city lights.

After Arcturus suggested that everyone look out for meteors, children from the shadow of trees began a song to these hide-and-seek stars, inviting them to join the festivities. The night had been well chosen or perhaps they were just lucky, for presently someone shouted, 'There's one!' 'Where? Where?' Others were spotted and pointed out; wishes were made.

Then the apparently impossible happened. Lights in the outstretched city began to oscillate, to rise in twos and threes, then in clusters steadily higher, into the garden, then up into the glade, dancing around and upwards into the sky, but brighter, much brighter, than the stars.

Cries of astonishment: something never before witnessed. Then, still greater surprise, when it began to be seen that the mysterious lights were on wings, were flying. The party had been found by fireflies: hundreds and hundreds of fireflies.

A lady guest in the know explained. Down near the pond, at an agreed signal, two big crates had been opened to release their fireflies. The idea had been Poppaea's. Of course, who else but Poppaea? Everything she touched turned to art. Where was she? They wanted to tell her how much pleasure she had given. But her lady confidante explained that because it was Arcturus's party, Poppaea wished to remain behind the scenes.

As the evening grew cool, the guests formed into groups or walked in the garden and Nero found Poppaea after some searching. At his suggestion, they seated themselves on a bench by the pond. The compliments came tumbling from his lips: how brilliantly she had arranged the evening, compared to other spectacles, it was like poetry to prose, and how lovely she was looking. 'Poppaea, you are the fourth Grace!'

'As Callimachus wrote about Bernice.' Then, with a mildly reproving look, 'You must find something more original.'

She wondered aloud about different kinds of light, how at dusk it became pure white and more precious. This was the kind of talk never heard from his mother or Octavia and, on an impulse, he confided a memory of Antium when he was a boy. He'd been hauling up his rowboat on the shore, the sun had set, darkness had begun to close in. The waves curling onto shingle suddenly began to glow and emit flashes and sparks. No moon; the glow and flashes came from within the waves, from phosphorus. That was how her presence affected him, wherever they happened to be. When would she let him see her again?

There were obstacles, she reminded him. But these with a quick gesture he dismissed, saying they shouldn't let so special an evening be spoiled, and he laid a hand on her wrist.

Gently she drew away. 'When you first came to my house, the very first time, I thought here is a man who is strong...'

Nero said quickly that of course he was strong.

'But in one area, just at present, you have... difficulties... Because she is strong.'

He averted his eyes, tried to slip his arm around her shoulders, only to have her again draw away.

'You must ask yourself this. Do I care enough for Poppaea to be strong?'

He assured her that he did; how could she doubt it?

'Strong enough to do the one thing necessary?'

The seriousness of her tone disturbed him and he did not answer at once.

'Well...?'

'Yes. Yes... I will.'

In the pause that followed, she seemed to assess his look, as if weighing up his determination. At last, she leaned forward and kissed his brow, just long enough to show limited approval. Then, as he sought to return the kiss, she said it was time he left and, taking his hand in hers, led him to the gate.

It had become habitual for Nero to spend Thursday afternoon in his mother's house. On one such Thursday, soon after Arcturus's party, mother and son were to be found in the aviary playing with the minahs: it was a simpler way of communicating. They fed the birds, laughed at their mimicry and taught them new tricks. Nero was still making pretexts to see Poppaea at the music school but his mother did not voice her irritation. She seemed preoccupied.

Leaving the aviary, she motioned for him to sit beside her on a couch. 'This house was your grandmother's and it was here that I lived until I married your father.' It held many memories and one she intended to share with him now. She took his hand and squeezed it affectionately.

When Tiberius retired permanently to Capri – recalled Agrippina – he left Rome in the charge of Sejanus, a tough ambitious knight whom he trusted. Tiberius's brother, Germanicus, Nero's heroic grandfather, had died on active service, leaving his widow, the first Agrippina, who was greatly loved by the people in honour of Germanicus, with seven young children, of whom the elder son was Tiberius's most likely heir. All of them lived in this house.

Sejanus rose to be consul and aspired to become the next *princeps*. With an unscrupulous henchman named Titus Ollius, he managed to convince Tiberius that Agrippina and her sons were plotting to seize power. They poisoned two of her sons and exiled Agrippina to Pantelaria, where a centurion beat her with such violence that one eye was blinded; she died soon after, still an exile.

Too late, Tiberius discovered the truth about his trusted agent. He denounced Sejanus and Ollius to the Senate, who sentenced both to death. When the two emerged from the House, an infuriated mob pounced on them, dragged them through the streets with hooks and threw their bodies into the Tiber.

'Why am I telling you this? Titus Ollius had a daughter, Pulchra. But such was the shame attaching to her father, she changed her name. The woman who styles herself Poppaea Sabina is in fact Pulchra Ollia.'

Nero rose to his feet, deeply shaken. Hammering his brow with the palm of his hand, he cried out. 'It can't be true. Can't be. I'd have heard.'

'Why? People prefer not to talk of past horrors. But be sure of this. Every educated person in Rome knows that this woman's father poisoned two of your uncles and caused your grandmother's untimely death.'

Nero protested. Terrible though these happenings were, they couldn't have affected Poppaea. She'd have been a mere child.

'And therefore all the more impressionable. Those horrors will always be part of her.'

Rising and still holding his hand, she led him across the courtyard to a portico. Here stood a row of statues, the paint on their faces making them look like real people in the dim light. She passed to the far end, stopping in front of the life-size figure of a soldier in full armour. 'Mark Anthony! Conqueror of the East. Look at those shoulders, the thrust of the jaw! And beside him his daughter, Antonia, so clever, my favourite grandmother.'

The charisma of statues and of glorious names was awesome. With as much or perhaps more respect than if they had been alive, mother and son bowed in homage. They moved on to Germanicus, his high forehead long familiar to Nero, next to his wife, the first Agrippina, idolized by the people of Rome. Then her two sons, who'd been poisoned...

He had seldom known his mother so moved and, when she turned to him, there were tears in the eyes that looked into his with such intensity. 'You belong to them.' Her voice was low and grave. 'Their blood feeds your marrow and liver. Every one of them was brave – the women at least as brave as the men. For family and country, they were ready to give their all.'

Nero saw himself outnumbered: he felt the snare tighten and fought back in near panic. Poppaea had made her own life. She was a fine person, in every way superior. No matter what her father might have done, his feelings for her were unchanged, and his dealings with her a private matter – for himself alone.

'Private!' she scoffed. 'Whoever heard of a *princeps* with a private life? You belong to Rome. The shades of your glorious forebears are watching to see how you match their sacrifices.'

Nero drew back, fearful. His voice shrank to a whisper. 'Does one owe so much to the dead?'

'To the great dead, yes.'

A long pause followed. Then she led him, his head bowed, back to the couch. Here she sat while he remained standing, his face contorted by inner conflict. At last he turned on her, accusingly. He wasn't a boy any more, he had his own life to lead. She mustn't hem him in. What he needed was space, space, space. These last words he shouted then, turning his back with a groan, pressed his forehead against the wall.

A silence followed.

'You have hurt me,' said Agrippina quietly. 'I await your apology.'

He said he hadn't meant to hurt her.

'Then give me our special kiss.'

That wouldn't help, he growled. But he turned to face her nevertheless.

'You have always done the right thing. Always... I'm waiting for that kiss.'

He did not want to give it. He was the man. Yet what had he done to prove his manhood? He was still just a bundle of unrealized projects, whereas she had achieved so much. Her imperious look, the upward tilt of the head, the diction that made every request a command: she was so sure she was right. Could it be that, as so often before, she was right? Then he owed it to her to ditch Poppaea.

Was he lacking in filial piety? He didn't want to pose such questions: why then was he doing so? Under her gaze, with a faint smile adding to its comeliness, his will always weakened and every situation became its reverse. He felt as he did when thrown in a wrestling bout, knee in the small of the back, both arms pinioned.

'I'm still waiting.'

With something between a groan and a guttural cry, he crossed to the couch and knelt before his mother. Slowly, almost solemnly, he kissed her eyes, the left side of her neck, then the right, still so smooth and firm, then her lips. As he moved to draw away, her hand came up to press the nape of his neck. 'No one loves you as much as I do.'

Nero felt a need to let matters settle. He suspended his music lessons and took to frequenting the race track opposite his stables where he practised driving a two-horse chariot fast on a circular track. Excitement eased his disquiet over the clash with his mother.

One afternoon, as he unharnessed his horses, a messenger handed him a sealed papyrus. Opening it, he found a few words in beautifully shaped cursive on expensive Augustus paper fragrant with lemon blossom. 'How sad that a budding friendship should be left to wilt.'

Touched by her words and the absence of reproof, Nero lost no time in replying. He had agreed to attend a poetry reading two days ahead and suggested that Poppaea meet him there, knowing that Octavia, who found such functions boring, would not be present.

News spread that Nero had sat beside Poppaea at the reading and afterwards held a long conversation with her. His mother ensured there were repercussions. Nero had submitted to Cabinet plans for a new meat market to replace the old one which was in poor repair, overcrowded and difficult to access. He had consulted those concerned and produced a first-rate dossier, which Cornelius in particular praised. Agrippina however said that she had studied it closely and had come to the conclusion that the new site was too close to a fashionable residential area: she would refer his dossier to a committee. Another name for letting it sink into quicksands.

Disappointed but not discouraged, Nero outlined a scheme for a new road up to Tusculum at the next meeting. This was urgently needed and pleas had reached him from several quarters. He had gone over the ground with surveyor and engineer and calculated the likely cost.

Agrippina agreed in principle to a new road but objected to this particular route. It would cut through property belonging to Calpurnius, an influential consul with pamphleteers in his pay. It would not do to displease him. Calpurnius might agree to cede the land if compensated, but he would certainly demand more than the land's true value, at a guess ten million. She certainly could not advise the Treasury to disburse so large a sum.

Nero sweated out his exasperation on the race track, and his skill reached a point where his trainer assured him he was good enough to compete against professional charioteers. He therefore gave notice that he intended to take part in the following month's championship.

Agrippina vented her anger in Cabinet. Had her son gone mad? If he won, people would say the race was rigged; if he lost, he would look a fool. Nero replied that spectators went to bet and to experience thrills, not specially to assess the drivers.

'And what if you're thrown? In your position, that becomes symbolically disastrous.' As he continued to argue, then to plead, she cut him short. If he were so foolish as to override her wishes, authority would be seen to be divided. It could be the first loose rock in a land slip.

Lucius took note but, being unaware of the strength of Nero's feelings for Poppaea or of Agrippina's opposition, he attached small importance to the altercations between son and mother. To his own surprise, but not Paula's, he had become absorbed in the reconditioning of his house. Further inspection having revealed no structural damage, the rendering had already been done, followed by redecoration. Paula's little man proved a giant of ingenuity, adept at replastering crumbling ceilings while Paula set about refurbishing doors and frames and polishing door-handles. Three months after they had taken possession, the atrium and one bedroom had been repainted as Paula wished and their original furnishings moved back in. Most of the day, when he was not on call, Lucius spent working on the house.

An hour after Agrippina had balked at her son's plan to race publicly, Nero burst into the room where, atop a stepladder, Lucius was inspecting the frieze. Words came tumbling from his lips, expressions of anger, acrimony and abuse. His brow and cheeks shone with perspiration and his eyes darted with a feverish glow.

Astonished by this unprecedented call, Lucius quickly came down the steps, removed his spattered apron and, taking Nero by the arm, drew him into the hall, where they would be out of the little man's hearing.

Here the unhappy man became less incoherent. Week after week, his best schemes had been frustrated or blocked, and he had been made to look a fool. Recriminations, real or imagined, were listed, and all led back to his mother. Through boyhood, she had kept him on a leading rein and now, when he had a right to run free, she tightened her grip. Why shouldn't he race his chariot? He could win, felt certain of it. And that was just what his mother didn't want. All eyes had to be focused on Augusta.

He paused for breath and Lucius cut in. 'Control yourself, don't overdramatize!' But the flow of recrimination resumed pell-mell: how in Cabinet his mother continually belittled him, plus the minor annoyances, such as her insistence that when reviewing the Guard he wear pointed boots that chafed his toes.

Again, Lucius urged calm, but the other only grew more excited. 'I've got to get it out Lucius – or it'll choke me.' He and a lady in every way superior had found one another, 'a lady of character who can't be managed, as Mother manages Octavia, and for that reason she has to be kept out of my life. Imagine the cruelty! You know what I'm beginning to think? She wants to cut off my balls!'

Breathing heavily, he now looked Lucius directly in the eye. 'What's your opinion?'

'You're making a very serious charge, and I think it's because you're so angry.'

Nero dropped his gaze, and it appeared that he didn't really want to hear what Lucius thought, for he asked anxiously, 'But you do support me?'

Lucius chose his reply with care. 'I want what's best for you as *princeps*.'

Nero bowed his head for some moments, as though reflecting, then again met Lucius in the eye. 'Thank you for listening.' The tone was formal, curt. He made his way hurriedly to the door and was gone, leaving Lucius with the impression that his main motive in coming was to hear himself voice his anger and thereby strengthen his resolve.

Lucius sat down and went over the scene. If Nero felt that his very manhood was threatened, the consequences could be serious. Lucius asked himself whether he should try to mediate. His first reaction was steer clear: Nero's love life was his own affair. But then he reminded himself that he was working for cohesion. That evening, he went to Agrippina's house.

Madam was busy, or so her manservant said, showing him into an anteroom smelling of the sage he so disliked. As he waited, he recalled with amusement that, before going to bed, Agrippina totted up to the last penny what she had spent that day.

When at last she called him in, he saw that her face was drawn; her glance seemed to say: 'What brings you here at this time of night?'

So Lucius began cautiously. No one would wish to intervene in an issue between mother and son, certainly he would not dare to;

nevertheless when the welfare of Rome was at stake he felt it his duty as a citizen to make certain points.

First-cousin marriages often proved childless as Nero's had so far been, whereas Poppaea had proved herself fertile. Nero's attachment to this lady appeared deep and lasting, they had tastes and interests in common. Since she found politics dull, she would not meddle in his public life. Lucius respectfully suggested that to live separated from Poppaea would divide Nero as a person, weakening his authority and harming Rome.

After nearly interrupting him several times over, Agrippina heard him out. Then her tirade struck with all the more force. Why was her son drawn to this married woman from the underworld of Naples professing Greek values and living for expensive pleasures? 'Because you, behind my back and against my orders, encouraged him to read Greek poetry, then to write it. Because you taught him to put the so-called finer feelings before *pietas* and family. And now, instead of bowing your head in shame you dare to advise me to crown your error with an unjustified divorce! Leave – before I get really angry.'

Politics is not my business but here I must say I took Agrippina's part. For years she had consistently fought for a certain idea of Rome and its *princeps*. In public life, she was everything an Augusta should be: handsome, assured, dignified, radiating the confidence a mercantile city needs. She was right to ask of her son a similar devotion to the State. By antagonising her, Lucius may have made things more difficult for Nero.

Events now gathered pace. Agrippina continued to dismiss, block or delay any suggestion her son made in Cabinet. Nero sat there sullen, speaking less and less, while his mother did most of the planning. Evidently, thought Lucius, she wanted to break his will and save the marriage, but later developments pointed to another motive.

The temple dedicated to Claudius had now been completed and the consul whom Agrippina chose to inaugurate it was a man who owed his advancement to her: he spoke little about the late *princeps*, nothing about his adopted son and heir and much about his widow. It was Agrippina Augusta who had paid for the temple and its priesthood: such munificence proved virtue of the highest order. How fortunate Rome was in her great ladies: Livia, Augustus's wife and partner, and now Agrippina, the wise ever-watchful guide of her young son.

Not content with polishing up her image, Agrippina began to push herself to the fore on public occasions. When a new Armenian ambassador came to present credentials to the head of State, Agrippina stepped forward to accept the ambassador's obeisance, and only quick thinking by Cornelius, who held Agrippina back by the arm while pushing Nero forward, prevented a shocking violation of the *princeps*'s prerogatives.

Senators watched with increasing unease, and decided to debate in the House what they saw as a dangerous marginalization of Nero. Agrippina had no right to sit in on debates so, in order to discover who might speak against her, she took the unprecedented step of concealing herself behind the drapes at the head of the cellar and listening to the speeches.

Lucius viewed all this with concern. Agrippina had engaged him as tutor in order to work with the Senate but, in Cabinet, she was beginning to act as though senators were her rivals for power. He recalled that she had received part of her education from her grandmother, Antonia, a keen admirer of the Pharaohs. Could it be that, like Messalina, she had ambitions to be a Roman Cleopatra? Lucius had no objection to a sufficiently gifted woman ruling Rome, but everyone he could think of would implacably oppose such a violation of age-old tradition.

Nero and Poppaea had been discreet about their meetings from the start. Nero did not wish to affront his mother, while Poppaea was mindful of her good name. But, as the months passed, each felt the need to see each other without restriction. And so, one afternoon, Nero entered Poppaea's house alone, remaining there for a full hour.

For a man to call on a lady in the absence of her husband was viewed by society as a first decisive step towards a declaration of love, and the gossips chitter-chattered.

Agrippina's reaction came quickly and in a form Nero did not expect. She summoned him at a very late hour, when her servants were in bed, opening the door herself, a lamp with a mica shade in her hand that showed a face pinched by stress, insomnia and possible tears. Nero sensed he was to blame and experienced a momentary twinge of shame.

She led him down a corridor to a part of her house he did not know, unlocked a door into a small room, windowless and undecorated, and turned the key behind them. He began to feel very uneasy.

She motioned him to one of two stools on either side of a low table and, placing her lamp on the wall-shelf in such a way that its light fell on his face leaving hers in shadow, she began to speak in an unusually low voice. She began by recalling the prelude to her husband's death three years before. He had been on the point of declaring Britannicus of age preparatory to appointing him heir. For Nero, his death had been exceedingly opportune.

'You remember the dinner the previous night? My devoted servant Locusta picked the mushrooms and prepared the sauce.' Agrippina described the mushrooms, and they were not the species Lucius and I had supposed. 'There are different kinds of *amanitas*: *amanita caesarea*, with an orange cap, and Fly Agaric or *amanita muscaria* with red cap marked with fly-sized white flecks. Both taste delicious but Fly Agaric has toxic properties which can be fatal to an already weak constitution... That night, one dish held *amanita caesarea*, but Claudius was served with Fly Agaric.'

Here she paused, as though to let her son picture the dinner. 'One person – only one – had the authority to tell Locusta to act as she did.'

At these words, as he was later to tell Lucius, Nero felt as though he had fallen down two flights of stairs. Dazed and confused, he thought that it couldn't be true, not his adored mother. Claudius – cruel, yes, but still her husband, whose bed she had shared. And yet, who else?

'It had to be,' his mother continued. 'Time was short. And now you understand why... others might fail to understand. Senators in particular, devoted to legality in its strictest form, would they understand why Caesar had to go? They would immediately arraign us both before their tribunal, pronounce the succession null and void, strip you of your *imperium* and send us both into exile for life. Inevitably. They could not do less.

'So what you have learned tonight the Senate must never learn... It is after all a family matter.' She paused, then put her first question of the evening. 'Can I count on you to keep it secret?'

Still partly dazed, he nodded. 'Madness not to.'

'Locusta too I can count on. So our secret will remain locked in this room, on one condition only, that you never see the Ollia woman again.'

Thinking he must have misheard, he gaped and looked at her uncomprehendingly, whereupon she repeated the condition. He drew back, almost trembling. How could this mother who had loved him so much and for so long bring herself to act so cruelly? She who had always been straight and candid with him now stooping to blackmail?

She pressed home. 'Should you continue to see her, I shall inform the Senate and you will cease to be *princeps*. That will be your doing, not mine. You will have ruined not only yourself but also your mother who bestowed upon you life and *imperium*.'

On that last most resonant word, she stopped and transferred her thrust to her gaze. From the shadow, she examined every nuance of fear on his features. This lasted a full minute, then she adopted a terse matter-of-fact tone: they understood each other and there remained nothing more to say.

After unlocking the door and picking up her lamp, she led the way back down the dim corridor. Nero found himself alone. Uppermost in a jumble of half-perceptions was the impression of his mother's strength, how she had him prostrate, his whole self and immediate future pinioned, and how she must hate Poppaea. He saw this not as loyalty to kin wrongfully killed but as jealousy of a gifted rival.

Octavia was in bed and asleep when he returned but, instead of joining her, he sat in his study with no light but for the dim star glow. Without consciously choosing to do so, he found himself drifting to the dining room. He pictured the fatal dinner. Claudius savouring the tasty dishes. Food of the gods! The mushrooms' poison circulating through his heavy frame. His last sight of the plump face faded to waxy pallor. And later his widow burning incense in front of his temple statue, invoking his protection.

At dawn, he washed and shaved. He had to see Poppaea – now, immediately – and so gain strength. Strength for what? He did not yet know. He sent a message asking her to meet him in a friend's safe house.

Uneasy at receiving so sudden a call, Poppaea was first at the rendezvous and when Nero glimpsed her at the far end of the hall, he did feel stronger. But as she approached, he felt that strength ebb. He felt suddenly inadequate.

They passed into an anteroom where they could be alone. A ray of sunshine from a window caught the pale pink of her cheeks and, with a start, Nero recalled Claudius's waxy pallor and his mother's words. He'd begun to rave like a Dionysiac. Impossible. And yet... if she'd done the other, she might perhaps do this. Poppaea must be warned. She was brave, had chosen to leave Otho. She could bear it.

He forced himself to inquire calmly about her doings since they'd last met. Then he spoke about their friendship, how he intended it to continue, but that certain persons might wish to see it end.

'One person?'

He nodded gravely. So it was best if, from then on, she prepared her own food, avoided pickled fish and any caterer's dish, and washed all fruit.

He saw her flinch, heard her breath quicken, but he had to go on. 'Your little boy too. Watch the goat being milked and bake his rusks yourself.'

She began to cry softly, discreetly, raising an arm to hide her eyes. It pained him to watch and to resist the urge to get drawn in. She asked what he proposed to do to protect her and her child.

Nero said he was locked in a battle of wills, which would perhaps be long drawn out, but that their love must prevail in the end. In company he had admired the easy way she handled quarrelsome people and awkward situations, choosing the right word, the calm note, never ruffled or thrown. So it came as a surprise when she tremblingly said, 'I cannot live under siege. It's not what I'm made for.' She would return to her husband. With Otho, she and her child would be safe.

He had been counting on drawing strength from her. Had he misinterpreted the harmony of her face as strength? Deep down, she was an artist, with the taut nerves of a thoroughbred racehorse. It struck him now that he would not just be fighting his mother, but looking within himself for the resilience to support Poppaea. On no account would he let her go. Stroking her brow and hair, he assured her that he would die rather than let her or her child be harmed. He promised the situation would not drag on and asked her to trust him to find a way to end it.

As he felt himself into this new role, he became more convincing to himself and to her. Very slowly, Poppaea let herself be comforted. She made him give a solemn promise to be her protector. Nero took his leave.

As pontiff, Nero had ceremonies to attend, rites to perform, prayers to offer; as commander-in-chief, it was his duty to present silver shoulder armour to those who had shown conspicuous gallantry on the frontiers. Always Agrippina accompanied him, but gone were the days when they travelled in the same litter and shared a covert smile at some contretemps. Now their relations were cool and they avoided each other's eyes.

There was unease among the observant and, with time, alarm. The denarius fell slightly against the drachma, recovered, then fell again; gold trickled out of the city, business confidence shrank. In the

House, a majority of senators placed the blame on Agrippina but feared to protest for fear of making matters worse.

In Cabinet, Nero spoke only when obliged to, in a disinterested tone and sometimes losing the thread of his argument. He never looked his mother in the face. One day he slipped out of Rome without a word of explanation and Lucius feared he was planning to resign and retire with Poppaea to one of his estates. A few days later, he returned. He had visited the naval base at Misenum, no one knew why.

Within the city walls, only the *princeps* had the right to a small armed bodyguard of six men of the Praetorian Guard. When Agrippina appeared in public with an armed bodyguard of her own, it caused widespread concern, all the more since she chose tough German mercenaries with allegiance not to Rome but to whoever employed them. She had informed neither her son nor the Senate and her action was seen as provocative, perhaps even as a decisive step in marginalizing her son.

Mid-March sees the celebration of a five-day festival celebrated in honour of Minerva, patron of all the arts and trades. Nero decided to spend it in Baiae, 100 miles down the coast where, like many prominent Romans, he had a summer villa. He asked Lucius to accompany him. Octavia, still hoping for a pregnancy, could not risk the bumpy road, and Poppaea would of course stay at home. As for Agrippina, she announced her intention of making the journey too, but would occupy her own villa three miles from the town.

The little seaside town was on holiday. Fishermen and their families, in best clothes, paraded the cobbled streets, decorated with foliage and bunting, speculating about pleasures and parties in store. Their gaiety infected the visitors. Rome's pressures yielded to something even more tremendous: the promise of spring.

A thirty-foot yacht rode at anchor in front of Nero's seaside villa, her crew smartly turned out in jackets of emerald green, his favourite colour. She had been built in Misenum to Nero's specifications. 'Tomorrow,' Nero informed Lucius, 'she will bring my mother here. I'm giving a dinner in her honour.' With a little laugh, he added, 'Parents have to be humoured.'

Next day Agrippina sent a message saying she had chosen to come by road, news that Nero received with a show of annoyance. Lucius, one of 20 guests at dinner, noticed with surprise how Nero gallantly offered his arm to his mother as she stepped down from her silver-fitted carriage, and again as they climbed the steps to the terrace, where fishermen's children presented a basket of wild flowers.

In accordance with her dislike of conspicuous spending, Nero served locally caught mackerel steamed in a white wine sauce, followed by crystallized fruit in soft white cheese. A team of jugglers performed between courses. Lucius knew nothing of Agrippina's threat to her son and, from snatches of conversation, he concluded that their quarrel had been patched up or at least forgotten for the evening.

They strolled on the terrace. The sea had calmed, the starlit sky was clear and Agrippina accepted to return home in the gleaming new yacht. Chatting to her easily, Nero installed his mother in the deck cabin abaft the mast. There she was joined by her maid Acerronia and her aide de camp Creperius. As the crew bent to their oars and the yacht glided away, Nero waved goodbye.

Lucius was sleeping soundly in the comfortable villa belonging to our elder brother Novatus, who was also in Baiae for the festival when a messenger burst in: Nero wanted him urgently. A glance at the window showed not a glimmer of dawn. Never at his best before breakfast, Lucius grumpily lit a lamp, pulled on the first clothes to hand and accompanied the messenger down to the waterfront.

Nero met him in the hall, dressed in a white bath robe: his feverish eyes looked everywhere except at Lucius. In a jerky voice, pitched higher than usual, he said he'd been receiving alarming reports about his mother, that she was plainly manoeuvring in order to seize sole control as head of State. At two that morning, an officer from her German bodyguard had been discovered skulking on the terrace. Challenged by the duty patrol, he had run his sword through one of the patrol before being stabbed in the abdomen. About to die, he revealed that Agrippina had ordered him to kill her son.

Lucius struggled to understand. How did this fit with the convivial dinner? And what legal form for her new powers could she have intended? In their last interview, Lucius had detected a note of determination verging on mania, but could this have driven her to so extreme a step?

By attempting to kill him, Nero continued, his mother had in fact made herself an enemy of the state and such he had declared her to be in front of his officers, ordering three of them to place her under arrest before she could head for Rome. When they arrived at her villa, her German bodyguard had rallied to her defence and, in the ensuing fracas, Agrippina had been killed.

Agrippina, so vibrant, so strong, not yet forty, always in control; no, it couldn't be... Nero was hurrying on, asking him something, pleading almost, and he must pay attention. 'I'm too overcome to perform funeral rites. Do me a favour. Ride at once to her villa. See that everything is done with propriety. Then gather up, seal and bring back to me her personal belongings and papers.'

Buckling a bridle on one of Nero's horses and tossing a sheepskin onto its back, Lucius set off and half an hour later, he stood in Agrippina's bedroom, beside him her housekeeper, a middle-aged peasant sturdy enough to wrest grain from a meagre soil. For quite some time he remained motionless, overcome, telling himself that he stood in a death chamber and trying to make the necessary mental adjustment.

Only then did he reverently lift the tip of the sheet covering what lay beneath. Pale, eyes closed, nose taut and pointed, the voice that had made every sentence Sibylline now silent forever. She had been too strong for her own good; all the same, thought Lucius, I shall miss her. He drew the sheet down further and saw that the right shoulder was deeply gashed: the wound was a hand's breadth wide, purplish-black with congealed blood.

'That happened in the fight?'

Without answering, the housekeeper averted her eyes from his and Lucius repeated the question.

'What fight? There was no fight.'

Puzzled and uneasy, Lucius drew the sheet back over the corpse and left the bedroom. He immediately began to question the housekeeper and, fortunately for him, under the weight of the night's horror and the loss of a mistress she had served for years, she was ready, even willing to unburden herself. Lucius heard from her lips an account of the night's events different from Nero's version, into which he later fitted details as they emerged.

The yacht had been built as a death trap and manned by unscrupulous thugs. On the masthead, concealed behind a furled sail, a massive hunk of lead hung suspended on a pulley. Halfway across the bay, a retaining line was cut and the lead crashed through the cabin's thin roof. Creperius died instantly. Agrippina and Acerronia lay resting inside the cabin; both were injured but saved from death by the thick oak side-panels of their couch.

The women clambered out onto the deck to find that a crewman had opened the starboard ports: water was pouring in and the yacht was listing. They at once jumped overboard. Agrippina, who could swim, pulled away. Acerronia floundered and, hoping for assistance, cried out that she was Agrippina, whereupon a crewman crashed an oar down on her skull.

A fishing boat working by the light of a flare picked up Agrippina and took her to her home. From there, she sent a freedman to Nero to report the shipwreck and reassure him that she was safe. She then told her housekeeper to prepare her departure for Rome. Nero's officers arrived two hours later. Agrippina understood but it was not in her character to run. In a steady voice, she ordered her bodyguard to drive off the intruders, standing behind them as sword impacted on sword, steel rasped and blood spurted.

Her guards gave ground before superior swordsmanship and Agrippina retreated to her bedroom, standing in the doorway as the lead assailant burst in. Looking him fearlessly in the eye she parted her gown to show her abdomen. 'Strike here, in the womb that bore Nero.' According to the housekeeper, she spoke this as a challenge, hoping the frightfulness of such an act would stay the soldier's hand. But the officer damped down shame with savagery, thrusting his sword through the white flesh, and Agrippina fell to the floor.

His years in court had taught Lucius how to spot a liar. This housekeeper was not lying. Lucius realized that Nero had planned and ordered a crime so horrible, so unnatural that lexicographers excluded it from the dictionary.

One name was missing in the accounts of Agrippina's death. For Lucius, Nero's attachment to Poppaea had been a determining factor in the crime, but Nero had preferred to invoke his threatened authority as *princeps*. By overreaching her power, Agrippina had lost her son's love and there came to his mind an inscription he had encountered when posted in Egypt, carved on a barracks wall:

I, the Captain of a Legion of Rome, serving in the desert of Libya, have learned and pondered this: There are in life but two things, Love and Power, and no man has both.

Lucius examined his own conscience. Here he was, smugly apportioning guilt to others, when he should be assessing his own complicity. By acting more wisely, perhaps he could have forestalled the killing. He had tried with Agrippina but doubtless too late, when battle lines had already been drawn. Earlier, much earlier, he should have gauged the latent tension, worked less on Homer and Pindar, more on the living. The relationship had been three-way; he should have acted as fulcrum, keeping mother and son in balance. He had failed as Nero's mentor.

Finding his way to the garden, thinking only of what he had seen and heard, he began to collect and pile up dry windfall branches. The gardener brought myrtle branches to place atop what became a four-foot pyre. Together they carried the body onto this wooden dais. The rasp of a flint, a spark on oiled rag and the pine branches began to crackle and spit.

When the pyre had slumped to a low smoking heap of ash and bone, a stranger appeared and seeing the purple stripe on his gown, approached Lucius. This was the mayor of Baiae, 'desiring speech' as he put it, one of those officials whose self-importance is in inverse proportion to their authority. He had that morning received a circular addressed to local municipalities, informing them that Caesar had decreed his mother to be an enemy of the State.

Lucius disliked the man's tone. 'Well, what of it?'

'The decree's effect does not end with death. By reason of the gravity of the offence, the mortal remains are to an extreme degree impure, would pollute and bring disaster to the community in whose soil they might be laid. Hence the law forbids inhumation.'

Lucius was annoyed by the man's intrusion. He recalled the ancient text in question and replied that he had no intention of burying the lady's remains. He told the gardener to fetch him one of the urns from the terrace balustrade and a trowel. He transferred the ash and bone to the urn and, with the mayor eyeing him suspiciously, he placed it in a secluded corner under a clump of pines. The smell of charred wood amid the spring greenery was depressing him. Without pausing to examine them, he packed up Agrippina's jewels, her toiletries and papers and headed for the coast road.

In Baiae the festival had been forgotten. People huddled in groups, feeding their fears with the latest rumours. One piece of certain news proved more than disquieting: Agrippina's two bodyguard officers had forced the checkpoint at Volturnum, heading for Rome.

Nero was not in his villa. Lucius eventually found him standing quite still at the far end of the beach, head cocked, unshaven jowl rough as sandpaper, bloodshot eyes fixed on a point across the bay. As Lucius came up, he gave a start, then gripped his arm tight. 'Listen... Now... You hear it?... Sad, sad, wailing. Her voice.'

Lucius said he could hear nothing, at which Nero snapped that he was getting deaf. The voice came from the direction of her villa, she was trying to tell him something, but the lapping waves drowned her words.

After listening out further and becoming more and more agitated, Nero asked Lucius about his mission. When he heard that cremation had not been followed by burial, Nero gave an angry snort. That was what she had been trying to tell him! Unless her ashes were returned to mother earth, her soul would wander homeless and grieving. With a moan, he squeezed his head between his hands. 'Ride back immediately and perform inhumation!'

Lucius reacted sharply. 'Did you or did you not declare your mother an enemy of the State? .. Well then, there can be no question of burying her ashes... Put it another way: if you order them to be buried, you declare to the world that she was not in fact an enemy of the State! Why then did she have to die?'

Nero's face twisted angrily. 'The legal mind... Can't you help me for a change?'

Help demanded frankness so Lucius brought himself to say that he knew about the shipwreck and how Agrippina came to be killed. Nero became taut as a lyre string. Half to himself, he muttered, 'There was no other way.' A pause followed. 'So now you'll...?' He shot Lucius a look of dread.

Lucius waited before answering. 'We'll see about that when you've had some rest.' He then persuaded Nero to return to his villa and, only after he had seen him swallow a sleeping powder, did he leave.

Even with three grains of laudanum in his system, Nero had too much on his mind to find rest. Next morning, Lucius found that a troubled night had compounded his state of nerves by turning his thoughts from dreadful past to menacing future. The post would soon apprise Rome of his decree, but Agrippina's two aides would be following close behind to proclaim their version of events and doubtless to try and suborn the Praetorian Guard. Powerful friends of his mother stood to gain by her will which his decree would render invalid; men like Calpurnius Piso who had long coveted the principate, might well demand that the consuls carry out an investigation into the circumstances of Agrippina's death. Incapable of standing still, his eyes bulging with fear, Nero seemed to picture his fall in detail. 'She will have won!' he groaned.

'Not if you act at once, with conviction.' He must hurry to Rome to convene the Senate and explain that *salus respublicae* – the survival of Rome – had required him to act as he did.

Nero met this proposal with a rush of objections. By leaving Baiae before festival rites were over, he would be insulting Minerva. Even before a friendly audience, he was a poor speaker and, in front of a suspicious Senate, he would dry up. He wasn't good at dissimulating; his expression would give him away, and who was to tell what an angry Roman crowd might do...

Too many excuses, thought Lucius; he's afraid. Terrified. As I am beginning to be. They really were in trouble, both of them.

Nero had adopted an appealing tone. 'Only one man can save me. A fluent speaker, respected and trusted by the Senate.'

Not this, thought Lucius, fear scooping a hole in his stomach. It was one thing to offer advice, quite another to wade waist-deep into the muck. 'How could I bring myself to do that?'

Nero's face hardened. 'I thought you were my friend.'

'You've made a proposal of the utmost gravity. You must leave me time.'

'To write and polish an essay?' His tone had turned nasty. 'Sorry... retract. But every hour counts.'

Lucius said he needed space to think things over. Having agreed to meet later, they went their separate ways, eyes averted.

This was the time of day, when Novatus exercised his dogs, and Lucius took a seat in the rotunda hall to await his return. Animal heads and trophies of the chase looked down on chairs with leather seats, stout oak tables and life-size effigies: marble dogs, bronze eagles and silver-plated geese.

He was feeling unwell. A grey sadness pervasive as double cataract dulled his perception and his thoughts. He told himself the morning air smelled of spring, poplars showed their first bronze leaves, finches were calling. The world was not about to be consumed by fire. But he could not console himself. The animal trophies drew his eye, assuming human form, as poor decapitated Cicero, as Claudius's victims, as Agrippina, as himself.

Had the previous day's events really happened? Could it be that he was being asked – no, implored – publicly to defecate loud and plentifully on the civilized world's lawmakers? For what purpose? To staunch blood that would otherwise flow. But could it be staunched? Was there not a spring of blood bubbling under the floor of Caesar's House, as his father used to aver, and from there flowing outwards to dye senators' shoes red? Could a single lie cap that spring? Was it that sort of world? The wild boars' tusks and the stags' dagger-sharp antlers gave him an answer.

He began to feel afraid. He told himself that it was reasonable to feel afraid. It followed that he must clear out. Altogether, before it became too late. Go to ground in Spain with Paula. Seven years' solitary – he'd done more than his bit to stop the flow of blood.

A servant appeared and offered a collation, which Lucius declined. He pointed out that the hem of Lucius's gown hung loose, evidently torn while collecting firewood. Lucius asked for a needle, cotton and scissors and set himself slowly to steady his nerves by neatly stitching up the tear. As he snipped the thread, the servant commented on his ring. 'Yes, it's unusual,' Lucius said curtly, then nodded the man away.

His momentary calm shattered, his mind now turned to the alternative. Nero, he thought, is my friend, my protégé, almost a son. I cannot lie to the Senate, but I cannot leave Nero in the lurch.

Firm footsteps and noisy panting announced the appearance of a tall, straight-backed man in his fifties accompanied by a pair of pure-bred wolfhounds. The dogs were wary until they recognized Lucius then, at a nod from their master, they folded themselves down at either side of a chest on which the new arrival seated himself.

Even as a boy, Novatus had always had a dog at his heels: a tubby-tailed mongrel for ratting in the wheat-barn, a pointer to follow him into the hills he loved for partridge. As the eldest brother and the most athletic, he saw life as a hunt for a quarry, a race for a prize; and 'Master Who Won?' intended to win that prize. He had succeeded in the fiercely competitive sports competitions of Corduba, at school in Rome, then as an army officer and finally governor of a whole Roman province. But always the rules had to be observed; Novatus was a stickler for rules and for doing the right thing. He had made a marriage in every respect correct into a consular family; his wife had recently died, leaving him with a sixteen-year-old daughter, Novatilla, currently staying with Paula, who was her favourite aunt.

It was typical of Novatus that, even after reaching senatorial rank, if he met a stranger in the street looking lost, he would go and offer help. Such was our brother, admired by Lucius and me though we always felt somewhat in awe of his rigour.

On entering the hall, Novatus threw a sharp glance at Lucius. 'What's this we hear? Is there truly some emergency?'

Lucius was sure his brother could be relied on for discretion and he thought it would help to clarify his own position if he disclosed what he knew. This he did briefly, starting from the moment the yacht drew out to open water until Nero's panic request to him that morning, ending simply: 'There you have my dilemma.'

Novatus frowned, stretched out his long legs and stared reflectively at his well-polished ankle boots. 'What dilemma? I see no dilemma. I see only a law and the duty to obey it.'

Raising his left hand, he slowly pulled at the fingers, one by one, his habit when marshalling points for a speech. Then he cleared his throat and adopted a grave tone.

'The Senate meets on the holiest of our seven hills, each sitting preceded by sacrifice to Jupiter. Proceedings – all of them without exception – take place under the watchful eye of Jupiter. There you took the most solemn vow open to a Roman and you took it of your own choice. As a lawyer, you were aware of its gravity, its binding force and its importance for government. To break that vow would be sacrilege. And this is something the people know, for when they discovered that Sejanus had lied to the Senate about Germanicus's children, they dragged his body through the streets on hooks and threw it into the Tiber.'

I recall an art lesson we had as boys when we had to depict a landscape from life. Novatus chose to draw a cascade of white water falling sheer from a steep mountain peak circled by Jupiter's eagles; Lucius by contrast depicted our river Baetis gliding across a level valley lined by farms and rows of olive trees. Even then, Novatus's mental grid was etched vertically, up and down whilst Lucius's was horizontal and connecting. Was Novatus's vision conditioned by his being eldest, which meant he almost always won and came top or was it because his heart belonged up in the hills? Whatever the explanation, for him, Rome – the city on seven hills – guarded and dispensed justice to those below and beyond with the unquestioned authority of a general commanding in the field.

I return to his discourse, delivered in best gubernatorial style. 'Consider also those who would be listening to your lies – for a whole string of falsehoods would be needed to make your story convincing. Would you lie to me? To Mela? Probably never. Or individually to your friends in the House – Junius Fronto, Publius Cano? Probably not. Why then to the House collectively?'

Lucius reflected with a twinge of envy how Novatus had never in his life had doubts. He reminded his brother that Nero and he had been colleagues and close friends. Friendship no less than the law had obligations. He became aware that three pairs of eyes, his brother's and his wolfhounds', had turned hard and hostile.

'You call Nero your friend!' Novatus's voice came like a whiplash. 'Now he's become a matricide any such link is annulled.'

Lucius retorted that Nero had been pushed to extremes, that he could be said to have killed in self-defence.

'Sophistry, Lucius! He intended to kill with his collapsible ship and kill he did. If you were to maintain otherwise in the House, on top of sacrilegious perjury, you would be covering for a criminal, thereby breaking a second fundamental law.'

The servant reappeared, bringing the post. There was nothing for Lucius, but Novatus had a letter from his daughter, which he opened and read carefully without comment before taking up the next strand of his argument. Given Lucius's conviction that civic cohesion was underpinned by respect for the law, if in this crucial situation he broke the law, surely he would be reneging on his beliefs.

'Agreed, but this is a special, perhaps unique case. Civic cohesion can exist only if there is a city to cohere. I would be breaking the law only in order to preserve the city.'

Novatus met this with irony. 'As Julius said when he became dictator a second time! Our city will be preserved only on the basis of principles and law, not on this or that man's prognostication.'

So far Lucius had been arguing defensively. Novatus having lapsed into temporary silence, he now had a chance to state the advantages of supporting Nero. Agrippina had grown up in dread of Tiberius and reacted with a manic need for control, but Nero was free of any such trauma. He had told Lucius many times that he intended to rule in the people's best interests. And Nero would probably back the major reforms his mentor longed to implement.

'All very desirable. But crystal-gazing can never be a substitute for duty here and now.' A pause ensued. Then he solemnly gave his advice. 'Hurry to Rome by all means. Address the Senate. But apprise them of a hideous crime committed almost on our doorstep. Then you'll be acting as the law and your vow direct. And I believe you will win considerable respect, even honour – for your family too.'

Lucius combed his hand nervously through his hair, wondering whether to confide his conviction and risk causing a rift. At last he spoke.

'Between two courses of action of apparently equal merit, I believe only one tribunal has the authority to decide...'

'Family elders...'

'No... Conscience.'

Novatus's composure deserted him. He rose brusquely, signing to his dogs to remain couched, and began to stride round the hall, shaking his head and clasping and unclasping his hands behind his back.

Here I must explain how Lucius came to adopt the opinion so at variance with his family ethos. As a boy, he viewed our estate not as a fenced-off domain but as part of the surrounding hillside, dependent on the same cosmic forces, notably wind from the west that brought lifesaving rain just when drought hurt. The routine pattern of living within our home he saw as a continuation of that order in nature and, when he did well, whether in class or in field sports, he viewed his fortune as somehow linked to the general order. It happened that, one summer night when he was too excited to sleep, he had got up, thrown a cape around his shoulders and gone into the garden. The double row of cypresses, the rose bushes, the sundial, all merged in the pale light of a nearly full moon, adding intensity to his mood. To his surprise, he saw his mother seated near the sundial. She said she had been unable to sleep and asked him what he was doing out at that time of night.

'I'm too happy to sleep.' He felt part of a larger order, wonderful and fearsome in its vastness. He thought it must be arranged and felt the need to give thanks for it. 'Novatus laughs at me, and father doesn't understand. But say you understand.'

She put her arm round him and drew him to her. 'I've had feelings like those. Perhaps you get them from me.'

'But who should I thank?'

She suggested Terminus, the tree stump protecting our boundaries, and the little bronze figures beside the hearth protecting our house.

But these, he said, were disproportionately small and did not satisfy him. And he sat beside her for a long while staring at the sky until both of them were ready for sleep.

Only when he went to law school did Lucius get an answer that met his needs. Spirit or Breath, Attalus the Stoic had explained, is not confined to nature. It's at work in each one of us. It was Spirit that prompted Lucius to feel wonder at the cosmos and a vague but deep need to give thanks for life, and he could best show his gratitude by acting on the promptings of Spirit. From then on, Lucius tried to put this view into practice.

I return to Baiae and Novatus. Still striding angrily about, at last he spoke. Civilized man had always operated on the basis of objective right and wrong: *pietas* learned from parents, laws of the land publicly displayed. When we do right, the Graces show favour, when we do wrong the Fates harass us. Plain and effective. 'Along comes Cicero,' his tone turned scornful, 'reads Zeno's books, borrows one of his fancy Greek concepts, translates it as *conscientia* – which had hitherto meant "holding knowledge in common" – and gives it a brand-new meaning...'

Lucius nodded. 'Inward perception of the rightness or otherwise of one's actions.'

'A fancy way of saying the individual decides for himself what he *thinks* he should do. Objective right and wrong go down the drain. It's one of the most subversive notions in history.'

'It's not just Cicero's doing,' said Lucius soothingly. 'Already our younger jurists were shifting attention from the deed itself to the agent's intention.'

'Or rather, what the agent *declares* his intention to have been... Cicero's conscience opens the door to wholesale subjectivism and to the Sophists' lie that man is the measure of all things.'

Lucius shook his head. 'We Stoics believe just the opposite of that lie... Although we've been brought up to accept the broad principles of right and wrong, these may not give clear guidance for particular decisions. Then we turn our attention outwards – to nature and to the beneficence at work there.'

'Beneficence?' He shrugged doubtfully. 'Only in a general way.'

'And in particulars. When your dogs get worms, what makes them nose out...'

Novatus ran his hands complacently along his wolfhounds' shaggy backs. 'My dogs never get worms... But continue.'

'The immanent God we call Spirit, Breath or Wind makes itself heard.'

This elicited a faraway look and a near-smile, 'Remember in Corduba, how you used to lie awake listening to the wind from the hills, telling us which tree produced which sound. That's what you're rationalizing, dear Lucius, as the voice of conscience.'

Lucius replied that a room could be observed through a chink in the door no less than through a window.

Novatus chose not to pursue his objection and a silence ensued. Novatus wanted to help, perhaps had helped by highlighting the seriousness of the issues, but Lucius was disappointed that the brother whose approval he most desired opposed his plan of action. Suppressing a sigh, Lucius rose and grasped Novatus's arm affectionately, saying he needed solitude to decide.

'One last thing,' Novatus called after him. 'Bear in mind the penalty for perjury. Thrown a hundred feet down from the Tarpeian Rock.'

From his window, Lucius looked out on a grey sky and choppy sea. By temperament, he rarely envisaged possible failure, but Novatus's last words gave him pause. Any account of Agrippina's end must be lengthy; any contradiction would be pounced on by Thrasea Paetus, a Stoic of extreme views who was determined to bury the principate.

He wouldn't slip up. Wouldn't admit that he could slip up. And even if he were to – well, he had several times put his life at risk, danger couldn't hold him back. He was tense and restless. As a way of shaking off the dismal prospect, he began to tidy his belongings left in disorder by his early call. His eye fell on an unframed hand-size portrait of Paula. The outline and planes of her face had been accurately caught but, as in any portrait, the subject was reduced to passivity, and Paula was all animation. It was enough of a likeness to set Lucius remembering their parting embrace, their promise at dusk to watch for the Pleiades – 'their stars' – to appear, and to feel the ache of separation.

He composed a letter. While he liked – perhaps needed – to put what he felt for her into words, Paula preferred to express her feelings in some well-chosen gesture. It occurred to him that he had been wrong not to take account of Paula in his assessment of options. After all, were he to be detected in perjury, she would be the one to suffer. His own fleeting dismay would be her lifelong burden.

What choice would Paula advise? Fully aware of all she would lose, she had nevertheless urged him to take the tutoring job all those years ago. Would she now again conceal her fears and did he have a right to accept her unselfishness? He thought, I'm overcomplicating, sidetracking. Get back to the crux.

He opened his overnight bag and took out a conch the size of his fist, its white upper side gnarled, the lipped underside, polished pink shading to amber. It stood on his desk at home and accompanied him when he travelled. Drawing the shutters to and seating himself at the table in the centre of the room, he laid the conch beside him. Closing his eyes, he repeated the procedure Attalus had taught him. Away with mood and whim. Void yourself of phlegm, choler and bile. Put aside comfort, convenience, whatever others may think. Place yourself in the presence of Spirit.

Lifting the lips of the conch against his right ear, he heard the sound of waves rising and falling and began to time his breathing to that rhythm. It helped. He felt his mind being slowly smoothed, as sand by eddying tide. He listened to the rhythm of order rippling out to nature as a whole, and tried to align himself and his options. He had given the best part of his life to seeing the tables of the law upheld in the courts, and he thought of that particularly sacred law obliging him to speak the truth and only the truth in the House. He pondered the compelling beauty of the law, giving himself time to picture it without distraction. Then he turned to the city of Rome. Rome as it could be under reasonable rule, freed of spies and informers, freed from fear, able to realize its founders' hopes, growing, improving, sending out daughter colonies, sharing with others its civilization. This too he pictured calmly, considering his obligation as a citizen.

He passed from one image to the other, from law, embodying the wisdom of the past to the city, full of promise for the future. He could point to no discernible certainty, but sensed a growing awareness of which had the stronger claim. Laying down the shell, he drew lungfuls of intense relief, comparable he fancied to what followed parturition. He must hurry. Success would depend on arriving in Rome before rumour built up.

Quickly he packed and took his leave of his brother. Novatus expressed deep concern. Lucius thought this was for his safety until the other said sharply, 'Novatilla. You're to tell the girl's governess to hire a carriage and bring her here without delay. I want my daughter safely beside me.'

Paula would be heartbroken at losing the companionship of her niece. Lucius thought, I should have foreseen this and taken it into account. His feeling of having made the right choice began to waver.

Next Lucius sought out Nero and found him pacing the beach. Wreckage from the yacht lay washed up on the shore. He had ordered it burned but the wet wood was slow to take and he cursed his men fiercely. When he caught sight of Lucius, he hurried towards him. On hearing of his intention, he flung himself on the older man's shoulder. 'Thank all the gods for that!'

Lucius was issued with an authorization at each post to use Caesar's relay horses and a chitty for meals. And what should Lucius do with Agrippina's belongings? Nero told him to take them with him and deposit them securely in his mother's house. Lucius warned Nero not to be lulled into a mistaken sense of security. He couldn't afford the slightest slip. 'Speak little,' he said. 'Damocles' sword hangs over your head.'

The two embraced and, minutes later, Lucius was galloping through heavy rain on the coast road.

PART THREE

Power at last

Lucius accompanied the senior consul to the raised sanctuary at the far end of the Temple of Jupiter, placed himself beside the gold statue of Victory and looked down on the three long rows of benches running each side of the temple. A few faces from the Cato Club he recognized, as well as certain distinguished ex-consuls. Shrewd, all of them, on the alert for any attempt to hoodwink. Latecomers were finding every seat taken and had to stand.

As the consul recited the customary prayer, Lucius only half listened, busy giving himself last-minute cautions. One lie only. Defend that lie and on no account add a second. Keep Poppaea out of it. Look confident. You're acting in the interests of Rome.

Every New Year's Day, even with frost in the air, he made himself go for a swim, and the shock of cold water then was equalled now as he plunged into his prepared speech, watched by an array of cold eyes.

Caesar's mother had encroached on her son's authority: listening to debates from behind a curtain, taking decisions rightfully his. And he, the head of State acclaimed by the people, his *imperium* granted by you in this very House, he resisted, did well to resist. Hungry for sole power, his mother could wait no longer. She sent one of her bodyguard to perform an unthinkable act – to kill her son, kill Caesar. Providentially the killer was intercepted. Nero ordered his mother's arrest. Dreading exposure, she told her bodyguard to resist, and in the fracas received a fatal wound.

Gasps and indignant murmurs; fear swept the upturned faces as from spreading fire. Lucius waited until he held attention once more.

'Picture our *princeps*. He's escaped assassination and lost his mother – unworthy yes, but still a mother. In a state of deep shock he has sent me as his emissary to inform you of what happened and to say he counts on your support.'

Were they swallowing it? He sensed a certain malaise. They would have preferred the reassurance of seeing Nero in person, or at least being given a date for his return.

A young quaestor stood up, unknown to Lucius. 'Where were you when the assassin was caught?' Not aggressive, just curious. Answer openly.

'Asleep. In my brother Novatus's villa nearby.'

'When were you wakened?'

'An hour afterwards – approximately.'

'Why weren't you sent for at once?'

'Nero had no special need of me. His priority was prompt action. If his mother were to reach Rome, she would achieve her purpose.'

The quaestor nodded, sat down and other questions followed. Was he addressing the House as a senator or as Caesar's Friend? What further examples of Agrippina's encroachment could he give? How did she behave at the festive dinner? These he answered crisply, his confidence growing. But now at the back of the left-hand benches, a small man with a big bald head stood up: Thrasea Paetus, a Stoic of austere life and proven integrity, so pure a republican that he refused ever to let the name Caesar sully his lips. He expressed himself in a dry, rasping voice.

'Two of the last lady's officers arrived here yesterday. They say their mistress was compelled to embark on an unseaworthy vessel.'

Dangerous ground this. Very. Hug the truth. 'It was the lady herself who chose to return to her villa in her son's custom-built yacht. I was present and heard her words. There was no compulsion.'

'These officers say the ship foundered, their mistress had to swim for her life. After such an ordeal would any lady have been in a fit state to set in action a complicated coup involving the murder of her son?'

Every cell in his body was on alert as Lucius searched for a safe reply. 'It is not for me, nor for you, to speculate on the state of mind of someone no longer alive. What I would ask you and the House to do is assess these officers' credentials. They are foreigners, Germans: they swore loyalty to their mistress, not loyalty to Rome. What could be more probable than that they try to commend their mistress in order to draw their pensions, which otherwise would be withheld?'

A mistake. And Thrasea pounced. 'The law makes no distinction of nationality. If these men have pertinent evidence, they should be heard. Otherwise you are contravening the principles you've upheld these 20 years.'

Cornered. A pounding in his left breast. His heart kicked into tachycardia. Fight it. Slow the beat. Then think. Should he invoke that ultimate proviso inscribed on the Twelve Tables: *salus populi suprema lex esto*, that all other laws are void if it is a question of saving the country? That would keep out the Germans, but wouldn't it open wide the door to Thrasea? 'You say the coup was foiled, you saw the alleged perpetrator's body burn on her funeral pyre, how then can you pronounce our country in desperate danger?'

He sensed legs being crossed and uncrossed uneasily. Look for some other way. Fast. But perjury you must avoid. Flung from the Tarpeian Rock. Flattened into a slab of butcher's meat. The image blocked out clear thinking. But as one's body will reel away from a hurtling chariot by involuntary reflex alone, so now some reserve source of help flipped up a single word: procedure. But he must put it across cannily.

'The House is sitting in order to hear a message from Caesar. If at some future date the Germans wish to bring their allegations before us, let us then sit as a court of law to hear them. But the officers should bear in mind that, by resisting Caesar's order for his mother's arrest, they have laid themselves open to a charge of treason, punishable by death.'

Murmurs of approval from the House. It had worked. Thrasea stood silent, scowling, but he did not sit down. Consulting a file, he resumed in his dry cricket-like voice. 'The *princeps* is said to wish to divorce his wife in order to marry another lady. And his mother forbade it.'

This had to be blocked fast. At all costs keep Poppaea out of issue. 'Do you speak from personal knowledge of the lady in question?'

A pause. 'I have heard from reliable...' While Thrasea searched for a convincing noun, Lucius cut in. Though he scorned rhetoric, rhetoric it would have to be.

'Thrasea Pateus has *heard*!... Is this House to be swayed by hearsay? Nero has been gracious enough to let me visit his house on many occasions. There I have observed his wife, the young lady you in this very hall gave Caesar dispensation to marry. Not once have I heard Caesar address her with hard words, not once the shadow of a quarrel. Does Thrasea Paetus choose to cast doubts on this most suitable marriage, a union approved by all here present and by the Roman people? At the very moment when a detestable crime has been committed and we have an obligation to reassure our citizens, would Thrasea have us chew the cabbage stalks of street tattle?'

It worked, or seemed to, for Thrasea, looking confused, sat down.

Senators measure a speech not by its words alone but against the speaker's known character. So now. They recalled how persistently Lucius had defended their liberties against both Gaius Caligula and Claudius. When Lucius blocked the former's bid to be allowed a raised seat in the Senate, Gaius sought to cow him by forcing him to run like a criminal behind his golden chariot through streets slippery with mud for a full hour and a half, while onlookers, worked on by agents, added their jeers to Gaius's and pelted Lucius with rotten fruit. At the end of that ordeal, reining in his pair of horses, Gaius turned triumphantly on his mud-stained victim, panting from an asthmatic spasm and now close to collapse. Expecting submission, he was met by a scornful look and words that became famous: 'Same time tomorrow, sire?'

Lucius sensed he had the House's confidence. Quickly now. Profit from his advantage. 'I move that this House send congratulations to the *princeps* on his providential escape with the hope that he will return speedily to resume his functions as head of State.'

The presiding consul called for a vote. One by one, senators walked to the podium, their right hands grasping wooden counters, ready to place them in the box of their choice. An attendant used an abacus to make the reckoning and then the consul announced the tally. Eight negative votes, no more than eight. Lucius's heartbeat eased. Nero could return in safety; the State had escaped fragmentation. He wanted to rejoice. But at this moment Thrasea chose to walk out before anyone else, pacing slowly between the facing benches. His expression was not that of a beaten man. Head high and eyes flashing: he believes I'm hiding the truth, Lucius thought bleakly.

Fifteen days later Nero returned. That same afternoon he summoned Lucius together with Burrus, who had lately proved a welcome ally to my brother. He told them that, before attending to political business, he intended to put his domestic affairs in order. The crowds who had lined the streets to cheer him that morning showed he had nothing to fear from a quick divorce.

'With respect, sire,' said Lucius, 'the crowds weren't cheering you. They were cheering the Nero I described to the Senate.' He added that, if he were to marry Poppaea at once, Rome would draw the obvious conclusion. Burrus put it more sternly. 'Divorce Octavia and you lose her dowry,' by which he meant the *imperium*. After long discussion, and with the terror that had seized him at Baiae still fresh in his mind, Nero reluctantly agreed to wait.

From there, Nero went straight to Poppaea's house. She was expecting him but showed no special excitement, though he did notice a new respect in her manner. Once seated in her favourite room with a view of the patio, he told her how much he'd missed her and how he'd longed to return.

She took his hand and pressed it. 'And now no more separation.'

He broke his news gently, but not gently enough, for she uttered a cry, screwed up her eyes and began to sob. Nero felt as though he'd knocked over a precious vase. Slowly she regained control. Eluding his attempts to take her in his arms, she inquired the reason for delay.

Nero said he had to respect public opinion.

'But for how long?... Just a short while? Very short? You promise?'

He promised and was allowed to stroke her hair. She tended to avoid unpleasant subjects; even so, it came as a relief to him that she asked no questions about his mother's death.

She was wearing a new dress of pale rose, with slashed sleeves and turned-up cuffs, made to her own design. He complimented her on the redecoration of the room which, before leaving for Baiae, he had agreed she should undertake and charge to him.

Poppaea said hesitantly, 'While the workmen were here, I had the whole house done... While you were away, I needed to console myself.' She gave him a soft appealing look. 'You don't mind, do you?'

By now he was familiar with her ways and found them endearing. He nodded agreement, following up with a request to know when it would be convenient for him to call – 'to sing a duet'.

Her reply was prompt and gracious. 'Any Tuesday morning at the music academy.'

'I meant... our other kind of duet.'

'Ah!' She looked at him archly. 'There we must respect public opinion.' She had a great deal of entertaining to attend to. She would have more free time, she continued as though thinking aloud, if she could employ a nanny for her little son and take on a second housemaid.

Nero was hungry for her body. He hastened to assure her that he would look after their salaries. Poppaea softened. She would review her engagements and let him know when he might visit. Nero decided he would have to be content with her assurance, and took his leave to attend a less welcome meeting.

When Agrippina had begun to devote all her attention to the struggle with her son, her place as Octavia's adviser had been taken by Manilius Messala. Second cousin to Octavia, aged 42, Manilius had trained for diplomacy but was barred from ambassadorship by the bigamous marriage and execution of his kinswoman Messalina. He now managed the family's extensive interests in the silversmiths' trade while presiding over the Ancient Families' Association and the Genealogical Society. He was tall and lean, with a long face and an admired scimitar nose, fine dark eyes and a weak liver. His aim in life was to restore their former influence to the Messala clan, and to this he brought a supple mind and suave manner. He was helped by his wife Priscilla, from the Silani clan, a pushy and persistent character.

In Nero's absence, Manilius had organized a family gathering in Octavia's honour, with some 80 of her kin from all over Italy, many of whom she had not met before. They were an impressive lot and some held key posts. They made a fuss of Octavia and their unspoken message was: rest assured, you are not alone.

Priscilla advised Octavia on how to win favour with the populace. She must show herself often, enquire about their hopes, sympathize with their misfortunes, contribute generously to provident funds. At home, she should try to meet her husband's tastes. Finding that she had nothing more alluring in her scent cupboard than lavender water, Priscilla took her to a perfumier's where they bought half a dozen unusual unguents and oils. She emphasized the importance of conjugal relations and gave her a herbal potion helpful in promoting fertility.

When Nero arrived at the agreed time in her apartment, Octavia was waiting for him, hair newly curled in the way he liked, with, as she eagerly put it, 'a welcome-home surprise'. Explaining that she had been to pottery classes, she handed him a small unglazed clay tray.

Nero inspected it uncertainly, 'For asparagus?'

'No, no. For your desk, to put your pens and styluses.'

It was beginner's work, irregular and uneven, the sort of object one places in a cupboard and forgets. That perhaps was why it touched Nero. She had taken trouble to please him, while he had come to hurt her.

He thanked her with a kiss on the lips she hadn't expected then, softening what he had planned to say, he recalled how their marriage had been arranged when they were still children: now as adults they had to allow for each other's diverging interests. As his lawful wife, Octavia would continue to be treated with respect and honour. But he intended to go on seeing his musical friend discreetly. Nothing would be done to offend her feelings or harm her status. Could she bring herself to accept that?

Octavia had a good opinion of herself. She saw Poppaea as a mere performer with a siren's voice, momentarily seductive to Nero but bound soon to cloy. Until that happened she was ready to wait, but she did make one stipulation. The aim of marriage was procreation; she had a right to children, and so she must be allowed to come to Nero's bed when conception was possible. A child would make divorce more difficult but the risk seemed worth taking and Nero agreed to her demand.

Having tidied his personal life, Nero threw himself with zest into the work of governing. It fell into three parts, first in importance being the dispensing of justice in the many appeal cases brought by provincials. Here, advised by a panel of lawyers, he followed Lucius's advice of avoiding snap decisions, getting troublesome cases set down in writing and deferring judgement to the day after the hearing.

Second in importance came foreign policy. Unaggressive by temperament and under the influence of Lucius's pacifism, Nero proposed to reduce military commitments. In Britain, the legions faced constant harassment and Nero wished to pull them out altogether. The issue was so important that, on Lucius's advice, he summoned the Senate military committee for consultation. They judged that, for Nero to undo his adoptive father's most glorious achievement would unsettle the army and cause a public outcry. In the interests of good relations with the Senate, Nero reluctantly deferred to their view, but he ordered the commander in Armenia to advance no further and to open peace talks with Parthia.

The third aspect of Nero's work involved the enlargement and embellishment of Rome expected of every *princeps* and here his artistic sensibility made itself felt. Many vacant lots had become unsightly, cluttered with debris from building works and overgrown with weeds and rubbish. Nero had these cleared and levelled, himself showing an example by joining in the work with pick and shovel.

Rome was full of street vendors of honey cakes, flavoured water and roasted chestnuts. More stalls had sprung up of late providing hot meals: sausages fried in oil, beans in sauce and various kinds of doughnut. More and more people had taken to eating their meals in the street. Arguing that Rome was becoming an open-air kitchen and the narrow streets were impassable, Nero had the stalls removed. Save by the stall holders, this was generally considered a gain.

It was Nero's ambition to provide Rome with a new gymnasium worthy of the city, with adjoining hot and cold baths. He opened the project to competition and himself chose the architect. Together they worked out in detail all the many new facilities it should provide. When building began, he regularly monitored progress with the site manager. To encourage senators to keep fit by using the gymnasium, he promised to provide them with free oil for use in the baths.

In the little free time left to him, Nero improved his technique as a chariot driver and learned to play the lyre. Lucius watched all this activity with mixed feelings. He believed it reflected youthful gusto as well as an almost febrile need to avoid dwelling on the recent horror at Baiae. He regretted that all this momentum obliged him to defer proposing his own cherished schemes, but drew hope from the fact that Nero consulted him regularly. Their exchanges of views took place in the open air, preferably near work in progress, by an aqueduct under repair and once at the stables so that Nero could lend a hand when his favourite mare began to foal.

One such meeting took place beside the as yet unroofed gymnasium, where new foundations for the baths were being re-laid after unexpected soil subsidence. Several tons of broken rock had to be tipped in, pounded tight and carefully levelled. Lucius drew Nero's attention to the contractor's steeply increased estimate of costs, from which it became evident that expenses were outrunning available funds, three-quarters of which came from Nero's privy purse, the rest from municipal rates.

'We'll borrow,' said Nero, unperturbed.

Aware that Nero's open-handedness could all too easily become reckless extravagance, Lucius explained that borrowing would be most unwise, given high interest rates, and they should cancel some other scheduled project. The list of these was produced, accountants' reports attached. One item caught Lucius's eye: a new recital hall at the music school costing no less than 25,000 denarii. Why so expensive? Nero explained that the hall interior had to be faced with acacia because it provided best acoustics.

Aware that Nero was already making over generous sums to Poppaea, Lucius said bluntly, 'If you want to complete the gym complex this year, I'm afraid you'll have to scale down the baths or else delay the recital hall.' After discussion, Nero chose to complete the gym as planned and they paused for a break.

As a result of speaking often in public, both men had developed slight throat irritation and huskiness. Lucius offered Nero one of his aniseed lozenges and, in return, Nero handed him one of the liquorice sweets he liked. Sucking these emollients, they strolled contentedly round the site, watching the arrival and unloading of marble plaques to face the future baths. Then they separated, Nero to inspect the guard, Lucius to Caesar's House from where he reported to Nero on Octavia's arrangements.

Poppaea meanwhile was building her reputation as a singer. She gave recitals in friends' houses, choosing now only sophisticated pieces with long runs and demanding leaps. She declined offers to sing in a public theatre: she could give of her best only in intimate sympathetic surroundings. She organized a music festival featuring guest artists from abroad that won high praise and entertained the visitors afterwards in her home. She also gave weekly singing lessons to two girls believed to show promise.

Thanks to Nero's gifts of coin, she took to visiting fashionable shops, carried there in her curtained litter. The curious pressed in to the first shop she entered and were rewarded by seeing her draw back her veil with a slow flourish, as an ear of wheat is revealed to the faithful at Eleusis. Poppaea bought only what could be specially made to her own design or taste, scorning anything duplicated. Soon shops were fighting to win her custom.

The milk of she-asses is known to keep skin smooth and fair. Poppaea had a churn of such milk brought weekly from a nearby farm to fill her onyx bath. This caught the public imagination and the more adulatory compared Poppaea stepping out of her bath of milk to Venus rising from the foam. Clearly this lady differed from any other. It was said of her that servants jumped to her every wish and she never had to lift a finger. Quite right too. Who ever heard of Venus exerting herself?

Nero had been welcomed back from Baiae in May. One evening early in August he left his house on foot, intending to spend the night with Poppaea, one of two she allowed him monthly. He was enjoying his many new responsibilities and sensed he was doing his job well. That afternoon his gymnasium had been roofed and he sang to himself in the street.

Poppaea had rare new hyacinths from Lydia to show him. When they had settled in what she called her snuggery, he told her that he heard her praises sung on every side. To his surprise, her expression clouded.

What people said gave her no pleasure, none at all. If she kept busy, it was only in order not to grieve at her sadnesses. Yes, sadnesses, there were several. Her little boy had no father to steady him, the great families snubbed her and, saddest of all, just at the season when orchards and vineyards were heavy with fruit, she was denied her longing to bear him a son.

Nero saw her distress was not artifice. He tried to reassure her, telling her that if he had his way, he would marry her tomorrow, but they had to wait. For how long? she cut in.

Until certain events were forgotten, so his advisers told him.

'Advisers! Why do you need advisers?'

'They're thinking of your good too, Poppaea.'

Getting up, she paced the room, tossing her head and swinging the ends of her silver-tassled belt. Why, she asked sharply, had work stopped on her recital room?

Not stopped, just delayed, Nero replied soothingly. Funds had run low and he had been advised not to borrow further.

'Advisers, advisers! Are you sure they know best – or indeed are impartial?'

Work, he promised, would begin again in January, but this did not help, for Poppaea objected that recitals had already been planned for that month.

Nero saw that nothing he said softened her frown and, as they drifted into an uneasy silence, he tried flattery before reaching out and lightly squeezing the back of her neck. Usually a prelude to caresses, this time it caused Poppaea to draw away, rise abruptly and say that she did not wish him to spend the night. She had begun to feel very insecure, and that did not go with making love. Nero protested, begged her to reconsider and then dejectedly took his leave.

A crane lowered a keystone into the marble entrance arch of the gymnasium, while workmen cheered this symbolic act of completion. Vaulting horses, parallel bars, trampolines, dumbbells and the rest were wheeled in, ready for opening day. Burrus was told to install fire protection equipment and Lucius to purchase fifteen giant barrels of oil. Lucius went to his regular supplier of oil, placed the order and gave the matter no further thought.

Nero had business in the law courts on the morning of his next informal consultation with Lucius and, since heavy rain was falling, chose to hold it in the Forum portico. His comments on Lucius's reports were curter than usual and, once they had been dealt with, he opened a file, took out a bill and looked accusingly at Lucius.

'Why did you buy Spanish oil instead of Italian?'

Lucius replied that it contained less acid and was better for the skin.

'But more expensive. I find that odd, since you're forever urging me to slash costs... Does the oil you bought happen to come from Corduba?'

Lucius said the dealer had not specified the provenance.

'But Corduba is Spain's main oil-producing region?'

Lucius conceded that the oil might well have come from Corduba.

'Where I believe you own an olive estate?'

'My father did; now it belongs to my brother.'

'Mela the banker?'

'Novatus.'

'So, in making a purchase on my behalf you chose to benefit your brother Novatus?'

Lucius contested hotly. His sole aim had been to satisfy Nero's desire for quality in everything touching the gymnasium.

Nero sniffed, looked unconvinced and dropped the subject, leaving Lucius disturbed by the pettiness of the charge and the hostile tone in which it had been made.

Minutes later, when Nero had closed the meeting, Lucius took out his enamelled box and, as usual, offered Nero an aniseed lozenge. To his surprise, Nero pretended to ignore him, produced his own liquorice sweets and, without passing them to Lucius, placed one in his mouth, saying he preferred his own.

'Is anything the matter, sire?' Lucius enquired anxiously.

Nero gave him a dark look. 'Not on my side.'

By now, Lucius and Paula had settled in to their house, and it was there that evening Lucius unburdened himself. The oil bill was clearly a pretext, not a cause, and why had Nero adopted so oblique a reproof? Lately his opinion had been asked for less often in Cabinet yet Lucius could recall no action on his part to explain such coolness. Bad enough at any time to lose Nero's friendship, but disastrous now, before he had had a chance to achieve anything important.

Lucius had enemies, perhaps more than most since he had never formed a cabal to ward them off but, as far as he knew, none had access to Nero's ear. Perhaps he had offended someone important? It was then that Paula hesitantly spoke Poppaea's name.

Impossible, said Lucius dismissively. He never saw Poppaea, had said or done nothing to offend her and, since politics bored her, why should she wish to make trouble in that area? Paula stuck to her suggestion. Lucius had urged Nero to make cuts in arts spending. Every week, he went to Caesar's House to talk privately with Octavia. In the Senate, he advocated measures for strengthening marriages by granting financial and social benefits to couples with more than one child. And they had never invited Poppaea to dinner.

It turned into one of those dreadful evenings, Paula pulling nervously at skin on the soles of her feet, Lucius rolling and unrolling himself in the curtains. Finally, long past midnight, Lucius suggested that Paula should act as peacemaker: invite Poppaea to call on her when Lucius was not at home. It could do no harm and might do some good.

Paula had enjoyed Novatilla's presence in the house and had begun to look on her as a substitute daughter, whom she could help in the difficult adolescent years. Greatly depressed by the girl's abrupt recall to Baiae, she felt in no mood to receive a stranger and doubted whether she could handle it. 'Either the lady won't accept and we'll be snubbed, or she'll show up my ignorance of the arts and gloat. From someone younger, that will be very painful.' But when Lucius explained Poppaea's key role and the danger he felt he was in, she eventually agreed to co-operate.

Poppaea arrived one morning soon after breakfast. Paula, always an early riser, received her in a tidy, freshly aired living room. Her visitor wore an expensive but studiedly simple primrose cotton gown fitted at the waist and overstitched on the pockets, while she wore only a loose blouse with wrap-around linen skirt.

Poppaea murmured a cool, offhand greeting, took in the room at a glance and turned to the furnishings. A little rosewood table having won a nod of approval, Paula mentioned that Lucius had begun to collect dining tables and had purchased it at auction. This brought no comment but a moment later Poppaea stopped with distaste before a little landscape in charcoal. 'Where on earth did you get *that?*'

'From the artist, my favourite aunt. It's a view of my family home.'

Poppaea drew a breath. 'The provinces. Somehow so… unshaped.' It was a sad general truth.

They seated themselves. Raising her eyebrows, with the very slight drawl she affected with strangers, Poppaea said she had been rather surprised by Paula's invitation.

Paula had already prepared an explanation. 'With my husband close to the *princeps* and you his intended, we have interests in common, sufficient perhaps to try to become friends.' And why had Poppaea accepted?

'You're said to be all a senator's wife should be and naturally I was curious to see what that entails.'

Paula deflected the other's irony. 'Giving many dinners… listening to senators tell the same stories many times.'

Poppaea frowned. 'I find senators unbearably stuffy.'

'Only some. And a little flirtation makes them quite amusing. As well as keeping one's husband up to the mark.'

Poppaea assumed a studiedly offhand tone. 'Does your husband ask your advice on State affairs?'

Paula smiled humbly. 'Politics aren't my skein of wool.'

'Isn't that rather irresponsible?'

'We can't all be perfect,' Paula replied sweetly.

A chilly pause ensued, broken by Poppaea expressing surprise that Paula's husband never came to her music recitals.

'Lucius isn't musical. I'm sure you wouldn't wish him to pretend.'

'And a man of *ideas*. Such people have little feeling. Only principles. But you know about that. When he threw away seven years of marriage just to score a point against Claudius.'

'He did what he did,' said Paula staunchly, '*because* of feeling… Feeling for the citizens of Rome.'

Sensing that she might be drawn into indiscretion, Paula decided on a change of scene. She was good in the kitchen and knew it. If she could get Poppaea there, she thought she would be able to handle her. She rose with mock seriousness and said, 'Another thing a senator's wife has to learn: do what has to be done now! I have ten pounds of pears in my kitchen and with this weather they won't keep. Would you care to help me peel them?'

It amused her to read the other's expression. At this very first meeting, the extraordinary idea of adjourning to the kitchen! Not to decorate a cake, but to do a cook's work. Paula opened a door invitingly but Poppaea held back. The kitchen wasn't her world: she disliked the smell of cooking, and steam spoilt her hair-do.

Poppaea stood her ground so Paula said they could chat through the open door.

She tied on an apron, chose a sharp knife and began to peel the first of a pile of pears, chatting easily about where she'd bought them, how she never bothered with a recipe, just followed her instinct. Having peeled the fruit, she made to fill a large copper basin with water. 'It's rather heavy. I wonder whether you would give me a hand,' she called coaxingly. Poppaea was drawn in to lift the basin onto the stove whereupon Paula pressed an apron on her and invited her to peel a second pile of pears. Poppaea gingerly took a knife, held a pear at arm's length and laboriously removed thick pieces of peel. 'It won't bite you,' laughed Paula and showed her how to hold the pear close, to cut the peel towards her in thin slivers, then to core each quarter in one quick movement.

The rind was deftly cut off a number of nobly citrons and then honey was added to the mix. With each step, Poppaea took a little more interest. Could it be that this lady, admitted by all to be elegance and refinement personified who, after peeling a single grape would wash her hands, should be stirring jam in a hot kitchen? This was happening and, what's more, she seemed to be enjoying it. Poppaea expressed curiosity about the hood over the stove and Paula explained how a cowl on top of the flue turned in the breeze, drawing out steam. There were very few in Rome. With a teasing glance she added, 'It comes from my part of the world – the unshaped provinces'.

Together they added wood to the stove and watched for the jam to boil. Paula recalled how as a child the kitchen had been a place of wonders: a cache of supposedly indigestible goodies where dough became hot crusty bread and servants exchanged grown-up talk which she wasn't meant to hear. She and her brother used to launch midnight forays for liver sausage. 'I expect you were too well-behaved for that?' As she hoped, this drew an admission that Poppaea too had raided her larder – for cream and raisins. 'I see we were both little terrors,' said Paula and was pleased at Poppaea's answering look of complicity.

After the jam had started to simmer and they had returned to the living room, Poppaea prepared to leave. Paula's offer of a pot of last year's pear jam met with hesitation. Poppaea had dismissed her litter and would be walking home: she did not want to be seen in the street carrying a pot of jam. 'Unthinkable,' agreed Paula, masking her amusement. She fetched a wicker basket with cover and handle into which she placed the pot. Poppaea departed and Paula threw herself on her bed with a loud sigh of relief.

Nero remained cool with Lucius. Paula feared she had made no impact and, though gossip-writers pushed to learn about her surprise two-hour visit and the contents of her little basket, Poppaea knew the value of mystery and said nothing.

Lucius judged that, even if he was right in imputing Nero's change of mood to Poppaea and even if Poppaea felt Paula to be well-disposed to her, it was by no means sure that her sympathy would extend to him. He had to assume that she would continue to suspect him and would work for his dismissal. Before he lost his influence altogether, he determined to lead out of their stables one of his winged horses, as he privately termed his radical plans for reform. His choice was determined for him when the Treasury suddenly announced the closure of Corduba's mint.

Lucius came to my office one afternoon, looking through me rather than at me. The weather was sticky and humid so I sent out my errand boy for iced drinks. I asked him whether Poppaea's reactions to Paula were known. Nothing definite, he replied, save a snippet quoting Poppaea as saying that, though no artist, Paula makes something of being natural. 'Perhaps apocryphal, and anyway it might mean anything,' he shrugged.

Settled with his favourite roasted pistachios and a glass of pomegranate juice, Lucius listed developments since becoming Caesar's Friend. Nero had improved the amenities of Rome, enlarged the vegetable and fruit markets, eased the housing shortage by building four new apartment blocks, brought running water to more homes, speeded up refuse collection and made numerous small improvements. Nero was sensitive to people's needs for he regularly walked the streets unattended, questioning artisans, listening to complaints and talking practicalities. The Senate busied itself with Italy, paving roads, dredging harbours, cutting new canals. All this was good to see, but what of the frontier provinces under Nero's jurisdiction and the others administered by the Senate? There inertia prevailed. Taxes were collected, roads kept passable, justice dispensed though often too slowly. But no attempts were made to better conditions. All 34 provinces existed for Rome's benefit and pride.

'That's the situation that troubles me, and I approach it like this. Why does a man choose to come and live in Rome? He seeks companionship and the stimulus to self-improvement that comes from competition. But once installed, what then? I think he will find himself looking beyond the city walls, to Roman citizens dwelling abroad and, more generally, to the other peoples of Europe. He may then say one of two things: these foreigners look different, speak a language I can't understand, wear different clothes, worship horses, even crocodiles – they are altogether different and therefore no concern of mine. Or he may say: before becoming a citizen of Rome, I was born an inhabitant of the Earth. That status is something I share with non-Romans whatever they may look like and wherever they may be. We are all, so to speak, citizens of this bountiful Earth. We have no constitution but we are nonetheless a community. It follows that I have obligations to them.'

'There speaks the Spaniard!' I couldn't help interposing.

Lucius agreed that being born a provincial had helped him view the situation more dispassionately than a born Roman, but his stance had firmer roots. 'Observing harmony in the natural world, the Stoic believes it to be work of Spirit, and that this same Spirit would wish a like harmony for mankind. I go a step further. I say that, for Spirit's goal to be realized, all of us have a part to play, a duty not to shun or impose on those who happen to look and speak differently.'

'Your views hang together I suppose,' I replied, 'but they're more likely to carry weight at a meeting of the Philosophical Society than with the Treasury, on whom the fate of Corduba's mint depends.'

Lucius agreed. But, just as he had concealed his pacifist convictions when dissuading Agrippina from waging war on Parthia, so he would use strictly empirical arguments with the Treasury.

As he rose to leave, I reminded him that Poppaea felt only scorn for the provinces. His pro-provincial stance could motivate her to set Nero against him still further. Lucius said he was prepared to take the risk and we parted amicably.

The hearing took place in a small committee room adjoining the temple of Juno Moneta, guardian of our national wealth, in the cellars of which gold bullion is stored under guard. The three Prefects, middle-aged equestrians, spelled out their case clearly and logically in numerate language: figures for income, figures for expenditure, figures for transporting minted coin from Spain to Rome. Lucius wondered whether their dreams also came to them in numbers. All the figures pointed one way: money would be saved by closing Corduba's mint and moving production to Rome.

Lucius opened his defence by recalling how he and his brothers used to watch copper ore being mined, then smelted and brought in from the foundry. One day he had sat up with the carter as he drove his mules into town, noting how people stopped to watch admiringly. Their comments were naive but deeply felt: 'Rome's given us roads and an aqueduct but it's we who keep their coffers full,' they would say. Just as a coin has value over and above its metal weight, so their mint had value for them as a source of self-esteem. They had harnessed their considerable skills to a local resource to turn out a product that found its way into pockets throughout the Republic. Their mint fuelled local development as wages went into new businesses. 'Corduba is Rome's child but now the child is growing up. If Rome continues to treat her as a child, love will curdle to rancour.'

Lucius expanded his argument into a plea. Let the Treasury allow Corduba to retain her mint and thereby mark a symbolic turning-point in Rome's treatment of the provinces. Of the millions Spain paid annually in taxes – more than enough to cover garrisons and road repair – let Rome in future spend the surplus on encouraging provincial development and building schools and libraries.

Here I should mention that Lucius personally set up a local fund in order to provide Corduba with its first library, to which I as his banker had recently paid in 200,000 denarii.

Lucius ended by declaring that investment would bring long-term gains, since development would increase wealth and yield to higher tax revenues. The Prefects convened briefly, then returned to announce their decision. The existence of two mints far apart was a wasteful duplication, while the monthly transport of coin to Rome under guard added to costs. Corduba's mint must close.

Their decision, against which there was no appeal came as a blow. Why, Lucius wondered, had the Prefects been so unimpressed by his proposals? Had it merely been a dialogue of the deaf? Or could it be that he was at fault, wrapped in a self-assurance that concealed self-deception: what he believed to be self-evidently advantageous to the Republic merely a product of nostalgia for his home town? He was too involved to be able to judge. But if it *were* so, there were far-reaching implications for any and every argument he might advance. He was cast into depression.

Soon afterwards there came his way what looked like a stroke of luck, though it was actually the result of behind the scenes moves. As suddenly as it had appeared, Nero's cold manner passed. In Cabinet he again asked Lucius's opinion first and praised any suggestion he found useful. Trivial but more significant: at their next weekly consultation, having worked through the agenda, he offered Lucius his pastilles, a new variety flavoured with blackcurrant. Lucius took one and offered his own: then they began to stroll easily side by side.

In a studiedly offhand tone, Nero mentioned that Poppaea had enjoyed her visit to Paula and was thinking of inviting her back – not to a party, but alone. He turned to face Lucius. 'I think it would be good for Poppaea to have a friend outside her musical set...' He rippled a hand suggestively.

'I agree,' said Lucius. 'I'll encourage her to go.'

The mood seemed right, the moment too good to miss. Lucius described the Corduba case and his extreme disappointment, hoping Nero might make a suggestion. But he said only that Hispania Baetica was a senatorial province, and he had no jurisdiction there.

Quite, said Lucius. But it was the competence of the Treasury that troubled him. 'We take it as axiomatic that no one should be a judge in his own case. Here we have three individuals doing precisely that.' The situation, he explained, had come about gradually. Ad hoc limited powers had been granted at a time of danger during the first Punic War when money was extremely tight. The Treasury had gradually extended these powers to their own advantage, as Claudius did with the *lex de maiestate*.

Lucius recalled that some of the provincials who arrived to appeal to their *princeps* claimed they were victims of unfair taxation. Nero had to refer them to the Treasury, aware that they would not receive there the satisfaction he might have been able to give them. Lucius concluded that much injustice and resentment could be avoided if in future appeals against the Treasury were decided in the Forum by independent magistrates. Nero listened attentively, put several questions, then said the issue was important and he would think it over carefully.

At their next consultation, the two agreed that it was a matter for the Senate to decide on the *princeps*'s initiative. Lucius would help him draft his speech and would prepare the ground with friends in the Cato Group.

Events turned out even more favourably than Lucius had hoped. Pleased at being treated by Nero as partners in government, the senators voted – by a majority of over a hundred – that future appeals against the Treasury should be heard by independent magistrates.

Next day, a court heard the Treasury prefects and Lucius repeat their arguments. They ruled that Corduba should retain its mint, a decision that caused little stir in the capital, for Romans had nothing to gain from centralized coining. In Corduba and the provinces generally, the ruling met with rejoicing.

Lucius was pleased at Cordoba's reprieve but what gave him more lasting satisfaction was his belief that the court's ruling would serve as both example and symbol to the provinces. The benchmark would remain Rome's convenience and immediate financial advantage, but he believed there would be a growing demand for improving education and resources in the provinces as the logical sequel to pacification and urbanization. Rome would thereby gain a welcome influx of trained manpower.

Lucius immediately began to consider mounting his second winged horse, bigger, less manageable than the first, any fall from which could put a disastrous end to his political career. And here once again I must go back in time.

Among the outdoor servants at Corduba, our favourite was Cadi, a stocky man with a round open face and jug ears. As small children, he let us ride on his shoulders and steer by pulling his big ears; later his duties included hustling us out of bed, seeing us washed and giving us breakfast. He lived in a room in the commons, smelling strongly of the ferrets with which he netted rabbits for the pot. He spoke survival Latin with an Iberian accent and there was little he did not know about insects, lizards and snakes.

He was held in respect as a useful member of the household and, only when I was eight and Lucius nine, did we learn that the iron ring Cadi wore on his left hand meant that he had a different status from paid workmen: he was a slave. This prompted a stream of questions. Father responded that, just as tainted water had to be filtered through sand three times before becoming potable, so three generations were needed to bring a slave from savagery to the level of a free person. Cadi was a first-generation slave, born into a marauding tribe and taken prisoner on the battlefield. Under certain conditions, his grandson – if he had one – would be a free man.

Cadi married late and sired one son, Lado, also robust but with nimble hands and a quick intelligence. When Lucius became quaestor, he brought Lado to Rome, taught shorthand and took him on as amanuensis. Lado too wore the iron ring. He received wages, but would have his board and keep for life.

Part of the slave's lore is to slack off whenever possible to remind yourself that you're not just a living tool. Lado proved a reliable amanuensis but he idled whenever he thought he could get away with it. The master's lore is to ensure servants don't take advantage. In return for security for life, a master expects his servants to pull their weight during working hours. Having more than once caught Lado snoring lightly at his desk, Lucius took to making spot checks, though it broke his flow and annoyed him to think he was spying. But it had been impressed on him that a man of equestrian rank had a special obligation to ensure high standards from his household.

There is osmosis between master and slave. Lado took note of everything Lucius said, of his attitude to visitors and his perseverance in adversity. In time, he shed his shyness and began to show an understanding of the cases in hand, even making perceptive comments. If it wasn't for his iron ring, no one would believe Lado was a slave, for he now possessed the attitude and values expected of a freedman. Lucius considered emancipating Lado. The change of status would work to his own advantage too, for he would no longer have the nagging worry of having to watch him and scold him for wasting time.

Lucius questioned friends who had freed their slaves. They warned him that, all too often, a manumitted slave left his employer out of embarrassment at working as an equal for the man he had served so long as a slave. Often too, they gave themselves airs, Narcissus and

Polybius being notorious examples. It was normal practice for a master to write the manumission of a deserving slave into his will, to take effect only after his death. Despite these warnings, Lucius decided to go ahead. But he was careful to avoid appearing the bountiful master. When Lado did a job well, he would compliment him, adding that, if he continued in similar vein, he would win himself free status.

The day came when Lucius went to the local magistrate, submitted the required papers and paid the heavy manumission tax. Lado bent on one knee, while Lucius placed a hand on his shoulder and proclaimed, 'I hereby set you free.' With a jig saw, Lado's ring was split and discarded.

At first there was awkwardness between them, each not quite sure what tone and manner to adopt. However, Lado showed no sign of leaving: he knew Lucius to be demanding, often impatient but seldom unfair. Soon he talked of marriage and children.

The most surprising result was the changes Lucius noticed in himself. He no longer fretted about maintaining the uneasy divide between master and slave; he could unburden himself about small everyday troubles arising from his work, ask Lado's advice and even reward good performance with an occasional gift. Before long, he was viewing his amanuensis as a friend. Lucius too had been freed.

His changed relations with Lado yielded other returns. Though no one loved the city more, Lucius paradoxically clung to country habits. Meals in the patio, bedroom window wide open summer and winter; he kept a pet tortoise in the garden and often cited its prognostic powers: if the animal moved less sluggishly than usual and ate a breakfast of cabbage, it was sure to rain. Lado shared Lucius's affection for rural Spain and its habits. Once a month, they would go off together to an inn kept by a Spaniard to enjoy fish baked in salt garnished with red peppers and black olives, washed down with heavy dark red wine. Lucius enjoyed the kind of slapstick theatre he had watched as a boy in Corduba where a clumsy workman carrying planks might knock over his apprentice or a husband dress up as a ghost to frighten his henpecking wife. Paula found such antics too obvious, but Lado loved them and the two would buy seats for the latest farce and sit doubled up with laughter. The conclusions Lucius drew from his experience with Lado helped to shape an increasingly critical attitude to the law on slavery.

When the first settlers on the seven hills began to expand their territory by force, they brought back as prisoners cowed helpless men roped together like cattle, most unable to speak a word of Latin and those who could so incoherent as to seem mentally deficient. Some came from tribes practising human sacrifice, some had no religion and no notion of *pietas*. Lawmakers of the day decided that these uprooted creatures lacked a sense of right and wrong, the defining attribute of a person in law. Without going so far as Aristotle, who held that those who let themselves be taken prisoner are born with an inferior nature and are fit only to serve their betters, legislators declared that the prisoners of war could not be accounted persons in the Roman sense of the word. They were non-persons, devoid of legal status.

In the countryside, where slaves worked the fields alongside their owners and were respected as indispensable, no one considered them non-persons: they had no cause to act resentfully, so the rigours of the legal system existed only on paper. But in Rome the situation was different. Here the rich kept dozens of slaves, many of them superfluous, as a sign of status. One millionaire kept one slave whose sole duty was to bring his clothes, another who escorted him to his litter, and a third to tuck him in. A pert Asian youth might be purchased simply to amuse visitors with a flow of shocking remarks. Huddle 40 slaves under one roof and, if they feel themselves to be figures of fun, ornament or occasional convenience, the result is a ferment of discontent to which the master reacts by meting out punishment. Punishments drive his chattels, as he terms them, to theft, aggression and even murder. In the event of murder, every slave under the master's roof would be presumed privy to the killer's intent and, having failed to prevent the crime, all would be led away to die on a T-cross.

Lucius's feelings were those of any humane person who has looked closely at an evil generally taken for granted, but with this difference:

he took trouble to fight it by publishing essays on the subject and in conversation with friends. Slavery, Lucius contended, was not a natural condition but a consequence of warfare, itself an unnatural condition.

If a slave comes straight from a backward tribe, his conscience may be poorly developed but is still operative. Instances of noble conduct are well attested: a slave risking his life to save his master from drowning, undergoing torture rather than falsely impugning an innocent. Slaves can behave as virtuously as free men and should be treated as persons. Drawing on the Stoic belief that all free men share the cosmos and therefore the status of 'cosmopolitan', Lucius extended the concept to cover slaves also. They were citizens of the cosmos and, with their first breath, imbibed the divine Spirit that would later guide them to make moral decisions. To all who are good, the divine Spirit acts like a father. It followed that, whoever maltreats a good slave with cruelty is affronting Spirit no less than if he ransacked the shrine of a Roman god.

After his success with the Corduba mint, Lucius felt sufficiently sure of himself to move from words to deeds. He would introduce a measure in the Senate to check one at least of the abuses he had denounced in writing. Stoic tenets and pity would carry no weight so, once again, Lucius decided to appeal to self-interest. He felt sure the Cato Group would vote with him but, needing further support, he decided to turn to the influential senator, Calpurnius Piso.

Calpurnius had been blessed with an illustrious name, handsome features, a full head of silvery grey hair – an important asset in Rome, where baldness is chaffed – an easy manner and comfortable fortune, part of which went to subsidizing young writers. Known as 'Moderation Piso' from his habit of keeping to the middle ground, he was respected in the House, though some believed he nurtured higher ambitions. Asked once why he hadn't voted for an unpopular measure of which he was known to approve, he replied that he wanted to preserve his influence for the day his country needed him.

The two men met in the portico adjoining the Senate, Calpurnius arriving in a newly laundered, freshly pressed gown fragrant with juniper and cinnamon. His grey eyes hovered slightly above Lucius's head during the initial exchange of civilities. As they strolled in the shade of a plane tree, Lucius aired neutral topics before slowly broaching the damaging effects of keeping a large number of slaves in one household.

'I'll cite you a case from my own experience. With someone at hand to perform the simplest task, the master of the house grows lazy. His muscles grow weak through inactivity. Carried everywhere in a sedan, he suffers from constipation, poor circulation and irritability. A cup is broken, a letter read too slowly, a couch-cushion disarranged and he rages and rants for an hour. To keep his retinue docile, he thinks he must continually blow them up. Soon it becomes a habit. Visitors, friends, family – all incur his anger. Meanwhile blood and bile mount to his head, his face grows bloated and purple and eventually apoplexy strikes. Doctors induce sweating, apply leeches, drain off a pint of blood – without effect. No one thinks of draining off the slaves.'

Calpurnius nodded gravely. 'Longinus, wasn't it? People judged him severely. As a knight, he had a duty to serve the Republic and, as a very rich man, he should have made his money circulate.'

'Longinus is only one of many. An excess of slaves invariably results in a diminution of civic duty. And when the well-to-do fail in their obligations to the city, decent people become indignant. Rome, they think, is a mill grinding out wealth, but if wealth so transforms the wealthy, what is the point of the mill turning? Then you get the first cracks in civic cohesion.'

Calpurnius agreed that the situation was far from healthy.

A huge retinue of slaves, continued Lucius, acted on their owner like poison. The sale of poison was forbidden by law: why not a law preventing the sale of slaves to any householder beyond a certain number?

'That might be desirable in a perfect state.'

'And we want Rome to be perfect.' He sought and held Calpurnius's eye. 'I'm ready to bring a motion to that effect before the House if I can count on you seconding it.'

Calpurnius looked up at the treetops and paused before replying. 'There would be grave objections. Infringement of personal liberty; not for the State to tell us how to run our homes.'

'Granted. But we can answer those objections. At a first try we may not get sufficient votes. But at least we'll have aired our disquiet, thrown the issue into the arena of public debate.' He placed a hand lightly on Calpurnius's arm, so that the other turned and Lucius held his gaze. 'I can count on your support then.'

The other drew back, his body suddenly tense and Lucius saw, just for a second, an expression he had glimpsed years before. During an outdoor party, a wasp had buzzed around Calpurnius's handsome head, he had jerked away but the insect nevertheless landed on his neck. Lucius, standing close, had been struck by his look of panic. While his wife fetched calendula and dabbed it on his neck, he had uttered little gasps of pain, then, leaning on her arm, staggered inside to lie down. Later it became known that he hadn't been stung at all.

Lucius had attributed his behaviour to a fear of insects. But now, as Calpurnius regained his composure and, avoiding the question, began to describe Lucius's proposal as extremely interesting, one that merited serious consideration, for which he was ready to sound out his circle of friends to discover their opinion, Lucius realized that it wasn't only wasps that caused him to panic. Calpurnius feared for his precious reputation and would never lend his support.

For five years now, Lucius had found in Burrus not only a close friend but also an ally in steering Nero towards what both believed to be his best interests. They felt at ease in each other's company and confided their worries and setbacks. On the question of slavery, Burrus took a characteristically straightforward and uncompromising stand: We label the wolf our natural enemy; this entitles us to harass the wolf, causing him to turn on us. Similarly we label a slave as dangerous, and this we consider entitles us to be cruel to him. But cruelty turns the slave into an enemy. In both cases, the trouble lies in mistaken labelling.

Burrus valued self-sufficiency. He considered it an admission of weakness to be dependent on a slave and had never felt a wish to keep one. But the commander who in battle made every effort to spare his men's lives did not close his eyes to the suffering of slaves in certain Roman households.

One evening shortly after the meeting with Calpurnius, Burrus and Lucius were sharing a friendly jar in a tavern. When the conversation turned to slavery, Burrus confided that he'd recently had a most disturbing experience. At the corner of his street stood a big kennels, where the owner bred bulldogs and mastiffs. He had a ring-shaped pit in his garden where he trained them for attack. Lately he'd begun to hold regular contests, pitting slaves against his dogs and charging people to watch. Burrus had joined the spectators. 'Nasty business. Messy. Something should be done.'

Lucius went to see for himself. The slave's only protection was a leather jerkin and gloves reinforced with metal strips. The mastiff, weighing perhaps a hundred pounds and unfed for two days, tugged wildly at its chain. Once released, the beast leaped up at the slave's face. Side-stepping, the slave threw himself on the dog's back, trying to grip its throat. The animal slipped free and renewed its attack: fury versus desperation. For a while there was no advantage either way, but gradually the unfortunate man tired, his parrying slowed, the dog closed in, tearing skin from his calves, jumping up to claw at neck and cheeks. The more blood flowed and the more the slave howled, the louder the spectators' screams of pleasure. To avert a kill, since this would result in an inquiry, the bleeding man was dragged out of the pit at a signal from the owner.

Afterwards Lucius sought out the owner, a bull-necked individual sporting a yellow kerchief fastened by a pearl pin. What, he asked, was the point of such carnage?

'Slave gets above himself, we cut him down to size.'

'I take it you've never done military service. Otherwise you'd have known what that man's just gone through and been disinclined to stage it for cheap thrills.'

The dog-breeder glared angrily at Lucius and pointed the way out with a bloodstained finger. '*Now*. My dogs don't like pussycats.' Lucius left, careful not to hurry.

Lucius and Burrus discussed what might be done to curb such acts of cruelty. As commander of the guard in touch with the city police, Burrus knew it wasn't an isolated case. The victim was often an upright slave, whose integrity a dissolute owner felt as a reproach.

Lucius took the view that, since the Senate feared to call in question the traditional grading of society and were reluctant to touch slavery, their best hope would to be interest Nero. Only a slim hope, for the *princeps* had no household slaves and slavery never came up in Cabinet. Besides he was busier than usual overseeing the building of the road to Subiaco which had been vetoed by his mother. Lucius suggested that, while he sought a possible opening, Burrus should put together a file of authenticated cases.

Once a month, Nero left his house on foot for a curious assignation. Entering the poor Aventine district, he would climb five flights of stairs to a modest tenement flat belonging to a woman who remained striking in her middle years. She would kiss him when he entered and called him Dominus. Her name was Eclogue and she had been Nero's nurse from birth until he was seven. They would sit reminiscing, joking and sharing a plateful of scones such as she used to bake for him as a child.

Lucius arranged to have business with Nero on his return from a visit to Eclogue. He brought the conversation around to Nero's loyalty to his former nurse.

'She was very good to me, I couldn't begin to tell you.' His eyes assumed a faraway look. 'No amount of sulks or tantrums could make her cross or withhold my bedtime story. When I had measles, she sat by my bed three nights without sleep. Now, poor thing, her sight's almost gone but she doesn't complain, says she has plenty of good memories to last her out.'

Lucius nodded with feigned casualness. 'I suppose she came from a good family in distressed circumstances.'

'Not a bit. She was born a slave. In fact she was emancipated only after she stopped being my nurse.'

Lucius expressed astonishment: even certain physicians agreed that a slave couldn't feel the finer emotions and had a higher threshold for pain than the rest of us.

Nero shook his head emphatically. 'I'd go on oath that Eclogue is as sensitive as you or me. Probably more so, being a woman.'

Having made his point, Lucius mentioned that Burrus wanted a private interview on a matter of great personal concern to him. Nero frowned and objected pressure of work, but Lucius persisted, reminding him that Burrus rarely made calls on his time.

For some months, Burrus had been suffering from chronic sore throat. It had reached the point where he sometimes found difficulty in enunciating. When a soldier who has survived wounds in a score of battles is thus incapacitated, his predicament arouses more than usual sympathy. As it happened, the painful throat was about to prove helpful. When he carried his bulky file to Nero and began in a croaky voice to cite instances of brutality, Nero listened with more than usual attention, sympathy for the veteran's condition spreading to concern at what he heard. Burrus emphasized the suffering of his womenfolk when a slave was carried home on a stretcher beaten to pulp. He ended by alluding pointedly to Nero's promise in the Senate that his principate would see no bloodshed.

Nero was sufficiently affected as to want to take action. Lucius might have suggestions, Burrus suggested. The sequel went according to plan. Lucius proposed that, since the Senate would not act, Nero should invoke his jurisdiction within the walls of Rome to issue a decree allowing any slave inside the city boundaries to bring a complaint of cruelty to the City Prefect. He could then use his powers to investigate the affair as a *prima facie* breach of the peace. If the complaint was substantiated, he would publish the name of the owner who would face shame and public disapproval as a result.

This was the first measure ever taken to curb cruelty to slaves. Lucius had also hoped to abolish the tax for freeing a slave but that proved impracticable. This milestone decree and his own writings prompted a larger debate about whether slaves possessed natural rights and, if so, whether these should be enshrined in Roman law. It marked, I believe, a decisive shift in opinion.

For Lucius, it had been a long run over a tricky obstacle course. Now he'd breasted the tape, his body could revel in deep lungfulls of air, his mind aglow like poplars at sunset. Forgetting hesitations and false moves, he told himself it wasn't a time for false modesty. He'd done something important and proved to himself at least that he hadn't lived in vain. Slaves had souls like the rest of men, there were two decrees to bear that out.

Paula acknowledged his achievement but, so intense and persistent was Lucius's euphoria, that he needed to feel appreciation all around him. Decrees did not address the whole problem and might even be repealed, but he expected those whose opinion counted to recognize that the whole city had gained for now giving slaves some dignity. Naturally the plutocrats did not take kindly to his so-called 'affront to their freedom'. They accused Lucius of intolerance, a wrong which ranked high in Rome's list of transgressions. Lucius considered the slur grossly unfair since he had always sought to practise and defend tolerance! Tolerance requires strong beliefs. To tolerate something, you must also disapprove of it: otherwise what looks like tolerance is mere indifference. By accusing him of 'haemophobia' and of baiting the rich because they happened to be rich, his critics were trying to make disapproval into a crime. While pretending to attack intolerance, they were actually displaying it.

Lucius could get along with few comforts: what he found difficult to bear was the imputation of unworthy motive. Especially when this came from Rome's patricians since, for all his efforts to master his weakness, Lucius retained a provincial longing for acceptance.

After the decree on cruelty to slaves, Lucius started behaving with more than customary impatience. He even became more abrupt with his own servants. When he wanted an errand done, he had been accustomed to frame a request: now often his tone was peremptory and snappy.

Lucius refused to call himself a philosopher, preferring the title 'sophomore', wise up top, foolish below. But he undoubtedly was a philosopher in the fullest sense. Such men, in my experience, are at their best in extreme adversity, but often fail to treat with equanimity the irritations, disappointments and snubs of everyday life.

It is customary for transcripts of Senate proceedings to be delivered in the evening by messenger. A servant would sign and place them on a salver in the hall, from where Lucius gathered them after supper. One evening, Lucius shouted for Paula and complained that the first page of his transcript was missing. She made a search and found the paper under a chest of drawers. Not liking his manner, she handed it to him with studied casualness, saying that a breeze from an open window had perhaps blown it from the salver.

'See it doesn't happen again. Every paper delivered to my house must be treated as an important State document and in future brought to me immediately.'

'Yes, lord and master,' said Paula with a deep bow, hoping that would bring a smile – but no.

Soon afterwards, Lucius was stretched out on his study couch at the end of a stressful day. Paula knocked, entered, knelt on one knee and proffered the salver with a flourish. It held a leaf of paper.

'Arrived this minute, excellency.'

Lucius stretched out a weary hand, took the paper and glanced at it, then sat up sharply. 'This is our butcher's bill!'

'Has to be considered a State document,' said Paula innocently.

Lucius tossed the paper across the room. 'Not funny.'

'But it is.' She skipped around his couch, laughing impishly. 'Very, very funny.'

Usually she could ease Lucius out of his pomposity, but that night Paula failed. Curtly, he ordered her out of his study. Why this unease, she wondered, just when he had achieved so much.

Since the first year of marriage, entertaining had meant much to both of them. Lucius liked seeing friends eating heartily and enjoying themselves. As Lucius had been exceptionally busy drafting the new measure to protect slaves, more than a month had passed since they had had guests. Paula dropped hints which were ignored by Lucius until he suggested the idea of a big festive dinner as though it were his. They made up a list of guests. To Paula's surprise, Lucius passed over old friends for recent acquaintances, mostly former consuls or members of Rome's exclusive patrician families. Paula, for whom these were but names, objected that she would find it difficult knowing so few of her own guests, but Lucius insisted it was time they broke new ground.

Fashion called for surprise dishes: the cap of what seemed a large mushroom would turn out to be minced meat; terrine of sweetbreads proved to be meringue filled with chestnut purée. Reluctantly Paula agreed to concoct a novel menu, but she demurred at Lucius's suggestion that they hire a footman to take mantles and announce guests, saying it wasn't their style.

'Paula, we have to move on.'

She looked him full in the eye, concerned, 'On – or up?'

'Both... I'll see to the footman.'

Paula received Lucius's new acquaintances with characteristic graciousness. She noticed their close observance of etiquette and how they enjoyed airing family history. There were no mishaps but she described the evening to Lucius as 'sticky', adding that she had overheard one guest whisper, 'Lucius is too much the innovator... he'll never be one of us.'

To win acceptance from an exclusive group calls for regular attendance at the functions they consider important. Hitherto Lucius had avoided these as time-consuming but now he took to frequenting the spring dance and chanting of archaic verse in honour of *Pia Mater* by the septuagenarian Arval Brethren. Here he met people whose opinion mattered and formed the impression that he was on the way to recognition.

His absences distressed Paula, who had expected to see more of her husband now that his long sessions with Burrus lasting often until after midnight were over. One evening she confided in him. 'When you're not with me, I get bored and listless. To cheer myself up, I want to go to the kitchen and nibble. But then my figure will suffer. So I force myself not to go to the kitchen, and then feel very hungry and cross.'

It was rare for Paula to complain, so this confession and the pathetic look accompanying it touched Lucius. 'Am I making you unhappy?' Lucius promised to go out less frequently: he kept his promise for he had decided on another path to his goal.

The visible sign of having arrived socially is the acquisition of a collection. This may consist of effigies of ancestors' masks, busts or statues; or perhaps antiquities or else objects of exceptionally fine workmanship and the like. Unlike Novatus and me, Lucius had been born with little interest in possessions. Later he grew to see them as time-consuming, hostages to fortune and a barrier between persons. Yet now he began to acquire tables, small ornate marble-topped pieces for two or three guests that would stand level with their dining couch.

Once you've bought a table, you have to look after it, wax the wood, polish the marble, make the metal shine as regularly as you would curry a horse. And, as your collection grows, you need somewhere to show it: Lucius proposed to Paula that they build on an annexe.

Paula had put much hard work and imagination into her house and garden. She considered them an expression of herself, a minor but distinctive accompaniment to Lucius's achievements. An annexe would block the afternoon sun from her rose bed. She felt that, seeing a collection of tables virtually on her doorstep, visitors would associate her home with a depository. Lucius thought these objections overemotional but, after a long discussion for and against the annexe, their views remained far apart. Since Paula felt so attached to her home and Lucius clung to his new acquisitions, the row escalated to the extent that Acilia and I became concerned. Why had Lucius become so difficult? We wondered whether he was suffering the frustrations of senility, but Acilia's discreet enquiries disclosed that Priapus still smiled on the Annaeus bed.

Lucius enjoyed the esteem of people he valued so why did he want more? Had success gone to his head? That I doubted. Often he'd confided how far short he thought he fell of the standard set by his teacher Attalus and his hero Marcus Cato, and every winter he read a life of Zeno, Socrates or some other admired figure because this checked any urge to self-satisfaction.

In an effort to help, I put it to him that his proposed collection was a means to an end: what he really wanted to collect was acceptance in the spirit of fellowship by ex-consuls and other personages. But that could never be. Always he would remain a 'new man', Spanish-born, an outsider.

Lucius threw back his head pugnaciously. Just wait and see: he would end by winning them round.

'And what would that get you?'

He didn't want to *get* anything, he retorted. He wasn't doing it for himself: he was fighting for a principle, so that future 'new men' from the provinces would be accepted as equals.

We argued the point at length but I got nowhere and had to drop it. He could have been sincere. On the other hand, most of us harbour some wild ambition, too wild to be avowed. From a chance remark to me at a wine-shop table, I can't help feeling that Lucius nursed a wish to be made full consul so giving his name to the year he held office and seeing every amphora wine produced that autumn inscribed 'vintage of the year Annaeus.'

The rift between Lucius and Paula widened and looked as though it might end badly. Then three little words went round the city, marginalizing everything else: *Poppaea gravida est.*

Eight men, including secretaries, were present in Cabinet when Nero strode in, whooping and waving a silver rattle. 'How about this! Father to be!' Lucius found his elation endearing and was first to offer congratulations.

'So much for malicious rumours, eh Lucius? Proved myself one with the best of my stallions!'

The child needed legitimization. Opposition would have come from Burrus, but his doctor had discovered that the unfortunate man had a tumour in his throat; he was too ill to be present and argue that Poppaea was frivolous to a degree unsuitable in Caesar's wife. Most of those who gave an opinion said a new marriage would be good for the succession provided the child proved a boy. Lucius also spoke in favour, remembering that, after he married for love, Augustus had become markedly less aristocratic.

After the meeting, Nero hurried to Octavia's apartment, anxious to get the break over quickly. He found her at her dressing table, pinning up her difficult hair. Standing behind her, hands resting on her shoulder and looking at her in the mirror: he began gently. What he had to say would hurt her but it needed saying. Circumstances demanded an immediate divorce; her dowry would be returned in full; she could no longer continue to live in Rome, but he would make over to her a large estate in Tuscany.

On learning that Poppaea was with child, Octavia showed neither surprise nor anxiety. She stood and turned to face her husband, eyes set hard, her pretty little chin thrust forward.

'It was I who brought you the succession.'

Nero had his answer ready. 'And now because of the succession you're asked to step aside.' This brought no response save a look of contempt. 'Your father sacrificed a scholar's career to accept the principate. That showed devotion to Rome. He would wish you to show a like devotion.'

'Haven't I already?' her tone was bitter. 'I've helped you more than you've ever admitted. I deserve better than to be cast aside, and my lawyers will oppose any attempt to do so.'

Nero was rattled into attack. 'Your mother caused a political crisis, do you wish to cause another?'

Looking him fiercely in the eye, Octavia revolved her wedding ring slowly on her finger. 'One does not divorce Caesar's daughter.' She spoke as though stating a self-evident truth. Hating quarrels, he chose to leave the room for his study whence he summoned the City Prefect and ordered him to remove statues of Octavia from eight prominent points in the city, to be replaced with wooden statues of Poppaea which he had already commissioned for their marriage day.

Next morning, Poppaea left home for the seamstress. Ears sensitive to lyre and flute, she disliked the hubbub of the street. 'Hurry!' she ordered her bearers. As she passed down the Esquiline's main street, shoppers stopped to stare in disapproval of the lady whose effigies had replaced Octavia's. 'Go back to your husband!' they snarled. 'Take your paws off our *princeps!*' 'Neapolitan slut!' Drawn by the shouting, more shoppers pressed forward and her progress was slowed. Poppaea called out sharply to let her pass. The crowd pushed closer. She turned to threats: 'I'll call the Watch,' she shrieked.

The crowd turned nasty. Two hefty market women pushed the bearers away and, seizing the litter, tipped it over, causing Poppaea to tumble onto the flagstones. There followed a moment of silent shock before the enormity of what had been done. Then a litter-bearer blew urgently on his alarm whistle and, as four men of the Watch came running, the crowd hurriedly dispersed. The new arrivals helped a pale and trembling Poppaea back into her litter and she was hurried home.

On the Calends of June when shops closed for the day, men and women began to gather in the Aventine marketplace. Raucous rollicking crowds are part of our Roman scene: supporters of the Reds, Greens or Blues, of a champion gladiator, a popular singer or a triumphant general. This crowd, numbering perhaps two hundred, was curiously muted as it surged eastwards. I watched from my office balcony, reminded of a stream of dark grey magma flowing down the slopes of Aetna. The crowd came to a halt outside Caesar's House, where one of their number handed in a petition. When Nero emerged looking uneasy, banners were raised variously inscribed: NERO AND OCTAVIA – ROME'S HAPPINESS; WE LOVE OUR LADY OCTAVIA; SABINA TO NAPLES and the like.

The crowd's spokesman, a master silversmith, bellowed out their protest. Rome at present was thriving. Why? Because of Claudius-with-the-gods. His bright star watched over the city on behalf of his beloved daughter. Sending Octavia away to marry a divorced mother from an alien city would precipitate anger among the gods who protected Rome. His people respectfully urged him to drop all thoughts of change.

Unprepared for such a show of protest, Nero ran his eye nervously over the expectant faces while preparing his reply. At last, jerkily, he began. Like any married man, he wanted a son to carry on his name and, as *princeps* he wanted to give the people a prospective heir. Since Fate had decreed that his wife could not bear children, he intended to marry a lady who could.

Nero's tone was conciliatory but his words did not please. Shouts of 'Shame!' punctuated angry complaints. Poppaea spent on a single dress what would feed a family for months; the people's hard-won tax payments would be squandered on singers and actors from Naples. Her musical offerings were black magic designed to make Nero her slave. Nero held up a hand for quiet. 'Poppaea will give us the son we want and need. Your next *princeps*.'

'No,' retorted the silversmith leader. 'She's Otho's wife. Used goods.' And the crowd backed him up. 'We don't want her!' 'Drown her in asses' milk!' As the shouting grew louder, banners were lifted and lowered in unison. 'Poppaea out! Poppaea out! Octavia our mother!' With a rhythm of their own like that of incoming waves, the demonstrators moved slowly up the flight of steps hurling insults with eyes flashing and fists clenched.

Nothing had prepared Nero to face a threatening crowd. Raising both arms imploringly, he called for calm. The crowd had a tongue but no ears. On they surged, up the flight of steps. Nero drew back and flung an anxious look at the doorway as though hoping for rescue.

Then the silversmith took charge. Turning to face the human tide, he held up his arms and the flow of bodies slackened, then stopped. 'Quiet!' He repeated the order until it was obeyed.

In a flat tone, from dry lips, Nero spoke. 'You've made your point. I will reconsider.'

A few cheers were drowned out by doubting voices. 'How do we know?'

With firmer voice, Nero repeated, 'I will reconsider.' Then he turned and re-entered his house, whereupon the crowd drifted slowly towards the Aventine.

What Nero meant by 'reconsider' is anyone's guess. Finding himself for the first time dangerously at odds with the people of Rome, he probably wanted advice. But the crowd interpreted his words differently, as he discovered at dawn from the Captain of the Watch and City Prefect. During the night, all statues of Poppaea had been overturned. It was a deadly serious act of defiance.

'With respect, sir,' said the City Prefect, 'The crowd last night did not speak for the people. The Messalla clan is strong on the Aventine. The silver trade is theirs and they own many tenements, shops, manufactories. Our men were watching closely. We happen to know that last night's demonstrators were mainly their tenants or dependants, coached and paid.'

'So we're dealing only with a clique?'

'No, with a faction. They are highly dangerous because their leaders are determined to cling to the influence which your wife affords them.'

Plans were discussed and adopted, orders given: the Watch to be armed with oak clubs, the Praetorians to be placed on standby, overturned statues to be set up and secured with iron clamps, and a date announced for Nero's marriage to Poppaea. The day passed calmly but at dusk masked men took to the streets. One gang set Poppaea's favourite dress shop on fire, another broke into the music academy and smashed every instrument they could find, another marched through the streets chanting slogans in praise of Octavia.

These were blinds for a more important foray. Manitius Messalla's son Junius, a naval officer with a creditable record against Carthaginian pirates, and his nephew Caius, who had won a silver shoulder piece in Armenia, joined in a carefully planned raid on Poppaea's house. Using a ladder from a nearby construction site, they climbed over the wall into Poppaea's garden, threw poisoned meat to her watchdog, prised open an outside door, and silently moved to Poppaea's room. Stifling her screams by bundling a flour sack over her head, they lifted her out to a waiting covered carriage.

They drove fast to the Appian Gate. Halted by the guard, Regulus explained that their passenger was an old woman suffering from smallpox: they were taking her out of the city lest she infect others. This guard happened to be a conscientious young fellow with an eye on promotion. He unstrapped the canvas flaps at the back of the carriage pulled off the sack covering the passenger's head and found himself looking at the one lady's face familiar to every Roman.

Next morning, Rome was unnaturally quiet: streets empty, shops shut for fear of looting, business stagnant. Though the Messallas were behind bars and Poppaea back in her home protected by a platoon of Praetorians, nothing had been resolved. No one, I believe, was more shaken than Lucius, for he saw the violence as a threat not only to the person of Nero but to the rule of law. Measured against the collapse of civic cohesion, his striving for social recognition now seemed trivial.

Lucius pondered the causes. He had warned Nero against arbitrary, angry or self-centred rule but never against vacillation, half-granting a concession only to weakly withdraw it. For this omission, he considered he had only himself to blame. Next, the Messallas. If he could discover what had motivated them to act lawlessly, he might be able to offer a prognosis, and at the same time improve his understanding of what held a city together. He asked and obtained permission from the City Prefect to enter the grim Mamertine and question the prisoners. His notes on that interview I have before me.

Recent history as viewed by the prisoners: Claudius an inadequate husband, neglected Messalina, then drew perverse pleasure from letting her cuckold him. Her so-called marriage to Sirius no more than a party spoof, played up by enemies. Claudius panicked: the axe fell on an innocent neck.

All Messallas thereafter bear a wholly unwarranted stain of dishonour. Rebuild family reputation, vindicate Messalina in the person of Octavia whom Nero, following Claudius, treats disgracefully.

For them, 'city' is no more than a mental construct, the reality is closely-connected families. I said that city wasn't something found in nature, but that didn't make it a mental construct.

Their reply: '"City" is vague, slippery. Who belongs? A North African vagrant who drops over the wall on a moonless night? Family you can name with certainty and cite their traditions.'

But where does family end? With a cousin once removed, a son-in-law's half-sister? We all know what family and city are, though the edges of definition are ragged. The city is wider, less exclusive than family, unites more people, therefore our obligation is more binding than to kin. Total disagreement. Their presuppositions incompatible with mine, and mine can claim no absolute authority. Habits no less than upbringing act as filters to values. Only someone who keeps himself tidy will recognize tidiness when he sees it.

Shift to related *palaestra*. 'Caius, you were in the army, Junius, you served in the navy. You didn't say, "I'm a Messalla, it would demean me to serve under an officer not a knight." On active service, the legion or your ship becomes more important than personal distinction. Living side by side engenders fellowship and loyalty. Having served as long as you did, presumably you value that arrangement?' They admitted as much. 'Then surely you should value wider loyalties in civilian life. Without perhaps being aware of it, your presuppositions and mine aren't all that different.'

Returning from the prison, Lucius recognized that his analysis of civic cohesion fell far short of completeness. The Messallas were not an isolated phenomenon: other patrician clans nurtured proud traditions and ambitions. These energized the city and shouldn't be stifled. But since each clan vied to be top, they had to be treated as a group and their respective contributions suitably honoured. Lucius penned an interim definition: civic cohesion requires general respect for the law, a *princeps* acting consistently and in co-operation with the Senate, and public recognition of the role played by the great families.

Extra benches were carried into the Forum's biggest courtroom: even so, tickets for the trial changed hands at sixty denarii and brought their money's worth of sensation. The Messalla duo had intended to hurry Poppaea to Ravenna and thence to an island off the Dalmatian coast where the family owned property. An armed crowd of five hundred was to march on Caesar's House demanding Octavia's reinstatement. Given his earlier vacillation, Nero could be expected to comply and Octavia would then persuade him to adopt as his son her Messalla cousin, Valerius, a promising seven year-old.

Lucius could not attend, being present at a sadder kind of trial. Burrus lay on his camp bed, unable to swallow the prescribed purple sage cordial. Lucius sat by him two nights in a row, watching the callused hands that had wielded a sword on seven frontiers lovingly stroke his grey fur coverlet, lips shaping the wolf's name he could no longer articulate. Lucius felt all the more grief on his friend's behalf as he was powerless to lend the least help and knew he was losing an irreplaceable ally.

On the day following Burrus's burial, Lucius went to hear the judge's summing up, from which emerged alarming implications. Half a dozen witnesses had attested to a master plan that did not limit itself to Rome and involved high-level accomplices in several provinces, motivated by ethnic pride or resentment. Despite an astute defence, the court found the accused guilty of abduction and incitement to rioting. Sentences of death were passed, subject to confirmation by the *princeps*.

Though the court's verdict conformed with the law, Lucius stood by his conviction that every execution reverberates down the years, that blood is the one stain that will not wash out. Nero had promised not to sign a death sentence and keeping that promise had changed Rome from a rat-run of spy-holes and informers to a free thinking environment. Nero's promise had set an important boundary for the characteristically impulsive *princeps*.

Fury is too bland a word to describe Nero's reaction to the Messallas' plan. Like a ship caught in cross winds which yaws, veers and puts about, he swung round the audience room, his face like a ghastly Saturnalia mask. At one point, he recited an elegy Poppaea used to sing him: 'You are good to me, oh so good, but each treasure you bring me hurts more than it pleases, for you withhold what I most want.' To think that, on the eve of her satisfaction, this living Terpsichore had been dragged from her home, terrorized and humiliated caused him agony. Octavia too came in for a lashing: self-righteous, sly little fox cub, nudging on her cousins. The hired mob rankled him especially as it had caused him to behave in a manner unbecoming of Caesar.

Rome remained in danger, so much was plain to Lucius. If I intervene, he thought I may do more harm than good. If I don't, Nero may act in such a way as to precipitate even more serious rioting. He sent Lado to request an interview with Nero. Although he received no reply, Lucius decided all the same to go. He found Nero with a damp cloth knotted round his brow to ease a headache, still ranting to a handful of uneasy officials, his eyes fever-bright, angrier than Lucius had ever known.

Nero hailed him sarcastically. 'Enter one philosopher! Come to douse my anger? Spare yourself the trouble. Nothing will keep me from sinking my teeth into those postulant necks. Pity they're citizens or I'd hoist them on the ignominious tree...'. There was a malicious, almost feral glint in his eyes. More snatches of acerbity followed. Only when he'd picked over the Messallas' actions one by one and he paused for breath, did Lucius have a chance to speak.

He reminded Nero of his promise not to sign a death sentence. 'For your own safety, if nothing else. By putting two individuals to death, you'll have a hundred of their kin out for your blood.'

Nero replied reasonably enough. Pardon was out of the question. It would mean overriding the court's verdict and, as a lawyer, Lucius wouldn't stand for that.

Lucius corrected him. He was suggesting clemency, not pardon. Clemency implies recognition that the sentence is just, and the determination not to apply it for good reason. The distinction was lost on Nero. 'Those who attempt a coup have always been put to death. Always.'

'Only because Rome has mostly been at war. With enemies at our gates, it was either kill or be killed. But thanks to you, we've entered an age of peace and have a better model – the gods... Does Jupiter strike down criminals with a lightning bolt or let them live out their lives side by side the good?'

Nero sniffed contemptuously. 'Where were the gods when those devils abducted my future wife? And your famous Divine Breath? On holiday?'

'We've been over this before. The gods respect our freedom to act badly.'

Was it the calm tone that set Nero off? 'Lucius, I'm angry enough as it is. Say another word and I'll start getting violent. You've been warned.'

So Lucius left with the taste of bile in his mouth.

Later, Lucius called at my house, looking unusually pale. He intermittently struggled for breath as his frustrating interview had brought on an attack of asthma. He flopped down on a chair, silent and mournful. Presently he told me what had happened. 'If Nero's as angry as you say, he may well kick you out of Cabinet,' I warned him.

Lucius shrugged in a rare gesture of helplessness, then delivered himself of one of his generalizations. Faction, even when foiled, could ram a hole in consistently sound government, therefore faction must be accounted the first enemy of cohesion.

We faced up to his dilemma. Nero was more influenced by real-life situations than by abstract advice, however wise. Lucius had lived through a situation that might possibly induce Nero to show clemency. But it would mean digging up an episode of which he was deeply ashamed. I was of course curious and invited him to confide. He did so, and I write my account now as he told it.

In her fifth year of marriage, Paula conceived and, as her body swelled, Lucius swelled too with pride and became almost a caricature of the uxorious father-to-be. With the delivery date drawing near, the midwife arrived. Lucius described her as the quintessential poet since she apparently looked on her thousandth delivery with as much wonder as her first. She soon shooed him out of the bedroom, treating him as an extra who, his business done, must withdraw to the wings.

During a difficult labour, Lucius pictured every possible complication and, when the midwife told him he had a son, he was so close to tears that all he could do was gulp. Paula unwrapped her pink bundle like a Saturnalia present. 'Just look at those long fingers.' Lucius decided he would go at once to register the birth, causing the midwife to stare. Paula explained, 'My husband needs to get things down in black and white.'

Lucius shared his excitement with the registrar and said the boy was to be called Marcus Annaeus Seneca after his great-grandfather. 'Remember that name. One day he may be consul.' On the way home, he bought the customary branch of myrtle to hang outside their door.

For Paula's mother and her lady friends, Lucius now became 'Marcus's father': they cited dubious resemblances and kept pressing the baby into his arms. Lucius was impressed by how easily Paula had made the transition to mother. As she bent over her suckling child, he saw her in profile, the love once reserved for him now radiating to their son, as was right. From what she had falteringly tried to explain, he understood that this love was limed by the intense elation felt in the lee of labour pain at participating in creation.

From a soggy bundle, Marcus grew into a crawler inquisitive as a puppy; by age three, he was a cheery little fellow with curly brown hair and winning brown eyes, who tried to befriend whoever came his way. I'm no lover of small children, but Marcus's bright trustful manner captivated me and I understood why Lucius doted on him.

Lucius made him a wooden mouse on wheels with black bead eyes and a wire tail which he would pull round the courtyard, calling on neighbouring cats to chase it. In summer, tired of trying to catch grasshoppers, he would rest at midday under a pine, where Lucius showed him how to focus a burning glass on a heap of needles.

At a children's party, Paula became uncomfortably aware that Marcus, then aged four, was markedly less tall and plump than boys of his age. She took him to Lucius's doctor, 'Query' Telethus, so known because of his caution. Telethus painstakingly palpated, weighed, measured, scrutinized his urine and concluded, 'Inadequate *tonus*, query.' He prescribed goat's milk and a course of exercise.

Three months later, Marcus again stood on the scales and was found to have lost two pounds. Telethus advised treatment at Mons Celani, for which Lucius obtained leave of absence.

The spa's hostel housed the doddering and incapacitated; its sulphur baths smelled of rotten eggs. When an attendant started to smear Marcus's body with mud, the boy shrank away. Lucius reassured him that it was a new game to see who could get dirtiest. When his parents tucked him into bed, Marcus noticed their anxious faces. 'Don't be sad,' he pleaded and Lucius told a second lie. 'We're not sad, Marcus.' Back in Rome, Telethus called in two specialists who declared that Marcus's muscles were slowly wasting: a condition both incurable and irreversible.

The weeks of grief that followed were agonizing. Like Zeno before him, Attalus addressed the question: Why does a beneficent God permit suffering and early death? After years of finding no answer, he had pulled down the shutters on that and related questions. But Lucius needed to find a reason for everything: day after day, he sat brooding in his study trying to make sense of his little son's brave clip-clop walk – iron braces had now been fitted to his flimsy legs – then he too pulled down the shutters.

Paula could no more accept the doctors' prognosis than she could stop swimming if she felt herself drowning. She turned to friends, acquaintances, even strangers, desperately seeking news of a possible cure and finally, from a market vendor, she learned that a friend of a friend had a master whose daughter showed Marcus's symptoms and who'd been helped by seaweed treatment in Gaeta.

She told Lucius that they should take Marcus to Gaeta, 80 miles down the coast. Lucius objected that indulging false hopes on such flimsy grounds was unreasonable. Moreover, the Senate would not grant him a second leave of absence but, to his astonishment, Paula said she would take Marcus to Gaeta alone. Unable to persuade Paula to change her mind, Lucius hired a two-horse carriage and driver.

From Paula's first letter, Lucius learned that the seaweed cure had improved Marcus's appetite but her next letter said the treatment was tiring him. As Lucius prepared for their return a third letter arrived: a lady at Gaeta spoke highly of the stimulating effects of mountain air and Paula had decided to take Marcus to the Dolomites.

Lucius's apartment had become untidy and dusty, while anxiety and hurried meals had brought on dyspepsia. From admiration of Paula's persistence he had passed to resenting her for her absence. After six weeks on his own, Lucius went one evening for relaxation to Cleopatra's Cellar, a tavern he found amusing because of its sham decor of lotuses and papyri, made-up hieroglyphs and friezes of females in profile with snakes in their hair. One of the servers caught Lucius's eye: in her early twenties, she had widely spaced eyes with little creases in the lids he found most attractive. During the lulls, she watched customers with a faint air of amusement. Lucius's cribbage partner said she was new, name of Melissa.

Lucius thought the girl bore a strong resemblance to Gaius Caesar's youngest sister Julia. His partner dismissed the idea emphatically: Julia was stewing in exile on some godforsaken island. At closing time, clinging to his hunch, Lucius waited outside the staff entrance. When Melissa appeared, he went up to her, said who he was and added that he felt sure he'd met her three years before at a party in Caesar's House. The girl drew back frowning, saying he must be mistaken but, when he reminded her of what they'd talked about, she admitted to being Julia on condition of secrecy.

What, he asked, was Caesar's sister doing waiting on tables? 'It's a living,' she replied easily. Lucius didn't like to ask how she had come to such a pass. 'I enjoy it. Like being in a play.' With that, she said she had to hurry and left him. He was stupefied by his discovery. Julia was the youngest of Germanicus's nine children. With her mother then living in exile, she received no schooling but picked up country lore from servants. Married off early as an item in a political deal and soon discarded by her worthless husband, she was taken in by her brother Gaius, newly *princeps*. First he had made a fuss of her but his increasing paranoia had prompted him to exile her to distant Kerkenna.

Lucius went again to the tavern, choosing a table served by Julia. He felt a pleasurable complicity as their eyes met during the evening. Next day, the feast of Minerva, being a holiday, he suggested a meeting to which she agreed.

At her wish, they went to the Campus Martius to watch jugglers and acrobats, monkeys and a dancing bear. Julia staked small change on games of chance, winning more often than losing. They shared a dish of lentils and she asked to read his palm, explaining that she always did so with a new acquaintance. She traced a line at the base of his little finger which she termed his line of honesty, and said it ran straight and deep. She then considered their birth signs and, on finding they matched, linked her arm through his. 'If you like, we can be friends.'

He asked about Kerkenna, knowing it to be a treeless waste, swept by desiccating winds. To his surprise, she didn't complain, recalling only how she used to watch small crabs playing on the sand until a wave sent them scurrying to their holes like shoppers in the Forum at a sudden downpour. It was she who broached her reduced circumstances. Claudius's wife Messalina had 'seconded' her property – she meant 'sequestered' – but a friend was working to recover it. She then drew from her purse a crumpled paper which she handed to Lucius to read:

Demons of the night, I summon you to join in aiding this spell. Bind, enchant, thwart, strike and conspire against Messalina. May she fail to please her husband and lovers, may her face be blemished with acne, may she take to her bed, refuse food and languish until she restores to Julia Livilla all her property, including her jade zebu amulet. Now, now! Quickly, quickly!

Julia explained that the spell had been cast by her neighbour, a woman well versed in magic who once put a spell on Eutychus the charioteer and he never won another race. The throats of three black cockerels had been slit on three nights of the moon's last phase and their blood scattered over Messalina's name written on the ground with pebbles. Lucius realized that this resort to magic was a logical step for a girl with no schooling who refused to be crushed.

The combination of a serious-minded senator of forty-three and a happy-go-lucky young woman almost half his age would appear unlikely, yet Lucius began to find himself very attracted to Julia, not only for her looks but also for her calm in adversity such as he, for all his efforts at self-discipline, hadn't achieved. He recognized that he was falling under a spell – and enjoying it. He suggested Julia pursue her cause in the law courts and, when she looked nonplussed, he offered to take up her case. Lucius began to divide his time between the State archives and Julia's rented room where he questioned her about Messalina and about Claudius, who had refused to intervene on his niece's behalf.

He enjoyed these sessions, sensed that she liked his company and felt he could easily slip into a liaison. Then he pictured Paula having a wretched time on a doomed mission. He wrote to her, telling her she had done everything possible to restore Marcus to health, but enough was enough. Pressure of work had built up and he needed her beside him: he would expect her home at the end of the month. But Paula replied that she had learned of another spa, on the Adriatic, and she was going to take Marcus there. Why, after his summons, did she continue with pointless treatment unless she now put Lucius second in her life? Lucius reacted as I'm sure I would have done, giving all his spare time to Julia's petition; he also stopped his nightly examination of conscience. The paper work completed, he jumped a queue to bring the case to court. Narcissus, who was not yet Secretary, acted for Messalina and sought to show that Gaius was already of unsound mind when he gifted property to her but Lucius produced doctors' reports to the contrary.

The court ordered Messalina to return Julia's possessions, notably her house in Rome and villa in Baiae. When Lucius brought her the news, Julia whooped for joy. 'And my amulet?' 'That too.' She threw her arms round his neck and hugged him. They drew apart, their eyes met, jubilant but hesitant. When Julia calmed down, Lucius broached a serious matter. Claudius had recently extended the law *de majestate*. Should any person unauthorised by the *princeps* enter into close relations with a member of his family, both laid themselves open to prosecution. 'Now your case is settled,' Lucius explained, 'it would be dangerous for you to go on seeing me. You would risk another island holiday.'

But she wanted to go on seeing him, she protested. He was her friend, he'd helped her, and she wasn't the sort to drop a friend. Lucius was touched but insisted. 'You'd be spied on,' he warned. 'Just like a play,' she replied merrily.

A plan took shape in Lucius's mind. While disapproving Claudius's arbitrary extension of the law *de majestate*, the Senate had feared to provoke a new, unpredictable *princeps* by contesting its legality in the aftermath of Gaius's assassination. But now, were Claudius to decide to charge him for associating with Julia, his case would be judged by the Senate sitting as a court. That would be a heaven-sent opportunity for Lucius to make a major speech denouncing the law, tracing its roots in the dynastic pretensions of Persia and Egypt, demonstrating how it infringed basic liberties and could in no way serve as a basis of prosecution. He saw himself inviting the House at its next legislative session to vote that the law be repealed.

Lucius found that his attraction to Julia was increased by this new sense of danger, and the two grew closer. The time came when she had to catch the ferry to Baiae to take legal repossession of her villa there. Lucius accompanied her to Ostia, only to find that a storm had delayed the ferry's departure until next morning. They found an inn where they spent the night together in a bedroom with spy-holes in its ceiling.

Lucius's trial did indeed take place before his fellow-senators but in a nightmare inversion of his plan. Cajoled by Messalina who hoped to divert attention from her own indiscretions, Claudius came to the House to preside in person, and there ruled that it would endanger the State if Lucius were to use his privilege as a senator to conduct his own defence. A lawyer would conduct his defence; Lucius could answer questions of fact put by the prosecutor, nothing more. With this ruling, as unprecedented as it was unexpected, Lucius's carefully prepared scheme collapsed.

Adultery having been proved, Lucius was found guilty. Claudius commuted the death sentence to indefinite exile in Corsica and was thanked in abject terms by the House for his magnanimity. At a private hearing Julia was exiled to Pantelleria.

Lucius found himself assigned to a dry-stone, earth-floor, one-room cottage, a mile from the main harbour with its tiny garrison and excise office. Once a week he collected the rations he had to prepare and cook himself. Behind the port rose sheer gaunt peaks, negation cast in granite. He understood little Corsican apart from a few words similar to Celtoiberian, and so was effectively cut off from the islanders. Privations he had trained himself to cope with, it was isolation that cut to the bone. At the dockside Attalus, bowed and leaning on a stick, had offered advice: 'Welcome adversity, it allows you to prove yourself self-sufficient. You'll suffer, but that will be bearable if you think persistently of the Greater Harmony.' Helped by the companionship of favourite texts, Lucius tried to live up to his mentor's call. In a rare smuggled letter to console his widowed mother, he assured her that while his body was undoubtedly imprisoned, his mind was free and took pleasure in consorting with men wiser than he.

Two months of solitude showed Lucius that this had been wishful thinking. Zeno, Panaetius and Plato were all mind whereas he was mind *and* body. The Greater Harmony couldn't satisfy him; he needed to be with his fellow men, deploying his energy for some purpose greater than his own peace of mind. So ended what I call Stage One of his exile. Stage Two was marked by his determination to get back to the Forum and Senate.

News reached him that Claudius's treasurer, a Lydian named Pallas, had lost a favourite brother. Lucius, who knew Pallas, decided to write to him since unsealed letters to State officials were permitted. He offered his condolences and urged Pallas to seek consolation by beginning a great poem in praise of Claudius's recently announced campaign to conquer southern Britain. For himself, Lucius wrote, he hoped he could share the joy of standing amid the cheering crowd to welcome Caesar home from the military triumph. Nauseating stuff, but that was what Claudius's circle demanded. Pallas coolly let it be known that he had left the letter unanswered, thus rubbing Lucius's nose in the dirt before the Cato Group.

Lucius saw no other way of softening the government and he turned his thoughts in a different direction. His mother had Novatus and me for support. Julia would likely be freed soon, for her sentence had been in the nature of a warning. As for Marcus, the last news was that his weight had dropped to forty-eight pounds and his voice to a whisper. By now he had certainly crossed the Styx, there to wait a hundred years before entering a new body. Even if he were to see him in another world, he would not recognize his one and only son.

The same held for Paula. She had hurried to the west coast only to find the ferry had sailed. There had been no farewell endearments: there was still a gulf between them. He thought miserably of Paula, quite alone, deprived of Marcus and associated in her husband's disgrace. In his first days of shock at finding himself cut virtually dead as far as family and friends were concerned, Lucius had asked how beneficent Spirit could permit such an injustice. Now he thought he saw the answer. In taking offence at Paula's efforts to cure Marcus, he had been wrong. He was paying for Paula's solitude in the spas with an equivalent solitude. This was justice paid out in the same coin.

Loneliness he could slowly learn to put up with. But another consequence followed from his awareness of wrongdoing: an urgent need to put things right, to explain his mistake to Paula, and offer her sympathy, comfort. But communication of any kind was forbidden, so this need began to fester in him. He saw his hut as a squirrel cage, with himself pacing the enclosure to no conceivable purpose, and he stopped notching the days and weeks with his fruit knife.

Furnace heat gave way to marrow-freezing cold and, after a hasty spring, again to the burning-glass sun. One day a wicker basket addressed to him arrived. Prisoners were allowed food parcels and, in the basket, lay a cake with no indication of its sender. Lucius divided it mentally to last twelve days and cut a first slice. It was a plain raisin cake but, compared with the local chestnut-flour bread, it tasted exquisite. Half-way through eating the cake, his knife struck metal. Easing out the object, he found it to be a ring set with a large amethyst, the very ring he had given Paula as a replacement for her wedding ring, lost one hurried day in the steam baths.

As he puzzled over why Paula should want to send him a cake containing her wedding ring, he concluded that she intended to divorce him, as was her right when a husband had been absent a year. Lucius plunged into despair. Some sort of future, however improbable, however distant, reunited with Paula was now cancelled. He'd been found unsatisfactory and dropped.

Stoics believe that when, for whatever reason, life plainly becomes pointless the reasonable man may take the emergency exit with which God in his goodness has provided him. Lucius held this belief and began – tentatively – to act on it. He swam in waters where the current ran strong, hoping to be flung onto rocks or swept out to sea and, when rainclouds capped the steep granite peaks, he took to climbing those slopes most subject to land slip. From one such climb, rain-soaked and shivering, he took to his bed. All next day, fever squeezed sweat from his pores like water from a dishcloth. In the evening, he found himself being shaken awake by an excise man from the harbour. Lucius must hurry down to the ferry as the captain wanted him.

He knew his way in the dark and eventually staggered up a narrow gangplank to be hustled by the ferry captain into a cabin dimly lit by an oil lamp swaying from the ceiling. The floor too swayed disconcertingly. Someone on board, said the captain, wanted to see him. For half an hour, no more. Then the ship would be sailing.

The captain left and a figure in a hooded cloak came in and drew back the hood, revealing a young woman: slim nose with a lift to it, high cheek bones, eyes downcast. Lucius gave a start, then shook his head. He was feverish, groggy, seeing what wasn't there. The woman raised her eyes to his. Crossing the swaying floor, he took the woman's hands in his, noticing that the cuffs of her sleeves were frayed. Two years since he'd put her on the road to Gaeta; three months since the cake. Now she had come to get him to return her dowry. It was all over. He let her hands go and took a step back.

'You've brought papers for me to sign.'

She appeared puzzled. 'Papers?'

'For the divorce... You sent me back your ring.'

'Oh, the ring... That was for you to pawn or sell and buy necessities.'

He couldn't take it in. 'Then why have you come?'

'To see you.' She added, matter-of-fact. 'Sestilia made the arrangements. She's good about that.' Lucius began to understand. So things were less bad than he'd thought. She wouldn't have taken the huge risk of coming to see him if he wasn't worth it. The half-hour would soon be up and he plunged into an apology. He had hurt her when she had been most vulnerable. She had to bear Marcus's death alone. Now he'd left her impoverished.

Paula's expression softened. Yes, he had behaved badly, and she'd suffered. But she'd decided to draw a line under the past. She still loved him. She'd come to say she would wait for him, wait until he returned. It was the last thing he had expected to hear, and again he experienced confusion. She couldn't, mustn't do it. He wasn't worth it. He had forfeited his rights as a husband. She was still young and attractive. Why should she live like a widow in the hope of a one-in-a-thousand chance?

The captain reappeared: 'Time to sail.' This brought a low groan from Lucius. Now he stepped up to Paula, took her in his arms, pressed her cheek against his neck. He searched in vain for words to match his feeling, but all he could manage was to speak her name possessively a dozen times.

Paula had said she would draw a line under the past, implying that she'd behave as though it hadn't happened. It was this that Lucius found incomprehensible. His attitude had its roots in boyhood. If a neighbour's livestock smashed in our fence and strayed into our garden, Father would furiously stand over the neighbour until he'd put right every bit of the damage. Many times he had told his sons: 'No excuses or promises – get it put right immediately. If you don't, it's you who'll be in the wrong. Rome didn't achieve greatness through leniency.' Natural justice, Father termed it, but he imparted it to us as basic common sense.

Lucius couldn't fit Paula's waiver of her rights into his rigorous way of thinking. It wasn't right of her to make the offer and it wouldn't be right of him to let her do so. Lucius found himself bowed down by the weight of her forgiveness. She had given him back the life he had intended to throw away. He felt he could only go on if he could lighten the weight a little by giving something somehow in return.

Among his neighbours, was a soft-stepping, sharp-eyed trapper, who had picked up a few phrases of Latin in the harbour. The man's unpronounceable name Lucius had simplified to Quercus; he would stop outside Lucius's hut to hold up proudly a hare or partridge. Quercus had two young sons, for whom he wanted to secure jobs in excise but, for that, he said, they would need Latin and arithmetic. Lucius had hitherto ignored the hint.

When Lucius had thrown off his fever, Quercus dropped in again and pottered round the hut. He spoke gloomily of his sons' prospects. Some part of Lucius – not his conscious mind – sprang alert. Here in a most unlikely shape was something that might meet his need. As he described it to me long afterwards, he felt like a drowning man who's been thrown a lifeline. Hammering declensions and conjugations into the heads of nine year-old Saldo, shy and silent and Bardo, a restless puppy of seven, would not be the most fulfilling of tasks. But, said his inner voice, the humility of the task would relieve him of the load that so oppressed him.

With the boys cross-legged on the ground, each with a pointed stick and a trayful of sand, Lucius imparted the magic signs that could change their lives. As the lessons progressed, Lucius began to experience a surprising cheerfulness. He attributed it to the fact that, for a change, he was engaged in an act of generosity.

With winter drawing near, he and Quercus built a rudimentary schoolroom out of logs from a fallen chestnut tree. There, with home-made styluses and a roll of Cicero's speeches cut into pieces of paper, the boys progressed to writing and sums. By spring the school was exciting envy in the village and Lucius accepted two more pupils, thereby establishing what enemies in Rome scoffingly termed Seneca's Backwoods Academy. It would keep him busy as long as exile lasted.

Here ends what Lucius told me about the great wrong he did to Paula.

After his first appeal to Nero for clemency on behalf of the Messallas had been cut short, Lucius found his further approaches dismissed. Finally he decided to wait no longer.

Passing through a ring of guards, Lucius found Nero in the hall of Caesar's House. Clad in officer's uniform – pleated leather skirt and ankle boots – he leaned over a city plan while the City Prefect and the new co-commander of the Guard, Faenius Rufus, pointed to areas where they expected further trouble. Around the chamber, tough faces new to Lucius had bubbled up like grease on a simmering cauldron.

Nero looked up on hearing Lucius's name. Apologising for arriving unbidden, Lucius asked permission to resume their interrupted talk.

Nero frowned, saying he had urgent matters on his mind.

Lucius met the younger man's gaze. 'So have I... For your future's at stake.'

'Very well,' he announced in a vexed tone.

In Nero's study, they faced each other across the desk. At their last meeting, said Lucius, Nero had appeared to view clemency as a form of weakness. He then described Paula's visit to him in Corsica. 'It took courage to come, courage to wait for me. Clemency is not the easy or weak option you think...'

Lucius then described how Paula's compassion had effected a positive transformation in his life, from self-disgust to a desire to make amends, and how he'd eventually been offered ways of doing this.

'Such as?'

'Taking the thankless job of teaching a difficult boy, name of Domitius.' This brought a half-smile and an easing of tension.

Lucius went on to say that he had talked to the prisoners, considered them misguided, not hardened criminals. Once freed, he believed they'd put faction behind them, rejoin their units and once again loyally serve Rome. They should be given that chance.

Nero wiped a hand over his brow. 'I wish I'd heard all this before.'

'Before?'

'The order for execution has been signed and sent to the Mamertine.'

This Lucius knew. 'But not carried out... I sent an order in your name saying you'd received new information and to defer execution.'

Nero flinched as though struck by a whip and, thrusting his jaw forward, he smashed both fists on the desk. 'You took it upon yourself to countermand Caesar!'

'I acted on behalf of Caesar. Of his better self. The self you were trying to conceal but I knew was there.' Nero was breathing heavily. 'Was I mistaken?'

Nero raised a threatening arm. 'I could have you tried for treason. Get out before I have you thrown out!'

Five months later, Nero invited the whole Senate to Antium to see the daughter Poppaea had brought into the world. Astonishingly, they all made the thirty-mile journey, even arthritic septuagenarians, clear evidence that they approved Nero's release of the Messallas. Nero informed them that the baby would bear the name Claudia and Poppaea the honorific title Augusta. Three days of festivities followed.

After a short stay in Ravenna, the Messalla duo had rejoined their units and Octavia had gone to Tuscany protesting loudly. We Romans are vain enough to believe there can be no life away from Rome and when someone prominent suddenly disappears from the scene, we assume the worst. Rumour had it that Poppaea – who incidentally was known to faint at the sight of blood – in a fury of revenge had ordered Octavia decapitated and her head brought to her house so that she could be sure she was really dead!

With Rome again calm, no one was surprised to see Nero composed and smiling. Only towards Lucius did he behave coolly. Lucius possessed a nose for detecting potentially important trails following the sometimes trifling incidents in the daily round. I say 'nose' because he couldn't have given a reason for his sudden alertness, this being an expression of a temperament that accorded supreme value to fellow-feeling.

Paula had been to a ladies' dinner and, at breakfast next day, described it to Lucius. The main dish, sausage and cabbage was left unfinished and their hostess, disliking leftovers, suggested to her sister-in-law that she take home the remains for her dogs. 'Oh dear no,' said the other. 'For Mimi and Nana, it has to be best fillet. Dogs have become so choosy.' Cats too, added another lady. Her angora insisted on boned fresh fish, lightly poached in milk and flavoured with cumin. 'Forget the cumin and she'll stalk off in a huff.' For the rest of the meal, conversation turned on pets and their needs. Paula added that yet another pet shop had opened in the neighbourhood, this one providing a beauty salon: 'Let us shampoo your dog to bring out his character.' The salon even offered a choice of fragrance, including essence of violets – and charged ten times a worker's daily wage!

'Won't violets turn off the bitches?' laughed Lucius as he recalled how at Corduba, after a morning's ratting, he and Novatus would take their terrier for a swim in the Baetis. The terrier wasn't short on character and would have bitten anyone trying to shampoo him! On leaving the breakfast table, he made a mental note of what Paula had told him.

Lucius was reluctant to part with old clothes but at Paula's insistence he agreed to replace a tatty belt. At the outfitter's, he found the shopkeeper engrossed in helping a newly-qualified young lawyer choose a neckerchief. On the counter were spread linens from Batavia, cottons from India, silks from China, in various colours and patterns, while the the shopkeeper extolled the virtues of each. But the customer kept shaking his head; this pattern was too conventional, that one had too little impact. 'I want something elegant to bring out my personality.' Finally the young man settled for a very expensive silk and, while it was being folded, he turned to Lucius with a self-satisfied smile: 'One owes it to oneself to be discriminating.'

The word struck Lucius as odd. In his student days, discrimination had meant pulling apart what should be united; but the young man had obviously used it in the sense of having a keen eye for shades of difference. 'Elegant' also seemed to have shifted from 'fussy', its meaning in Lucius's youth, to 'cutting a figure'. While the shopkeeper laid out his range of belts, Lucius noted how he and his friends used to dress to conform; was the young man unusual in wishing to be out of step? Gracious no, said the shopkeeper, a majority of his customers now took immense pains to assert their personality through clothes that set them apart.

Lucius's musings on the subject were forgotten, surfacing later in a different kind of encounter. His old friend Lucilius, whose statue of Brutus nearly cost him his head under Claudius, served the State ably as a procurator. He regularly sought consolation from my brother to relieve his obsessive dread of death and of what might follow. His lifelong interest in sculpture stemmed from his desire to ensure survival after death. He had now decided to donate his famous collection of statues and busts to the city and, before doing so, invited friends to a private viewing.

Lucius and I were among those who went. The works had been placed in chronological order in a long gallery open to the garden on one side. Lucilius acted as our guide. Starting with statues of his forbears going back two centuries, he pointed out that, under the influence of Athens, faces then were idealized. Long heads, noses running straight down from the brow, close-cropped hair, benign expressions – and nearly all virtually interchangeable. By the time of the Civil War, sculptors were indicating their subject's profession: broad shoulders, muscular arms and a thrusting chin for a general, for an orator arm uplifted, palm outstretched. Then, with the principate, heads suddenly became smaller and rounder, the chin less obtrusive. Augustus had that shape of head, Lucilius explained, and patrons wanted to look more like him.

Contemporary statuary sought out individuality. 'This fellow with jutting underlip and deep lines from nose to mouth – you see him brooding, melancholy, sunk in inaction. And that one – rosebud lips, dreamy eyes and long slim hands – you can almost hear his high-pitched voice.'

Men hadn't suddenly acquired recognizable faces, so why, asked Lucius, this turnaround? Lucilius believed that the new generation had become interested in what sets one man off from another. 'That's what the sculptor is asked to show, and he's only too happy to oblige, to prove his own distinctiveness too.'

Lucius recalled the young man with his neckerchief and saw a connection. I suggested that Rome's prosperity since Nero had become *princeps* gave people more leisure to dwell on difference. But why value difference? asked Lucius. To this neither of us then had an answer.

It is one of our longest established beliefs that the gods communicate with us by means of a few chosen birds, notably the eagle, raven, crow and owl. The College of Augurs is the official body charged with translating their behaviour into messages.

One morning, an unusual pair of birds alighted on the pediment of our most sacred building, the Capitoline Temple of Jupiter. They were less large than eagles, the male grey, the female brown. First they carried out a careful investigation of the roof, then preened themselves and gazed down curiously at the crowd gathered to watch. They returned next day and again three days later, attracting onlookers who speculated about their significance.

In due course, the College pronounced. The birds resembled buzzards but did not soar as buzzards do and therefore they probably belonged to an unfamiliar species of eagle, Jupiter's preferred messenger. They flew in from the right half of the sky – as viewed by College observers from their *tabernaculum*, a tent-like hide in the Campus Martius – and most likely signified Jupiter's approval of the government. If they nested on the Temple, that would promise fecundity for the city.

Normally the College's pronouncement would have been accepted as final. However, a long defunct body re-established by Claudius calling itself the College of Soothsayers thought fit to take issue with the Augurs. They pointed out that the male bird had grey plumage and that grey, the colour of ashes, portends the death of a public figure. This caused a flurry, for never had anyone publicly dared to contradict the College of Augurs. More was to follow. The Ornithological Society, only recently formed, declared the birds to be harriers, therefore closely related to the hawk, a species whose habits were without significance to man.

The College of Augurs issued a statement ridiculing the two dissenting views and reasserting its own interpretation. In the past, this would have been sufficient to silence differences but now, as the pair of birds continued their visits, people of all walks joined in the debate, each siding with this or that recognized body, others putting forward their own interpretations, often far-fetched or plain silly.

So far the battlefield had been circumscribed. Now a registered association calling itself the Original Haruspices went so far as to reject altogether the principles of avian divination; far more reliable, they claimed, was the ancient Etruscan practice of divining from the folds of an ox's liver. This sparked further division, with some demanding that an ox be slaughtered and its liver examined in public, monitored by impartial observers, to learn whether the portents revealed corresponded with those of the College of Augurs.

Into these troubled waters, certain Greek residents now tossed a rock. After tracing Roman cults to their Greek origins, they pointed out that, from time immemorial, Athenian augurs greeted the left half of the sky as propitious and the right as ominous. On what grounds had Romans opted for the reverse? To this most radical objection, no one ventured a reply, with the result that any and every view of the mysterious birds now appeared to have claim to validity. One group actually called for an end to the time-honoured practice whereby qualified observers scanned the sky from dawn to dusk for signs of a thunder storm on the left at which any business in the Senate would be adjourned for the day.

Lucius and I were astonished by the uproar and questioned some of the disputants. Their answers suggested that the strange birds were merely its occasion, not its cause. A deeper rooted attitude appeared to be at work, one not seen in the fearsome years of Tiberius, Gaius and Claudius. Then we Romans had sought reassurance by focusing on likenesses to ourselves in our neighbours; we needed – and found – matters on which we could agree. In periods of unease such as the present, we notice and dwell upon differences: in defence of our own distinctiveness, such differences cause us to contest publicly any divergent opinion.

The variety of views on so fundamental a subject as the gods' favour or displeasure and the intensity with which they were voiced engendered scepticism, and a tone of irony new to the city entered into people's discourse. Accepted opinions on subjects far removed from augury were met with a shrug of the shoulders as though to say, who are you, or anyone else, to tell me how to think? A month passed. Evidently deciding not to nest on the Capitoline, the harriers departed for good, thus precipitating further argument about why they had appeared in the first place.

Lucius had inherited from Aunt Sestilia a small vineyard in Noventum, 14 miles north-east of Rome. I usually accompanied him there in October to harvest his grapes and make the wine. Not having seen him for some time, I decided to call on him to agree plans one evening in September.

His house and ten neighbouring residences are reached by a quarter-mile private road. I was halfway along it, driving fast in poor light when, without any warning, my chariot lurched violently to the left and came to a jarring halt. I found the left wheel deeply embedded in mud and only eased it out after much effort. Heavy rain had caused part of the road to subside but Lucius said the residents' association would be meeting shortly to put things right and, to ensure I didn't again 'imperil life, limb and your custom-built chariot', he would keep me informed.

So he did. The association's chairman, a retired civil engineer, made up for his unimposing presence with good sense, thoroughness and tact. At the residents' meeting he proposed that the collapsed section of road should be re-laid with improved drainage, and that the entire road be re-gravelled and sanded. Discussion ensued. A quiet householder, hitherto reputed a yes-man, claimed gravel was a mistake as it caused jolting and eventual damage to chariots: only sand should be used. This brought a sharp reply from his neighbour: unless mixed with gravel in dry weather, sand would envelop road-users in clouds of dust. Argument between the two was interrupted by a third, who insisted the road was so deeply rutted, only complete relaying would provide an acceptable surface.

The chairman answered all three courteously and reiterated his proposal whereupon a young businessman got up. He had lived five years in Alexandria, where private roads consisted of sturdy flagstones a chariot's wheelspan apart, with sand between. These gave long service, the high initial cost being soon offset by low upkeep. One man praised the idea, another objected to it as foreign, a third warned that wet flagstones on a slope would cause skidding. The chairman concluded that, while the proposal had merits, it was inappropriate to their needs. The proponent proved touchy and moved a vote of no confidence in the chairman, arguing that he was too old for the job. He lost the vote but soured the general mood.

Cost was discussed, a surprise suggestion coming from the owner of the smallest house, a man close with his money and a late payer. His villa stood near the bottom of the road, so he got less use out of the road and should pay less than other owners. This immediately divided home-owners according to their position up or down the road. Tempers rose and, when the chairman could at last make himself heard, he declared that it would be impossible to calculate fair proportionate payments.

This brought further bickering. Lucius, who had long experience of calming disgruntled committees, decided to speak. What in essence, was a road? Not just a means of getting from A to B but an indispensable link between citizens, a symbol of neighbourliness. As the mother of road-building, Rome kept thousands of miles in excellent repair without argument, and here were we counting pennies while our one short line of communication with each other and the city was rapidly becoming impassable. We were twisting and snapping like a basketful of crabs, and he invited the chairman to put total costs to a quick vote.

At this, the businessman who'd lived in Alexandria rose huffily. He wasn't prepared to take lessons in citizenship from anyone, however prominent, and he promptly walked out of the meeting. The breeder of guard dogs chose this occasion to get his own back. Lucius Annaeus received more visitors than any two owners together, chariots continually racing to his house, some accompanied by outriders. It was that exceptionally heavy traffic which had caused subsidence and Lucius Annaeus should bear the whole cost of renovation. Although rejected as unfair, this suggestion opened the way to further radical suggestions, from which it became clear that each householder with the exception of Lucius and the chairman considered the road his and intended its upkeep to be done his way and no other.

When I next called on Lucius, the road had become impassable. I had to leave my chariot with my driver and walk part of the way along a verge. At the house, I was obliged to remove my mud-encrusted shoes and wash my feet, while teasing Lucius about his inaccessibility.

He took the criticism in good humour and explained that there were two matters at issue: temporary repairs and funding, a majority refusing to vote the first without the second, on which however, no consensus had emerged because many of the neighbours were no longer on speaking terms.

He decided to look up old minutes out of curiosity. In the past, members had put forward suggestions with due deference, allowing differences to be resolved without ill feeling, whereas now each appeared convinced that his proposal was far and away the best and, if it didn't win support, took it as a personal affront. This gave the chairman virtually no range for manoeuvre. Lucius placed the situation in a wider context, suggesting that it had much in common with disagreement over the birds: one had led to the metaphorical impasse called scepticism, the other to a dead end.

'You've long believed civic cohesion resides largely in law-abidingness,' I pointed out provokingly, 'yet none of your obstructive neighbours is breaking the law.'

This episode would not have been worth citing but for the fact that it prefigured a comparable and far more wide-reaching rift. In February, the head of the Statistics Bureau, Fabius Cerealis, presented Cabinet with the past year's figures for births and deaths: live births 15,090; deaths 24,350. Set against the average for the previous decade, the death rate remained stable, while the birth rate was declining. Nero, much displeased, said he couldn't understand the drop. Rome was flourishing, business excellent; numbers ought to be rising.

While refusing to comment as a statistician, Fabius suggested two causes. Young couples were choosing to spend their money on show-off items rather than on having more children while an increasing number were divorcing or choosing to live apart. To reverse the trend, some proposed taxing pigs' bladders, used as contraceptives; others an increased bounty for each child after the first, or else at least two children as a condition for advancement in the *cursus honorum*. Nero closed the meeting by calling on Fabius to provide a breakdown of figures according to social group.

The falling birth rate set off serious discussion especially after Rome learned with shock that Poppaea's baby, less than three months old, had suddenly been taken ill and died. Baby Claudia, so long awaited, had been a source of joy and pride to Nero, both as father and *princeps*. She symbolized a direct continuity that was his only by adoption. He proclaimed a day of public mourning and, when presiding at her funeral, did not – or could not – hide his tears. He was now so popular that many in the city shared his grief. They wanted to know the cause of Claudia's death and condemned the infant mortality figures.

Anyone good at figures could calculate exactly the year when Rome's population would shrink by a quarter, by a half, and so on. But no one has ever been able to predict when and why public opinion will suddenly turn such data into alarm. It happened now, at first hesitant and muted, as though citizens were afraid to say out loud: 'The stock is effete; Rome has grown old.' Only gradually did citizens become articulate, drawing strength from a range of analogies. After outgrowing its optimum size, a city becomes intractable: voices multiply, individuals shout to be heard, co-ordination slows; then, like an ageing elephant, it staggers under its own weight and at last sinks to the ground, unable to rise.

Another analogy. Which living thing has the longest life? The oak. One such tree, in Placentia, is held to be 800 years old, but now its branches near the crown are bare of leaves, sure sign that sap is failing. Eight centuries would appear to be the likeliest terminus for living organisms, and Rome was founded 814 years ago.

Again, a walled garden produces prize scented red roses until roses of other varieties are grown in a neighbouring garden. Their pollen transmitted across the wall causes the prize roses to become less sturdy and no longer only red. Thus Roman vigour is confused and weakened by immigrants' values and habits.

And what, in humans, are the signs of senescence? Immobility, idealization of the past, garrulousness, nitpicking – all plainly discernible in our behaviour today. But why this ageing *now*, academicians asked. One replied that Rome had been founded by Mars as a military city; with peace, it had outgrown its function and was now just a husk. Another recalled that Romulus, seeing 12 eagles flying in line from east to west, predicted that Rome would last 12 decades and, when in due course that span was exceeded, 120 was multiplied by the sacred number seven to predict a life of 840 years. Plainly the end was not far off.

Epicureans disputed such views. Rome, like any other complexity, resulted from the random hooking of innumerable atoms which were now starting to come unhooked by chance alone; but no one could be sure that the process of unhooking would not be reversed, again by chance.

The seriousness of the subject meant that differences were aired less stridently than when the harriers frequented the Capitol, but they were held more tenaciously. Again, no consensus emerged, with the result that fear was compounded by fatalism: 'Rome going downhill? Too bad; nothing anyone can do about it.'

Call it as one will – loss of direction, failure of nerve, boredom with concord – as a banker, I knew it meant trouble. Pindar said: 'Gold is good but water is best' – I believe that gold is good, but confidence best. With confidence ebbing by the day, gold began to trickle abroad. The new mood had emerged in a period of rising living standards, but expectations had been rising as fast or faster. Far from reviving, markets also suffered the effects of the new mood. Interest rates rose, business dragged, borrowers defaulted, bankruptcies increased.

Wherever he looked, Lucius too found cause for gloom. Nero had taken his daughter's death so hard that he cancelled four Cabinets in a row. In reaction to their earlier elation, senators murmured that Poppaea was far too highly strung to bear healthy children, while the more superstitious among them saw Claudia's death as a sign that Claudius-with-the-gods was dissociating himself from Nero and his offspring.

Lucius took some of the blame for this dangerous mood on himself, for in speeches and conversation he had asserted that law and law-abidingness were in themselves sufficient to hold the citizenry together, that those two ingredients were the lime and sand of cohesion. He'd been wrong. Something essential had been lacking to check dissension and its concomitant, gloom; now speedily he must find it.

He told Paula that he must go to ground in his study in order to concentrate. She gathered several sprigs of parsley from her garden, pleated them on a thin reed circlet and placed this round the top of her husband's head in order to stimulate his thinking.

Lucius drew together the observations he had made over recent months and identified three separate, though related, disorders. The first, lack of confidence – call it failure of nerve – stemmed from belief that Rome had grown old. It was a legacy of our dazzling past in comparison with which the present looked dim, the future doomed, so that childbearing went by the board. One would somehow need to combat the notion of ageing with something more positive.

A second disorder took the form of exaggerated self-centredness, together with its mirror-image, fear of being submerged in the crowd. This led to the over-assertion of personal distinctiveness, petty differences becoming magnified out of all proportion to their intrinsic importance. Lucius recalled his access road which was now steadily deteriorating as differences hardened to bloody-minded obstructiveness for its own sake. Other examples came to his mind: tax money in hand but payment deliberately withheld until long after the due date; fishermen's failure to agree a standard mesh for nets, thereby forcing the Ostia's old Tunny Co-operative into liquidation.

Lucius turned to the third related disorder: the acid of irony. After eroding key accepted values, irony was now targeting and eating away the very possibility of objective truth. Lucius then began to examine critically his own earlier reading of cohesion. Respect for the law, necessary and indeed vital, could perhaps be seen as unenterprising; it didn't lift people's spirits or excite their hopes. It might be politically correct but it was stagnant. In the negative, almost nihilistic present situation, what was more necessary than belief, bright with promise, in something that stirred the heat and that all could share? That something, for Lucius, must centre on Rome – but a Rome guaranteed immune from ageing which satisfied our longing as mortals for continuity, for survival through generations, a longing second only to self-preservation. Only so could it withstand the acid of irony.

The outflow of coin and bullion reached a point where Nero had to take action. He appointed commissioners chosen from across the social spectrum to propose a remedy. Lucius was not originally chosen but later, the co-commander of the Guard, Faenius Rufus, a close friend of Lucius, persuaded Nero to include him in the commission.

As expected, sharply different solutions were mooted. The military wanted a morale-boosting campaign against the Friesians or against the Iceni. Knights called for the biggest lottery ever, finances from the privy purse, with freehold villas being offered as top prizes. Guilds demanded a ban on Greek entrepreneurs who undercut Romans by employing unskilled labour, while bankers called for the amount of silver and gold in the coinage to be reduced by a tenth.

Lucius was one of the last to speak. The danger, he warned was one of morale and lay in the perception of ageing. 'Ageing is a phenomenon that scares us and, seeing no way to counter it, we turn in circles like sheep. Yet all the while the answer lies to hand, in the first book of the *Aeneid* where Jupiter, addressing Venus, assures her that he will lay no bounds of space nor bounds of time upon the Roman people. "*No bounds of time.*" He is promising Venus, protectress of the refugees from burned-out Troy, that their future city will be immune from ageing. Now the first part of Jupiter's promise has been fulfilled: Rome has in fact spread far and wide, is still spreading – and that is a guarantee of the second part.

What we should do now is proclaim Rome eternal – Rome today, Rome tomorrow – in a manner everyone can comprehend, by holding festive Games. If I may make a suggestion, competitors from each of the provinces should be invited to take part with their travel expenses paid, as a visible sign that, in whatever latitude Romans have chosen to settle, there, for good, is part of Rome. This will direct our gaze not only forward in time but outward in space.'

Lucius had slanted his speech at Nero, with his fondness for poetry, Virgil in particular, and his love of sport. When a respected banker rose to object that Lucius's proposals were no more than verbal sleight-of-hand, Nero cut him short.

'I like Lucius Annaeus's plan. Games will restore much-needed confidence, and I intend to play an active role.'

'The *princeps*'s traditional right,' Calpurnius Piso slipped in smoothly, 'as chairman of the judges.'

'No, Calpurnius. I intend to compete, out in the stadium and on equal terms with others.'

A date was set, four months ahead, which would allow distant provinces to prepare, train and send competitors, and Rome to organize not only the practicalities but also the appropriate pomp.

Always eager to encourage physical fitness, Nero added to the traditional programme new athletic contests open to senators and knights, and others open to women. At Poppaea's suggestion, he scheduled musical and dramatic events, with the festival as a whole dedicated to Apollo.

Artisans worked around the clock fashioning the best in javelins and discuses; the Theatre of Marcellus and the Circus Maximus received new triangular sunshades on adjustable poles; names of householders offering free accommodation to visitors were posted in the Forum, and contestants entered on intensive training. Already skilled with the two-horse chariot, Nero learned to handle the more demanding quadriga, in which the two outside horses are loosely attached to the shaft by ropes. The horse on the left is closest to the marker at each end of the circus; if, in cornering at speed, he is allowed to come too close, the chariot risks crashing; if he swings out too far, valuable yards are lost.

An excited crowd of 10,000 turned out to watch the inaugural ceremony in the Circus Maximus where the contestants paraded to the beat of the Guards' band and the first sporting events were held. Nero competed that day in the medium-weight wrestling contest and won second prize. On the morning of the third day, a large crowd watched the ladies' running and jumping contests. They came ready to laugh and left impressed.

In the afternoon, I joined Lucius to watch the important quadriga final. Nero drove a chariot made to his own specifications from the outer part of the trunk of a mountain ash, which bends under intense strain where the customary oak may snap. How flimsy it looked for the job in hand! With two shafts and four pairs of reins, you have to direct almost a ton of horseflesh while standing steady on a lurching platform three foot by two. Get those reins entangled, mistime a turn and presently sweepers will be raking up bits of your liver and brain.

The presiding praetor checked the ages of the horses by examining their teeth, then climbed the steps of his podium. With a flourish, he raised his white starting banner, assured himself that the four finalists had moved roughly into line, then swished it down. Whips snapped, forelegs thrust up and forward, hindquarters strained at their harness and the chariots rolled forward over the raked sand, heaving at first like swans gathering speed for takeoff.

Nero had drawn the outside lane and, on the first lap, narrowed without closing the gap between himself and the rest. As they raced back to their starting point, the praetor unhooked the first of eight brass dolphins, one for each lap of the five-mile race. By the sixth lap, three drivers had drawn ahead: Argentarius, an experienced professional driving North African horses, a Sicilian newcomer, Thysis, who had come second in the Olympics, and Nero. At the far end of the track, Thysis cornered too fast and his wheels skidded, sending his chariot slewing against the stone parapet. He just managed to cut his reins before being vomited onto the track, while his terrified horses fell, then scrambled up to gallop wildly after Argentarius, who was now in the lead.

Nero had been coming up fast behind Thysis and it seemed certain he must hit the prostrate driver but, by pulling hard on his right hand pair and leaning so far out to the right that his left wheel lifted, he managed to clear the huddled body by a few inches. On the last lap, Nero crept up on Argentarius. Wild with excitement, spectators stood up on their seats to urge him on, snapping their fingers, flapping their togas, some blowing toy trumpets. The finish proved so close that we in the crowd could not be sure who had won. Nero had given express orders that he was not to be favoured in events in which he was competing, and presumably the judges acted accordingly. They decided that Nero's chariot had passed the finish inches ahead of Argentarius's. Nero received paeans of praise from the delighted crowd, which personally I think should have gone to his horses.

On the evening of the fourth day, we saw the artistic side of Nero. His training as a singer and lyricist had progressed behind the closed doors of the musical academy. He had worked hard to become proficient and win Poppaea's esteem and, after their marriage, music became their favourite evening activity. They often sang together, with Lucius playing the accompaniment.

Under Terpnus's guidance, he had mastered the cithara, which has a sound chest of wood larger than the lyre's and which, no less than a quadriga, demands very strong wrists and fingers and highly developed co-ordination. It is played standing, strapped to the left wrist and pressed against the left side of the body. The left hand is held behind the seven strings, plucking, strumming or dampening, while the right plucks with an ivory plectrum. When his name was called, Nero walked confidently up the steps to the platform, bowed to the judges and spoke the time-honoured formula: 'I have full confidence in your decision.' Placing his right foot firmly on the square marble block, he closed his eyes briefly, then struck the opening chords before singing one of his own poems set to music by Poppaea. The upper registers of his bass voice had been strengthened by a diet of boiled leeks and he pitched every phrase of his love song to the far end of the theatre. He followed it with two pastorals.

After a short rest in the dressing-room, he reappeared with a lion's pelt over his bare torso, held at the right shoulder with a silver clasp, and a lion's head, fangs bared, attached to his occiput, while gold chains adorned his arms and legs. Walking heavily to the centre of the stage, he waited for the flautist's first notes, then began his recitative. He, Hercules, had won fame through feats of strength, only to be driven by his jealous stepmother Hera to a pitch of madness so extreme that he had begun to inflict grievous harm on his own children. In self-defence, they had had to restrain him with chains. Was any fate more wretched than his, the strongest man on earth a prisoner of his own kin?

Recitative is not my favourite genre, but I have to admit that Nero conveyed admirably the pathetic tension between physical strength and a mind weakened through no fault of his own. During the long performance, he observed the rules scrupulously, never daring to clear his throat and wiping sweat from his brow with his arm, a handkerchief not being allowed. He was warmly applauded and the judges awarded him second prize.

An unusual event followed. From his interview with the Messalla prisoners, Lucius had concluded that the safety of the State required that patrician families be sweetened. At his request, the presiding praetor staged a pageant in which members of all ten leading families enacted chosen deeds of bravery or public-spiritedness by their forebears. Lucius had taken pains to see that each episode should be dramatic and not too long, so that spectators wouldn't be bored; in fact novelty alone ensured the pageant's success and the families concerned, suitably gratified, endorsed and made fashionable the new catchphrase: Eternal Rome.

So the Games came to a close. Visitors from Italy and competitors from the provinces, who had scooped many of the prizes, took the road home. It had been a communal event, with all citizens involved. Shared pleasure and excitement had renewed a waning solidarity. This had been the point of the exercise. What no one had foreseen was Nero's immense overnight popularity. By his youth, vigour and prowess he was seen to embody the message of the Games. I will cite one small example from many. At our local butcher's, I found a display made of white lard. It was of a four-horse chariot modelled in careful detail showing wheels, spokes and traces. Leaning forward was the driver who, from his full cheeks, rounded chin and curly hair, was plainly meant to be Nero. This butcher is close to his money – even a bone for our dog is added to our bill – but he had thrilled to the quadriga race and this was his tribute to the winner: two nights' painstaking work without a penny profit.

PART FOUR

Fighting the Furies

By pressing Nero to include song and recitative in the Games, Poppaea had contributed greatly to his success so it was surprising that she should afterwards have voiced apprehension to Paula. 'Before the Games, Nero thought only of me, but now he thinks only of Rome, of how Rome views him and how he can continue being a favourite. Do you see?... He's become so big and I... I'm beginning to have worry lines.'

She ran a finger along the corners of her eyes and the edges of her mouth. 'Worst of all, my hair's getting darker.' Putting it into words made her shiver. 'The day I lose my looks, I should wish to die.' Paula tried to reassure her: the pain of losing little Claudia had brought on depression and fears quite unjustified since Nero certainly still loved her.

But Poppaea believed she was slipping. She went on a shopping spree, spending heavily on undergarments, complexion lotions and rare scents. She wept when Nero scolded her for extravagance. Her show of tears won him over and helped her regain calm. At length she dared to ask him for a suitable building to replace her wrecked music centre and suggested Agrippina's old house. In his determination to put his mother out of his mind, Nero had placed Lucius in sole charge of her property and effects. So it happened that, following his wife's request, Nero – accompanied by Lucius – re-entered his mother's house – and his past.

The conscientious housekeeper showed them the public rooms and fussed in expectation of compliments on the polished brass fixtures, then the garden, with its topiary smooth as polished diabase. Passing under the netting, they entered the aviary to be greeted by a flutter of wings and a voice Lucius could have sworn was Agrippina's. 'Dearest boy, how are you?'

Nero stepped back in alarm, his hand gripping Lucius's arm. Moments later, a white minah flew down and perched on his shoulder. 'Give me a kiss. One of our special goodnight kisses.'

The scene was eerie. Lucius wished he hadn't come. Nero quickly recovered his composure and showed pleasure at finding the feathered companions of his boyhood. He began to stroke the white bird, smiling as it fluttered under his touch. 'Mother's favourite. She spent hours teaching her the right intonation.'

Since leaving Baiae, Nero had never referred directly to his mother's death. Occasional veiled allusions led Lucius to believe that he saw it as her own doing. She had tried to destroy him and he had acted in self-defence. Evidently the grisly drama of her end did not prevent him feeling nostalgic pleasure in remembering their earlier good times together, to which the creatures fluttering about him were living witness. He talked to the birds and had the housekeeper fetch raisins with which he rewarded the cleverest.

Agrippina's office was a small bare-walled room containing a desk, a chair and a tall cupboard. Lucius unlocked the desk and Nero began to work through the contents of its lateral compartments. Varied accounts, notes on the conduct of servants, Nero's boyhood letters fastened with a ribbon and a drawing of him aged six seated in a dogcart, flicking his long whip with an air of assurance. The last set him musing for a while. Then he turned to the cupboard: African beadwork, a sandalwood box inlaid with pistachio, a gourd painted with figures, and other singular items, each docketed with the name of the ambassador who had offered it as a gift to win Agrippina's favour. A few of the objects were of sufficiently fine workmanship to engage Nero's attention.

Seated at the desk, Lucius was studying the accounts, written in Agrippina's own bold hand. Expenses were listed under separate headings; payments for toiletries included hairdressing, bath oil, face creams and hare-blood, an exfoliant for legs. In each category, Lucius found that expenses had kept within a modest monthly budget.

A decorated rectangular panel caught Lucius's eye. On finding that it was set in a groove, he slid it open. Inside lay a cluster of scrolls. One by one he pulled them out, six in all; they were of finest blanched papyrus, covered with sections of writing in black ink in Agrippina's clear cursive. Some were short, others longer, all dated. Lucius realised that he was holding Agrippina's diary.

He felt squeamish about diaries: prying into intimate secrets was like a surgeon cutting through flesh to a vital organ. He thought about Agrippina's cool controlled character: her diary would be as matter-of-fact as a ship's log. He placed the scrolls in chronological order and began to read sample entries. Soon he realized he had in front of him a highly personal record. He read on. Alone at the top, constantly under pressure and with Claudius too weak to be her confidant, Agrippina had confided her hopes and intentions, doubts and disappointments to her diary. Many entries concerned her son: her interview with Lucius for the job of tutor was noted. Claudius's sudden death was recorded without comment. When 'the odious Ollia woman' came on the scene, the diary's tone turned bitter and at times so enraged as to verge on incoherent. The last entry recorded the departure for Baiae.

Nero had finished perusing the curios in the cupboard and now crossed to the desk. He was startled by Lucius's find. Seating himself in the chair vacated by Lucius, he picked up a scroll at random. For a few minutes, he read in silence. 'Look at this,' he indicated.

Claudius's behaviour does not improve. Tonight he told guests to break wind freely at table in both directions, because it is good for the health. Any other lady of rank would have left him. Why do I stay? For my dearest boy, and for Rome.

'And this.'

The Troy Game. My dearest boy handled his horse with aplomb. He is still naive, still inclined like his father to trust anyone who jollies him along. But with me to guide him he will become a second Germanicus.

Nero unrolled more scrolls. 'I will do everything in my power to keep the Ollia woman from my son.' Schemes to get the hated woman out of Rome were sketched out. With his head in his hands, Nero sighed intermittently as he read on. Suddenly his arms flopped onto the desk with a thud, his eyes closed and there came from his open mouth a hoarse gasp. 'It cannot be,' he groaned barely audibly. A silence followed which Lucius deemed it prudent not to break. At last Nero pulled himself together, reread the entry and passed the scroll to Lucius:

> As a last resort I told him I would go to the Senate. I would describe to the elected Fathers how, on my Orders, Lucusta added poisonous fungi to a dish of mushrooms to kill Caesar. This was my ultimate threat to make him renounce the Ollia woman. It is but a threat. For no folly of his will induce me to ruin the career of the one person in the world whom I love above all others, the one person for whom, despite the pain he is causing me, I will make any sacrifice.

In Egypt, Lucius had once entered a rock tomb alone to study frescoes when its heavy door swung shut behind him. He reacted to the diary entry with a similar cold dread.

The effect on Nero must have been a hundred times worse. I don't believe it,' he muttered defiantly. 'Can't believe it.' His mother couldn't have written that entry. It didn't fit with the deadly serious tone in which she had uttered her threat. Or might it be that, in confusion, she had jotted down an intention, never in fact carried through? Yet her handwriting here was neat and regular, with no sign of impetuousness. Could she have written those words in order to appear in a favourable light to posterity? It didn't correspond with the frankness of the diary as a whole.

Lucius scanned the entries before and after the passage that had so shocked them and, when asked his opinion, replied bleakly that there could be little doubt that those few awesome lines described truly Agrippina's intention: she would threaten her son but her threat would be bluff. A further silence ensued, during which Nero sat motionless gazing at the blank wall beyond the desk. Finally, calling the housekeeper, he asked in a dull voice for a box with a lid. Into this he packed the scrolls and still in silence the two men left the house of secrets. In the street, they parted, Nero raising a finger to his lips. 'Mum's the word.'

An incubation period followed. Nero read the whole diary, from which it emerged that this mother had had no wish to usurp her son's place as head of State. As the toxic implication was absorbed, the first symptom showed: a surge of compassion and tears for the shade of his mother, killed unjustly, followed by an order to Lucius to have her ashes brought to Rome for burial, a task deputed to Novatus.

Novatus set about the task with characteristic thoroughness. But Agrippina's villa had fallen into neglect, its garden turned into a public playground. Extensive search failed to reveal the urn which was presumed stolen or lost. To the wrong of an unjustified killing was now added Nero's frightful realization that he had sent his innocent mother's shade to wander homeless for 20 lifetimes, with no one to clasp her hand or share her pain. Stricken by remorse, Nero reacted with the wildest of wild plans. Why, he asked Lucius, shouldn't he place himself in the hands of the law, confess his deed, plead extenuating circumstances and ask leave to expiate through exceptional services to society, as Hercules did with his celebrated labours? Surely the court would see the logic of this and agree? Lucius raised the immediately obvious objection: the man who had struck Agrippina the fatal blow had since died; without a witness and the body of the victim, no court would touch such a case.

Each time the diary or lost urn came to mind, Nero's strongly visual memory threw up an image of some close and happy hour spent with his mother, often beside the sea at Antium. His days were an ordeal of self-reproach. As remorse fed on itself, his inner disquiet began to show outwardly. He held himself less straight and walked without assurance, often looking down at the ground. One day he appeared in a frayed tunic, buttons undone, and a stained unpressed gown. When criticized for wearing such shabby clothes, he replied bitterly that they were good enough for his likes. He would sometimes skip his morning shave, telling Poppaea that he couldn't bear seeing his face in the mirror.

He would pass associates without looking up and spoke seldom in Cabinet. This lapse from easy openness disturbed those in his circle; believing themselves slighted, they drew away, causing Nero to imagine that they guessed his secret and were coming to hate him.

It happened that the number of appellants from the provinces had been growing to the point where a bureau had been created to supervise them when they arrived in Rome. Knowing how Lucius cared about good relations within the Republic, Nero had persuaded him to head it. One afternoon, in the study of Caesar's House, Lucius read his monthly report as Overseer of Appellants. Instead of commenting on relevant points, Nero fixed him with a challenging stare.

'Know what you are, Lucius? A hypocrite.'

Lucius cocked his head in hurt surprise.

'You know very well what I really am deep down and it fills you with disgust. But you're too much the smooth courtier to say so.'

Lucius protested. He'd never gone in for flattery and took pride in always being frank with Nero. The other seemed not to hear. 'You know perfectly well I'm a heap of dung, and you loathe me. But you'll have to come clean and admit it. Then we'll know how we stand.'

Lucius replied placatingly that one could hate a certain deed which was over and done with, without hating the agent.

Nero laughed sardonically. 'The deed's in here, you idiot!' He thumped his chest. 'Suppurating, stinking. I feel it and smell it.'

Lucius saw the pathos behind the melodrama. He would have liked to show sympathy but knew this would be a mistaken reaction so he fall back on weak neutrality. 'Just as you say, sire.'

New symptoms began to show. Nero kept finding excuses for absenting himself from routine tasks. He missed three court sessions in a row. When Lucius warned him about the unfavourable comments being made about him, Nero rounded on him angrily. 'Would you have me hand down sentences knowing I'm guiltier than the accused?' He also shirked inspecting the guard, explaining that, when the duty officer marched up to him and snapped to attention, he could hardly hold back from trembling.

As he grew more convinced that those around him knew his crime and were shying away from him, Nero drew in on himself. There were moments when he could swear he heard his mother's voice, other moments, between sunset and nightfall, when he could swear he saw her face, the dear eyes and often kissed lips. In a rush of tenderness, he would stretch his arms for an embrace, only to enfold emptiness. Why did she continually elude him? Would her anger have no end?

One night, Poppaea woke to find Nero shaking and shrieking. She cradled his head in her arms, stroked his damp brow and gradually managed to calm him. Another nightmare, the worst so far: he had felt himself dragged down into a dark pit by strong hands with white fingers and long sharp nails. The pit was the inside of a huge anthill where a horde of giant winged ants began to eat away at his flesh – arms, legs, body, face. As fast as he drove off one swarm, another attacked.

Poppaea did all she could after her fashion. She put him on a light diet of young sorrel leaves scented with mint, steamed in spring water and seasoned with a first pressing of olive oil; she gave him sorbets of blackcurrants and clover honey. She arranged sweet-smelling bouquets in his study; played and sang sentimental music. She would be a new Ariadne, her voice the thread that would draw him slowly out of the labyrinth, away from the Minotaur's jaws. At bedtime, she rubbed his brow and mastoids with a syringa lotion of her own devising. Prettiness would defeat ugliness. Her cure might have worked had she not been so neurotic herself. Was he feeling a little bit calmer, she would anxiously enquire once too often, undermining the effects of her tender care.

Poppaea took him to a Menander comedy. He enjoyed the first scenes but walked out of the theatre at the interval in the throes of depression. Those smooth youths swapping jokes made him feel like an exile from normal life. That night, he awoke from another terrifying dream and, unable to regain sleep, stumbled into Cabinet

257

next day with the swollen eyes and mottled face of a badly mauled boxer. He nodded off listening to long-winded reports, causing those present to exchange frightened looks.

Lucius felt deeply sorry for the man and alarmed for the ruler. He looked for ways to help and finally chose one prompted by Poppaea's experience at the theatre. He suggested to Nero that he read him a play after supper, which he found particularly gloomy. After initial reluctance, Nero agreed and asked for a play by Euripides. Lucius chose *The Minotaur*. Nero listened closely, shuddering at the climaxes, and praised it afterwards as a real cauldron of horrors. That night, he slept uninterruptedly, and a couple of days later, he asked for another tragedy. This continued until the day when Lucius said he'd exhausted his library of tragedies. 'Then write me one yourself,' said Nero.

Lucius objected that he was no poet, had never written a play, didn't know how to construct one and, even if her were foolish enough to try, he'd then appear ridiculous to his friends.

Nero cajoled. 'It's not for the stage, Lucius. It's only for me.'

Lucius countered by proposing his nephew Lucan – my elder son – already prominent in Nero's Poets' Circle, but the idea was rejected. 'I don't want someone else knowing what we know.'

Lucius set to work, choosing the most chilling plot he could think of. Medea falls in love with Jason, king of Thrace, and bears him children. Then he deserts her. She looks for some way of doing him harm, but he is powerful and well protected. Finally she decides to poison their children, a little boy and girl upon whom Jason dotes; Medea exults in her revenge as they die in agony.

When he was composing a piece, Lucius would decide on a voice and tone appropriate to each character, then he mentally positioned the cast around his room. As the action began, he imagined lines being spoken from this or that chair, repeating them aloud and making changes until he felt they worked. In short, he had to be aware of voices coming *to* him rather than *from* him.

When Lucius read his play out loud, Nero seemed to live every scene. 'You've got it all there. Medea's feeling of being trapped, the breaking-point. Not a sign, not a word from Jason. Great Jupiter, what she went through! Pity her children!' And again, with his mind full of horrors worse than his own, Nero enjoyed a night of deep sleep.

The trouble with performing one helpful action is that you're expected to follow with another. For his second play, Lucius chose the hatred between King Atreus and his brother Thyestes, ending when Atreus tricks Thyestes into attending a banquet where the main dish is the minced-up bodies of his own sons. Lucius piled on the horrors, layer upon ghastly layer, for it was these that caused Nero to shudder cathartically. Lucius had to come up with tolerable verse, for Nero had learned from Poppaea to appreciate the finer point of poetic style.

Lucius started on a third play, the strain now beginning to tell on him. He arrived one day at my office and slumped on a couch. 'Such fun! I really get immense satisfaction turning out spine-chillers. What an achievement! My grandnephews will be able to boast: "That's what great-uncle Lucius did when he was Caesar's Friend." And so rewarding to know you'll have to start over again tomorrow, and the day after. What an appreciative audience! Write a heartfelt plea by Clytemnestra, not bad stuff, though I say it myself and what do I get but a frown and tongue-clicking: "Last line but one, your iambics limp." I'm damned if I'll put fine writing into three acts of abattoir-peeping...'

On the nights when Lucius read to him, Nero slept well and woke refreshed. But the time came when Lucius found he had dried up and couldn't manage another chilling scene.

Nero took it hard. 'Already? Plautus wrote 50 plays.'

'Comedies: fingertip work. Tragedy has to come from your guts.'

Nero pouted and frowned. As a poet, he had to agree that inspiration can't be forced.

Soon Nero's debilitating insomnia returned, along with a new symptom. Now that he was sure Agrippina's shade would never grant him her pardon, the three witch-like Furies took her place in his imaginings. He claimed he actually saw them with his fatigued eyes. At first, they appeared as indistinct prowling figures, then they took definite shape as more than life-size women with snakelike hair and eyes like glowing coals. They cracked whips close to Nero's face and thrust flaming torches at his hands and feet. He had to know whether they were real. He roused Poppaea and dragged her protesting onto the terrace so that she could decide. When she insisted that she could see nothing, he rounded on her angrily and accused her of lying.

He took to keeping his chariot whip at hand and, after dark, whenever he spied the hateful shapes, he would lash out with the four-foot ox-hide thong. If they still held their ground, he would pick up a heavy object and hurl it at them. Once he shattered a beautiful statue of Flora with an iron doorstop.

Early one morning Poppaea knocked at the door of Lucius's house, red-eyed and sobbing. Led to a couch by Paula, she described how Nero had awoken from a horrifying dream. Hearing a noise outside and thinking this to be the Furies, he had rushed out shouting insults. Poppaea's trusted maid had got up to see what the row was about. Believing her to be Alecto, leader of the Furies, Nero had grabbed her by the neck with both hands. Poppaea had tried to pull them apart, shouting at Nero until at last he came to his senses.

Her head resting against Paula's shoulder, Poppaea unburdened herself. Otho had had too little imagination, Nero had far too much. She was terrified that he might strike her a blow and kill or disfigure her. 'I daren't stay a day longer,' she kept repeating. Finally Poppaea begged Paula to come and stay in Caesar's House to protect her just for a few days. Paula didn't in the least want to leave Lucius and Lucius of course didn't want to see his wife risk assault, but the obligations of friendship prevailed.

So Paula was dragged into Nero's private life, sharing his meals, listening to his small talk, observing his mannerisms and noting his alarm as his water-clock marked the gradually diminishing hours of daylight. She noticed his habit after each meal of placing scraps of leftovers on a platter which he would lay reverently on the hearth in front of tiny bronze figures representing the Lares. It's a traditional rite rarely kept in highborn families and Paula attributed Nero's observance to Claudius's influence.

After his victories in the Games, Nero had publicly offered his laurel crowns to Apollo, laying them gratefully on his altar; he had also issued special coinage depicting the god. Paula shared his piety. She would often go to the Temple of Juno to pray and she belonged to an association for keeping the temple decorated with fresh flowers. In this respect she was different from Lucius. Lucius held to the Stoic view that we strengthen our character by fighting inner battles single-handed; praying for succour shows weakness and insults the Spirit divine, who knows our needs and will provide for them or not as and when, in his wisdom, he sees fit.

There were periods when Nero seemed his old likeable self, open-hearted and considerate of others. He chose a seat close to hers once while she embroidered, and spoke about Poppaea. He said he found her less anxious now that Paula had rallied to help her.

'Losing Claudia unsettled her... But of course you went through that yourself.'

His tone of sympathy won her confidence. 'Little Marcus was already a little person, so full of promise, I thought I didn't want to go on living. Later I turned to Juno and that helped. I offered a white lamb each year on her feast-day, and her priest chanted prayers for my intention. My little boy was irreplaceable, so I asked for a daughter.' She paused, distracted, as though carried back in time. 'Later, much later, a girl did come into my home.'

'A daughter?'

'A niece. But I love her like a daughter and she looks on me as her second mother.'

'So Juno heard your prayer?'

'So the priest says, and I believe him.'

Two days later, Lucius was making his way to the Temple of Apollo on Nero's command. After a long discussion with Lucius, Nero had concluded that, since his crime had angered not only his mother but also the gods, it was to them that he must turn. Lucius walked slowly, weighed down by apprehension. He esteemed Roman religion for its antiquity, moderation and for the dignity of its ceremonial, but it bristled with old taboos. A god could be invoked only through his priests, who must approve the faithful's petition before reformulating it correctly and then presenting it to the god in person. The Forum's intricacies were as nothing to those within a temple precinct.

Alphaeus, the priest who met Lucius by appointment, proved to be less than 30 years-old and was open-faced and bright-eyed, looking as though he had just eaten a juicy peach. The hair at his nape he wore long, gathered by a narrow ribbon, and the collar of his white gown was embroidered in gold thread with a device of Apollo's lyre. He showed Lucius around the temple. It was not large, Apollo's cult being a comparatively recent import from Greece, but Augustus had endowed it with coloured terracotta bas-reliefs and marble statues of Apollo, his mother Latona, and sister Diana. It happened to be the hour when worshippers were permitted to perform the gods' toilet: one old man was going through the motions of filling a bath and washing Apollo, another with empty hands mimed the action of anointing with oil, while two women dressed Latona's hair, one moving her fingers as if combing and curling, the other holding a mirror to the deity's face.

Lucius believed these activities to be misguided and passed them over in silence. He gratified his guide by expressing admiration for the outstandingly fine bas-reliefs. They sat down on a stone bench in the precinct; fantail pigeons circled and cooed beside a fountain and at first Lucius hesitated to disturb the serene atmosphere. He had come with an unusual request on behalf of a dear friend. A bitter protracted family quarrel had led to bloodshed, in fact – it pained him to have to say it – to a violent death.

From the corner of his eye, he saw Alphaeus flinch and bite his lower lip. He paused before going to the essential. 'For months, my friend has been tormented by guilt and remorse. He's on the brink of a breakdown. He wishes to invoke the help of Apollo.'

A long silence followed and, when the priest replied, his voice had lost its exuberance. 'Isn't your friend aware that Apollo is god of light and beauty? Anything foul and ugly he finds abhorrent. To become involved in the murky after-effects of a violent crime would defile him... It would be quite unthinkable.'

'Suppose this man had made generous offerings to Apollo?'

'That would make his dereliction more monstrous and alienate him still further.'

His recent immersion in Greek tragedy had provided Lucius with an apparently decisive precedent. He reminded the priest of Aeschylus's play, *The Eumenides*: Clytemnestra has killed her husband and their son Orestes has avenged his father by killing his mother. Pursued by the Furies, Orestes is standing trial in Athens, where Apollo comes down to plead in his favour. The priest knew the play. 'Apollo argues that the mother is not the creator of her child, only bears and nourishes the newly wakened life. So matricide, though evil, does not violate any fundamental law of nature, as Clytemnestra's murder of her husband did.'

Lucius knocked in the nail. 'The court acquits Orestes and Apollo drives the Furies back to hell.'

Far from being thrown, Alphaeus lost no time in parrying. 'Doctors in Rome have a much better understanding of physiology than the Athenians centuries ago. It is mother and father who jointly procreate, one reason why we accord our women higher status than the Greeks. Aeschylus's portrayal of Apollo is a highly improbable fiction. We deny that our god ever acted, or ever could act, in favour of a matricide.'

'Even in circumstances that might lead to a suicide?'

'No circumstances can change a god's essential nature.'

Lucius couldn't help being impressed by the young priest's firmness. After a courteous leave-taking, it was in a gloomy mood that he turned into a street full of shoppers and entered the first pastry shop, where he hurriedly downed three almond cakes, so adding heaviness to dejection. More perhaps than most men, Lucius hated to admit defeat. Recalling that Agrippina's patron deity had been Juno, protectress of mothers, next day he made his way to Juno's Temple, which is larger and more richly decorated than Apollo's. In its colonnade, peacocks arched their tail feathers and uttered their occasional piercing cries to ward off evil while vendors sold tin medals and quartz amulets.

The middle-aged priest charged with receiving visitors wore a russet gown embroidered with Juno's emblem, a diadem. His strong face bore lines like glacier striation on rock betokening a daily struggle against avarice, envy and perhaps despair. Lucius felt at ease with him and went straight to the point. A great lady, for long a votary of this very temple, had been killed as the result of a quarrel based on misunderstanding. The unfortunate person responsible for her death, though deeply repentant, was being hounded mercilessly by the Furies. He was sleepless, prone to rash decisions and threatening to his wife. Unless the Furies were called off, madness would probably lead to further bloodshed. Juno was propitious towards wives. Here was a wife in danger from a husband who had long endured his torments bravely. Could he not hope that Juno would grant him forgiveness and call off the Furies?

The priest, who had listened gravely throughout, said that this was not the first case of its kind, nor the worst, to come his way. How true that the human heart was clogged with filth. 'Let us be clear. A sacrilege, a blasphemy – these the god has power to forgive. But where a wrong has been done to one of her votaries, the god's prime obligation must be to the votary.

'The case you cite falls outside these categories. Blood has been shed, a life taken. It has moved out of Juno's power to help. It has become the concern of Themis, guardian of Right, and of the Fates, the three sisters who spin the thread of life which none may cut with impunity. It is they who have unleashed the Furies, and Juno is powerless to influence or intercede.'

At so stark a preclusion Lucius felt his stomach turn to lead. Half to himself, he murmured, 'Then our only recourse is to Jupiter allmighty.'

But this too brought dissent. 'With respect, you appear to be confusing categories. The gods live in another world from ours, their role here below is limited to averting evil and misfortune from their devotees. I'm talking about robbery, assault, disease, shipwreck, that kind of thing. Our primary role as priests is to offer our gods sacrifice and thereby protect our votaries from evil.

'We have a secondary role also. To protect our gods from mischievous stories put about by cynics, from illicit forms of worship, from irreverence, and above all from those who wish to demean our gods by attributing to them inappropriate feelings or powers that would sully their numen.' He looked reprovingly at Lucius.

'Are you saying that none of the gods can help?'

'I'm saying that what you came here to find – peace of mind for someone tormented by guilt – is not within the scope of any god.'

They parted with glum looks. On an impulse, Lucius entered the temple, hoping to find there what had so far eluded him. He walked up the length of the building, welcoming its cool calm. At the end stood a more than life-size statue of a mature woman with high forehead, hair crowned by a diadem and covered at the back with the veil that distinguished her as Jupiter's bride. For a long while Lucius scrutinized the face. What did he hope to find? What sign could there be from this block of marble, lifeless as the quarry from which it had been hewn? Lips that did not speak, ears deaf to suffering. She and her lord had used their power again and again to protect Rome from her enemies. Were they powerless to save Nero from himself?

He became aware of even more disturbing fissures in his own inner sanctum. How could Spirit divine, cosmic orderer and by definition forwarder of good intentions, remain aloof at this moment of crisis? If the Roman gods were absent – absentees absolutely – was Spirit too, at darkest midnight, an absentee?

Lucius left the temple with a sinking feeling. A vendor approached, urging him to buy a tin medal of Juno. He declined and instead slipped all his loose change into a cripple's outstretched palm.

Having promised to report at once, Lucius found Nero in his stables chatting with his most recent confidant, Ofonius Tigellinus. This man, son of a Sicilian innkeeper, strong and good-looking, had made his way to the top through horse-racing circles, where he had not been above fixing races. In one celebrated instance, he had introduced a potent mustard suppository into the rectum of a poorly fancied runner. Without formal schooling, he had picked up a smattering of law. This and more than a pinch of flattery had won him the post of commander of the watch, and most recently, though wholly lacking in military experience, co-commander of the Praetorian Guard.

Lucius described his encounters. Nero's face expressed disappointment and Tigellinus sighed dramatically. 'I wonder whether you handled it the right way. Shouldn't you...?' He rubbed a finger and thumb together. Lucius replied coldly that temple priests were not be bought as easily as jockeys.

After further inconclusive discussion Lucius left the stables much depressed. At least Tigellinus, with the latest racetrack stories, could provide diverting amusement.

Nero was too deeply shaken for diversion of any kind. Even the gods – his last hope – shrank in horror from his crime. What lay ahead was an unending struggle to outwit the unappeasable Furies. His behaviour in public became increasingly odd. On tours of inspection, he continually threw anxious glances over his shoulder and refused to enter enclosed spaces or dark buildings, lest he be trapped by the Furies. Intending to visit town A, he announced he would go on that day to town B. On the appointed date he turned up unannounced in town A, thereby eluding the Furies but angering the citizens of town B, who had hung out banners, festooned their streets with flowers and cooked a gala dinner in his honour. The goodwill won through the Games began to cool and one daring vaudeville portrayed a man stuffing down food, followed by a woman swimming for dear life.

Lucius considered that incoherent behaviour by a head of State must obviously lead to loss of direction by the State, hence to dissension and faction. Nothing now mattered so much as getting Nero back to normalcy.

'Prisoner escaped!' came the call an hour before dawn. Eyes half-opened, Lucius padded to the kitchen, pushed a pan of water onto still hot charcoal embers, dressed but did not shave, then mixed lemon and honey into heated water. Only with that in his stomach did he feel up to rousing his driver and joining the police captain whose shout at the window had wakened him.

A Cilician born Roman citizen had been living in the house of Domitius Graecinus, paid by the State to lodge persons in custody waiting for Caesar to hear their appeal. Domitius's wife, woken by footsteps and a scuffle, had found the man's bed slept in but his room empty, and raised the alarm.

The prisoner had been in Rome for several months and Lucius, as Overseer of Appellants, should have personally checked security. Preoccupied as he was, he had failed to do so. If the man wasn't caught, Lucius could expect trouble.

Arriving in Ostia, Lucius and the police captain were joined by two customs men and began to search the ships due to clear port. By mid-morning they had drawn blank of three and started on the fourth, bound for Joppa with a cargo of tar and hides. The master, a shifty-eyed Cypriot, escorted them to the hold where large barrels lay lashed to the beams. The customs men attacked the nearest barrel with chisels and mallets. When the top fell out, the master pointed. 'Just as I said: tar.'

Lucius's head throbbed from lack of air and the stench of newly-dyed hides, but he had a gut feeling which told him to carry on. When the top of the fifth barrel had been levered off, the men found wood shavings inside instead of tar. Suddenly excited as children at a lucky dip, they hurriedly pulled out the shavings in handfuls, revealing what looked like the top part of a plaster head. Then, to their surprise, the head began to stir.

Lucius ordered the barrel tipped on its side whereupon inch-wide holes close to the topmost hoops became noticeable. With the customs men holding it steady, the police captain inserted both hands into the shavings and got a grip under the armpits. Then, as though extracting flesh from a lobster claw, he began to ease the body upwards and out.

Cords on wrists and ankles were cut, a leather gag removed and the released man sat up blinking, shaking dust from his face and easing out his stiffness. Perhaps aware of his comical appearance, he gave a self-deprecating laugh. 'Will someone please tell me where I am!'

'In the hands of the law,' replied Lucius sharply. 'Slipping house arrest is a serious offence.'

The man said he'd been in his room writing a plea for his case to be speeded up when he'd heard footsteps in the passage. His door was suddenly flung open and, before he had time to turn, something heavy hit the base of his skull. The next he knew he was being packed for shipment. All this the man recounted in educated speech with a Greek accent. The grey-white hair at the sides and back of a bald head suggested he was about Lucius's age, and he had the wind-beaten face of one who has lived rough and hard.

Lucius knew him only as number 43 on a list of appellants. To avoid any further trouble, he decided to keep him safe in his own house until he had found out more about him and how he had been abducted from a secure lodging. The prisoner asked for water and was allowed to drink from the harbour fountain. Then he mounted beside Lucius in Lucius's chariot, and the driver whipped up the pair of horses.

The prisoner seemed surprisingly at ease and talked cheerfully. 'Ever been shipwrecked?' he asked Lucius. 'It's something you don't easily forget. I should know: last time was my fourth. The ship in which they brought me to Rome, as soon as I saw how low she lay on the water and her mast set too far astern, I shook my head. I grew up in a port, that's how I could tell. Sailed straight into a levanter. She couldn't handle it, broke up on the rocks. That's when you see what men are like inside. The quiet little fellow huddled in the stern, he's the one who launches a life raft and pulls out the drowning... Some lost, some saved – that's a shipwreck.

'Fine horses you have. By their step, I'd say Asturian. I've been as far east as Arabia, and when, or should I say *if*, my appeal's heard, I'll head west, as far as Spain. But not by sea, thank you. I've friends in Spain, pen-friends, that is.' He began to whistle quietly, a jaunty tune, then broke off. 'Doesn't annoy you? I'm certainly glad you decanted me.'

Very assured, very talkative and potentially a bore, thought Lucius as he neared home and turned into the private road, patched up now of necessity since most of the house-owners had had guests staying for the Games. A disused loose-box next to the stables would do as lodging, a canvas and straw palliasse as bedding. The police captain, who had followed in his chariot, fixed shackles to the Cilician's ankles and handed the key to Lucius. Connected by three hands' lengths of chain they allowed a slow, shuffling walk. While the police captain went off to fetch the man's belongings, Lucius locked the loose-box door and went to his study.

As he puzzled over how the abduction could have been carried out, the sound of whistling came through the open window. This added to his annoyance. Why should a man in chains be so damned cheerful?

Next morning, when he went to see number 43, he found that his belongings had been reunited with a tattered cloak neatly folded, together with many scrolls and, of all things, a loom. The prisoner was seated, rattling the shuttle backwards and forwards, while nodding a welcome to Lucius. He explained that he earned his living by weaving sections of sunshade awnings for a private open-air theatre. Then he asked Lucius politely whether he might receive visitors. A further annoyance but since the law permitted up to eight visitors a day, Lucius had to assent.

Next day, her duty done, Paula came home and very soon went to visit her surprise lodger. Afterwards she scolded Lucius, saying she'd been shocked to find the man's mattress crawling with bed bugs. When she'd asked him why he hadn't complained, he'd shrugged and said it wasn't important; in fact bed bugs had their uses, preventing him from taking too much sleep.

'Did you notice his tunic? Thin cotton in the middle of winter! He said his other clothes had been lost at sea.'

'And he treated you to his shipwreck, scene by lurid scene.'

'In his place, wouldn't you do the same? Then he said I shouldn't bother about meals, since he had figs and nuts; with bread brought by a friend, that was all he needed. He had two visitors. They left as soon as I arrived. He said he didn't even know them, that they came looking for comfort and advice. I asked him if he was a philosopher and he smiled. "No," he said, "but I do bring a message."'

Lucius sniffed. 'Every other arrival from the east claims to bring a message.'

Two days passed. Each morning, a line of visitors stretched down the road, a vendor of hot snacks doing a brisk trade. When a neighbour came to complain about riffraff on her doorstep, Paula tactfully calmed her down.

Lucius received the dossier on number 43, a detailed scroll covering 20 years' travels in a dozen provinces, during which he appeared to have been known by a variety of names. After studying the dossier, Lucius went to the loose-box, where his prisoner sat at his loom, heaving the shuttle from side to side while dictating a letter to a visitor cross-legged on the floor beside him. Guessing Lucius had private business, the visitor quietly rose and left.

Lucius explained that he was required to file a report. 'It seems you've had several aliases. One of them is listed as Mercury, but surely that's a mistake?'

The prisoner looked momentarily puzzled, then nodded, laughing briefly. 'That was in Lystra, a town of Lycaonia. I arrived there with a colleague and I was speaking about the good life when suddenly a man in the crowd, a cripple, threw away his crutches and began striding about like you or me. General amazement. In the east – but you know this – many live in hope that one bright day a wonder-working god will come down and do them a bit of good. And here, they thought, were two such wonder-workers. My colleague was a tall fellow, slow, dignified, authoritative. Evidently this was Jupiter and I, being quick and talkative, was Mercury. They invoked us as gods and wouldn't heed our denials.'

Lucius made a note. 'What about other names in your dossier? In Palestine: Rabbi Saul, a doctor of law; in Damascus, 'Scourge of the Nazarenes'. Then, suddenly, popping up here, there and everywhere, Paul of Tarsus.'

The prisoner explained that, for years now, he'd been known as Paul of Tarsus and that it was thus that he had appealed to Caesar. 'Eight months my case has been gestating.' He sighed, then smiled wryly. 'Let's hope next month it will come to term.'

So long a delay was unusual and it crossed Lucius's mind that someone at the top might be blocking the suit. Lucius learned that, on the night of his abduction, the Praetorian who normally kept watch outside his lodging hadn't shown up. Someone with authority must have dispensed him from duty. Could it be Tigellinus? But why should such a highly placed figure concern himself with this compulsive wanderer who spent his daylight hours weaving canvas awnings with the doggedness of a galley-slave?

Paula had become increasingly curious about their lodger. Solicitous for his well-being, she knitted him a woollen tunic and had a camp bed moved to the loose-box. She told Lucius that his visitors spoke of Paul with respectful affection and that, when she was with him, she had a pleasant sensation of calm, almost like being in a temple.

This brought a smile. 'Paula and Paul: you're beginning to see him as a twin-soul. What will come next?'

What came next was Paula's plea that, since their lodger needed fresh air and exercise, Lucius should take him along on his afternoon walks. Lucius had no objection and next day, unlocking the bolts on Paul's shackles, the two of them set off for town, Lucius slowing his usually fast stride in rhythm with the other's stiff-legged gait. When Paul mentioned pointedly that so far he had had no opportunity of seeing the sights, Lucius cheerfully proposed his 'Class One Guided Tour.'

Entering Augustus's Forum, Lucius showed Paul the court room where he'd won his first case and the Rostrum where poor Cicero's mutilated head and hands had been put on show. They had a quick look at the high gaunt Tabularium, where the documents of Rome's long history are preserved. In the broad Via Sacra, Paul inquired what battles were depicted on its triumphal arches. 'You're known as a practical nation, yet all these arches – what function do they serve?'

'None,' Lucius admitted. 'But they serve to emphasise a vista.'

'As well as the value you attach to victories?'

A cold north wind was blowing and Lucius hurried to the Campus Martius, where a marble milestone marks the navel of the Republic known as the golden milestone because all distances are measured from it. Lucius compared it to the hub of a giant wheel, the spokes of which were made up of roads, Roman law and the Latin language. 'Plus a reliable postal service,' added Paul.

All the while they had been passing temples, Lucius naming each god and his field of action. 'One to serve each of your needs,' was Paul's comment, at which Lucius murmured dully, 'not quite.'

Paul enquired about a new-looking temple. Not wishing to pass criticism in front of a stranger, Lucius replied that it was dedicated to Nero's adoptive father, who was believed by many to have joined the gods.

'But by one writer,' countered Paul, 'Claudius is said to be serving Aeacus in Hades as a legal dogsbody.'

The twinkle of amusement in his eyes told Lucius that Paul was referring to his satire *Pumpkinification*. Lucius was astonished to find himself facing one of his readers. He was already uncomfortable about the treatment accorded to Paul and now he was positively embarrassed. 'Could we put an end to this charade?' he enquired, half-appalled and half-amused at the vagaries of fate. He offered to take Paul to the nearby wine-shop where they served Falerian wine of the highest quality. Paul was only too pleased to accept. My brother lent him a clean toga and shawl. Even the sandals fitted perfectly as Paul had the same size feet as him. As they walked down the avenue planted with planes, Seneca had the impression that a lowly individual was loping behind them but he paid no heed. Paul was pleased to be treated like a fellow human and expounded on the Aristotelian golden mean. They reached the place. I know it well. It's a bit of a dive by the bakery with an informal brothel around the corner.

Once seated, Seneca ordered his favourite vintage from a rather buxom girl from Puteoli. The wine came in a terracotta jug and they drank thirstily to friendship, to luck and to the power of good over evil. That much they agreed on, and more. But Seneca was curious to find out more about the shipwreck. What had brought Paul to this pretty pass?

He had been arrested in Jerusalem and ordered transported to Rome for trial. On board ship, they had tied him to the mast because of his powers of persuasion: he was always distracting the sailors, said the skipper. They had not even allowed him to trail his fishing line, a favourite pursuit. Near Malta, a furious storm overtook them. With all hands on deck, Paul started offering advice in his commanding voice. The men paid more attention to him than to the bosun and the ship foundered All the men were saved, but the ship was a total loss for insurance purposes. 'All that grain gone to waste!' Paul sighed.

Paul's tribulations were not over. The next berth that was found for him was aboard a ship from Alexandria carrying ceramics and oil. None of the sailors would even talk to him as they saw him as bad luck. But at least he did not have to be tied to the mast and could get on with his fishing. Some fine fish he caught, he said, his eyes twinkling with delighted recollection.

At this point, the small man who had been shadowing them in the street made himself known as Juba, one of the seamen on the shipwrecked voyage. He wanted to talk about the storm and the shipwreck. His appearance was rougher than his manner. 'You were in custody – but still a citizen and proud of it. You wouldn't hear of anchors for'ard, swore they'd pull us abeam the waves. No business whatever of yours, but you yelled at the bosun to haul back the dinghy laying out anchors. Which, idiot man, he did. Dreadful mistake. Truly dreadful. The anchors astern couldn't hold us. All night the levanter drove us east. Then...' He banged his fist on the table. 'Crash! Guts torn out of her hull. A wreck... And every man of her fine crew without a place.'

The seaman paused, stared gloomily at his empty beaker then, eyeing Paul conspiratorially, resumed. The circumstances of the wreck were under investigation. Act of Fortune, no insurance would be payable; negligence and the insurers would be stung for a million or more. He lowered his voice to a husky whisper. 'What's it worth to you for me to keep quiet? Say I never heard you shout that order?'

Threats of any kind invariably enraged Lucius and he waited for Paul to do what he would have done, scoop this vermin off his stool, frogmarch him up the stairs and into the gutter. But Paul rubbed his chin reflectively, then beckoned a server, paid for three more measures of wine, touched his beaker to Juba's, and drank with him.

Lucius watched in astonishment as Paul addressed the seaman slowly and calmly. 'Go to Pomponius Acer in Ostia. Say you're sent by Paul of Tarsus. He will give you a place on one of his freighters. Remember: Pomponius Acer. Opposite the lighthouse... You're a first-rate seaman; don't become a second-rate twister.'

Whatever the bo'sun had expected, it clearly wasn't this. His face expressed astonishment, pique, hesitation and finally surly acceptance. Scowling, he left the table and headed sheepishly up the stairs. As he reached the upper level, Lucius observed a tall figure step from behind a pillar and lay a hand on his shoulder. The two whispered together and, as they turned into the light, Lucius saw that the lobe of the tall man's right ear was missing. This placed him. One of three spies employed by Tigellinus: his earlobe bitten off in a tavern brawl.

A minor unpleasantness now became disturbing. Why should Tigellinus be having Paul watched? Perhaps he'd arranged to have Paul abducted as a service to someone important or for coin. Paul's presence in Lucius's house would then alarm Tigellinus: he'd be thinking Lucius might learn of his conniving and use it against him.

Then again, if Paul had agreed to buying Juba's silence, Tigellinus would have had a case against Paul for misleading the shipwreck inquiry. Tigellinus would then emerge as vigilant while Lucius would be maligned for protecting a highly suspicious foreigner. Keeping these thoughts to himself, Lucius led the way out of the wine shop.

The snow had stopped falling. It had been trodden to slush on the thoroughfares, but lay an inch or more thick on the Ara Pacis and on the heads of the processional figures, so that the altar seemed no longer of marble but of snow. As they paused to look, Lucius remembered a conversation they had had about the absence of an image of Peace.

'Unless you see the snow as a fitting image.'

'Surely rather far-fetched.' They headed in the direction of his house and, to cap the subject, Lucius tossed out a countryman's saying: 'Winter white, plants delight.'

'And poor man's plight... But watch those boys throwing snowballs. For them, it's bliss. You could have a reasonable argument about the value or otherwise of a snowfall and never reach a conclusion.'

As they walked carefully through the slush, Paul grew confiding. 'You know, Lucius, it used to bother me that any non-human occurrence should admit of uncountable explanations, and any general concept too. Take integrity. We can argue on and on about its nature, how far it should or shouldn't override self-interest, but isn't it only when we meet a man of integrity, listen to what he says, watch his face, see how far he lives up to his words, that we truly understand what integrity is?'

'Possibly,' Lucius conceded.

'In your essays, you portray Cato the man living thriftily, avoiding ostentation, rejecting with scorn offers of bribes; your readers see integrity personified, like one of those statues we passed earlier. They admire and even come to love it.'

So Paul knew his essays! 'Cato's been my lifelong hero,' Lucius said feelingly. 'But such men are rare as plums in January.'

'I know such a one,' Paul said quietly.

'Yes?'

'He lived far from Rome in a remote part of Palestine, not marked on Agrippina's map, yet he brought news of a god greater than any yet glimpsed in Rome, a god who can bring peace of mind to the individual and peace to the nations.'

'Huh!' One more Eastern cure-all deity! In dealing with appeal cases, he had encountered many such: Atargathi the Great Mother and her flagellant priests, Mithras lifting his followers to the stars with a sprinkling of bull's blood, cuddly boy Bacchus, inviting devotees to a playground Elysium, all swings and seesaws; Gnostics promising an end to gender and its divisions. Vapours, all of them.

Either disregarding or not noticing Lucius's scornful grunt, Paul pressed on. 'He had no rank, no status, no influence, so why did people believe the news he brought? Because he possessed authority. Of which, perhaps you'd agree, there are two kinds. Official, such as Caesar possesses, and the authority emanating from someone who lives up to his teaching, the kind Cato had.'

They turned into a descent where the snow had drifted. Half-way down, Paul slipped and Lucius grabbed his arm just in time to prevent him falling.

'I'm becoming a nuisance.'

'Not a bit. Shackles have left you stiff.' For the rest of the way he supported his companion while reflecting on his polyvalent character. A manual worker, yet well read and a tireless correspondent: a foreigner conversant with Roman affairs; lively and quick yet calm under provocation. He had won Lucius's respect. Here was a man with a logical mind who said sensible things, but he was apparently lost to one of those dim cults we in Rome term superstitions.

Back at the house, Lucius replaced the shackles on Paul's legs. He did not want to be found remiss.

The following evening, Lucius visited the dimly-lit stables with a large beaker of red wine and two silver cups. Setting the tray down on a low table, he coaxed a slow-burning log into the stove. Paul joined him and they ran their hands along the warm iron. Lucius poured wine from the beaker; they touched cups and drank.

I now append an entry from Lucius's secret diary.

Paul: A fine nose and smooth on the palate. Samian?

Lucius: Yes, but grown on a small vineyard, planted with my own two hands. It helps to keep gloom at bay... I've noticed that you, the prisoner, are cheerful and sing aloud when you're making converts.

Whereas for me, all my moral writings have made few converts to Stoicism. I suppose it's because I'm only on the first rung of moral progress.

Paul (jokingly): Yet you've managed to acquire the good things of life – furniture inlaid with ivory and gold. And expensive vines.

Lucius: Stoics do not require the sacrifice of wealth, only the achievement of spiritual detachment from worldly goods. But we do tend to have gloomy thoughts. We know that despite possessing free will we cannot outwit Fate or Providence. To quote Chrysippus, "Virtue is sufficient for happiness, nothing except virtue is good."

Paul: An excellent recipe for living, but he added that emotions are always bad, and there I disagree.

Lucius: So would I. Religion is *not* emotions. It is logical virtuous behaviour.

More wine was poured out.

Paul: Tell me, how do you see an after-life?

Lucius: As a Roman? Cold, mouldering and dingy. Hades is a mirthless place guarded by the hound Cerberus who wags his tail for new arrivals but devours those attempting to leave.

Paul: And as a Stoic philosopher?

Lucius: I find it illogical to suppose that a virtuous life would end in such misery.

Paul: Yet you teach that virtue is sufficient for happiness.

Lucius: In this life on earth. There is no after-life.

Paul: On that we can't agree. But perhaps we can agree that life itself is given to us on trust, our parents being mere intermediaries?

Lucius: Certainly – and the giver is Fate.

Paul: By which you mean Providence. So we agree on the origin of life. However, you believe that someone in desperate trouble should end his life by suicide. How can it be virtuous to destroy the life bestowed by Providence?

Lucius: The virtue lies in courage. It takes a brave man in full health to slit the veins in his wrists and watch the blood ooze out, hour by hour.

Paul: If death is not the end and an after-life promised, you should not kill what has been given to you on trust.

Lucius: Let me think that through… You've got me into a corner and intend to convert me.

Paul: Never, Lucius. We are friends and I do not try to convert friends. Besides, I do not need to. Every virtuous man who keeps clear of evil emotions and seeks God will go to happiness in an after-life.

Lucius (after a pause): There's the bell for dinner. Until another talk.

Paula returned from her weekly visit to Poppaea with news so worrying that Lucius hurried to Caesar's House. There he found the lady, who had obviously been crying, in a state of shock provoked by new aggressiveness from Nero. It was for her sake that he had issued the order to end his mother's life; therefore it was her responsibility to deal with the Furies. She would find the words and tone to mollify the dreaded sisters. That was her role. Instead of arranging recitals in a vain attempt to calm him, she should be at his side on the alert, day and night, ready to act.

'If Poppaea cracks, Nero's finished,' thought Lucius. He hurried to Nero's apartment and told the major domo on duty to announce him. The man returned looking cowed, with orders to show Lucius off the premises.

Paula's response to anxiety was to bake a cake. Cutting it in half, she placed one half on a platter and asked Lucius to take it to Paul. Paul was busy at his loom and nodded a welcome while continuing to dictate in Greek to his scribe. Placing the cake within reach of the loom, Lucius took a seat and prepared to wait. Paul meanwhile continued what appeared to be a letter of encouragement to a community troubled by dissension.

Dictation finished, Paul reached for the letter, read it through slowly, made one or two alterations and folded it neatly. From a small pot beside him, he took a spatula with which he spread paste on the edges of the folded paper. 'Bluebell bulbs,' he explained to Lucius. 'More adhesive than flour and water.'

Lucius observed how deftly Paul spread the paste and sealed the letter. His orders to the scribe were very precise: how to find the ship, the passwords to be exchanged before entrusting the letter to the ship's master. If Paul is so practical, thought Lucius, then perhaps his message might be of practical use. It came to him that he ought at least to hear what it was about.

Once again he trotted out his familiar tale: a young friend, still in his twenties, deeply troubled by a guilty deed, at war with himself. What could be done to help? Paul showed no surprise: it even crossed Lucius's mind that he might have been expecting such an approach.

'He is searching desperately for peace of mind,' explained Lucius. 'The trouble is, he's not an intellectual. Everything has to be hard and practical as the mechanism of your loom.'

'That should present no difficulty,' said Paul quietly. A colleague of his, John Mark by name, now in Rome, had been one of the companions of Yeshua – the teacher whose message was peace – and he had noted down what Yeshua said as he spoke it. Paul could lend Lucius a copy of those notes to pass to his young friend. He brought forth a leather pouch secured by a strap and brass buckle, opened it, and took out two rolls, which he handed to Lucius.

'You say these were written down at the time?'

Paul nodded. 'Verbatim.'

Nero's aggressiveness alternated with less troubled periods of self-pity or self reproach. Lucius waited for one such calm day before securing an interview. The meeting began badly. When he asked permission to speak of a Cilician in custody who'd recently been saved from kidnap, Nero turned on him angrily. 'So it's a criminal you want to involve me with! As though you haven't brought trouble enough.'

Lucius changed tack. Drawing on Paul's notes, he spoke of a latter-day Socrates named Yeshua. He cited several of the man's sayings. Nero reluctantly agreed to look through the rolls Lucius had brought with him. 'The Greek is cloddish,' was his first comment. But he read on and, after a good deal of pressing from Lucius, agreed to listen to what the Cilician had to say.

An appellant is forbidden by law to communicate with Caesar before his appeal case has been heard, so the meeting would have to be *incognito*. Nero liked the drama. 'We'll meet in your house and I'll wear one of my recitative masks.' Lucius suggested he also remove his phoenix ring.

Whenever Nero glimpsed a ray of hope, he would bounce out of his misery. Arriving at the appointed time, he looked almost cheerful. To Lucius's annoyance, he brought Tigellinus in tow. And it was the Sicilian who fastened Nero's copper mask with slits for eyes and mouth, attached at the nape by leather thongs, tight on the brow and projecting slightly at the chin.

They seated themselves, Nero and Tigellinus facing Lucius and Paul, who knew only that Lucius's young friend had had a brush with the law and wished to conceal his identity. Nero spoke first, moving his shoulders and gesturing with his hands. 'I can see this Yeshua of yours. Lucius says he's the Socrates type, but Socrates owned a house and had friends in high places. This man has no house, no coin, not even a change of clothes but, wherever he happens to be, he takes charge. Socrates never stopped talking. This fellow does things. And does them with style. Crowd of thousands pressing him to speak; no rostrum, no auditorium, no high ground. So what does he do? Jumps into a boat, rows out, stands up in the prow and speaks from the lake! How's that for style!...

'Move to a wedding where the idiot groom has skimped on the wine. At the back of the hall stands the strong quiet man – must be strong to sleep rough and have a voice that carries across water. Observes the panic, knows he can put things right. Should he push forward and play Lord Obvious? More dramatic than that. Unassumingly – on the quiet – turns six tall jars of water into wine.'

'So what?' scoffed Tigellinus. 'I turn wine into water several times a day.'

Nero laughed. 'Fair enough. But that wouldn't save a wedding. I tell you, this man's a thaumaturge with a genius for showmanship.'

Tigellinus shrugged. 'So what's new? Healed the sick, so did Aesculapius. Fed the hungry: *you* do that every day!'

Paul had been sitting motionless. Now he raised his right palm as a plea to be heard and Nero assented by pointing a finger.

'You call Yeshua a showman and so he was. But what did he come to show? His power to put things right, and not just in the natural world. The wind and waves he was really concerned to calm were those within.' Lucius was struck by Paul's assured tone and by something in his manner that could only be called fervour. 'Your poet Ovid wrote: "The better way I see and approve, the worse I follow." I think he spoke for us all. Every day we fail to follow the better way, and every day add to our past faults. Ovid was living in exile from Rome but he suffered the more harrowing emotion of being exiled from his own better self. He felt – as we've all felt – that he had distanced himself from the gods, that they had turned away in disgust.'

Paul paused. Lucius noted that Nero had suddenly turned very still: the ruler of half the world was listening attentively to an unknown prisoner from the back of beyond.

'When men suffer Ovid's plight,' Paul continued, 'incapable of rescuing themselves, they look for someone to do it for them. The Romans are rescued from invaders by Curius Dentatus whom they hail as *liberator*. Aesculapius saves a dying man and is hailed as *soter*, the equivalent Greek term. Now in order to describe quite a new kind of rescuer, Yeshua chooses *soter*, extending its meaning to denote a god who frees and saves from past and present wrongdoing.

'While other gods shun wrongdoers, this god goes out of his way to help them. Even when we're sunk to our necks in the quicksands of past or present wrongdoing, such is the extent of his goodness that he drags us out, and such the extent of his mercy that he forgives us.'

From beginning to end, this extraordinary claim was recounted with an intensity Lucius hadn't encountered in Paul before: pride edged with excitement such as a vintner might show a customer when holding to the light a glass of rare golden Falernian.

A short silence was broken by Nero saying that Paul's meaning was difficult to take in but sounded important. If it was important, why didn't Yeshua proclaim his message in Rome?

Because, replied Paul easily, he hadn't been born a citizen of Rome and his tongue was Aramaic. But he did command his followers to spread his message in the Roman world.

'Are you one of them?' asked Tigellinus scornfully, eyeing his chained legs.

'Yes, though unworthy.'

'Sluggish too, apparently. When Festus arrived as Procurator in Caesarea, you could easily have lodged a formal complaint for imprisonment without trial. Then you'd have walked free. Why did you choose to appeal to Caesar and spend further months in chains?'

Lucius thought he detected the hint of a smile on Paul's lips. 'An inexpensive way of getting to Rome, a reputedly open-minded city.' Evidently a dig at his questioner.

Tigellinus turned to Nero. Every new cult, he reminded his master, is a superstition. Only when its god is formally recognized by the *pontifex maximus* can it be classified as a religion. Until then, it must be viewed as potentially subversive. Fishing a handful of coins from his pocket, Tigellinus selected a drachma and held it before Nero's masked face. 'Caesar's head, inscribed with one of his official titles: *Soter* – Saviour of the Republic. Transferring Caesar's title to a strange god seems to me a *prima facie* case of *lèse majesté*. Again, those notes you've been reading – are they authentic? Was Yeshua a real person? If so, his name should be on the census rolls. And that new bright star moving from east to west – did our astronomers record it?'

Quite unruffled, Paul said he would welcome any investigation. Then, at a sign from Nero, Lucius led Paul to an adjoining room. When he returned, Nero instructed him to check the points raised by Tigellinus. Lucius asked for his impressions of Paul. 'He spoke clearly and to the point. For a prisoner, I'm surprised by his assurance and his joyful expression.'

'Cockiness I'd call it,' grumbled Tigellinus. 'Obsessed by a single idea. We know what that means.' Rubbing thumb and forefinger under his nostrils, he advised that Paul's baggage and the lining of his clothes be searched.

As a busy young lawyer specializing in wills, Lucius had often had to consult early records, so he knew the archives well. He quickly traced copies of Augustus's census in Palestine and worked through them until he found the entry for Yeshua's birth. Then he crossed the street to the Office of Astronomers and Augurs. Here they had no record of anything unusual for the year of the census, but the secretary drew his attention to sightings by their sister observatory in Alexandria. These records did signal an unusually bright conjunction of planets or a comet moving in the opposite direction to the fixed stars. Having also ascertained that no hashish had been found in Paul's possession, Lucius hurried to Caesar's House.

'I told you that man was sound.' said Nero, pleased. 'Arrange another meeting.'

Lucius pointed out that Paul's appeal had been pending for many months and suggested that Nero should first hear his case.

'Tigellinus says it must wait,' said Nero impatiently. 'There are gaps in his dossier.'

'Anything specific?'

'It appears that 12 years ago he was charged with subversion somewhere in Greece and found guilty.'

Lucius confirmed that Paul had been charged – but not with subversion. He'd been accused of predicting an imminent end to the world, thereby causing a slump in trade. The case had been heard in Corinth by the Governor of Achaea, who pronounced Paul innocent and set him free. 'How do I know? The governor happened to be my brother Novatus ..'

Nero raised an eyebrow and lent his full attention.

'It's possible that Tigellinus also cited subversion on the corn ship bringing Paul to Rome, with a trainee bosun as witness. But that man has withdrawn his testimony and is now en route to the Black Sea.'

Lucius spoke of the night Paul had been abducted. There had been no guard on the house. Why had the guard been removed? So that Paul could be shipped back to Palestine before Nero heard his case. Only three men had the authority to remove a guard: the captain of the watch and either one of the co-commanders of the Guard. So why such trouble to prevent Paul's appeal being heard? Because Paul, a Roman citizen, had been imprisoned by Antonius Felix for two years without trial. That was illegal and would prompt serious reprimand, possibly dismissal. Lucius paused a moment. 'The son of Antonius Felix is married to Tigellinus's daughter.'

Nero's face registered annoyance. 'All well and good to act in the interests of family. But not to the detriment of an innocent party.' Hands joined behind his back, Nero paced the room.

'If you heard his appeal now, Paul would be eager to help you. The interview would of course be confidential.'

Nero heard the case the following morning. It presented no complication. Paul was formally declared free and unshackled. At Lucius's request, Paul agreed to speak further about guilt and how its horrors might be assuaged. This time, Nero returned to Lucius's house unmasked and without Tigellinus.

As he took a seat on the curule chair, with Lucius and Paul facing him on cushioned stools, Nero tried to disguise his edginess beneath an exaggeratedly matter-of-fact manner. Borrowing Lucius's face-saver, he cited a friend who had shed innocent blood and was being hounded by the Furies to the limits of endurance. Paul had described a god of forgiveness, but this man's hands were stained with the blood of his own family. Surely that was beyond pardon?

Paul assured him that no crime was too heinous for his god to forgive.

Nero was not satisfied. 'I'm a man who deals in hard facts. If am to believe you, I need proof.'

'It takes telling. Have you the time?'

'Try me and see.'

Paul lowered his head reflectively. At last, in an even tone and fixing Nero in the eye, he began.

'You'll have heard of Jewish law, the strength and mainstay of our nation, stricter and more all-embracing than yours. Some years ago, Yeshua's followers – now known as Nazarenes – began contesting that law, saying it should be replaced by a more merciful code. One day, a Nazarene named Stephen was expounding these views. He was young, good-looking and convincing. There arrived on the scene a doctor of law. He too was young, but a stickler for orthodoxy. It shocked him to hear Stephen picking holes in Jewish law and accusing lawyers of using it for gain. He interrupted, denouncing the speaker for hearsay and ordering him to retract. Far from doing so, Stephen went on to sing the praises of a new god different from Yahweh. The doctor of law flew into a rage. Shouting "Blasphemy! Blasphemy!" he picked up a heavy stone and hurled it at Stephen, striking him hard on the neck. He ordered those around to do the same, since Jewish law penalizes blasphemy with stoning. Such was his persuasiveness that the crowd too began to hurl stones. Presently, leaving a mangled young body in the dust for the beaks and pinions of carrion birds to jab and tear, the doctor of law went on his way.'

Paul's tone had become emotional: his brow creased and his eyes closed momentarily. Lucius and Nero exchanged disappointed looks. Would their carefully planned interview produce nothing more relevant than a banal story of cults clashing?

The lawyer, resumed Paul, tried to shrug off a regrettable incident, but the memory of Stephen's eager young face would not leave him. He tried to efface it by citing his duty as a doctor of law. But the memory remained and seemed to reproach him for his cruel and impetuous action. To justify his deed, the lawyer chose to champion his own sacred code of law by pitilessly hunting down any Nazarene who dared question it.

One day, he made a journey on horseback to rout out yet another nest of infidels. Swallows circled high in a cloudless sky and the air was fresh, yet from the heavens came a sound like the roll of drums and a voice deep as thunder. Twice it called him by name. 'Why do you persecute me?' the voice asked. What was happening? Whose voice could this be? And whom was he persecuting? The Nazarenes, yes, and by extension their god. Could the voice from the sky be the voice of that god?

Terrified by the thunder, his horse had thrown the lawyer to the ground, where, prostrate, he thought night had suddenly fallen. He couldn't even see his own hands. Total blindness blanked his vision. He saw himself led like a dog, fed like an infant. In his misery, the reproachful faces of those he'd sent for scourging passed before his mind. He began to understand that he had acted less for love of the law and more from hatred of Yeshua's god. And presently the voice from the sky spoke to him again: 'All this I forgive you.'

Three days later he regained his sight. But the world had changed. Now he found himself in a new world where he was able to walk freely and easily. Slowly it dawned on him that he had indeed been forgiven.

Nero looked confused. 'Forgiveness, out of the blue, just like that?' He snapped his fingers and shook his head doubtfully.

Was it because he had been composing tragedies that Lucius felt the drama in Paul's quiet narration? A violent killing, the voice of God, blindness, regeneration. Oedipus outdone. Cosmic, more than cosmic, since a cancer had actually been reversed. He found the sheer sweep of the story compelling, but Nero seemed less impressed.

'Who is this shadowy lawyer?' demanded Nero defensively. 'What do we know of him... I suppose he lives out of reach?'

'He was out of reach in custody for some time until he appealed to Caesar,' replied Paul. A moment's hesitation. 'Now he's living in the house of Annaeus Seneca.'

The room and everything in it suddenly blurred for Lucius. Was nothing and no one what they seemed? This apparently harmless weaver who talked feelingly about peace – a cold-blooded killer? Surely not! Yet one didn't invent a story like that. Then a nasty sarcastic inner voice piped up: First Nero, now Paul – you really must stop this habit of befriending murderers.

Nero looked almost as surprised but, prompted by the urgency of his need, he quickly resumed probing. 'Forgiven – so you claim. But how do we *know* you were?'

Paul seemed ready for the question. 'When those three days of darkness lifted, I saw I must make amends. I would give my remaining years to telling others about this god who offered forgiveness and peace of mind. I felt I was a new person and took a new name. This made my former colleagues treat me as a renegade; they hunted me down as once I had hunted Nazarenes. For 29 years, I've been on the run, telling others about my release from sin. Would anyone but a lunatic do so if what he was saying hadn't happened?'

Lucius seemed half-convinced; Nero shook his head dubiously. 'I need to know more about this man Yeshua. If his own people hated him, presumably he was just another of those dozens of bandits who regularly disturb the peace in Judaea.'

Paul heaved a sigh. 'I never met Christus, alas. I was not worthy to meet him. But I have many friends who knew him intimately and told me of incidents that proved he was no bandit. Once, when the authorities came to arrest him, Yeshua's best friend struck a soldier on the head with his sword. At once Yeshua ordered his friend to sheathe the weapon. There was never quarreling or backbiting among his closest followers. Like you, Caesar, he was a man of peace. Yet this kindly man who protected children was arrested, flogged and judged guilty of disturbing the peace, with no right of appeal.'

Caesar frowned. 'How so, if he was a pacifist?'

'Because he claimed to be King of the Jews.'

Caesar looked startled and angry. 'But a King is just what Judaea has long needed and clamoured for. Both Saducees and Pharisees agree on that and they are right.'

Paul nodded assent. 'So gentle a man gave no sign of being a suitable leader of a disunited people. And procurator Pilatus had to make that most difficult choice: judge Yeshua according to Jewish Law or judge him according to Roman Law. Each valid, each respected. Where did the truth lie? Pilatus could not choose both so he washed his hands of the affair.'

Caesar looked angry and thrust out his chin. 'Prisoner, remove, your clothes!

Slowly, Paul rose to his feet and said resignedly, 'I don't like to parade my misfortune but if there's no other way...' He loosened a brass clasp and removed his cloak, undid the toggles on the tunic Paula had made him and pulled it over his head. Wearing only his underpants, he slowly turned his back to Caesar and Lucius. Purple scarred ridges in uneven lines ran across its whole length and width, like rock strata or a message in runic. Lucius found himself flinching. He had once had to monitor a public scourging and recalled the thud of the metal-tipped thongs, the screams trailing into whimpers, then the silence of unconsciousness; the limp body cut loose, oozing blood, to be dumped like a side of beef.

'Fifty lashes in Philippi,' said Paul evenly, 'fifty in Caesarea; many more elsewhere. You don't submit to that for something that didn't happen.'

At the sight of Paul's stripes, Nero emitted a low cry and shut his eyes – the poet in him shrank from anything hideous. Only when Paul had dressed himself did he open them once more. 'You too have felt their whips,' he murmured.

After sitting silent for a while, Nero beckoned to Lucius and said in a low voice, 'Whipped like a flea-ridden mongrel, yet he seems perfectly at ease, while I slope about with shadows under my eyes and haven't been able to sing a note for months... Can this god of his really smoke out the Furies?'

His failure with the priests had taught Lucius caution. 'That's what the evidence suggests. But it's for you to decide.'

Nero resumed control, asking sharply, 'What must my friend do to be forgiven?'

Paul answered jubilantly as though telling Nero he'd won first prize in a lottery. 'He's already been forgiven,' he said.

This brought a frown. 'I don't understand.'

'Nor do I in the sense I think you mean. However, I do believe I *know* and, if you ask me how, the answer is that 30 years ago, Christus enacted God's forgiveness. He played it out before our eyes.'

Whether Nero fully grasped his meaning is doubtful, but he evidently accepted the statement and passed on to practicalities.

Having been brought up to believe that, in any transaction, taking must be balanced by giving, he said cajolingly, 'My friend is not without power and wealth. He has publicly honoured his patron Apollo, he has influence with Caesar who, as *pontifex maximus*, can grant a new cult official status. He will readily reward this god of yours with honour and rich votive offerings.'

Paul smiled. 'Your friend need hand out no gold, shed no animal blood, raise no altar nor temple for, as I've said, he's already been forgiven. What he should do is learn more about the person who performed that act of general forgiveness and try to live as he lived.' He paused, perhaps expecting a further query. 'I shall be leaving very soon for Spain, but the friend who wrote the notes you have read – his name is John Mark – will gladly provide all you need. Annaeus here has his address.'

The meeting ended. Nero was puzzled about certain details but partially reassured and Lucius was relieved to think that he might soon resume his equanimity.

Two days later, under the porch of Lucius's house, Paul bade a hurried goodbye to the couple who had offered him safe shelter. His loom had been returned to the weaver who'd lent it, his scanty belongings packed into a canvas shoulder bag. They included letters to Lucius's family and, at Paul's request, a copy of Lucius's essay on Mercy in the author's hand.

Paul said he wouldn't have time to write, but would try to send Lucius a memento and token of thanks, while Lucius promised to find John Mark. After the two had clasped hands, Paul embraced Paula with Lucius's permission and thanked her once more for the knitted tunic which, he said smilingly, was saving his life.

They watched their friend, for so they now thought of him, turn into the road, proclaiming his welcome freedom with long fast strides. All three felt the poignancy of hurried farewells when so much of importance remains unspoken.

PART FIVE

Fire, deaths and their aftermath

O ne evening in the following July, my wife Acilia and I sat
chatting in our garden over a leisurely supper. The air was still
and sultry. Midges clustered over the fruit bowl, moths butted the
shades of our table lamps. With no appetite for the smoked venison
and pickles, we ate sparingly of myrtle berries in soured cream, while
idly watching lights go on in the city.

Acilia, her eyes sharper than mine, noticed an unusual shimmering
near the Aventine. She thought it came from an open-air torch light
party. We speculated who might be celebrating and decided that,
since we hadn't been invited, the party couldn't be up to much.

The mosquitoes becoming a nuisance. Acilia went in to prepare for
bed and, as I snuffed out the lamps, I noticed that the shimmering
had become a glow, pulsating and flecked with what looked like
flames. Perhaps a small fire, I thought. Our excellent fire-fighting
service would deal with it promptly. But we own an apartment block
in that district, so it seemed prudent to go and take a look.

Ten minutes later I found myself hurrying in the direction of
voices shouting, screaming, shrieking – frenziedly, imploringly – the
one word city-dwellers dread to hear: 'Water! Water! Water!' This is
the district of emporia, many of which stock timber and lamp oil.
Edicts to move them out had been resisted as costly and it was from
one such yard that flames were rising to the staccato of crackling
wood. What frightened me most was the blast of intense dry heat, as
from a baker's oven. Bunching my gown over nose and mouth, I
limped on. One more step, I thought, and I'll shrivel like an autumn
leaf.

Pumps on wheels plunged down up, down up, forcing water through in a race to drown 'the beast' – the firemen's name for a blaze – while buckets of water sloshed along a human chain to leather-gloved masked figures in high boots. Patrols darted about, bludgeoning flying sparks with vinegar-soaked matting.

The flames spread to a big warehouse. Crafty as steeplejacks, they edged up the facade and ignited the upper courses. When the building was gutted, the masonry quivered for a full minute as though reluctant to take the plunge, then dived in a cascade of brick and stone. The firemen cheered in the vain belief that the masonry would entomb the beast. I asked an officer holding a plan of the district when his men would be able to put out the fire. He gave me the look reserved for silly questions. 'A blaze this size, you can't put out. But we expect to contain it.'

Satisfied that our property was in no immediate danger, I walked home for a few hours' sleep. When I awoke, I rubbed my eyes in disbelief: the sun was rising in the north! An overnight wind had set the fire amok: the blaze had vaulted streets to gorge itself on poor people's easily swallowed wattle-and-earth houses. Then it had massed before the city's monumental centre, throwing up triumphant yellow-red banners into a throbbing lurid sky, beneath which cowering survivors pressed toward the city gates clutching their few pathetic treasures.

From Antium, where he had been visiting Poppaea, Nero rode back at a gallop. When he caught sight of the conflagration from high ground a mile from the city, those accompanying him attested to his horror and pain. His city, his people, his home – almost everything he valued – trembled on the knife-edge of destruction. Nero experienced shock on a panoramic scale and it jolted him out of his imagined alarms into confronting a real situation even more terrifying.

At Caesar's House he immediately conferred with Faenius Rufus, veteran officer and trained engineer, who showed him a sketch plan. Wind from the south-west was nudging the fire towards the historic centre around the Capitol. It had to be saved at all costs with firebreaks.

Nero hurried to a belvedere north of the Circus Maximus. Here seven-wheeled siege catapults, elephant-high, stood in line. Nero took charge of the teams and joined in the loading, heaving block after block into leather slings, ratcheting up the capstans to bend the catapults to near snapping point. At his signal, the arms flew free, hurling their missiles in a low arc at the houses targeted for demolition. Destroy in order to save. Stripped to the waist, dust and ash sticking to his sweat, Nero toiled 20 hours with only one short rest. By his example and words of encouragement, he extracted the utmost from his men.

In a dozen different streets, firemen struggled to save particularly important buildings as volunteers ran in to remove their contents. From the smoke filled vaults of Juno Moneta's temple, five volunteers – of which I was one – staggered out, bent double under the weight of crates of gold bullion. As for Lucius, he and his house slaves, clothes doused, linen masks over their lower faces, made half a dozen forays into the crumbling Tabularium in order to rescue the oldest, most precious records, bearing grape-harvesters' baskets strapped to their backs.

Of the Great Fire, everything that could be said and written has been said and written. Along with orphaned Romulus and Remus suckled by the she-wolf, it has joined the stories every child learns with his abc. Let it be recalled that the city burned for six days before the last flames were beaten out. Of 14 districts, three were totally destroyed, seven more partially destroyed, leaving only four undamaged. So many bodies were burned beyond recognition that the number of dead has never been ascertained, but it exceeded 100. The loss of property extended to every class: Nero and many senators lost their homes, I lost my block of apartments, many artisans their workshops and stock. People's minds were permanently singed too: there were many who succumbed to pathological depression. It is perhaps ridiculous on my part that I have never again been able to eat sour cream with myrtle berries.

No one's mental picture was more radically altered than Nero's. He had twice talked with John Mark, his haste to obtain forgiveness countered by unease at forsaking the god to whom he owed his musical gift and athletic victories. But the disaster that had left half his people and himself homeless had made such concerns no longer urgent. Those hateful flames so high they seemed to lick the stars had dimmed the Furies' torches for good. They had left behind a pall of smoke and veil of soot, acid and sour, which thickened the saliva. The skeleton of his house looked like a ripe fig hollowed out by wasps. Nero moaned repeatedly that he had found Rome marble and left it rubble.

At 27, he was too energetic a man to remain passive before chaos. Hardly had he slept off his week-long fire-fighting when he summoned to the big open-sided tent he had erected on the Quirinal 20 civil engineers and architects. Then and there, they put on paper plans and a timetable for removing the hundreds of tons of debris and rebuilding the devastated city centre.

The day after the fire succumbed to inanition, we never glimpsed the sun, and no one was to be seen in the rubble-strewn streets. People were adjusting to bleak reality: food scarce, water no less so, for the Aqua Claudia had collapsed. The next day saw traders carrying in vegetables, bread, eggs but, with full stomachs, came awareness that business was at a standstill and the livelihood of many would have to be built up afresh. Sulky gloom quickened to anger. It was unthinkable that a fire on this scale could have been an act of the gods. Someone had started it and whoever was the culprit must be found and punished. Artisan unions, clubs sharing religious rites and workmen's funeral associations turned out in force. Shouting their demands and chanting anthems, they marched up the Via Sacra towards Nero's canvas headquarters on the Quirinal Hill.

Two platoons of Praetorians armed with heavy clubs stood on duty guard a stone's throw from Nero's tent under order from Tigellinus.

Not having served in the army, he took fright seeing this restive crowd and overreacted. His men charged, laying about the marchers' shoulders with their clubs and quickly dispersing them.

The crowd's anger now turned against Tigellinus who was in any case unpopular. Those who, like me, had seen the fire in its early stages, recalled that it appeared to have originated in a stockyard used by a construction firm belonging to Tigellinus. Word went about that Tigellinus himself had started the fire in the yard in order to touch insurance. That explained his haste to silence the demonstration.

In my opinion, the idea was fantastical but, when it came to Tigellinus's ears, he realized that, in the city's present mood, he stood in serious danger and that, if he was to extricate himself, he must quickly find a scapegoat. The Nazarenes came to mind. If he could incriminate the sect, he would not only save his own skin, but also score off his rival Lucius.

Tigellinus obtained leave to question John Mark in Nero's open-sided tent on the Quirinal. Paul's friend was tall and looked younger than his 51 years. His brown eyes held a shy look and his left hand had stump fingers, which he did his best to conceal in his cuff. In contrast to Paul, he seemed very much the countryman ill at ease in the big city.

The gist of the questioning follows:

Tigellinus: At dinner time on the night of 19 July, my men made a routine check at the house of Harbour Master Firmius Gallus, a suspected Nazarene. You and five others of the same superstition were gathered around a table. The only items on the table were a jar of poor-quality wine and a cheap loaf. Questioned, you said you were sharing a *sacramentum*. Is that correct?

John Mark: Quite correct.

Tigellinus: You know of course that, every New Year, our Praetorian Guards take a solemn oath of loyalty to Caesar, and the name of that oath is *sacramentum*?

John Mark: I didn't know. How could I, having just arrived in Rome?

Tigellinus: But your table companions are residents, they most certainly knew. I put it to you that while fuddling yourselves with new wine, you poured ridicule on Caesar's elite guard.

John Mark: Not at all. I think you'd agree that a word can occasionally be given a new meaning.

Tigellinus: Yes, for sinister purposes – as a burglar calls theft redistribution of wealth... I pass on to the scrolls found in your lodging. You have admitted writing them. In one, you say you eagerly await the return of your teacher, deceased. But before he can reappear, and I quote, 'The sun will be darkened and the moon will refuse her light.' Elsewhere you say that Yeshua will wash men clean and again I quote, 'With wind and fire,' while the unclean will be 'swept away and burned.' I put it to you that this is the language of arsonists.

John Mark: Not so. We speak of fire as a visible image of spiritual cleansing.

Tigellinus: Tell that to those with third-degree burns! I turn next to the odd fact that two of your table companions recently sold their houses in Rome. Truly remarkable foresight!

John Mark: They sold them to relieve the very poor.

Tigellinus: I put it to you that everyone at that table on 19 July knew what was about to take place, and you were celebrating what you hoped would be the collapse of Roman power.

So much for the questioning of John Mark. It was for Nero to decide what action to take. Over the course of two short meetings, he had not warmed to John Mark as he had to Paul, but he could not imagine him as a turbulent incendiary. Nevertheless he found some of the revelations shocking and, when Tigellinus asked leave to force known Nazarenes to prove their loyalty to Rome, Nero agreed.

Some 50 of that sect, including eight women, were rounded up. John Mark was not among them as the Harbour Master had confirmed his alibi for the night of the fire. Led under guard to one of the temples that had escaped damage, they were lined up in front of a great marble statue of Jupiter. The temple priest explained that each in turn should step forward, dip a spoon in the silver bowl of wine beside the statue and sprinkle drops on the god's feet, then take the thurible and proffer incense to the god. Finally all should recite after him, sentence by sentence, a prayer in praise of Jupiter Almighty, greatest and best of the gods, lord of the heavens and protector of Rome. Five amongst them refused the wine, incense and prayer. Warned by the priest of the gravity of non-compliance and invited to reconsider, one of the five complied. The rest were led away to be held in custody until Cabinet met.

At the meeting, Tigellinus argued that the fire had begun at nightfall therefore eyewitness evidence could not reasonably be expected. However, the Nazarenes were known to extol destruction by fire, while Paul in so many words had admitted that he hoped to displace our gods with his. The plan was plain for all to see following the repudiation, bordering on insult, of the deities who brought glory to our city, and this at a moment when Palestine was seething with revolt. It could hardly be coincidence that the Nazarenes venerated a Palestinian magician. These facts taken together provided very strong circumstantial evidence of political subversion; he therefore demanded the full legal penalty: citizens to be beheaded, non-citizens burned alive.

Lucius asked for a brief recess. He had been puzzled by the Nazarenes' intransigence, for he shared the general view that the cult of one god need not preclude sacrifice to others. So he rushed to John Mark's scantily furnished attic room, to find him slicing vegetables for a midday meal. Hurriedly he explained a plan for saving the Nazarenes. 'We dispense orthodox Jews from worshipping our gods because Judaism is even older than our religion.' Since Yeshua was Jewish and much of his message conformed to Jewish law, he urged John Mark to confront Tigellinus and inform him that the teaching of the Nazarenes was a form of Judaism and should benefit from the same dispensation.

John Mark's reaction was to recoil as though stung by nettles. The knife fell from his fingers, he threw Lucius a wild-eyed look and clamped both hands to his forehead. Breathing heavily, he then slumped on a stool, head sunk on his chest. With the strong smell of onion pervading the room, Lucius found the scene grotesque. But no time could be lost. Adapting himself to the other's hypersensitivity, he gently explained the need to meet malevolence with cunning: it was probably his only chance of saving innocent lives.

It was like addressing a dummy: the head remained slumped, the arms hung loose and motionless. Lucius had to use all his self-control to resist the urge to give him a good shaking. The minutes passed, precious minutes that Tigellinus might well use to wind up proceedings.

At last the slumped figure stirred, shook itself briskly like a dog after a dip, and turned to face Lucius. 'We're a very small group struggling to keep our identity. Gnostics, Jews and the many, many followers of the boy Bacchus would like to assimilate our creed to theirs and swallow us up. I ask myself what Paul would have done. I'm fairly sure he'd have turned down your plan... I must do the same.'

Lucius felt disappointment edged with reluctant respect. He returned to Cabinet, saying that there were no new points he wished to raise. When the meeting ended, he had a private word with Nero, urging him to sleep on the evidence before passing judgement.

600 and more demonstrators on the slope below Nero's headquarters were still waiting noisily for the government to act. Crowd behaviour interests me and I had been asking questions of some of them. A number wanted revenge for lost lives and property, others were intent on forestalling a second fire. About the culprits' identity there were acrimonious differences. Some accused Parthians, whose Magi were reputed to worship fire; some the Mithraites, who baptise initiates in gore from the severed arteries of a bull; others with a little learning and a taste for numbers recalled that the nineteenth of July was the very day invaders from Gaul had sacked Rome 418 months and 418 days before, and therefore pointed an accusing finger at Rome's Gallic community. As for the Nazarenes, they were few in number and kept to themselves but, since they refused to worship Rome's gods, they too were now suspect.

Fear and helplessness excited the crowd. Each group wanted to incriminate its own supposed culprits, and therefore sought to discredit the others. As the hours passed, invective turned to fighting.

A rumour began to circulate that Nero favoured the Nazarenes because he had set Paul free. The crowd had been without food all day and, when Rufus addressed them, explaining with tact and his natural air of authority that Nero would announce his decision next morning, they were persuaded to go home.

I doubt whether Nero got any sleep that night. He was pacing anxiously when Rufus arrived at dawn to report. A still larger crowd had gathered and their mood was aggressive. The situation was in no way comparable with the Messalla riots. These people were not being egged on: their anger was spontaneous and deep-seated. Unless Nero identified and punished the arsonists, the people would almost certainly take matters into their own hands. Those who accused the Nazarenes would butcher the lot; those who suspected other minorities would do as much to them. 'If you decide on force,' declared Rufus, 'I will give the order, but I can't answer for all my men, since many lost kin in the fire. You personally will be in no danger. I can race you to the Camp by back streets.'

Lucius arrived on the Quirinal to find the crowd massed along the slope and working itself into a fury. He told himself they were baying like wolves hungry for human flesh until, remembering Burrus, he withdrew the comparison.

'Burn them!' roared the crowd. 'Burn, burn, burn. Roast the bastards alive, we want to hear them sizzle!'

At headquarters, a nervous Tigellinus was briefing his spies in case he had to run for his life. Nero looked pale and drawn. Lucius saw clearly the terrible dilemma facing him, which only he could resolve. He felt obliged to make one last appeal. 'Will you condemn the Nazarenes, who have every appearance of being scapegoats, and lose your reputation for justice?'

'It's support I need, not moralizing,' he replied sharply.

After further discussion with Rufus and Tigellinus, Nero emerged from the tent to face the crowd. Raising his arms for quiet, he announced that the guilty would be punished that very evening. The news was met with cheers and much self-congratulation.

Our forbears enacted that the two situations most dangerous to the city – armed riot and arson – be punished by fire. Tigellinus decided that the crowd's fury called for the punishment to be implemented in an awesome spectacle. He had blacksmiths run up cylindrical iron frames with a hinged section like those for protecting saplings from livestock. 18 were set in two lines in the park adjoining Nero's racetrack.

Just before nightfall, three horse-drawn haycarts arrived carrying the Nazarenes who were not Roman Citizens, 36 in all, one having hanged himself in prison. Each had been trussed in sacking, only his head left visible. One spectator, closer to the carts than me, claimed he heard the sound of voices singing a hymn. Two trussed bodies were hurled onto the ground by each of the iron cages.

Along the road from the Tiber, illuminated for the occasion with naphtha flares, surged a crowd of several thousand. They were marshalled by men of the watch as they neared the eastern end of the racetrack. The western end had been cordoned off for the *princeps*, his suite and the Guards band.

A bugler sounded a fanfare, signal for two soldiers at each of the cages to tip a trussed body, head first into the iron frame. Another bugle call and they applied a flaming torch to the top of the sacking, producing a sharp hiss followed by spurts of yellow-white flame. Wax had been rubbed into the hessian to render it what the law stipulates: a *tunica molesta*.

The crowd had the spectacle it came for: two lines of outsize torches, their flames reflected in the foliage of adjacent ilexes; 18 human beings agonizing as fire snatched at their feet and then plunged down their legs to their vital organs. As their screams slowly died away, the flames continued burning to the base of each cage to become a mourning torch.

Again the bugle sounded. A soldier at each cage hammered open the catch: the charred body was pulled out and dumped on the ground and then the second trussed victim was hoisted into the cage. They lit the top of the waxed sacking and the crowd savoured a repeat performance. I will dwell on that horror no longer; it does us no credit and is best forgotten.

Ten days or so had passed when I chanced to meet Paula in the street. Her smile was less bright than usual. When I said I hadn't seen Lucius lately, her brow creased. 'He's not well.'

'Asthma?' He had suffered an attack after his forays into the Tabularium.

'That has passed, but he's become angry with himself, discouraged. And, for once, I can't seem to help him.' Given the closeness of their marriage, I was surprised and hinted as much. 'I think I'm too close. I get drawn into what he's feeling and that adds to his pain. In another way I'm not close enough. He sees his so-called failure in man's terms: ideas and concepts I can't relate to.'

I looked in on Lucius next morning, to find him in his study, carefully cracking an occasional walnut in his fingers to get the kernel out whole, a habit of his when stressed. His eyes had a dull, defeated look.

I made myself comfortable and, since he showed no signs of wanting to unburden himself, I started speaking about what I thought might be his trouble. I told him how saddened I was by the loss of our oldest buildings especially the destruction of the temple of Vesta, where the sacred flame symbolizing Rome's hearth kept alight for centuries by dedicated virgins had been extinguished in the ruins.

He nodded and, with a catch in his voice, named other irreplaceable monuments, adding that he felt their loss all the more keenly for having been an unwitting accomplice. I asked him what he meant. 'I've spent much of my life defining the nature of a city, writing about it, lecturing about it. My views gained wide acceptance and were acted upon. And now, recent events have proved them inadequate. Worse than inadequate: wrong. Fatally wrong. And I can't see where I blundered.'

I reminded him how he had been fascinated by the idea of civic cohesion as soon as we came to Rome. 'We'd been in Rome just a week and were still goggle-eyed and disorientated, when Novatus announced that it was like 1,000 Cordubas rolled into one, but you said, 'No, it's different. Here people in the street don't nod to one another.'

'Your memory's sharper than mine... Corduba had grown like a plant but Rome, so it seemed to me, was wholly man-made. From 100 different places, with 100 different trades, men had chosen to come here to make a living. Intense competition made them give of their best and so they flourished. But they remained virtual strangers to one another, knew only a few neighbours by name. By and large they were discrete, each striving to go one better. And so I kept asking myself, how did this improbably huge and diverse city hold together?

'At law school, I realized that part of the answer was an excellent legal system. And with Attalus I came to believe that Spirit was nudging us towards fellowship – but this my friends wouldn't swallow so I kept it to myself.'

'You entered the Senate – that gave you new insight.'

'I saw the importance of cohabitation by *princeps* and Senate. The *princeps* especially would get above himself. In a small way, I tried to keep him down.'

'Don't be so modest. You opposed Gaius's demand for a throne in the House and Claudius's abuse of *lèse majesté*: you twice put your life on the line.'

He shrugged dismissively. 'Ancient history... Then came Nero.'

'Preceded, you're forgetting, by a certain lady.'

He cracked a walnut aggressively, frowning as the kernel broke. 'She held an up-down view of government that no one could shake. Cracks at the top spread downwards and, to prevent dissension, I lied to the Senate... With Nero we have a ruler who respects the law, allows freedom of expression and works easily with the Senate. That was the point where I defined civic cohesion in two parts: law and law-abidingness, *princeps* and Senate at peace.'

'You told me then that you hoped your views would become part of the way people thought and so strengthen the cohesion you claimed to define.'

He nodded with a sad ironic expression. 'The Messalla riots blew up and Nero believed it his duty to execute the guilty. I managed to show him that his conscience was badly informed – by his mother, though I did not name her – and that mercy, far from being a sign of weakness, could do much to strengthen cohesion.'

'Then came that worrying general failure of nerve.'

'A falling birth-rate coinciding with exaggerated individualism led to parochial behaviour, petty obstruction as a form of self-assertion. No law had been broken yet here was cohesion beginning to crack... Our answer took the form of encouraging citizens to look outward to the provinces, and to the future. Concord was restored until the Great Fire. Then the good people of Rome screamed for the blood of scapegoats. Their demand was met. On the night that mere suspects – their guilt unproven – became human torches law, law-abidingess and justice crashed down like so many statues from their pedestals. Anyone with a grain of humanity must grieve. I grieve too, my spit tastes of bitter aloes.'

'You saw that civic cohesion isn't justice or fellowship or good government but animal self-preservation... But shouldn't you have seen that years ago when you lied about Agrippina's death to the Senate?'

'The two cases are different. I was trying to save a life. Did save it.' A short silence followed. When Lucius spoke again, it was with uncharacteristic hesitancy. 'My attempt to define cohesion has crumbled. So what do I do next? What does my hard-headed businessman brother advise?'

'If I'd bought into wheat and a run of poor harvests brought me no return, I'd switch to metals.'

Lucius threw me a shocked look. 'Not scuttle?'

'Turn your analytical eye on a less elusive subject.'

Here we were interrupted. Lado came in to announce that a messenger had arrived with an immediate summons from Caesar. Lucius had risen to his feet before Lado clarified that the summons was for me. We looked at each other in surprise and, when we came to say goodbye, Lucius thanked me for what he termed my understanding with a warmth I found touching.

Nero was still based in his open-sided tent on the Quirinal. Here he worked, ate and slept to show his identification with the homeless. Planks on trestles made tables, bales of straw served as seating. Clad in an athlete's knee-length tunic, he stood at one of the tables, looking from the plans spread there to the district immediately below where, to the ring of pickaxes and rasp of crane pulleys, the first new street was beginning to take shape. Architects and draughtsmen busied themselves with compasses, dividers and set squares. I had the impression of a team in good heart working flat out; when one of his recommendations proved its worth, Nero would break into song.

Half an hour passed before Nero had time for me. In order to rebuild a city, land, materials and workmen are not enough. Coin in quantity is needed, and he had sent for me to arrange a loan. First he explained his intentions: every new street at least six yards wide, every new house to be of terracotta and brick, with an agreed proportion of fireproof Alban stone. Each must have a flat-roofed porch, where buckets of sand and fire-fighting gear provided by the municipality would be stored. Each house would have an inner courtyard and garden to reduce the risk of any fire spreading.

'All the provinces, save the poorest, have agreed to help in kind or coin. We'll discuss that presently. But first there's a private project I want you to hear about.' Summoning a servant, he sent for Poppaea to join him.

Poppaea had returned to Rome on Nero's orders only two days after the fire had been extinguished. Shaken as much by the loss of her home as by the acres of twisted ugliness, and fearing the acidic air would harm her complexion, she felt inclined to order her carriage back to Antium. But when she reached Nero's headquarters, in place of the shifty-eyed husband of recent months, she was welcomed with a strong-armed embrace and a long loving look. He had regained self-control, had returned to his old affectionate self. Her months of exclusion were over, she could resume a normal married life. At her request, Nero had a tent for her set up close to his.

She glided in, lithe as ever, her figure a shade fuller than I remembered, looking assured and happy. She kissed her husband on both cheeks and it struck me that they appeared as a honeymooning couple. Nero introduced me – incorrectly – as 'the man with the money bags' and suggested that Poppaea should tell me how she envisaged their new home. First and foremost, she wanted her home to be spacious. This was only natural, for she'd spent her early years in cramped lodgings. Waste land near the Circus Maximus was available and could be reclaimed without difficulty. There was enough for the house proper, a large garden and an artificial lake.

Poppaea stated that she wanted a façade of three bays on either side of a domed central hall. I interrupted to object that a dome would prove very costly and technically difficult: so far, it had been managed successfully on only one temple. It might also strike the populace as overly ostentatious.

She lifted her chin haughtily. 'Since Nero is rebuilding Rome, he has a right to ostentation.' There would be two music rooms, she continued, one for song and lyre recitals, another – larger – for the water-powered organ her husband had designed and helped to build. Each bathroom would have three taps for cold, hot and sulphurous water. She wanted a nursery – her eyes met Nero's – with walls cushioned in blue silk. Her choice of words and rhythmical phrasing made even the central heating sound poetic.

'Tell Mela about the dining room,' said Nero.

'A mosaic floor depicting the fruits of earth and sea.'

'And a ceiling painted with the Four Seasons that revolves, driven by water power.'

As they exchanged satisfied looks, Paula tripped in, a little out of breath. She bowed to Nero and gave Poppaea a sisterly embrace. Nero had taken to using Paula's teasing manner against her. 'You're a danger to the State,' he complained. 'The one moment in the day when I see my wife you want to drag her away.'

Paula drew herself up condescendingly. 'There's a law lays down that Caesar shall share his wife with his people.'

'Nonsense!'

'It's inscribed on the bronze tablets. Lucius will look it out for you.' Then she turned to Poppaea. 'We must hurry or be late for our rounds.' They set off for the damaged Temple of Neptune, where severely injured victims of the fire lay on makeshift bedding, their burns eased with sap of aloes. Many had lost one or more relatives. They were the heroes of those horrific six days yet they felt forgotten, so Paula had persuaded Poppaea to visit them daily. Just to see that unforgettably beautiful face and to hear a few words of sympathy helped them through the long days.

Nero and I got down to the matter in hand. After reviewing Nero's desiderata, I summed up. 'You want perfection and like to astonish. Neither comes cheap.' He admitted as much with a laugh, then gave me exact figures for the collateral he could provide. Before I agree a loan, I assess the health of the borrower. Three months earlier, I wouldn't have lent him a piece of string but now Nero's obvious determination and measured confidence suggested that he was again the *princeps* of his first years. I believed I could interest a consortium of bankers, but of course did not say so then. I pointed out that money had been flowing out in the wake of the fire, that the Levant was stealing some of our markets, but I would do my best on his behalf.

He rose to his feet signifying that our talk was over. This was the hour when he joined builders on site, sharing their manual work until nightfall. As I prepared to leave, he called out, 'Where's Annaeus these days?'

'The philosopher in him has taken a tumble.' He shook his head, then was gone.

Lucius learned from his secretary that Nero was drafting an edict forbidding Nazarenes from proselytizing within the walls. Recalling Paul's farewell words, he hurried to warn John Mark, who had moved to still cheaper lodging, a minute attic room reached by rickety stairs smelling of boiled cabbage. On the table lay opened scrolls and kid parchment half covered with writing.

On hearing Lucius's news, John Mark gave a long sigh. 'I wonder whether it applies to the written word.'

'Why? Have you been writing?'

'Not getting far, but Paul said I must put my memories in writing.' Seating Lucius on a rickety stool, he explained that he'd been ordering his notes. But he wasn't a writer: he'd left school at 14 to enter the family tile-making business. He drew out from the cupboard a crumpled manuscript which he smoothed and read out:

> Simon Peter said to his friends 'Let Yeshua's mother Mary go out from our midst for women are not worthy of life.' And Yeshua said, 'See I will draw her so as to make her male so that she also may become a living spirit like you males. For every woman who has become male will enter the kingdom of heaven.'

John Mark's mouth screwed up as though he'd swallowed vinegar. 'Gnostic invention! Yeshua never said anything of the sort, but Gnostics are numerous and powerful and their garbled teaching is troubling our people... So it's a race for the truth.' After much hesitation, he spoke up. 'Now you're here, would it be too much trouble to give me some tips? As an experienced writer.'

Believing that writing cannot be taught, Lucius normally declined such requests but he felt sorry for this stranger and warmed to his modesty. John Mark admitted that he had thought of taking some Greek biography as a model. Lucius advised against: Greek biographers tended to choose some pet theme and forced their subject into that mould, squeezing the life out of them. He suggested instead Caesar's *Commentaries*, a straight account of what Caesar saw, did and said. No purple passages, no trimmings. He would lend him a copy. John Mark turned to the question of language. He'd been told to use Greek – but what style should he aim for?

'Who are you writing for?'

'The man in the street.'

'Then use the language of the street.'

When travelling through Palestine, recording what Yeshua said and did, there had been one or two others doing the same. He'd heard from Paul that they too had been told to produce a narrative. Ought he to return to Jerusalem and talk to them, to make sure his memories tallied with theirs?

Lucius was decisive. 'The best way to the truth is through more than one eyewitness narrative. Synoptically... So trust your own notes. Don't hum and haw. Start tomorrow.'

John Mark looked relieved. Then, in a burst of courage, he said, 'I'd be curious to hear your opinion of Yeshua.'

Lucius thought back to Paul's account of the man. 'He knew the law of his people inside out but went beyond it.'

'Yes?' said John Mark encouragingly.

'Goes beyond justice to mercy.'

'As a prerequisite to peace. Peace was a word he used often, and always with emphasis.'

'He castigates anger.'

'Like you, if I may say so. And again, like you, he abhors the mass murder we applaud as victory in the field.' Seeing he had his visitor's attention, John Mark continued with greater assurance. 'But he wasn't content with words. He knew words are soon eroded by old habits. If men were to put his words into action, the dead-weight of habit had to be lifted from their shoulders. And only one fulcrum could do it.' Passing beyond what he'd written in the Notes, John Mark explained that under Jewish law, unlike Roman, one man could pay the penalty of another by taking his place. Yeshua had chosen to do this.

John Mark began to describe Yeshua's trial but Lucius became too ruffled to hear him out. 'You're saying that, though he hadn't done anything wrong, he lent himself to a hideous miscarriage of justice!

He must have been mad!'

'You forget: he was doing it to save others from trial and condemnation.' John Mark amplified his point but it all sounded remote from common sense to Lucius and, when it emerged that the odious trial took place in a Roman court, he lost patience. 'Who was the judge?' he demanded.

John Mark told him. It was a name known to Lucius, one of which he would have preferred not to be reminded. He had been reprimanded and dismissed for treating Samaritans with unacceptable cruelty: a disgrace to the service and, on top of it all, a native of Tarrago. ' I suggest you omit the judge's name from your account.'

John Mark looked surprised. 'You recommended detail.'

'It would bring the Roman judicial system into disrepute.'

Lifting the oppressive weight of habit, substitution of the innocent for the guilty, the choice of silence in face of false witnesses – at so many preposterous notions asserted in a tiny room, Lucius began to feel a sickening claustrophobia. He asked John Mark for a cup of water. This had to be fetched from a tap on the ground floor and the room filled with the stench of cabbage when John Mark opened the door. Lucius had half a mind to cut and run, but two mouthfuls of cold water and shame at his cowardice kept him where he was.

John Mark started again with what appeared to be an unrelated topic. 'Paul used to talk to me about man's need for a guide. Socrates, Epicurus, your Zeno and Attalus, Plato as interpreted by Cicero and so on. One teaches this, another that, but none with sufficient authority to convince more than a handful that he is the one sure guide. In their predicament, some men wished and prayed for truth. If only guidance could come from a god. Paul told me that you incline to some such belief, but only the few with learning and leisure can arrive at that. For others, something plainer is needed, namely a person who teaches righteousness and lives up to his teaching day after day to a more than human degree. Such a person might convince even the uneducated.'

John Mark paused and suggested another cup of water or something to eat.

Lucius shook his head. 'I'm feeling better. And what you say interests me.'

'Men were given this longing for guidance. In my country, we see it in our prophets; the Greeks in Herakles, who repeatedly went to the rescue of those struck by disaster, and in Aesculapius, who cured the incurable. They held them to be gods and built shrines in their honour. They believed Paul to be Mercury: always this longing for visible certainty.'

Lucius pursed his lips. 'In Rome we're too level-headed for that.'

'Are you? You believe Mars begot Romulus, and Julius Caesar claimed descent from Venus. In your eastern provinces, you call Nero "Son of a god". If God were to send us an envoy who wouldn't be written off as just another wonder-worker, an envoy whose teaching would be authenticated by his actions, he must be different in kind from those I've described. There was only one solution. God himself must become the envoy.'

'That would be madness!' Lucius almost shouted. 'God transcends this world and everything in it.'

But John Mark continued to the end. 'God would take the form of a man and live here as we do.'

Lucius, appalled, threw up his hands. 'Impossible. A contradiction in terms. Worse – blasphemy. God of the mountains and seas, of the stars and planets squeezed into 20 ounces of brain in a sack of offal!'

'Yet our animal side is of God's own making... There is something else you should hear. The name of this envoy, the man who is God, is Yeshua.'

Lucius felt his chin drop and stared at the other in silent stupefaction.

'Paul thought you'd be shocked.'

'What else did he say?'

'That you see things as he did when young, in terms of the law.'

'Some sense at last. I'm proud to be a lawyer. It is we lawyers who are called to preserve common sense in an often foolish world.'

Lucius calmed down in the ensuing pause. 'If I follow you correctly, you're asking me to believe that the prisoner condemned to death by Procurator Pontius was God in the form of man.'

John Mark nodded twice. 'I'm afraid I've offended you.'

'No – and if you had, it wouldn't matter. What matters is that my plate just now happens to be heaped with injustice and the last thing I want is a second helping.'

In the long silence that followed, Lucius became aware that John Mark had sunk into deep gloom. He thought, I came on a protective mission and I've ended by adding to his troubles. He assumed a softer tone. 'At first I was drawn to a god with power to forgive and bring inner peace. But please understand, of a god who can lend himself to a monstrous act of injustice, I want to hear no more.'

He made to leave, grasping the hand John Mark offered him and pressing it warmly. 'Be careful whom you talk to. Tigellinus will be having you watched. And I wish you success with your narrative.'

Nero promised a phoenix trophy to the first district to arise from the ashes. With this and other incentives, his rebuilding programme acquired a momentum of its own. On every side, scaffolding rose, sand and lime were mixed into concrete and sloshed into wooden frames. Whenever a new apartment block was inaugurated, Nero would be present, always with Poppaea, who enjoyed sharing his new popularity.

Lucius had no advice to offer about reconstruction and found himself bogged down in mental quagmires. It was from Poppaea that he had glimpses of the happy evenings that fate had offered Nero and his wife in the fourth year of their marriage. In a house lent by a friend, Nero would accompany Poppaea's songs on the lyre or cithara and join her in duets: while he fitted the first pipes to his mechanical water organ, Poppaea would sketch designs for the interior of their new house.

A month before her child was due, Poppaea left for Antium. Nero was to join her nearer the expected date. One night she woke with severe migraine. Unable to strike a spark from the flint at her bedside, she rose without a lamp, intending to fetch a meadowsweet mixture to soothe her pain. In the darkness she miscalculated her step, tripped and fell heavily. Her cries brought help; she was carried back to bed and her doctor summoned. The child had been damaged and Poppaea had severe internal bleeding which he could do nothing to staunch. The end came eight hours later.

When he heard the ghastly news, Nero broke down in tears and for three hours could do nothing but sit alone, head slumped in his arms. Then he rode for Antium to bring back her body. At the elaborate state funeral, the populace marvelled at the huge quantities of fragrance: ambergris, jasmine oil, myrrh and other perfumes costlier than gold sweetened the air around the pyre. What I remember was Nero's moving eulogy of his beautiful wife, and his declaration that she had gone to join the gods.

Lucius of course called at once to offer condolence and listened helplessly as Nero intensified his grief by describing his loss. To Poppaea, he had been able to say whatever passed through his mind, though she would sometimes tick him off for grossness. She had borne with his insults and accusations through the worst of his illness. Her white lies over money had somehow made him love her the more. Not for nothing was her hair the colour of amber for she herself possessed the magnetic quality of amber. Irresistible, irreplaceable. Now he felt helpless, as though he'd lost the use of an arm or leg.

What Nero found that he missed especially was the inability to express his artistic side through talking to Poppaea about the best of the work being produced in Rome. He invited his Poets' Circle to meet more often, always in the evening, the hardest time to get through alone. The members read, discussed and criticized one another's latest productions. My son Lucan, a member of the Circle, had chosen to write a fierce epic about the war between Julius Caesar and Pompey, but most of his contemporaries followed the fashionable poet of the moment, Callimachus of Alexandria, who excels in allusiveness and displays of recondite learning. So much of their work contained names of forgotten heroes, rarely-invoked deities, place names fallen into disuse, mountains and streams culled from antique gazetteers. Nero more often than not followed that fashion. In Lucius's opinion he could produce well-turned lines worthy of an anthology but he lacked a distinctive poetic vision.

These evenings with like-minded companions helped him through the immediate aftermath of losing Poppaea. Among older members of the Circle, one stood out. Titus Petronius Niger, of senatorial rank, had recently returned from governing Bithynia. In his late fifties, he lived apart from his wife in a spacious house outside the walls, spending his inherited fortune freely on rare objects and on private performances by his troupe of actors. He was a connoisseur of fine living and a student of human eccentricities.

Yet nothing in Titus Petronius Niger's appearance suggested the connoisseur: heavily built, a big jutting nose, cheeks beginning to sag, small sharp eyes with an impudent look. His knowledge of poetry was encyclopaedic and he could cite apposite lines for any situation. Though he had not yet read his own verse in public, he brought a refined critical faculty to bear on others' work: he was merciless when it came to a line that didn't scan, a short vowel treated as long or a hackneyed adjective. His preferred authors were the old comic playwrights who treat the seamy side of life and he had no patience with pastorals. 'Don't your shepherds ever smell sour or step in a turd?' Likewise with the elegies of timid lovers. 'Who laid down that poetry should stop at the navel?' he would bellow.

He gave occasional parties about which little was known except that they were unconventional and reserved for a favoured few. The young poet Persius, never afraid to put a direct question, asked what was needed to qualify as a guest and was told that guests had to be prepared to cross the Rubicon.

Nero became curious about Petronius's other life but the older man kept his distance until one day after the Circle had dispersed he approached Nero with studied casualness. 'I suspect your evenings are sometimes dull. I'd ask you to my next little gathering except that it will go on until dawn and I hear you need your full eight hours – for the body beautiful' – the last words were spoken with tongue in cheek.

Manliness alone would have induced Nero to accept.

Ten guests came to the party, the youngest were Nero and my unruly son Lucan, about whose epic Petronius deigned to show interest. A few had ruddy predatory faces, the others a blasé look and the pallor induced by high living. It was from Lucan that I learned the run of events.

They were received by Petronius in a deliberately offhand way with none of the usual 'so delighted you found time to come' greetings and passed to roguish-looking servants who allotted them places under a portico, where couches facing tables in a sweeping curve looked onto topiary sloping to a large pool fed by a marble boy making water.

The servants returned carrying appetizers upon platters of pewter, not the customary silver. Exchanging sly looks, they bent over each guest, almost touching his cheek, and in a conspiratorial whisper recommended as aphrodisiac the trout eggs on roundels of crisp toast and the pâté of boar sweetbreads: Lucan spied one putting the tip of his tongue into a guest's ear.

From the adjoining hall a grey-haired master of ceremonies swaggered in: despite a preposterous red cloak trimmed with silvered tassels, his expression was solemn and self-important. Banging a table for silence, he gave his name as Sublimus and announced that, in Petronius's house, the drinking of wine was treated as a spiritual experience. He would be their guide.

A servant passed among the guests with a jug of white wine. 'No more than a finger,' cautioned Sublimus. 'We want no boozing here .. First savour the fragrance.' He lifted his goblet reverently to his nose. 'The moment of encounter, a new acquaintance. Scent of a yellow rose, warmth of amber. A hint of wonders to come. Linger over this. Anticipation is perhaps the supreme pleasure.' He eyed the company severely until their faces expressed attentive compliance.

'Now we taste. A few drops, very few, to roll on the tongue. Picture the grape as a buoy on which we float to new, less troubled lands. Let us share what we see. You, sir.' He extended a hand invitingly.

The designated guest giggled: 'A calm lake at dawn, with one white sail.'

'And a mauve haze,' added another.

'For me there is rhythm,' said a third. 'Gentle rhythm, like a poem by Callimachus.'

Sublimus raised rapturous eyes, then bowed his appreciation of the last spoken. 'You, sir, have a palate of rare refinement.'

The servant dispensing the wine had been looking increasingly cross and now strode up to Sublimus. 'Tell you what it tastes of. Gooseberries on the turn... with a hint of shoe leather.'

The master shuddered and moved the man away with a reproving look. 'Rise, man, rise! Give your soul a chance.' He turned to the guests. 'Breathe in the bouquet and sip again. Wine likes to be approached slowly, with good manners. Now depth is added to your pleasure. Share this new sensation.'

While the guests rolled their tongues and translated taste into beautiful phrases, Sublimus was surreptitiously sloshing wine into his glass and gulping it down. Gradually his speech became slurred and his phrases disjointed until the servant complained that he could not understand a word he was saying. 'Moron!' snapped the master, glowering at him fiercely. 'Prepare yourself: a vision is about to take form.' Downing one more glassful, he turned to the garden, spreading his arms wide. 'The promised moment approaches. Wine has lifted us to a higher plane.'

From the darkness emerged a procession of dancers: youths playing panpipes, girls rattling tambourines, followed by two tall figures masked with horned goat-heads escorting a very plump jovial-looking man bare to his protruding paunch, head crowned with bunches of black grapes that dangled like locks over his round cheeks. As they danced along the open side of the portico, Sublimus joined them, happily waving a hand, but very unsteady on his feet.

'Moderation ... the golden mean. Keep it spiritual. Extremely, exaltingly spiritual.' Then in a sudden booming tone: 'Tow the middle line.' By extending his arms as a guide and with exaggerated concentration succeeding in taking three or four steps forward, only to veer wildly to one side, he was saved from stumbling by the nearest pipe-playing youth, who led him away presumably to sleep it off.

With a glance at his major domo Petronius signalled for supper to be served. New guests like Lucan expected a then-fashionable delicacy, peacock tongues in savoury sumach, but Petronius evidently scorned the conventional. Servants dished out in an offhand manner undercooked beef in thick pastry, slabs of wild boar and whole young partridges. No fish, no sauces, only artichokes in oil and strong vinegar.

One guest politely complimented his host on the artichokes, saying they had evidently been gathered, as the gourmet Frantinus advises, just as the inner leaves were turning mauve. Petronius frowned. 'It's solid nosh. Let it speak for itself.' After which no one dared mention food.

The dancers withdrew, leaving the party more relaxed, guests enjoying their meal and exchanging thoughts on what they had heard and seen. This continued some time until a new performer stepped forward. Well built, wearing a senator's gown, his strong face marked with mascara to emphasize the brows, he was introduced by a now sober Sublimus as a famous doctor of natural science.

'I begin to speak.' His voice was deep, his tone solemn. 'Who begins? What begins? Words begin. My words. And what are words? Breath, shaped. What is breath? Breath is air in motion. I draw in my breath, I expel it. What do I expel? Air in motion. I fall asleep, I snore – disturbing to my bedmate, or bedmates as the case may be. What is snoring but air in motion? My stomach feels distended. I release air in motion, that is to say, wind. Call burping a north wind. There is also a south wind, not demonstrable in polite society. What have all these winds in common? They're essential to life. Can't do without them.

'Man is a microcosm. Don't ask how or why, just take it from me. Therefore – note the therefore – wind is essential to the cosmos.

What drives clouds to release rain that fills the rivers that fill the sea? Wind. What pollinates trees and cops? Wind. Everywhere in the cosmos wind. But what, you ask, of fire-belching volcanoes? They too are produced by wind: see my essay "Volcanoes: the hidden truth."

Here Nero and Lucan began to laugh aloud. They knew Lucius had published a youthful essay which he now regretted, claiming that in caves and fissures of certain mountains wind builds up with such force that they drove flaming lava out of the summit.

"To return to you and me. How can we best fulfil ourselves? How to climb to our pinnacle of being? How else, I answer, but with wind, with words. What words? Obviously those containing most air. Words that bubble, soar, skim the immaterial. Words like Uninterruptability, Omnitranscendoimmanence and my own favourite – Ultraincomprehesibility.' Bowing deeply, he acknowledged the applause and departed.

Evidently familiar with this performance, Petronius gave all his attention to his guests' faces, assessing individual reactions. By now they were getting accustomed to the party's unusual tone, applauded the satire on Lucius and beckoned for their glasses to be filled.

Ripe randy-making cheeses were served, with plum brandy to chase them, before the next performer came on, a muscular young man with curly blond hair – visibly a wig – a panther skin draped over his right shoulder and carrying an ivory eight-string cithara. He bowed, twice flexed the biceps of his free arms, sat on the ground cross-legged, turned his instrument upside down and began to tune it. After some moments of clowning – snapping a string and fumbling the business of replacing it – he leaned right back and lifted his legs until his feet squared up to the face of the cithara. He then began to pluck the strings with his toes, at first discordantly, then as expertly as a virtuoso with his fingers. From there he broke into recitative, pronouncing the tender words of Nero's most popular love song with a ghastly nasal twang, as though he were suffering from a heavy head cold.

Everyone was watching Nero. They knew he didn't mind literary lampoons if they were clever, but this was face-to-face mocking. But after his first surprise he settled down to laugh as loudly as everyone else.

A pause followed, then the same young man reappeared, divested of panther skin and cithara, and in a confiding tone started to share his views about animals. 'Some at least understand what we say and their feelings can easily be hurt. When they hear a boy scolded as a filthy little beast for guzzling his food like a pig, they become quite upset. You see, they're fond of us humans and would like to get closer. Mammals especially, since we have in common our beautiful mammas.' Here he cupped his nipples and agitated them. 'It's for us with, dare I say it – our superior intelligence, to make the first move.

'So when my companion left me – artful little bitch – my mistake, that word may offend and I retract – I turned elsewhere. I was looking for someone playful, a sporting type like me, not averse to high jinks. I'm happy to say I've found her, and my wishes – my desires – are fulfilled. We get along you might say swimmingly. If you're interested, you might care to meet her.'

Curious and glad to walk off a heavy meal, guests rose and followed him between clipped box bushes down to the pool, lit now by pine torches. The animal-lover stripped and dived into the pool, presently bobbing up with his arms round the neck of a porpoise. 'Isn't she a beauty? Presently, if you listen closely, you'll hear her tell me how much she loves me – in her own language of course.' With that, he swam off, the porpoise, some six feet in length, gliding beside him, churning the water with her stubby nose. After circling the pool twice, the man clasped Myrrha to him, legs astride her lower body. Some of the guests found this strong meat; they exchanged hesitant glances. But voyeurism prevailed and soon they were crouching down for a closer look.

Sounds began to rise from the joined figures: shrill peeps, bass sighs and lingering moans. The man surfaced for air, then returned to nuzzle Myrrha more closely and fondle her breasts. The sounds quickened and became more intense. Presently the young man pulled himself out of the pool, shook water from his hair and, looking well pleased, spoke feelingly of Myrrha's firm, supple body. 'Animals are too intelligent to say "yours" and "mine". So if anyone among you would like to know her better, give me a nod and I'll introduce you.'

The youths and girls who had accompanied Bacchus now reappeared, this time in weird costume: dhotis, chain-mail tunics, loose trousers, veils, hoods, yashmaks, flower tiaras, tall waving crests of osprey feathers. Racing down to the pool, they laid inviting hands on the guests. By now these were eroticized and needed no urging to single out a girl or youth to their liking and disappear into the dark. So Petronius's party ended as most wild parties begin.

For information I needed in putting together his loan, Nero had referred me to Tigellinus. I first went to see him at a time when Nero had attended three of Petronius's parties. After giving me the figures I needed, he asked with a worried look what I thought of Nero's new interest.

I said it was normal for a young man, strictly brought up and having lost the wife he loved, to enjoy a bit of night life. 'As long as he doesn't try to repay Petronius in kind,' I added. 'That would cost him millions.'

The Sicilian looked unconvinced. 'It's the people he meets that worry me. They're scoffers,' which I translated as 'men who will scoff at me.'

I shrugged off his alarm. 'All they're looking for is a belly laugh and a slice of tenderloin.'

In the world of horses, the first thing you learn is that you can't fool around with nature. For all his uppishness, Tigellinus respected the norms. 'I'm not so sure. Nero asked the point of the cabaret skits and Petronius said, "To lower the threshold of shame." That can take him into deep waters, wouldn't you say?'

'Perhaps he's just preparing Nero for the day he reads his off-colour poetry to the Circle.'

I thought no more about the matter until Lucius averted to it. He had found Nero in excellent spirits at Cabinet, though once or twice with a hangover, and enthusiastic about the 'revels' – Petronius's word. But he doubted whether Nero would be satisfied for long with erotica and a certain sloe-eyed Circassian with a double-jointed back who had caught his fancy.

'What puzzles me,' my brother continued, 'is Petronius's character. He governed Bithynia ably and honestly, staunchly defends the Senate's privileges, but is nearly always crying down and disparaging. His clan name you know is Niger, and he's certainly quick to denigrate. Beneath the surface, I detect a current of deep personal dissatisfaction. Yet he has everything: distinguished ancestry, wealth, status as a former consul.'

There was Petronius's purchase at auction of a wine dipper made of amortized fluorspar. Did he really value it as the price paid – 300,000 sesterces? Could it really impart a hint of myrrhine to wine, as he said, or did it amuse him to take people in with a bogus claim? Was he trying to demonstrate that 300,000 sesterces – what people imagine as the gateway to untold joys – can buy no more than a stone implement for ladling out juice of grapes that will quickly pass through the bladder, leaving not a trace? Was he a fribble or wrecker? And if a wrecker, why should such a man take an interest in Nero, healthy, positive-thinking and barely half his age?

'Curiosity,' I suggested, 'and the attraction of opposites.'

'Maybe you're right.' He shrugged and sighed. 'These days I'm so sunk in gloom I can't think clearly.'

When entering Petronius's house, guests are expected to leave behind rank, family and honours, so Nero was treated like any other guest and he welcomed the resultant informality.

One evening at supper he found himself at his host's table, with Lucan as a third. Attacking his teeth with a silver toothpick, Petronius enquired what he thought of his troupe. Nero said he admired their versatility but found some of their sketches improbable.

'They're taken from life, every one of them. And life itself is improbable. But each has a theme, as you'll see in a moment.'

Lamps in the portico were turned down and the short two-character sketch that followed I give as Lucan described it to me.

A young man, earnest but unassured; a girl, pretty, a dreamy look in her eyes. He tells the girl he's wild about her and proposes marriage. 'I may be just a gardener but I'm well proportioned... Where it matters.' He leers suggestively and is met with a look of disgust.

'That kind of talk will get you nowhere. You must know that I write poetry and value only what is refined. My future husband must protect me from what is crude and commonplace. He will be a soldier.'

The man looks discouraged, ruminates, then slowly perks up. 'Were I to join the legions, would you take me as your husband?'

She looks him up and down reflectively.

'You must serve with gallantry, then come to me wearing a plumed helmet and lay it humbly at my feet.'

The gardener pulls at his hair doubtfully, blows out his lips, sucks them in – this several times. Then, with gusto. 'Agreed.'

We see him marching, counter marching, then learning to make sword thrusts. Lights are dimmed, then go up to reveal the gardener in coat of mail, looking assured, wearing a scarlet plumed helmet. He lays the helmet at her feet.

The girl is pleased. 'My hero!' She allows him to give her a chaste kiss.

'There is something I must tell you,' says the man. 'Last summer I was wounded in action. Hit by a Parthian arrow.'

'Poor dear. Where? In the shoulder?'

'Lower.'

'In the chest.'

'Lower.' The girl begins to look anxious. 'Where it might matter to some! But not to a poet.'

She draws back, drained of warmth. 'You make a mistake. A poet deals in perfection, therefore anything incomplete or missing will jar. It would silence her muse forever.'

'But you promised... if I laid a plumed helmet at your feet.'

'How earthy you are! Don't you see I was speaking in symbols?'

She pulls the plumes from his helmet one by one and hands it back to him. 'Your thoughts would never commune with mine.'

Head bowed, between sadness and anger, he plods off.

Petronius poured more wine for Nero and Lucan. 'When young people believe they're in love, most often they're imposing a fantasy on each other. In effect acting out a falsehood. Why does that happen? Because when they were children their spinster nursemaids locked Priapus in a cupboard and warned them never, never to open it.

'Here we reinstate Priapus and the primacy of the physical. Where do meat and wine belong? Down in our bellies, not in upturned moonish eyes. When a philosopher encapsulates the universe in half a dozen slick lines, is that wisdom or absurdity? When we hand our coin to the priests, is that piety or buying insurance? Here we abhor such cant.'

He turned to Nero. 'How do you find that little Circassian piece?'

Nero's eyes brightened. 'She can bend and twist and coil like a cobra. She can knot a cherry stalk with her tongue.' Then, more dully, 'But she has almost no Latin.'

'So?'

'I can't say I know her.'

'Keep her like that. A cobra.' He then described a short cruise he proposed to make on his yacht with half a dozen friends. Would Nero care to join him? Feeling just then like a change of scene, Nero enquired the dates and, finding them convenient, accepted.

Eight days later, Nero stood on the fore-deck of a well-appointed yacht, watching the hills of Rome slowly recede as the Tiber widened. In contrast to Petronius's older, sophisticated dinner guests, his fellow passengers were well-built young sportsmen, one a prize-winning stunt rider, easygoing and eager to talk racing and athletics.

Petronius divided his time between the poop, talking to crewmen and his cabin, where he would touch up his latest verses before joining his guests in late afternoon to outline their evening's entertainment. Six numbered pavilions had been set up on shore. His guests would throw dice to see who would go to which pavilion. In each would be found a desirable female – not your common or garden art. 'Well-equipped as you are, they'll expect you to give of your best. It should be amusing. But remember – ask no names, give no names. Strictly carnal.'

Wine was served from a silver bowl with the precious fluospar dipper, in which Nero detected a lacing of aphrodisiac. Petronius returned to his cabin and the talk turned to transsexual games – and brawls – and to sexual exploits: how many laps you could take your filly, the ability of a certain Indian to prolong his pleasure for three hours, and more of the same.

At dusk the yacht cast anchor and a dinghy took the men ashore to find the pavilions furnished with every kind of luxurious fitting, the linen scented, the ladies elegantly dressed, well spoken and cool – at first.

Next morning, with the yacht under way, Petronius came to the main cabin, listened with relish to details of his guests' exploits and then murmured almost casually, 'It may interest you to learn that each of those agreeable ladies is the unsatisfied or neglected wife of a senator.'

General stupefaction. One man laughed nervously, another looked angry. 'Why didn't you tell us?'

'And ruin your evening?'

Nero disliked being tricked and feared the consequences. 'If this gets out, there'll be trouble.'

'On the contrary. Husbands will be delighted to find their wives for once in a good mood.'

A swim from the yacht left the party feeling more relaxed. The young men started to brag about their exploits, one claiming to have entered a nuptial chamber on the night of the wedding and to have keyed the bride twice while her husband snored. They then moved on to more dangerous exploits, tempting in the extreme but so far not attempted. One in particular was alluded to several times as 'top of the tree' and 'the hot one,' always with awe and a barely concealed shiver. Nero's curiosity was aroused and when someone mentioned that 'the hot one' had been performed only once before, he enquired when that was.

'The night Mars tupped Rhea Silvia.'

Lucan told me he could virtually see the gooseflesh on Nero's thighs. These young men had in mind the unthinkable: the deflowering of a Vestal Virgin, probably Rubria, the youngest and prettiest. And they went into the project thoroughly. The danger and near-impossibility of entering the Temple, patched up after the fire and always kept locked at night, the consequences if caught: the Vestal buried alive, the rapist thrown from the Tarpeian Rock.

They even compared possible ways of effecting entrance and, though they did not try to draw him into the discussion or look at him, Nero found this in itself suspicious. He, as *pontifex maximus*, was the one man with a right to enter the Temple at will; it was for him to rape Rubria.

He felt distinctly uneasy but, careful to contain himself, joined in the talk in the hope of discovering whether his suspicion was justified, and he then took part in the heavy drinking afterwards. Nothing new emerged, but he went to his berth with serious doubts about Petronius's intentions.

In the morning, when the yacht returned to its moorings and Nero went ashore, he asked himself whether he hadn't overreacted, whether he wasn't harbouring groundless suspicions. In two minds, he hurried away for a thorough tour of building sites and afterwards to the gym, where he stripped for a workout. Here, to his annoyance and dismay, he failed to clear the vaulting horse and was thrown twice by his wrestling partner. His trainer, watching closely, drew him aside and warned him that heavy meals, too much wine and too much of something else were sapping his physique. He reminded him that the annual Games in which he hoped to be a winner were only a month away.

Nero's pride as an athlete resolved his doubts for him. When Petronius next invited him Nero explained that he was back in training and wouldn't be able to accept. Noticing the older man's pique, he suggested he read the poem he'd written on the yacht and any other poems of his choice at the next Poets' Circle.

Young Roman writers then as now want their literature to equal that of Periclean Athens. Much was expected from Petronius and they also hoped that he might reward their praise with subsidies.

Nero placed Petronius on his right at dinner and, working to heal any snub the older man might have felt, let him into a secret: the famous Roman painter Fabulus who rarely undertook new commissions, had agreed to decorate the hall of his new house.

Once the Cos wine had passed around and the mood grown convivial, Nero introduced the reader: after serving the State he was now serving the Muses. At which Petronius unfastened a long gilded case and drew out a parchment scroll. He remained reclining, as was customary, and began to read. Helen's elopement as recounted by Paris in a pointedly anti-heroic way: casual, conversational, almost blasé, and the resultant launching of a hundred ships, landing on a distant shore, ten years' fighting – all this the people treated as a ridiculous and counterproductive overreaction. If only the Danai had let her love-affair run its course, Helen, bored by Troy, would have returned home; instead, Paris had to play up to the epic wished on him and assume a role he detested, that of perpetually faithful lover.

This satire Petronius had crafted into lines of the utmost complexity: dizzying inversions, subtle alliteration, daring amphiboly. It left his young audience gasping. A theme so at variance with accepted norms and Paris's anti-heroic character they could take, but they found that these jarred with the artifice of the verse. Mood and language cancelled each other out. They applauded for its originality but without gusto: only Lucan, an extremist by temperament, declared it a total success.

Petronius's second poem was also a satire, but shorter. A young man expects to come into a legacy on the day he marries. But he is not the marrying type. He persuades his boyfriend to let his hair grow and be curled, to mascara his pretty blue eyes and to put on a bride's dress whereupon they go through a form of marriage, with due festivity and, as they prepare to go off on their honeymoon, the promised legacy safely in the bridegroom's pocket, parents wish them many lovely children.

His listeners liked to write about love and marriage, mainly in the form of gently, happy pastorals, weighted with recondite allusions. The subject and tone of Petronius's poem rasped on them and the work drew almost no applause.

Showing no sign of pique, Petronius read his last poem, in which the youth Ganymede, seated beside an attractive young woman, relives the day he was spirited up to Olympus. His new master, the Thunderer, is getting old, his wrinkled cheeks sagging, his hair falling out. Instead of his promised job – passing wine when the gods have a party – Ganymede is told to procure an anti-wrinkle cream. He consults the gods; one offers him an infallible cure for wrinkles under certain conditions. But Ganymede is a good boy, he declines and returns empty-handed. His master scolds him and tells him to procure a hair restorer. So it goes on, all chores. He's been expecting to have his cheek stroked, perhaps a little cuddle and pickings after a dinner. But his master is on a diet and, because of his gout, won't touch wine. Soon Ganymede decides he's had enough of Olympus, finds a rope and lowers himself to earth.

The young woman listens with sympathy, for she too has had a disappointment. That very same Thunderer took a fancy to her, but he'd lost his looks – just as Ganymede said – and guessed that a bald head, warts prominent as molehills and a cracked voice wouldn't exactly entice. What to do? 'As you probably know, the Thunderer has quite a name as a quick-change artist. I was sitting in this very spot when a swan, just one cock swan, appears out of the blue; flapping its heavy wings, it circles the lake, skims the surface, pushes forward its webbed feet to brake, paddles towards me. No ordinary swan this but one that speaks. He tells me his name, sidles up, lays his long soft downy neck on my shoulder, then coils it round my neck. Well really!

'I enjoy having my breath taken away but not to the point of suffocation. Besides his long beak was rough as pumice. Every woman would like a heavenly lover, but only in *modo recipientis*. 'I broke free and pushed him away, at which he lifted his wings, spread them wide and paraded before me. "Don't you find me beautiful?"

'"Sublime. But I cannot be more than your friend. We ladies are adaptable but within limits."

'He protested, called me prosaic, urged me to soar, went on and on. At last in a huff he re-entered the water and flew back to where he came from.'

The young woman turned sadly to Ganymede. 'You've been luckier than me. At least you went to heaven.'

'And learned that our kind of pleasure is best.' Having kissed away her incipient tears, he persuaded her to let him prove it.

Normally a reading ends with brief comments, appreciative or otherwise, followed by detailed discussion. Petronius had chosen subjects generally considered offensive and, while his treatment of the first two could be thought of as broad satire, no one save Lucan I fancy felt happy about his last offering. Not only did it mock the gods but implicitly it condemned the Circle's pious poeticizing about them as rubbish.

No one knew quite what to say. Lucan hailed Petronius as a bold innovator but this found no echo. As the silence lengthened, Petronius looked hopefully at his host, but Nero had taken his measure. Behind the fun, he saw a man grimly concerned with what he hated in the age to which he belonged and unable to forgive Destiny for giving us limitless desires in a ridiculously limited body.

Nero felt a duty nevertheless to propitiate the feelings of one who was his guest and moreover possessed of considerable influence. Summing up the reading as an attempt to widen the field of satire, he was able to say – truthfully – that he greatly admired the cadences and alliteration in the last section of the second poem: models of elegant craftsmanship.

This was not at all what Petronius had been hoping for, but he was sufficiently master of himself to bow his head in acknowledgement, then to suggest that they pass to work by some other member. After that evening Petronius never again attended the Circle.

I might have known Lucius wouldn't follow my advice to stop brooding on how and why cohesion broke down after the fire. True, he immersed himself in Cabinet business and took pleasure in Nero's mental recovery and the speed at which he drove forward rebuilding, but he still wasn't at ease in his skin. Rubbing shoulders with me at a reception, he murmured that his choice of Eternal Rome as a civic ideal had probably been a mistake: eternity was really self-preservation writ large, with no moral sanctions. But then, to my mind illogically, he inveighed against our gods: they'd intervened often enough on behalf of Aeneas, Camillus, Scipio and many others in need, yet not one of their number had deigned to help Nero escape the Furies or those poor innocents the *tunica molesta*.

In search of distraction, he had renewed his interest in his collection of dining tables – housed, as a concession to Paula, not in an annexe but in an extension of the loose-box Paul had occupied. His political thinking might be askew, but these tables at least stood solid.

One afternoon, as he was polishing a tabletop of pink Pentelic marble with golden yellow traces of weathering, who should arrive but John Mark, not only unannounced but bruised and cut about the face: eyes swollen to slits, a deep gash on the forehead, another on the left cheek, and his upper lip raw and twisted.

Startled and much concerned, Lucius sat him down and learned what had happened. A bunch of tough young Gnostics had ordered him to clear out of Rome and when he refused beat him up. No, he didn't need a doctor or pharmacist, he'd come because last night in bed he'd got to thinking about their last talk and how inadequately he'd answered Lucius's objections.

'Sometime after midnight I woke. My head throbbed and I had a touch of fever. I found myself saying "Blinkers". Just one word "Blinkers" – aloud.'

'As on a dray horse?'

'They restrict and have to come off.'

Lucius frowned. 'I can't say I follow you.'

'Your blinkers as a Roman, your blinkers as a senator, I'm asking you to remove them and become plain Lucius Annaeus, one man among many...'

Lucius drew back, perturbed by what he was asked to do, and even more by the change in John Mark. His shyness and the hesitancy in his voice had disappeared; he spoke now with assurance, seemed indeed driven.

'Suppose we clear the ground. Is Parthia part of the Roman Republic?'

'No.'

'India? China?'

'What a question!'

'Then much of the world knows nothing of Roman law.'

'So much the worse for them.'

'Consequently cruelty and injustice thrive world-wide... Now for more blinkers. In Egypt you watched priests placing a bejewelled necklace upon a crocodile god. You saw the dung beetle worshipped and the bull Apis. In Gaul it's a horse god people bow down to. Would you agree that, in a world context, Roman religion is a minority cult?'

'If you choose to put it like that.'

'Suppose your God of the cosmos wished to send our world a messenger, would the message be framed for a minority or for the majority?'

'For the majority.'

'And he would proclaim it amid cruelty and injustice?'

'That would seem to follow.'

'If he wanted to shatter the prevailing mould of savage animal gods and powerful ruler gods, would he tell his messenger to live out the attributes of a quite different God of peace not here and there, not now and then, but right to the natural end of human life – dramatically too, to the point where there could be no contesting the seriousness of his claims?'

'I'm not sure that follows.'

'But you'd agree I think that it is not an unreasonable hypothesis?'

A long silence followed, during which Lucius reflected on the implications of John Mark's argument and on his earlier discussions with Paul. Slowly he found himself driven to admit that the manner of Yeshua's death was not after all an impediment to believing that he had been sent by God or was God. He found this brought a stir of excitement, not unlike the glimpse of a distant sail in his Corsican loneliness. But also it made him afraid. It would demand so much rethinking. When young, he had reached out bravely to such challenges but now, in his sixties, he found it hard to yield sure ground or move forward to new.

John Mark was looking at him expectantly beneath swollen eyelids. Lucius thought, it's good of him to care and to have mastered his shyness to call on me. Since it seemed that all that could be said at this point had been said, Lucius thanked his visitor and escorted him to the courtyard. 'Don't be surprised to find a watchman outside your lodging. He'll be there on my orders to deter Gnostics and others.' John Mark's demurring gesture he countered with a laugh. 'Can't have Rome falling into disrepute... On your way out, ask Paula for leaves of yarrow from her garden. Nothing better for healing cuts.'

Having found that orgies, even if he'd decided to continue them, did not fill the void left by Poppaea, Nero decided on a change of direction. He moved into a three-room suite in the completed east wing of his planned new home, brought his old nurse Eclogue in as housekeeper and gave all his free time to perfecting the decoration and furnishing which Poppaea and he had planned together. He saw the house as a continuation, a fulfilment of their marriage. At the same time, he invited well-to-do ladies to subscribe to a marble statue of Poppaea, which in due course was inaugurated on the Palatine with a public holiday.

Nero's return to domesticity received added impetus from an unexpected manifestation. It took place in an Ostia warehouse, where Tigellinus, in charge of donations from the provinces to the mother city, had insisted he come to inspect a shipment from Athens. Some 40 wooden crates stood in line, some of the smaller ones opened, their contents on display. Tigellinus explained that Greece had sent what only she could provide: works of art to embellish public buildings. Glistening on a trestle table stood 40 goblets and ten decanters of finest purplish-blue Alexandrian glass; next to them, hangings embroidered with scenes from *The Iliad*; ceremonial lamp stands, a set of matching tribal rugs from Macedonia; four bronze and beech wood curule chairs with silver lion claw feet.

At each item, Nero's admiration went up a notch. Lifting one of a dozen silver dining plates depicting the Labours of Hercules in raised relief, he examined the rendering of a horse, then passed it to Tigellinus: 'Look at those fetlocks. Every tendon correct.'

'No one can match Corinthian silversmiths,' purred Tigellinus, adding that Gaul, with all its wealth, had contributed four miserly barge-loads of timber, while Greece, mountainous and poor, had reached down to the bottom of her purse. 'They sent agents round each one of their cities with orders to accept only the very best.'

As workmen opened the larger crates and eased out their contents, the dim warehouse grew resplendent with gleaming marble statues of Neptune, of Triton, of Laocoon and his sons grappling with a sea monster. A painted marble statue of an athlete crouching and holding a discus brought a gasp from Nero. 'School of Praxiteles,' he murmured, only to hear Tigellinus say he'd been assured this piece was by the master himself. And beside the right foot they did discover Praxiteles's signature. Nero saluted the masterpiece with a burst of song. 'We'll set it up at the entrance to the Circus Maximus.'

'As you wish,' said Tigellinus, adding however that the Greeks had expressed a hope that the finest statues would go to Nero's new house, since no one could appreciate them better than he.

When the tour of inspection ended, Nero confided that he was quite overcome, never had he seen such an array of beautiful objects.

As rebuilding in the city proceeded and the fabric of his house attained its full length of seven bays, Nero gave more and more of his leisure time to embellishing the interior. He wanted its inauguration to cause surprise, so no visitors were admitted, and I was one of the very few allowed in so as to check the steadily growing account sheets against work completed, this being one of the conditions of our loan.

A team of three stuccoists, all from Athens, had been engaged to plaster the underside of the dome and the surround of the dining room ceiling panel. I watched them atop bamboo scaffolding, coaxing their refractory material into curves, coils, rosettes and arabesques with the dexterity of chefs piping a cake with whipped cream.

I was led by Nero up a narrow spiral staircase to hear how the ceiling panel revolved. Made of balsa, it was suspended on a bamboo shaft and geared to cog wheels powered by water running from a cistern concealed in an escarpment behind the house.

On the walls of the largest reception room, four mural artists, Greeks from Naples, were painting delicate architectural trompe l'oeil as a frame for cupids, small animals and ornamental bushes. This style, all the fashion in Naples, had been chosen by Poppaea but, instead of the usual red background, she had specified that it should be white. Again the men's skill and application impressed me. It didn't surprise me that Nero treated them as friends and he spoke to them in Greek.

Sarpedon, a Greek acoustics expert recommended by Tigellinus, having tested Nero's voice in respect of various wooden panels, completely rethought the music rooms and was now boarding the walls with mature beech wood. These men charged reasonable fees and their work was up to schedule, so I returned from my inspection satisfied.

While I viewed the house in terms of value for money, Lucius pondered its political effect. He believed that not only its lavishness but Nero's preference for Greek craftsmen would infuriate certain senators, and when I mentioned that Nero planned to coat the ceiling of the open portico with gold leaf he shook his head unhappily. 'People will call it the Golden House. Danger in that.' A deputation from the Senate did in fact soon call. By then, five of the statues donated by Greece had been installed, with the Laocoon under the dome, and the perimeters of the proposed park and of the future lake were pegged out.

The senators told Nero they considered the house's scale and magnificence inappropriate in a republic, one even suggesting that it was modelled on King Philip of Macedon's notorious palace – a point contested by Nero. To the main complaint that he was appropriating for his park land belonging to the city, Nero replied that he was in fact reclaiming long neglected waste land, and he intended citizens to have free access to it during daylight hours. While this met the senators' complaint, it added to their disquiet since such an action would add still further to Nero's popularity.

Lucius continued to attend Cabinet regularly, pleased by Nero's regaining of confidence, though concerned by bouts of anger when he couldn't get his way. There had been one awkward moment when Nero asked, 'Are you still seeing John Mark?' and Lucius replied, 'Yes and I've come to esteem him.' This had been met with chilly silence.

Upset by the deputation's criticisms and evidently feeling a need to explain his stand and gain support, Nero drew Lucius aside after Cabinet and suggested they take a walk together that afternoon to look at the newly completed lake. They had agreed to meet under the colonnaded entrance, its pediment carving of Apollo and the Muses dazzling white against a cloudless sky. Presently the bronze-studded cedar doors opened and Nero ran down the steps, dressed Greek-style in blouse, short tunic and slippers. Lucius could not help express surprise and was told that in hot weather Greek dress was lighter and besides, a toga would distance him from the Greek craftsmen gilding his portico.

'And at your last recital you sang in Greek.'

'More poetical than Latin,' adding with a laugh, 'so at least you taught me in class. And since I'm a poet ...'

They passed down an avenue lined by plane trees. Nero said they were fifteen years old, had been uprooted from a stand upstream on the Tiber, carted to Rome and replanted. 'Doing well, obviously like it here.' They arrived at the lake, an exact replica in miniature of the

Mediterranean Sea and its coastal provinces, each faithfully rendered as on a large scale relief. From Spain to Cappadocia, each province with its rivers and mountains had been delineated with small pebbles of varying colour, cities designated by one or more key buildings, harbours by ships, and even the lighthouses of Ostia and Alexandria had their place.

Nero headed for the lake's north-eastern shore and pointed out white-capped Mount Olympus, Troy, Corinth, Athens. 'Where it all began! It was you who made me read Homer and Pindar. How right you were! But you said they'd grown decadent and corrupt. There you were wrong. Where do we get the doctors who heal smashed legs and remove kidney stones? The astronomers who find new stars? Composers who work with quarter-tones? Did you know the wood of a lyre reacts to the breath of the lyricist? I didn't until yesterday when Sarpedon told me.'

The house's many Hellenic features had already grated on Lucius and this perfervid praise of an altogether too bumptious people he found unacceptable but, before he could get in a word, Nero continued.

'Yet how do we treat them? We levy 40 million annually, by way of a governor with sticky palms. We allow this most sophisticated people no say in the running of their own affairs. Yet they bear it with quiet dignity and, when I ask for contributions, they reach down into what we've left them of their patrimony and ship priceless adornments for our State buildings and more than a hundred statues. You've seen the Laocoon?'

Lucius nodded and agreed Greece had sent many admirable pieces.

'The time has come to make some return. They've invited me to visit their leading cities. I intend to accept. They hold sporting contests exactly as Pindar describes and in their next Olympic Games I shall be competing.'

In living memory no *princeps* had visited Greece and Lucius of course felt astonishment. But if he went as an athlete perhaps there was no cause for concern.

They had arrived at the water's edge. Nero snapped off half of a nearby reed and pointed to Corinth.

'It's still hush-hush but I know you can keep a secret. The Corinthians badly need a canal. Here, through the isthmus. I intend them to have it. I shall lend them my team of engineers, compose and read a commemorative poem, cut the first divot. And, on the day I sail home, I shall make them a stupendous parting gift. Can you guess?'

'A university?'

Nero snorted derisively. 'Think big, Lucius. Big, big, big. I shall address the people of Corinth in their own open-air theatre. I shall say, "Rome when she chooses can be generous." I shall then announce an end to taxation, to a proconsul telling them how to run their lives. I shall say, "People of Greece, today Nero grants you autonomy."'

Am I listening to a daydream, Lucius asked himself, or to the first symptoms of mania? 'You can't do that,' he found himself shouting. 'Greece belongs to the Senate. Or rather, we in the Senate hold it in trust for the Roman people.'

'The Senate will come round,' said Nero easily. 'I'll toss them a sweetener. Sardinia.'

'The rag-and-bone island! They'd take that as a kick in the face... My brother ruled Greece for three years, the lifetime ambition of every senator.'

'They must find other forms of vanity... Don't you see, Lucius, this is bigger than senatorial sensibilities. A world-scale gesture. Greece's gifts to the world recognized and rewarded.'

Not a daydream, not psychosis, thought Lucius, but a well thought-out plan coming from a *princeps* in Greek-style clothes silhouetted against a Greek-style house. But how to contain it?

'Your proposal goes against all you've done for eleven years to conciliate the Senate. You'd be breaking a fundamental law. You'd be on the road to autocracy.'

'How so? No bloodshed.'

'You're creating the conditions for bloodshed.'

'Whose?'

Without answering Lucius looked Nero long and hard in the eye.

Nero stiffened and clenched his fists. 'Say that again,' he hissed, 'I'll wrap you in wax and set you on fire.'

Lucius staggered back, stupefied. Some moments passed. Then Nero tossed his head, tossed it again as though shaking off an insect. 'Just joking,' he murmured and forced a smile. But Lucius was by no means sure, and they returned to the house in silence.

Lucius would have liked to take a long country walk, analysing Nero's declared intentions and trying to decide how to thwart them. But that afternoon he had a long-standing appointment with John Mark. Perhaps jealousy played a part, but I considered Lucius was seeing too much of John Mark. He has no teacher's diploma and I don't trust a man who lives from hand to mouth. His influence could be sinister.

As he crossed town, Lucius prepared for his meeting by recalling relevant data. Intellectually he had arrived not at conviction but at a truce with doubt. Once admit the reasonableness of theophany, what he did during his short life Yeshua could claim to be that theophany: as John Mark quaintly phrased it, to be the Word uttered by Breath Divine. In this Lucius found a satisfying coherence emerge between his past and the strange new present.

He had met 'the flock' – John Mark's curious term. Arriving unannounced for what he had been told was a prayer meeting, he had been puzzled to find six men seated on a bench holding their sandals in their hands, their ungainly feet exposed, bunions and all. He thought he'd wandered into a chiropodist's surgery until he saw John Mark at the back of the big room. Taking a seat, he watched an elderly man wearing a knight's ring, down on his knees, wash and dry all the feet, one pair of which belonged to a slave! An upside-down situation, Saturnalia – out of season!

Lucius managed to take it in his stride, which I certainly wouldn't have done, and after the washing got talking with those present. He expected the high-pitched vaporizing and stories about paranormal powers he'd met with in other new sects, so it came as a welcome surprise to find them concerned mostly with giving practical help to widows and the handicapped. And now he had come to learn what would be required of him if he joined.

John Mark ran halfway down the stairs to welcome him, his cuts at the scab stage, the top row of teeth missing an incisor. Once seated, he announced in an uncharacteristic tone of pride that he'd been approached by one of the consuls designate and that the flock had a new member, Ancasta, daughter of a British King.

Lucius repressed a smile. He knew the lady and emended the last word: 'Kinglet.'

'Oh...' A slight pause, and John Mark got down to business. Lucius treated religion as a private affair between himself and God; from now on he would be asked to become a member of a community, to worship alongside and with them, share their *sacramentum* and, most important, find in them support for his new way of life and in turn lend support.

That was one jolt; another jolt came from John Mark's insistence on petitionary prayer – Lucius believing that to call attention to one's pain or needs would be insulting to an omniscient Deity and demeaning to a self-respecting man. Lucius inquired whether he could continue to refer to God by the names he had used for a lifetime – Jupiter and Pneuma. John Mark demurred, provided he make a mental distinction.

Though unsure of his own capacities, John Mark was very sure indeed of what he believed and of what he expected from his community. From their hour-long talk Lucius came away impressed, relieved too at finding no apparent obstacles. Only on the walk back did John Mark's answer to one of his questions begin to echo irritatingly in his ears, and its implications to disturb him: 'How do you attest Yeshua in your circle? That will be up to you. You've always set great store by conscience.'

In his relations with Nero Lucius had arrived at a crisis and, though it was a political matter, for once he consulted Paula. It is my belief that what may be called Nero's Hellenism was the work of

Tigellinus, for business reasons promoting Greek interests, but Paula attributed it to Poppaea. It was she, with her troubled background, who had furnished luxuriously. It was she, with her musical gifts and artistic circles, who had converted Nero to the primacy of aesthetic values.

Poppaea's death had left Nero inconsolable and I admit that her influence endured. He had thought ribaldry and turpitude would fill the gap in his life only to discover that they sullied his memories of Poppaea and soon took the road to cruelty and worse.

At this point the generous gifts from Greece turned his attention to the Greek contribution to civilization generally, on which Poppaea with her Neapolitan background had often dwelled. Paula remembered Poppaea saying one day, 'The Greeks may have lost a few battles but they remain a superior people.' From there, given Nero's liberality, it was a short step to wishing to make some return, preferably one that would satisfy his passion for showmanship.

Lucius listened attentively to his wife, agreeing with much she said but adding a rider: life in the Golden House, as it was now generally known, had altered Nero, almost as though he felt the need to 'fill out' his proud surroundings. 'He's begun to see himself as bigger than he is, and that angers the Senate. There lies the danger.' He put it to Paula: Should he resign, thereby deserting Nero who was set on a collision course? Or stay on in the hope of limiting damage but losing his reputation for honesty?

Paula reminded him that he hadn't been able to prevent Nero burning the Nazarenes: since then he'd grown in assurance and also perhaps in callousness. She doubted whether he'd now heed Lucius's prompting, however sensible and tactful.

Lucius raised objections. Hadn't he a duty to put Rome's welfare before his own reputation? Above all, he felt for Nero something very close to love. To break with him would be like splitting himself in two. Paula gently brought him around to her view and, after some days of inner rebuke, to a line of action. 'Unless I see signs of retraction, I'll spell out the dangers of Greek autonomy, how it will fragment the Republic, lead to regionalism elsewhere, then to total break-up. In the coldest manner, I shall tell him that his behaviour obliged me no longer to call myself his friend. Like that I will shake him, perhaps even make him rethink.'

But Paula advised against this. For the sake of showing himself in the light he would be making an enemy. It would also turn Nero against the sound maxims Lucius had imparted over the years. She suggested he part without hard words, so that the link which had lasted so long and on the whole happily would persist. This evinced irritation and a form of pique. 'You ask too much of me.' He turned away and a pattern familiar to me repeated itself. He saw that the advice he had asked for was demanding and probably wise, but jibbed at admitting it straight off. His annoyance usually lasted a matter of minutes and so it was now. Turning abruptly he took her in his arms and kissed her.

Immediately after siesta time Lucius, who had the right of entry without appointment, arrived at the Golden House where he found Nero busy in the main music room with a workman, making minor adjustments to the water organ and so absorbed he did not notice his visitor. These completed, he seated himself at the keyboard and, while the workman activated the pump handle, struck the keys in turn, assessing the timbre of each note. Then he started to play and after a moment to sing in his strong bass the words of one of his odes. Eyes closed, he appeared totally absorbed.

Listening to his tremolos Lucius thought, perhaps this artist at the keyboard is the real Nero, and the statesman into which I have tried to mould him is Nero as I imagined him to be. With a last flourish on the organ Nero looked up, perceived Lucius and crossed the room to greet him.

'A Greek song?' asked Lucius, probing.

'I shall sing it in Corinth.'

Lucius noticed the firm future and decided to lose no time in speaking his carefully chosen words.

'After long service Augustus allowed Maecenas and Agrippina to retire. I would ask you to grant me the same favour.'

Nero's eyelids flickered uneasily. 'You're angry at something I said?'

'No. Just a natural wish to return to private life.'

'You still have all your teeth.'

'But they lack their old bite.'

In the silence that followed, Lucius thought he saw in the young face a slackening of tension that might have been relief, then a darkening that might have been regret. He unbuttoned the pouch on his belt, removed his seal and handed it to Nero, who accepted it without comment.

One more formality remained. Foreseeing that London would develop as a port, Lucius had bought land along the Thames, later selling it at a profit and entrusting the proceeds to me to reinvest. When a highly placed official resigns he lays himself open to charges of malversion by greedy enemies and there is a recognized drill for safeguarding property in one's possession before taking office.

'Here is a list of holdings acquired during my service with you. Kindly order your agents to take them over and register them in your name.'

The paper itemized vineyards in Italy, arable land in Gaul a collection of valuable tables. After studying it, Nero said, 'less deserving men have made a bigger pile than you... keep them. But should you wish to contribute to my rebuilding fund ...'

This was generous and Lucius said so, then stepped forward, intending a last affectionate embrace. Nero however chose a colder farewell, grasping Lucius's right arm and pressing it firmly but briefly in his strong fingers.

PART SIX

A disturbing gift

The parting of Nero and his closest adviser set Rome abuzz. Had Lucius resigned, and if so why? Or had he been sacked, and if so why? Lucius of course said nothing about Nero's secret plans for Greece, imparted in confidence, and let it be known he had resigned for reasons of health. But this did not satisfy gossips. Twice a week Lucius swam eight lengths of the gymnasium pool – was that a sign of failing vigour? And how had he managed to retain his property and tables? Most likely there had been a trade-off. Say nothing against my Golden House and I'll let you hang on to your loot.

Lucius knew public life well enough that, now he had dropped to being one senator among many, he would be a less useful person to his friends and acquaintances. He was prepared to see some – perhaps many – drop away, either for that reason or, believing he'd been sacked, because they feared incurring Nero's displeasure.

Prepared as he was, he took their defections when they came with Stoic calm, in fact he jokingly acted out to me the street behaviour of certain acquaintances. Some he said looked right through him, as if he were a wraith, some looked up at the sky as though worrying about the weather, some down at the pavement deep in thought, one blinked as though he had a midge in his eye and stopped to remove it, one slipped into a urinal, another lifted a hand, snapped his fingers as though suddenly recalling an appointment, and turned on his heel.

Most of his life Lucius had had to fight and he had no intention now of fading into obscurity. In Rome, reputation is eight parts in ten show; well then, he would show off his remarkable collection of tables and do it with a flourish. Invitations to dinner went out to 50 friends who had stayed loyal, and others not in politics whom he esteemed: scientists, natural historians, members of an expedition that had recently explored Ethiopia. With Lucius managing an air of calm assurance and Paula receiving each guest with a greeting attuned to his or her character, the dinner proved a success and the dining tables on which the meal was served excited interest beyond Lucius's expectations.

Among those I myself particularly admired was a cedar wood piece from Luxor supported by four cranes with bent heads, their slim legs glinting with gold leaf, as well as a sigma table of beaten brass embossed with a hunting scene, semicircular in shape so as to nestle beside three couches arranged as a half-moon, and there was also a rampaging snarling leopard in solid ivory bearing on its curved broad back and muscular shoulders a round grey-veined marble top: Roman work at its strongest.

That these and many more should belong to a philosopher, one moreover who had had to pig-it for seven years in an earth-floor hut and eaten from a wooden platter, made them all the more interesting. In answer to a guest's inquiry, Lucius said he intended to continue to acquire rare pieces and, on his death, leave the whole collection to the city of Rome. At which I overheard a whispered favourable comparison with that most famous of donors, Maecenas.

Lucius followed with more dinners. It gave him great pleasure to see people enjoying themselves, and to watch Paula bringing out the best in them. It gave him strength to treat adversity with Stoic contempt and to put on a brave face.

One afternoon, as a distraction, Lucius called at the shop of his bookseller, who was also his publisher and an admirer, to enquire about sales. The bookseller, a neat little man with a goatee, replied that they had fallen off lately; however he urged Lucius to let him publish as a book the letters he had written over the years to his friend Lucilius. They would, he believed, sell well and would confirm Lucius as the most eminent philosopher since Cicero.

This was unexpected and pleasing. Lucius agreed to look over the essays, which, among other subjects, treated cruelty to slaves, wars of conquest, freedom of expression. Holding them together like a keystone was his concept of the Deity: Breath Divine, a cosmic force, immanent, impersonal, unmoved by prayer. As he re-read them, a recent chance meeting in the street with John Mark came to mind. He had mentioned his pain at losing Nero's friendship, whereupon John Mark hinted that perhaps a higher power than Caesar wanted Lucius as his friend, a useful friend. Lucius shrugged off the adjective: 'My influence now is down to a single vote in the House.'

'And to your pen.'

Lucius, startled, reacted sharply: 'What are you suggesting?'

'Only suggesting.'

Each continued on his way, Lucius irritated – more than that, deeply disturbed. The hint was all too applicable to his proposed book. Retract the metaphysical basis of his ethical teaching? Out of the question. He'd lose all credibility. But his zest for the project began to wane and, when he got home, he replaced the essays in a cupboard and opened the catalogue of his tables.

Free of the pressure of Cabinet, Lucius was able to give much of his day to consulting dealers about possible purchases, to corresponding with his part-time agent in the East, to polishing silver encrustations, waxing marquetry, blanching ivory with lemon juice. He treated each table as others treat a pet, commenting aloud on its style – suave, bold, retiring – talking to it about its provenance: not so strange, for he had trained as an orator and spent much of his life speaking, either in court or in the House. And so he kept in check his pain at the break with Nero, his frustration at no longer having a hand in government, his disappointment at losing friends. In an imperfect world, his tables at least were perfect examples of their kind.

Paula understood Lucius's need for reassurance but she became uneasy as Lucius gave more and more time to his collection. One evening, she crossed the courtyard to remind him that supper had been served ten minutes earlier and was getting cold; outside his store-room she heard conversation but, when she opened the door, she found him alone. He explained that he enjoyed picturing the artisan who conceived a particularly stylish table and imagining him confiding his aim and technique. He added that he'd adopted the habit when writing plays for Nero: speaking aloud the lines appropriate to this or that character.

On the evening of 12 July – a date I find starred in his diary – two crates arrived by cart from Ostia and were carried directly to Lucius's study. Unpacking the larger he found a small waist-high oval table on slim serpentine bronze legs, joined midway by a convoluted bracket, its rosewood top inlaid in ivory and encircled by a narrow enamel frieze.

The table, made in Luxor, had been sent on approval, and Lucius circled it critically. 'Custom-designed as a serving table. Feminine grace. For fruit and sweets only, nothing to mar your smooth complexion. 'But are you steady, my girl?' He placed a bowl of water on the table top and checked that it did not tilt, then jogged one side and found the table stood four square.

'Passed fit and ready for active service!' He gave a mock salute and lifted the table nearer the window, to catch the light.

Opening the second crate, he found a plain rectangular table of pine or similar inferior wood, the top upheld by two panels, each swelling to enclose a trefoil aperture, then receding to lock into a plain base, the panels being held firm by a squared shaft. The table was devoid of any decoration, and the strokes of the maker's adze blade had been left unsmoothed, giving a wavy effect to the surface, which was waxed but without patina.

At first astonished, then extremely annoyed at having been sent a worthless piece, Lucius looked at the shipping label on the crate. Caesarea Philippi. His agent did business only with cities of repute; why order from a town with no tradition of fine art? Perhaps, though, there had been a mix-up. Intended for someone else and delivered in error. Tomorrow he would have it removed.

Picking up the bits and pieces of the crate for kindling, he noticed a card on the floor; evidently it had fallen out during the unpacking.

On the card was a line of neat writing: 'A gift from your mercurial friend.'

Mercurial? Paul! How could that be? He seemed to recall him saying he wouldn't write but might send something. But why this piece of junk? As a joke? Paul had given no sign of black humour though about such idiosyncrasies one could never tell. Probably a joke. He looked again at the table. It annoyed him and he carried it away from the light to a far corner of his study.

He turned back to the Egyptian table, and began to feel soothed. It brought back pleasing memories of his service abroad: of grey shadows under mascaraed eyes, inbreeding, subtlety, conversation skimming the surface like dragonflies. And with these came a whiff of pride, much-needed pride. From the days when the Prefect had tossed him muddy boots to clean and polish, he had made his own way up the *cursus honorum*, right to the top. Done it all himself.

A table like this with an aura, it would cause quite a stir, and on that pleasant note he went to bed. Shortly after midnight he woke with a vague feeling of unease. He lit his lamp, began to read, only to find that the puzzle of the pine table distracted him. Putting on his cotton dressing-gown and slippers, he padded to his study. From halfway up the sky, a second-phase moon made of the room a black-and-white etching and the unsmoothed surface of the pine table shimmered like ripples on a lake.

A total misfit as far as he was concerned but curiosity made him decide to give it a closer look. Carrying it to the moonlit centre of his study, he turned it upside down and ran his fingertips over the mitre-joints. No overlap, no play. He felt the butts, and found them neat and tight in their rabbets. No glue anywhere, no cover-up with paste. Next he examined the feet. On one his fingers met a small excrescence. Lighting a lamp he found that it represented a bird, wings spread, seen from above, carefully carved. He was familiar with some of the animal emblems used by craftsmen in the East to sign their work, but not this one. He consulted his catalogue of emblems, but could find no entry for a bird in flight.

Returning to the table and holding the lamp close to the carving he saw that it exactly resembled a bird he had seen embroidered on John Mark's collar. Lucius had asked its meaning and was told it was a dove – not just any dove but the one that had designated Yeshua as God's chosen messenger, a belief Lucius found easy to understand, since quite often in Rome's past a leader had been designated by Jupiter's eagle alighting on his shoulder. Could this be a table for use by Nazarenes? Paul was clever with his hands: perhaps he had made it himself? No, a tent-maker would not wish or dare to impinge on joiners' territory.

But if Paul wished to offer such a table, he could have had it made in Rome. Why go to the expense of shipping a table all the way from far-off Palestine? Palestine... The word, though unspoken, jolted Lucius. He considered the table anew, in that context. Not a mistake, not a misfit, something possibly altogether other. A workaday piece such as this might have been ordered by a customer in Nazareth. Perhaps even made by Yeshua. Aware of his role, what more appropriate than to sign it with a dove? A guess, no more than a wild guess. Yet it might explain why Paul had had it sent all the way from Palestine.

Lucius now began to feel uneasy, had a vague sense of being cornered. It was his habit to get to know a table as it arrived, putting questions and imagining answers. Though his nerves were beginning to be on edge, he decided to adopt that line. 'So here you are, dropped in like a meteorite, unexpected, unannounced. I didn't like your looks, didn't know what to make of you.'

He paused, trying to gauge the table's mood, its likely response; before formulating its reply. For once, nothing came. He waited; still nothing. Perhaps his ungracious welcome had put the table in a huff. He tried again.

'I've begun to warm to your quiet strength and to wonder about the man who made you.'

This time he felt he was getting closer, sensed the kind of reply that might come. He dropped his voice a tone. 'You can tell by looking at his style. A craftsman who made wood give of its best. Did you notice near one of my feet a barely visible knot? Most joiners would have thrown that piece away, but he put it to good use.'

'And his character?'

'Like mine. Unpretentious. And with the warmth that wood imparts. For tables he had a special fondness, because they bring friends together. It may interest you that he never owned a table. Even for his last meal – a borrowed pine table. And in Emmaus it was over a hostelry table. He shone out as a friend.'

Yes, now it was flowing. Lucius began to feel easier.

'Why did Paul send you to me?'

'As a message.'

'As a message?'

'We'll come to that later... As a boy, what sort of table did you eat off?'

'Nothing fancy. Plain wood; ilex, I think.'

'His sort of table. And when you did well for yourself, you kept to a simple style of furnishing, never went in for showy stuff. My maker would have liked you for that. Because for one kind of table he had no use – expensive, showy tables that lure, like those he overturned angrily at the Temple entrance...'

Both sides of the dialogue had stemmed from Lucius – he had been aware of being in charge – but these last words with their implied sharp criticism seemed to slip out involuntarily – surely they could not be his? Whose then? he asked himself. As a musical score carries a melody, could a table carry a verbal message imprinted on the wood by its sender – or maker – which in his state of taut nerves passed to his vocal cords? No. Too far fetched. Belongs with the trickster's rope coiling of itself high into the air.

Certain men claimed the gift of transmitting thought – even through walls from a distance. Perhaps John Mark possessed that gift? Yet this voice was too assured to be his and bore no trace of a Greek accent. Unsatisfactory. He decided to leave trying to understand how and why and returned crossly to the table itself.

'For someone uninvited, your allusion to my collection was considerably less than polite.'

'Do you want smooth talk – or my message?... You have come to know my maker – your maker too. You have come to believe his claims. Then what? In one of your essays did you, or did you not, write: "If I couldn't share my wisdom with others, I'd rather not be wise?"'

Lucius admitted the words were his.

'Yet your belief in my maker's claims, you have chosen not to share. You have chosen silence – behind a barricade of tables.'

Lucius felt the taunt like a whiplash. 'You don't understand. Or if you do, you're heartless. Don't you see, I'd be numbered with the arsonists, have to resign from the Senate, declare most of my books mistaken, be treated with derision.' A short pause, then, quietly, 'Like Paul... Like your maker.'

This was too much! Effrontery, insolence – he wouldn't stand for more. He turned and made for the door, but so wrought up was he that his hand shook and it took some moments to grasp and lift the latch. Then he crept unsteadily to safety and threw himself onto his bed.

I've beaten a retreat, he thought, but from what? From a table that talks. It flashed though his brain that he was thinking nonsense, and then came something close to terror. His behaviour had all the signs of dementia. He'd passed into a madman's world. But then, he thought, if I've gone mad, I wouldn't be aware that I am mad.

What followed? When he held his conch shell to his ear, he sensed not exactly a voice but his conscience being nudged from outside. Could this be a similar but more direct phenomenon? A table through which an unwelcome nudging made itself known? At this less terrifying possibility, he began to calm down. Only to become worked up again as he brooded on the unfairness of the charge against him. He had left it unanswered; perhaps given the impression that he couldn't answer it. That wouldn't do.

Easing himself off the bed, he regained the study, determined to put himself in the right. The moon had begun its descent, casting just enough light to delineate the table from which, before he had time to speak, he heard the now familiar voice, firm but less hostile: 'I'm glad you've come back; we left our talk unfinished.'

Lucius struck a defiant tone. 'You may not know it, but I've spent my life trying to find reasonable solutions to knotty problems: inheritance disputes, how to prevent Caesar behaving like a god, whether or not to continue a bloody war. If you mention the name Seneca, an educated Roman will say, "Ah yes, the philosopher," meaning a man who acts reasonably.

'With that in mind, perhaps you'd be so good as to answer a question. Would I be acting reasonably if I threw over a lifetime's loyalties in order to attest the teaching of a stranger I've never even seen, never spoken to.'

The answer came pat, annoyingly pat. 'You never spoke to Zeno, I believe, or Socrates or Cato.'

'That's different. Their teaching accords with reason: Yeshua's goes beyond reason. And another thing. Constancy's been one of my watchwords. Avoiding wild leaps in the dark.'

A pause followed and Lucius thought he had made his point. But no, the voice continued, quietly. 'Once before you took an important leap in the dark.'

'When, may I ask?'

'On your travels you happened to meet a stranger, were drawn by unusual qualities. That person lived far off, led a life quite different from yours. Background, fortune and age divided you. Family and friends warned that it would be unreasonable for you to join your lives. And you too saw that it would be in many ways unreasonable, for it would alienate influential members of your family and do your career no good. Even up to the appointed day, you sweated helplessly on your bed: "I shan't be able to turn my life around. I can't go through with this." Then you remembered the stranger's qualities. And, as you've said over and over again down the years, marrying her was the best thing you ever did.'

It astonished Lucius to hear his inner pre-marital anguish thrown in his face, since he'd never breathed a word of it to anyone. Even Paul, supposing the voice was his, could have no means of knowing.

At the same time, he saw himself balked by the other's latest move, looked in vain for some way of avoiding checkmate. The table meanwhile had lapsed into a silence that could signal victory.

More exhausted than after pleading a life-or-death criminal case, Lucius slumped into a chair. He became aware of the gravity of what had been happening, and at the same time of its improbability. Has the whole debate been illusion? he asked himself, and answered with a textbook maxim. An experience can be understood only as one of a series; a unique experience therefore cannot be understood, but that does not imply its non-existence. Was this voice that knew his secrets in truth unique? He remembered Paul, the voice which changed his life, the voice with no visible source, from somewhere in the sky. But exhaustion and perhaps also awe slammed a door on that.

The consequences at least were plain. He had lost his case, and therefore would be morally obliged to pay up, with all that that entailed. First and most painful, he must tell Paula of his commitment to Yeshua and, for the first time in their married life, they would no longer be of one mind on an important issue.

The last glimmer of moonlight had faded, leaving him in darkness. He reached out a hand to the table he had called a misfit, feeling the ripples on its surface, assuring himself that it was real and still there. Only then did he order the court to be cleared and allow his tired eyelids to fall shut.

At breakfast, Paula inquired about Lucius's restless night. Had he felt unwell? Just a few squirrels, he lied and followed with the suggestion that, after so much strenuous party-giving, a break would do her good. They agreed to take a two-day holiday in the hills where, in quiet surroundings, he planned to break his shattering news.

He spent that day in a Senate committee and an hour after sunset headed for a thick clump of pines at the north end of the Gardens of Marcellus; here, in response to an urgent message, he was to meet my son Lucan. Lucius had canvassed for his nephew when he stood for the Senate and got in; since then, he had found the young man impetuous and over-prone to view life in terms of villains and heroes.

A taste for melodrama showed in this summons to a nocturnal meeting with its warning not to wear senatorial dress.

Among the close-branched pines, darkness fell early and bats were already flitting through the resin-charged air. Responding to a sudden hiss, Lucius found his nephew hard up against a pine trunk, a mesh of glossy black hair dangling over his sallow brow, dark brown eyes fierce.

'You weren't tailed?'

Lucius signalled a negative. Aware that his nephew thought conventional politeness unworthy of the bold and free, he refrained from embracing him and instead asked news of his mother Acilia, for the two were close.

'Sick in her soul,' snapped the other, 'as everyone with spirit must be under tyranny.'

'Tyranny? I don't follow.'

Lucan replied by citing Nero's remark on moving into his new house: 'At last I can live as a human being!' and his reported proposal to change the name of Rome to Neropolis.

Unimpressed by what he knew to be street tattle, Lucius challenged Lucan to give him an actual example of tyrannical behaviour, to which the younger man replied sombrely that Nero was a literary despot who crushed originality.

So that's it, thought Lucius. At a recent Poets' Circle, Nero had criticized Lucan's propensity for witches, black magic and gruesome poisonings, and the offended poet had stormed out in a huff. No fury equals literary pique. Lucan ate a pound and a half of green plums and next morning hurried to the main Forum latrine, a meeting-place for idle gossips. There he lifted his gown, squatted on one of the fifteen marble seats and at the top of his voice roared out a half-line from Nero's best-known pastoral. '*Sub terris tonuisse putes*': You might suppose it had thundered beneath the earth.

He had then voided his bowels tumultuously. Consternation throughout the latrine! A second time he boomed Nero's sonorous phrase and again produced a thunderous rumble, causing a dozen occupants to rise from unfinished business and scurry like startled rabbits into the street, where onlookers gaped at them and laughed.

Lucius reminded his nephew of this incident, which had become the talk of Rome. 'Gaius or Claudius would have punished you under the law of *maiestas*, whereas Nero had a good laugh and told his friends about it at dinner.'

Lucan scowled and divulged his more recent, more painful grievance. Only yesterday Nero had asked him not to publish Books Three and Four of his *Pharsalia*. 'He's jealous, madly jealous. Knows my poetry's better than his but doesn't want the world to know.'

Lucius had read the *Pharsalia* and considered it a misleadingly slanted version of the catastrophic war between Julius Caesar and the Senate party, with much emphasis on betrayal and poisonings. Quietly he told Lucan that such a work could re-open wounds beginning to heal and encourage faction to become armed rebellion. Nero had done right to ask him not to publish – while allowing him to circularize Books Three and Four privately.

Annoyed at his lack of sympathy, Lucan hardened his tone. He wasn't the only one to be treated unjustly. Every month, men of talent were being passed over for high office. Petronius Niger deserved a full consulship and had been fobbed off with an end-of-year deputization; Plautius Lateranus had been refused a cash grant to supplement an income depleted by losses in the fire. Flavius Scaevinus had been counting on a priesthood and still hadn't got it.

As Lucan growled these and other names, Lucius most, he suggested, exemplified a sentence in one of his essays: 'So great is the presumptuousness of men that although they have received much, the fact that they could have obtained more serves as an injustice.'

Curbing his impatience, Lucius began to explain why these charges too were quite unjustified, but Lucan cut him short. 'There comes a moment when a free man has to say no.'

'You mean you'll leave the Senate?'

Lucan snorted derisively. Lifting a hand to the scabbard on his belt, he pulled out his dagger and held it point upward inches from Lucius's face. 'The tyrant must go!' – words he spoke like a line of verse. Then, as Lucius tautened and took a step back, 'I'm asking you to join us.'

A sharp stab of pain in Lucius's scrotum and his testicles lifted, a bat's wing grazed his face; from afar off a hoopoe's wailing call. Slowly, with Lucan making things worse by prodding for a reply, Lucius confronted this wildly improbable situation. From his day-to-day dealings, he knew that influential senators, though piqued by the Golden House, by and large approved of Nero and his success in rebuilding the city. The discontents named by Lucan were probably not of a stature to mount an effective coup. However, a failed coup would damage the State almost as much as a successful one, since it would bring executions, reprisals and lasting hatred between executive and legislature.

Lucius began with Lucan's invitation to join the plot. He said that one maxim more than any other he had tried to put across was that assassination doesn't put an end to tyranny, since the next ruler will invariably use terror as a way of pre-empting a similar fate. Though he'd written thousands of words against autocracy, he reminded Lucan that he had never formed a cabal, never joined one; Gaius and later Claudius he had opposed openly, man to man. So he refused point blank to take part in the plot, then urged Lucan to drop it and instead to renew friendly relations with Nero so as to help counter the influence of his Greek flatterers.

Even as he spoke, he sensed that Lucan, an all-or-nothing young man, would not be swayed. In fact, taking his uncle's refusal as a personal affront, he charged him scornfully with writing as a hero and acting as one of the spineless *humiliores*. Lucius found it all extremely unpleasant. The meeting culminated in Lucan's abrupt departure with a scornful toss of his head.

Next morning brought a second unexpected encounter, as suave as the first had been abrasive. Antonius Natalis, in his early fifties, belonged to the equestrian order, though Lucius privately classed him in the order of lizards. With his carefully trimmed tuft of hair at his chin, smooth manners, quasi-continuous smile and rubbing together of long white hands, he saw himself as everyone's friend, an intermediary, in every sense of the word a mixer. His income came from furthering equestrian interests with senators but he had a penchant for patricians with a chiselled profile and regularly attended the lavish receptions given by Calpurnius Piso. Though Piso had never lifted a finger to help him, Natalis liked to remind himself and his cronies that he had the ear of a man descended in direct line from King Numa.

Natalis came in smiling and oily-tongued: Lucius was looking his best. Should he ever retire, the Forum would be a dull place, and more in that vein. He had taken the liberty of making a goodwill call on behalf of former consul Calpurnius Piso. Lucius's defences went to full alert. Why should someone at the peak of success make overtures to him at his nadir? A link with the conspiracy? Given his extreme caution, Piso was unlikely to have joined a firebrand but might he not see himself as Nero's successor after the dirty work was done? Best to tread as though on eggs.

He explained to Natalis that he wished to spend his remaining days quietly, in fact was leaving that morning for the hills. Natalis persisted, declaring that friends ought to meet regularly.

'A meeting in this case would benefit neither party,' said Lucius decisively. 'Please tell Piso that.' He saw that his peremptory manner had hurt Natalis's pride. Too bad. Leading the way to the front door he saw his visitor out and, knowing how slippery Natalis could be, minuted the conversation and his message to Piso in his daybook.

Lucius and Paula took rooms in a guest house near Sublaquem overlooking the lake. In the morning he rowed out to fish perch and returned with a basketful. In the afternoon, they took a scenic walk together and as the sun went down seated themselves on a bench in the garden, where Paula busied herself hemming a scarf.

Lucius had mentally shelved his nephew's conspiracy, real or imagined. His thoughts were wholly on Paula. Since girlhood, she had been a committed worshipper of the triad: Jupiter, Juno, Minerva and on feast days he had accompanied her to the rites in their temples, seeing there the best available manifestation of Spirit divine. To date, he had told her only that John Mark's teaching amounted to a subversive attack on the Roman system of justice. Now he must share with her his experience with the table which, after much heart-searching, he felt sure had been neither projection nor hallucination, and his decision to join John Mark's little community. His about-face would come as a shock; she would see it as a step unworthy of him, a desertion. He dithered and a dozen times tried to find the right approach.

As Lucius began to speak, from the other end of the garden a boy and girl came out to play, children of the householder. Their game was to balance, spin, flick into the air and catch a bobbin on a cord fastened to sticks held in their hands. Paula laid down her needle to watch. 'The little boy is just Marcus's age.'

Though Lucius had long ago put the loss of his son behind him, he well knew that Paula refused to do so and suffered accordingly. He took her hand and pressed it comfortingly. 'You gave him all the love a child could wish for.'

To his surprise, she began to speak of Paul, how from the start she had felt drawn to him. Much that he said was beyond her and in his busy life she held no importance, yet he had taken the trouble to show interest and had asked her, with his usual tact, whether she had children. She told him about Marcus. When he asked to hear more, she described his unusually affectionate nature, his sense of fun, and the cruel illness that had cut short a life full of promise. Each morning when she woke the first thing she felt was the pain of his loss.

Paul had expressed sympathy then, to her surprise, said almost brightly, 'Marcus was taken from you – but only to be kept safe.'

Here Lucius interrupted Paula. 'A little heap of ash – safe?'

'"Safer," said Paul, "than he would have been in your arms. And when your life is over he will come running to meet you."'

'How could that be, I asked, with iron braces on his legs?' At which he explained that a more perfect form of existence awaits us when we die.

'When Paul left for Spain, I turned to John Mark. He told me of Yeshua's promise, and that, if I accepted his teaching, I would rejoin

Marcus and all the pain of losing him would be worthwhile...' After a pause she resumed hesitantly, dropping her eyes: 'Lucius, I should like to belong to John Mark's community but of course I will do nothing without your leave.'

Lucius gaped, paused, screwed up his eyes as he tried to adjust, then found himself laughing. Paula's hurt look brought that to a stop and he explained that, unknown to each other, they'd arrived at the same destination. She, it was plain, less hesitantly than he and by a more direct route.

Now it was her turn to be surprised and about his route she wanted to hear, saying she had noticed for some days that he'd looked distraught: 'But sillily I thought it was some trouble with one of your tables.'

'It was. The table to which I now attach most value. But it all came right in the end.'

The children ran up to demonstrate how well they could balance and toss their bobbins. Meanwhile the sinking orange-red sun balanced momentarily on the distant hills. Happy at having confided, happier still that their secrets should have kept them united, Lucius felt the place and time to be unusually propitious and suggested they stay a further two days. They would return on the afternoon of the dinner Novatus was giving to celebrate their wedding anniversary.

PART SEVEN

Serving Rome to the end

Meanwhile the conspiracy in which my misguided son had joined was taking shape and a leading role assigned to Flavius Scaevinus. As a young senator, Scaevinus had belonged to the Cato Club but, inclined to laziness, he never made his mark in the House. With middle age and the death of his wife, he skimped the hard work of law-making for the pleasures of the table: Caspian sturgeon, hazelnut flavoured North Sea oysters, flamingo tongues and lush black hothouse grapes – with these, accompanied by gourmet friends, he literally consumed his patrimony. Glimpsing him alone at parties, puffy-faced, scarlet capillaries in his cheeks, stomach flopping over his belt, I felt sorry for him but not sorry enough to go up and chat.

He applied for one of the grants awarded to needy senators but Nero, spending heavily on his house, could not oblige. Then he borrowed and began to sell family furniture.

Scaevinus had been blessed with a sweet-tempered daughter, Antonia. He thought the world of her. She was now of marriageable age but since he could no longer provide a dowry, no suitors came forward. In alarm he reapplied for a grant, was again turned down and felt hard done by. It was then that he thought up a desperate remedy. He would redeem a wasted life by, as he saw it, one glorious deed which would bring him fame and money and so save Antonia from spinsterhood.

The assassination was scheduled for the festival of Ceres, when Nero presided over lavish Games in the Circus Maximus. One of the consuls designate, Plautius Lateranus, would approach the tribune;

adopting the customary kneeling posture, he would ask Nero for a cash grant for the extra expenses he would incur in his new office. As Nero turned to an aide for the relevant file, Plautius would grab Nero's legs and throw him to the ground. This would be Scaevinus's cue: he would plunge a dagger into the back of Nero's neck.

In the nearby Temple of Ceres, Calpurnius Piso would be watching and, when Scaevinus struck, would dash for the Guards' Camp, where millionaire Petronius, a key figure in the plot, had distributed bribes. Co-commander Faenius Natalis and those who had been bought would then acclaim Piso as *princeps*.

With the Cerealia a few days away, Scaevinus planned a dinner for the eve of the festival and invited half a dozen friends. On the afternoon before the dinner he called to his study Milichus, his trustworthy manservant whom he had recently manumitted. He told Milichus that he had just added a codicil to his will, whereby his stableman and his charioteer would receive their freedom. He then unlocked a drawer in his desk and took out a dagger of old-fashioned design, with a slightly curved bronze handle and a long straight tempered blade. Describing it as a family heirloom with a history, he handed it to Milichus, telling him to sharpen the blade on the scullery grindstone. 'Be sure you put a good edge on it.'

At dinner Milichus noticed that his master appeared preoccupied and his attempts at jollity were forced. He remarked on this to his wife, who did the cooking, told her about the codicil and the dagger and said he was afraid Scaevinus was planning suicide. This brought a scornful laugh. 'Just before the asparagus season? You don't know your master.'

She closed the kitchen door and lowered her voice. That very morning, she said, Scaevinus had closeted himself with a visitor whose face she didn't know. Later, as the visitor was leaving, she made a point of passing through the hall, at which both men averted their eyes. She recalled Scaevinus's bitter complaints at not receiving a grant from Caesar and advised her husband to tell the authorities about the dagger and the name of the visitor, Natalis. For this he might receive a reward.

Milichus was fond of his master and owed him a debt of gratitude for his freedom. He objected that he couldn't bring yet more trouble into his life on such doubtful evidence, sentiments pooh-poohed by his wife who warned him sharply that if he didn't hurry at once to Caesar's House and tell what he knew the two of them would be implicated as accomplices.

An hour later Milichus stood before Tigellinus and told his story. Nero, informed, snapped, 'Impossible, no one would want to kill me.' But Tigellinus arrested Scaevinus and Natalis and questioned them separately about their meeting. Their accounts did not match.

Meanwhile Lucius and Paula were returning by chariot. At the city gate they joined a queue. When their turn came and the guard made to frisk him, Lucius pushed the man away: 'Can't you see I'm a senator?'

'Yes, and it's your sort we're out for.'

Only then, from the officer at the gate, did Lucius learn of the plot and exactly how it had been discovered. What a fiasco! When you've sworn to kill Caesar, you don't ask your servant to sharpen the dagger.

Lucius's immediate concern was for Lucan. He still had friends at the top whom he could call on to delay prosecution. But perhaps Lucan had had time to get away and go into hiding.

And Calpurnius Piso? Who would have imagined that paragon of circumspection in an ill-advised coup? Thank heaven he'd declined Piso's offer of a meeting.

When he and Paula arrived home, his secretary provided further news. Tigellinus had arrested half a dozen senators, including Plautius Lateranus and his co-commander Faenius Rufus, imposed a curfew and put the Guards on alert. Shocked at learning of the coup and relieved that Fortune had preserved their young *princeps*, never had public opinion run so strongly in favour of Nero.

Then they made plans for the day. Paula would rest in preparation for their anniversary dinner with Novatus that evening, to which her favourite cousin was coming, having sailed to Rome from Gades in his private yacht. Lucius would reply to the usual backlog of letters and wait for his secretary to return with the latest news.

This when it reached him was sparse. Along with the knight
Natalia, Flavius Scaevinus, Pomponius Lateranus and Calpurnius
Piso were being held. No other names had been made public.

Even though he had expected it, Lucius felt the shock. These were
fellow senators, colleagues with whom he had conducted the State's
business. He had shared meals with them, betted together on horses.
They had acted rashly, doubtless in part from misplaced patriotism
and now they would die, their blood once shed a dividing line
between Nero and the Senate. The aftermath he preferred not to
envisage.

Instead he went to his study and unrolled his favourite Symposium
but, halfway through the first paragraph, his thoughts turned to John
Mark. He seemed to remember him saying he was in touch with one
of the consuls designate. Could it be Pomponius? Concerned for his
friend's safety, he decided to find out.

He walked fast across town, where eyes had become shifty, talk
muffled. At John Mark's lodging, the protective watchman was not
to be seen, removed doubtless by Tigellinus after Lucius resigned.

When the door was partly opened by just a few inches, he found
himself looking at a badly frightened face. Eyes bright as an addict's
blinked jerkily and very fast, activated by twitching of the cheek
muscles. The mouth was tight-shut, lips drawn in, the complexion
alarmingly pale. For quite some time, it gave no sign of recognition,
then the door was pulled back and a hand offered: damp, cold and
limp.

Lucius quickly took charge, putting an arm around the
unfortunate man and steered him to a seat on his unmade bed, while
perching himself opposite on a stool. There he waited, thinking John
Mark resembled nothing so much as a scarecrow knocked askew by
a squall. Minutes passed. Finally, judging him so frightened as to
have lost all initiative, Lucius adopted the role of prompter.

'You've been seeing Pomponius... Is that the trouble?'

No answer. Lucius repeated his question in a different form. This
time it elicited a whisper. 'Once ... once only.'

'Go on.'

'He made the approach. And I wrote him a letter.'

With an effort Lucius hid his vexation. 'When?'

'Two days ago.'

'What about?'

'The theatre. Pomponius never misses a first night. He'd heard a rumour not true that Nazarenes may not watch plays.'

Like a broken dyke, John Mark's terror poured out. His letter would be found. Tigellinus hated the community, he'd be arrested and charged with proselytizing, with knowing about the conspiracy, perhaps aiding and abetting it. Then the death penalty.

'Lucius, I want to be brave, but look at me. Scrawny arms, narrow ribcage, skin so thin it bleeds at a scratch. How could a body like mine let me be brave? I see it all. "Give us the names of your superiors and we'll let you off with deportation. Otherwise rivets through your wrists, rivets heavy as horseshoes." I've seen it, I know... That's when I will crack. To save my despicable grade-three body.'

Lucius had never seen anyone behave like this. It rattled him. He didn't know how to handle it. Finally, hesitating between severity and gentleness he opted for the second. He moved to the bed and put his arm around his friend's hunched back. 'It may not come to that, John Mark. And if it should, God has provided you with an emergency exit.'

But the back did not straighten. 'So I thought once.'

'And rightly so. A man's life is his. No one else's. To dispose of as he thinks best.'

'Is it his? Or is it on loan – until the lender decides to take it back?'

'Did Yeshua say that?'

John Mark dropped his eyes. 'Not in so many words.'

'Well then.'

Lucius's triumphant tone had a curious effect. John Mark got up, head high, his facial tic eased and his voice challenging.

'Your special field is testamentary law. When a man dies and his will is read, what is the usual cause of dissension?'

'The will itself. Every will, however carefully worded, imperfectly expresses the testator's wishes.'

'The testator will choose one of his friends, fair-minded – one only. In the light of his personal knowledge of the testator, it is he who decides what is intended by his will.'

'Yeshua left a will: his teaching as written down by those who heard it with their own ears and in order to settle disputes about its meaning he appointed one of his friends to be his executor. It is that friend – his name is Cephas – who decides how the terms of the will should be applied to matters not specifically mentioned by the testator.'

'But conscience should do that for us.'

'It can – when well-informed. Too often it is badly informed, as when Nero set innocent Nazarenes on fire. It is Cephas as Yeshua's executor who tells us that no man should take his own life.'

'In effect limiting our freedom.'

'What value does freedom have outside the boundaries of truth?'

In the pause that followed, Lucius thought back to other concessions he'd been asked to make. Ever since Paul's arrival he'd been running an obstacle race, and at this latest obstacle he balked. It didn't suit him at all. Nor obviously did it suit John Mark. His state of nerves suggested it was likely he'd crack under arrest, therefore he ought to be free to take his own life. He was still grappling with these and other issues when there came three sharp raps at the door. These sent John Mark into a new burst of trembling. 'I won't answer,' he whispered.

Further rapping was followed by a man's voice. 'Is Annaeus Seneca there?'

Lucius motioned John Mark to hide under the bed, then opened the door a handbreadth to find his secretary Lado. 'Colonel Galvius to see you.'

'Here?'

'At the house.'

'Did he say why?'

'Orders from Caesar.'

What could this mean? Lucius knew he was in the clear, but an unexpected call by one of Nero's aides de camp worried him.

Telling Lado he'd be with him shortly, he considered what to do with John Mark. Calling him out from under the bed, he explained who the visitor was and why he must leave immediately. When this brought an anguished look and a plea to stay, Lucius did his best to reassure him. 'Don't dwell on a situation that may not arise. Think of your flock, they need to see you calm. And that letter to Pomponius, he may well have destroyed.'

'And if he hasn't?'

'I have friends in the department dealing with suspicious evidence. I'll try to get the letter mislaid, presumed lost.'

After embracing his friend, he joined Lado and hurried across town, encouraging himself by reminding Lado that Galvius was one of Burrus's protégés, whom Lucius had twice helped to higher rank. Honest, discreet.

When he arrived home, Lucius hurried to his bedroom where Paula, preparing to dress and still in her négligée, threw herself into his arms. He dried her tears, tried to reassure her and helped her back to her bedroom.

Galvius announced his message crisply: Nero saw ramifications of the plot on all sides; Tigellinus, fearful for Nero's safety and for his own, was urging him to pass summary judgement – as was his right after an attempted coup – on those who confessed or against whom there was evidence deemed sufficient; Natalis, hoping for leniency, was trying to implicate the man Tigellinus most wished to see out of the way. 'He informed Tigellinus that you ended your reply to Calpurnius Piso with the words: "My welfare depends on his," meaning Piso's.

'He was lying,' Lucius retorted angrily. Taking his daybook from his desk he pointed out to Galvius the relevant memorandum, explaining that he made it a rule to write up any unsolicited visit.

'Go back to Nero and deliver the following message: "I could have no reason to value any private person's welfare above my own. Nor do I stoop to flattery. Caesar can vouch for that: he's had more frankness than servility from Annaeus Seneca."' He then made Galvius repeat the message verbatim and got his assurance that he would deliver it in person.

'To me,' said Galvius respectfully, 'your case looks irrefutable. Having the honour to be your friend, may I add that I'm greatly relieved.'

Lucius hurried back to tell his wife. 'So you see, Paula, nothing wrong has been done and there's no evidence against me save that of a confessed criminal. Tonight we celebrate. Let's hurry up and enjoy it.'

Novatus's villa stands four miles out on the Appian Way, a commanding old-style mansion in spacious grounds. The oak-panelled hall with its bossed ceiling smells of leather and dogs and the game hanging in the nearby larder. Family portrait busts and masks gaze proudly at the heads and antlers of animals killed. Here, when I arrived for the anniversary dinner, I found Novatus appraising his latest trophy, an admirably stuffed full-grown bear with open jaws. Already at age twelve, Novatus knew what he wanted from life and went for it, laurel-wreath after laurel-wreath, with the same accuracy he showed in hurling a javelin brought to bear on a bear's throat. I admire him, as do his many friends, but still find him a shade overpowering.

Novatus's house guest, Valerius, joined us. He is the son of mother's elder brother and owns the family fleet based in Gades, from where he had arrived the previous day: middle-aged, tanned face with as many lines as a chart and the calm assurance of one who's sailed the world's seas in every weather.

'What news of the plot?' he inquired. Novatus replied that they'd pulled in Petronius Niger: but the whole affair was odious to him and he asked us not to mention it at dinner.

We spoke next of Lucius. I said I was shocked that so many fair-weather friends were snubbing him and that his stock had plummeted.

'Not where I live,' Valerius slipped in. 'You know he gave Cordoba its first library as well as saving its mint from closure.'

Novatus said he understood Lucius was flirting with the Nazarenes and went on to praise Rome's attitude to sects in general. 'We let them have their say knowing that soon they'll appear as ridiculous as last year's fashion for men to wear small gold earrings. In the case of the Nazarenes that's just as well. If the eternal city is up there,' he pointed a finger towards the ceiling, 'what would become of Rome?'

A crunch of chariot wheels on gravel heralded the arrival of Lucius and Paula, holding hands and apologizing for being late. 'We thought you'd slipped off on a second honeymoon,' laughed Valerius.

I was pleased to find Lucius looking fitter than when I'd seen him a month before. Wearing senator's gown and red shoes, he held himself straight with a vigorous step and a firm voice. Though his brow was 'barnacled' (his word) with rosacea, one would have given him ten years less than sixty-five. He was certainly deeply shaken and saddened at what he saw as an unjustified plot and the victims it would claim but his face did not show it and he began to join readily in the light-hearted talk.

Paula had kept her looks too, as fulfilled busy ladies often do. Her closely fitted décolleté dress of warm pink satin showed off her slim figure and shapely shoulders, while a gauze stole draped over the back of her head accentuated the light in her fair hair and her only jewellery: a pearl at each ear.

Lucius as chief guest took the long couch to the left of Novatus's, with Paula on a cushioned chair beside him, while Valerius and I shared a couch opposite Novatus. His daughter Novatilla was now married with her own home, so there were no flowers or other decoration and the roast shoulder of boar was carried in with no attempt at novel presentation, to be carved expertly by Novatus, using the sharp-edged hunting knife that had killed the animal.

We Senecas are shy about voicing affection, preferring to show it in persiflage, and it was in that vein that Valerius addressed Paula. 'We know what a trial living with Lucius must be. Fastidious about food, beats the servants, sneaks away to his mistress. How have you stood it so long?'

Paula met this with a smile. 'You could have added that he doesn't utter a syllable at breakfast and regularly forgets my birthday. But he does have minor redeeming points. When I tell him what trouble I have deciding between two samples for bedroom curtains, he doesn't say "Yes dear," while thinking of something else. And when I have linen to press, even if he's busy on a speech, he'll come and heat my iron, only he can get the temperature right.'

I joined in the banter. 'When Lucius came back from Provence, he never stopped talking about a pert teen-aged dryad who kept him twiddling his thumbs a whole morning while she calmly picked apricots... But how did you see him?'

Paula put on a mock solemn expression. 'Very self-important. The world's troubles on his broad shoulders... And with other bachelor faults a woman fondly believes she can change.'

'Unfair!' we chorused. 'Shame!'

Novatus stepped up the pressure. 'When Lucius sailed off to Corsica, we expected you to remarry. How do you answer that?'

'Perhaps no one asked me!' We murmured disbelief. 'Perhaps I thought no man could match the Seneca brothers, and since you and Mela weren't free, I'd better just wait for Lucius.'

'Flatterer!' we laughed, while Novatus whispered to Lucius, 'Paula's fidelity – when will you give us an essay on that?'

Lucius chose to answer seriously: Latin had evolved in a man's world, the words to do justice to Paula didn't yet exist, at which Novatus pointed an accusing finger: 'Blames his tools!'

When we were boys mother sometimes let us cook our own evening meal outside: always pork and garlic sausage, and Novatus had had the happy idea of serving exactly that kind of sausage, with a variety of garnishes. It set us reminiscing and joking. Then came ripe apricots, accompanied by walnuts and roasted wheat grains as at a wedding, white Falernian mixed with wine from Cos. It pleased me that, after their recent misfortunes, Lucius and Paula should see how much they meant to us.

A police order had gone out that no one that night should leave their homes so when through the talk and laughter I heard the castanet rattle of hooves, I wondered who could be defying it. Moments later the main entrance bell rang, to be answered by a servant, and in strode an officer in uniform, Colonel Galvius.

Conversation came to a stop in mid-sentence, a glass fell to the floor and broke. Galvius bowed to Novatus, whom he knew by sight, and continued to Lucius's couch, where, bending his lips to my brother's ear he whispered, 'I'm off duty and here as a friend to give you advance warning.'

Lucius's head jerked back. 'Warning?'

'Caesar believes Natalis. Or chooses to.'

Lucius registered disbelief. 'Against the word of his lifelong friend? Not possible.'

'He is very frightened.'

'Of a lonely man grown old?'

'But much admired. I heard the order given in a low, sad voice. When darkness falls – an hour from now – you're to be arrested.'

Lucius tightened his lips and hardened his jaw, 'To be tried by my peers in the Senate.'

Galvius's correction came in a half-choked voice: 'To be executed as an enemy of the State.'

If you're involved in a chariot crash you don't notice how others behave. At Galvius's words, I recall only that I threw up my arms, blurted out a curse and an invocation, then found myself on my feet, chest thrust out, fists tight in an absurd vestigial posture of defence.

Valerius remained reclining and, accustomed to emergencies, was first to find words. His yacht lay in Ostia, her crew on call, provisions in her galley. She was ready to sail. In half an hour – less, if he galloped – Lucius could be aboard her and on his way to Rhodes or one of the remoter Dodecanese. And Paula with him, why not?

Novatus said that was an excellent plan: nothing shameful about escaping a sentence passed without due trial. He pressed Lucius to accept, as did I. As for poor Paula, her face hidden in her hands, she was breathing heavily, apparently in shock.

Lucius I found terrible to look at, the enjoyment of a few minutes earlier replaced by a granite grimness. He was doubtless thinking of Nero and what could have prompted his fatal order. Minutes passed before he answered Valerius, speaking more slowly than usual, and with emphasis.

'If I allow the State to sever my head without hearing my case, I shall be lending myself to an act of injustice. But if I accept your offer and run away, it will be seen as an admission of guilt... However, one other course is open: it will keep Nero from committing a needless crime and allow me to die as a free man.'

He appeared now to be straining to hold back intense emotion. Like someone who's drunk too much, he proceeded very slowly and with almost exaggerated caution to feel for the pocket of his gown, to unbutton it and to draw out Cicero's silver fruit knife and to pull open the blade.

Raising his left hand and shaking down the cuff, he swept the blade through the air above the inner side of the wrist.

Yes, he intended to open his veins. Declining a second plea by Valerius for escape, he asked Novatus to allow him to do what had to be done in the room where they were, surrounded by family.

Novatus hesitated only a moment: he saw Lucius's choice as the most honourable one. With his gift for practicalities he summoned a servant and told him to remove the food, now a cruel mockery, to fetch straw and a horse blanket to spread on a couch wider than the dining couches. This done, Novatus sent the man to fetch Statius, his own doctor, who lived three houses away. Paula meanwhile knelt by Lucius, her head on his shoulder, not speaking, too overcome to be of use.

Presently Statius arrived, aged about forty, brisk in manner, leather bag embossed with a caduceus slung from his shoulder. Novatus introduced him and explained that his brother had decided to make of his death a protest against Nero's monstrous illegality.

This drew a quiet correction from Lucius. All his political life he had worked for peaceful partnership between *princeps* and Senate.

Now that the Senate, then Nero, had chosen the path of bloodshed, he saw only one course: to dissociate himself from both and make a freely chosen death the keystone of his life's effort.

Learning how important it was to hurry, Statius called for linen napkins or their equivalent, two fingerbowls and a shallow metal basin containing a little water.

Recognizing Corduba copper, Lucius stroked the bowl with signs of pleasure.

Installed on the more spacious couch, Lucius rolled back his sleeves to the elbow. Turning his left wrist upward, a delta of blueish veins, and inhaling deeply, he drew his fruit knife blade across the wrist at the point indicated by Statius, making a cut two inches long.

'Deeper,' said Statius. Lucius reinserted the blade, pressing until his arm muscles ridged, while Statius disposed a fingerbowl underneath on the blanket.

With a scalpel Statius cut the right wrist. Swabbing a trickle of blood as it flowed out, he told Lucius that our body contains some twelve pints of blood; when four pints are lost, consciousness clouds, coma ensues and soon respiration stops. In a healthy man that might take two hours.

As I watched the level in the fingerbowls rise, drop by drop, while Statius prevented coagulation, so my anger rose. Against Nero, against the gods, against the Fates. But then, hadn't I dreaded some such finale from the day Lucius stood for the quaestorship and father warned him that to put on a senator's red shoes was to take the first step into a bloodbath?

For everyone present this was ordeal enough but soon, unexpectedly as in one of the tragedies Lucius had written for Nero, ordeal doubled. Paula, kneeling quietly beside her husband, suddenly shrieked and threw her arms round his neck. 'Let me come with you,' she begged. 'Let me, let me...' Then, more quietly, a catch in her voice: 'Remember our wedding day, how we said we'd share – not just the good things.'

Wives have occasionally chosen to die alongside their husbands, always elderly women, with little to live for. But Paula – pulsating with life, still very attractive, not yet forty!

Lucius gave every sign of being touched but at once began to dissuade her. She had no reason to feel anxious. Nero had nothing against her, his brothers would care for her. And, as she persisted, 'My dear, death is a door we pass through single file.'

'But holding hands,' she whispered with insistence, placing her fingertips on Lucius's left palm in a gesture that drew his gaze downward to her wrists. Perhaps he then pictured the painful red abrasions caused when the brigands tied her up, saw her ordeal and bravery, as a prefiguring? Did she truly want to join him?

This brought an emphatic 'I do, I do' and from Lucius, 'So be it.'

Statius immediately protested. His vocation was to heal the sick and ease the dying, not to help a lady in the bloom of life to an untimely grave. He had started to pack up his instruments and dressings when Novatus laid a hand firmly on his shoulder. 'Consider, my friend. Lucius's death will have more chance of doing good if his wife shares it, as she has chosen to do. It is your duty as a citizen – I would say your privilege – to lend her all help.'

Novatus's status and authoritative manner, no less than his words, had the desired effect. Sullenly Statius helped Valerius to push a couch next to Lucius's. Paula took off her stole, lay down and carefully arranged a coverlet in such a way that her dress wouldn't be spoiled. Then, closing her eyes, she submitted to Statius's scalpel.

Lucius had trained himself to accept death as the natural limit of life and to meet it with reasoned calm. His own death, that is. But with Paula beside him, seeing the red trickle from her smooth slim wrists, measuring out her departure from him like a water clock, clearly he felt a great surge of pity, the one emotion he found difficult to master. And with it something else. Her frightened eyes were fixed on his, looking to him for support, support he could not refuse, and yet he knew deep down that by trying to give it he would lose the strength to face bravely his own end.

Abruptly and somewhat incoherently he tried to explain this to Paula and said it would be easier for them both if she were moved to another room. Holding back tears she gave a nod of agreement. Lucius then asked Valerius to carry her to one of the bedrooms. As he lifted her in his strong arms and made for the door, I was reminded of a vase painting of Pluto abducting Prosperina.

It is customary for a famous man in his last hours to recall notable achievements and to hand down wise counsels – Roman showmanship to the end. But this was not in Lucius's character nor was it his style. He declined to pontify, indeed he showed an almost embarrassing humility.

I asked whether he had arrived at a satisfactory definition of cohesion.

'All my attempts I see now were foolish mistakes. I glorified cohesion, which presupposes that the city is a *summum bonum*. That leads to the view that preservation of the city is above every and all the laws, and this led to a mass crime: burning of scapegoats.'

'So what follows?'

'Cohesion must become subordinate to something other than the city's laws. Some restraint, but not of course a forcible restraint. It must come from the citizens themselves.

'I believe it will come only from conscience, civic conscience when interpreting and applying the laws. It will act according to certain moral imperatives. But these are not to be found, as I once believed, in the natural world. Probably the citizens will work them out for themselves, generation by generation, and I think they will be accepted by a consensus only if they are seen to have been practised by someone they cannot help cherishing and admiring.'

All this was quite new to me. I said so and asked whether he'd put these ideas into an essay.

'I intended to do so but had no time.'

'At least you've made notes?'

'Not even that.' Then, after a pause, 'if you're interested you could do worse than talk to John Mark.'

At the mention of this name, I saw Novatus frown, and he quickly changed the subject.

'What,' he asked, 'has been the most satisfying thing in your life?'

Lucius thought for a few moments. 'Helping those who need help.'

'And the most difficult?'

'The same. To do it without hurting their pride and without becoming proud oneself.'

To Valerius, who said it must be comforting to leave behind a famous name, he replied, 'A ship which large in the river seems tiny when on the ocean.'

Here Statius interrupted. A man of Lucius's age loses blood more slowly than a man in his prime, and in Lucius's case a muscular body and good tone still further slowed the loss. Three quarters of an hour had passed and Lucius had lost only one pint of blood. To hasten death he proposed to cut the saphenous veins of both legs, one vein near the knee, the other near the ankle. This would be painful.

With some apparent difficulty Statius found the veins in question and, as he cut each in turn, caused Lucius to stifle a cry. More bowls were placed beneath the severed veins.

Lucius asked after Paula. Novatus went to see and was able to reassure him that she was in no pain and beginning to look drowsy.

More practical discussion followed. I spoke of my Memoir and asked if I might read and draw on Lucius's copious diaries. To this he gave assent, adding with a smile, 'Don't be too hard on me, Mela.'

Presently there came a most unwelcome intrusion: a maniple of six soldiers under a commander deputising for Galvius, who could not bring himself to arrest in person a man he admired and knew to be innocent. Novatus dealt with the commander in his best governor's style. The eminent person they intended to arrest had opened his veins and was on the point of death. He would allow the squad to surround the house but not to enter until the end came.

We continued to try to read Lucius's expression, hoping for signs of a speedy end, with Statius increasingly uneasy, monitoring pulse rate and swabbing coagulating blood. 'Your body disobeys your will. Valves and muscles are straining to check the flow.'

Lucius made a wry face, comparing his exit to an overlong play that has spectators yawning. 'Tortoise Seneca! How people will scoff!'

All patience gone, Lucius asked Statius to administer hemlock, knowing from Socrates' death that it acts on the respiratory organs, a fatal dose usually causing death promptly. Statius agreed and went off to his house for corium leaves, while Novatus's servant heated water.

Presently the appropriate dose had been weighed, the leaves infused and the mixture poured into a goblet. Lucius swallowed it in three mouthfuls, grimacing at the bitterness.

Instead of watching for unfocussed eyes and nodding head, we now looked for much faster respiration, the prelude to depression of the lungs and morbid blueness of the skin. But we continued to converse. To the question whether he believed the soul survives death, Lucius replied with a boyhood memory. We'd been set an important arithmetic exam and sat puzzling over difficult square roots, maddeningly aware that the answers lay just out of reach, on the master's desk, at the back of his teacher's scroll. 'It may be so for the big questions we can't answer here.'

Half an hour passed but brought none of the predicted symptoms. Statius decided blood flow was too weak to carry the poison from stomach to lungs and so bring breathing to a halt. He proposed immersion in a warm bath. This should counteract the body's efforts to constrict the veins, while water would inhibit clotting.

Supported by Statius and Novatus, Lucius shuffled to the villa's sunken marble bath. Stripping to his modesty clout, he inched down the shallow steps and sat on the marble surround. After some moments he dipped his forearms in the water, and closing his eyes, bent his head in an attitude of prayer. Cupping the water in his right hand, he sprinkled a little of it as a libation on Novatus's feet and on mine, saying in a firm voice, 'I give thanks to Jupiter the Deliverer' – words later to be the subject of heated debate, for John Mark claimed he was invoking Yeshua the Saviour. This I could not believe. If Lucius had intended to join the Nazarenes, I think he would have told me.

The water around Lucius's lower body turned to a reddish nimbus, and I thought, at last. But soon the red faded away to pink. The Fates seemed to shrink from cutting the thread of this far from ordinary life.

Throughout, Statius had appeared in control. Now, however, concern for Lucius and hurt professional pride ruffled him and in an almost angry tone he told Novatus and me to help Lucius into the adjoining steam chamber.

Lucius by now was short of breath and showing signs of dizziness. The exertion of taking ten paces set his heart racing. He had always dreaded the thought of asphyxiation and his eyes had a frightened look as he turned to Statius for reassurance. The doctor explained that asphyxiation was painless and much like falling asleep.

We eased Lucius into a sitting position on the slatted pined couch in one corner of the booth, allowing support for his back. Novatus opened three vents, steam eddied in and we closed the door: through the selenite panel, we could see his body fade into the enveloping vapour. Presently we heard a quick succession of hard sounds from the throat.

We carried his body, wrapped in towels, to Novatus's room, laid it on the bed, closed his eyes and eased up the chin, holding it in place with a linen band. We called in the maniple, who satisfied himself that the State now had one enemy less, then covered the body with a sheet, placed a lighted lamp beside it and closed the shutters.

In another room we found Paula. Acting on orders that Lucius's wife should come to no harm, the maniple had tied up her wrists with bandages. Her face was chalky, her eyes shut, but she was still breathing. Statius took her pulse, examined her eyes, called for blankets and said he would remain at her bedside. I shall speak of her again presently.

At dawn we prepared for the last rites. Lucius had bequeathed me his pyramid ring, and I transferred it from his marble-cold hand to mine. We lifted his body onto a pyre of cypress branches and set it aflame. When the embers had cooled, we collected and placed in a brass urn three handfuls of grey-white ash: this was the moment when I could no longer hold back tears.

The arena has hardened us to dying but not to the fact of death. Of the person Lucius had been, that nothing should remain but a dole of grey-white ash, this I conceived as something so wasteful, so futile as not to be borne. More than that, to be resisted. It came to me then that all that was best in Lucius – his spirit if you like – resided now in me, his close companion since childhood, and that on me fell the full responsibility of taking up the pen Lucius had laid down in order to rescue that spirit from the ashes. Perhaps in bequeathing his ring to me, he had hoped I might do just that.

With this in mind, I accompanied Novatus, the brass urn in his hands, to the end of the garden where a gate gives on to the Appian Way. There on the roadside, for his journey into who knows where, we buried his ashes, marking the spot with a pegged wooden sign until a suitable headstone could be found and inscribed with the words: *Si terra levis* – May the earth lie lightly upon you. The air had been still all day but, as we completed our sad task, a gust of wind blew up, ballooning our gowns and bending a nearby cypress.

As the father and brother of condemned men, my life was also at risk and I had no option but to go to ground. So I am writing this epilogue in a remote valley of the Dolomites, its mood far different from that in which I began my Memoir.

Before leaving Rome, I visited Paula. For two months after her ordeal her cheeks were white as linen and she was pointed out in the streets as 'the pale widow'. Helped by John Mark, she turned her house into an orphanage for children whose parents had died in the Fire. Lucius's ring with the pyramid of constancy had come into my keeping and before saying goodbye, I gave it to Paula. It was she who most deserved to wear it.

Petronius Niger, condemned for his part in Piso's plot, had used his last hours for a deadly Parthian shot. He wrote a will imputing to the *princeps* his own excesses. Petronius's formal betrothal, in feminine dress, to a dashing young gladiator, followed by a torchlit procession to the bridal chamber, he ascribed to Nero. Nero, he asserted conceived the boat journey designed to dishonour senators' wives. Most damaging of all, he declared that Nero had raped Rubria, youngest of the inviolable Vestals.

Wills have to be published, even when composed of lies, and certain unscrupulous senators decided to play this up as the basis of a smear campaign. By osmosis, it spread to the provinces and there Nero began to be discredited as a libertine.

Lucius's funeral did not, as Nero hoped, take his friend and teacher out of his life. Just as he had brooded on his mother's death, believing it to have been necessary for Rome, so now with Lucius, who had been almost a father to him.

Lucius had chosen to protect a member of his family for having shared in a plot to murder Caesar. Unforgivable. Whereas, what he should have done was to have forewarned Caesar of the plot, whereupon five senators would have paid with their lives. For that the Senate would never have forgiven him.

Lucius had chosen to believe that lifelong friendship would have made Nero merciful. And he had misread Nero's mind when the plot was discovered to be a farce. The senators had to pay for their lives; how much more the one man who could have forewarned him.

'Perhaps I made the wrong choice,' Nero explained to his close friends, 'but at least I did the right thing by saving Lucius's wife from suicide. Perhaps that too was a mistake, since I cheated them both out of that rare agreement whereby a wife pledges fidelity to the last drop of her blood. I have to face up to the fact that I've done Lucius an unforgivable wrong. The blood I ordered him to shed is upon my head.'

A senior member of his staff spoke up. 'Since Caesar had good reason to do what he did, surely he will find one of the gods to forgive him.'

The suggestion was well meant but produced the opposite effect. Nero recalled his mother's death and how in vain Lucius had gone around the temples, offering the priests rich presents if only they would pray their gods to forgive, and the answer was invariably, 'Matricide is unpardonable.'

It would be the same or worse with patricide: Lucius had been in many ways a father to him and he must expect the Furies to return. Sleepless nights, hearing their shrill cries which no one else could hear. The precincts of madness.

Yet one man had offered to free him from guilt and its consequences. After granting his appeal, he had received Paul of Tarsus in his still uncompleted house and there described the horrors that followed from his misdeeds. Paul had shown sympathy and promised to help him receive forgiveness by following the teaching of Christus.

Days later came the shock... Lucius told him that Paul had decided to take ship to Spain in order to teach Spaniards the way to Christus.

Why? Lucius could only guess. Perhaps he had found Romans unwilling or hostile listeners, perhaps feared civil disturbances. And chose to forget that Nero had freed him from his chains.

Nowhere could Nero find help. So be it. He would fight the Furies by action.

He turned to face his advisers.

'I am still Caesar, by birth and the people's will. I have ruled Rome and its Empire for seven years and ended unnecessary wars. At twenty-nine I am still vigorous.'

He paused and lowered his voice. 'My first thought is for Corinth. Once Achaea's proudest city until a misguided proconsul sacked it, leaving its four miles of wall a tumble-down ruin. That wrong should be put right. I do not know how, but somehow I shall find a way.'

His team of advisers was by no means happy about his proposal. A journey to Corinth by sea would take weeks, leaving Rome without a ruler. And Caesar could not travel alone. He must protect himself with a contingent of his own praetorian soldiers. Loyal friends must accompany him and, once they had judged the mood in Corinth, advise him on how to proceed. But if all this proved complicated and risky, it was better than seeing so gifted a Caesar lapse into melancholia.

During the voyage, Nero as always set himself to learn the various skills new to him. First from the long experienced captain, then from the steersman and finally from the crew, who taught him how to hoist sails and lower them fast at the first sign of storm. On the fifth day out in rough sea, the captain allowed him to handle the ship for a full hour. In the first day of calm weather, he assembled the crew and treated them to some of the popular songs he had made famous. Then he called for their sea shanties, listened appreciatively and applauded.

In the autumn after Lucius's suicide, Nero and his suite landed at Corinth's harbour in the Gulf of Corinth, which faces Asia. The western part of the city lies on the isthmus, that narrow band of high ground which separates the city from the Mediterranean.

Its favourable position as a seaport early raised Corinth to commercial prosperity as an emporium of trade between Europe and

Asia. At Corinth the first triremes were built. It colonized in several directions and later Rome made it the capital of her province of Achaea. This gave the Corinthians ideas above their station; they sought independence, whereupon a proconsul, Mummius, taught them a lesson in a barbarous manner. He levelled every yard of their miles-long wall and most of their public buildings. Later it was partially rebuilt by Julius Caesar, who peopled it with a colony of veterans. But Corinth had no statues or other treasures to fund Nero for the rebuilding of Rome.

In choosing to honour this neglected city by a visit from Caesar, Nero showed an acute sense of history, of Rome's obligations towards her Empire as well as his famous Graecophilia. He planned to join Corinth to two seas, the Mediterranean and Asiatic. This would be achieved by demolishing the isthmus, five Roman miles long. Julius Caesar had dreamed of this shortly before Brutus struck him down. If and when the work was achieved, Corinth would rise again as a great city, with a commanding position on all shipping, both commercial and naval. This was now Nero's serious intention.

Nero planned to spend a year in Corinth, intending to take part in Greece's many Games and musical contests. He would conduct the affairs of Rome and its provinces from his headquarters and travel to the Games and contests according to their dates. He would personally study and decide the engineering work required for demolishing and removing the isthmus. This plan he put into effect immediately and it soon proved satisfactory. He felt fulfilled by helping the Corinthians while competing on equal terms in sporting and musical events. A weekly report from Rome informed him that the city was calm and his popularity as great as ever.

Exactly a year to the day after his arrival, Corinth held a special celebration of the Isthmian Games in which he took part. After the last race, before a massive crowd, Corinthians and their guests, Nero stood up on a rostrum, called for silence and made an extraordinary announcement: 'From this day forth, Corinth and the whole of Greece will be liberated from Roman administration and taxation.'

As he had foreseen, the crowd could not believe him and he had to repeat in a booming voice the priceless gift he was bestowing on his beloved Greece. Slowly applause grew from a ripple into a series of waves.

Nero then drove by chariot, with a crowd following, to the isthmus, where he had assembled his strong praetorian soldiers. He addressed them, describing the beneficial long-term project they were undertaking and encouraged them to begin their Herculean task.

At a signal from his trumpeter, he walked down to near the water's edge, struck the ground with his mattock several times and carried off a heavy basketful of earth on his shoulders. No speech was needed. The crowd knew that he had drawn up plans for a canal. As well as freeing them from taxation, he intended to return Corinth to wealth.

Mindful that Corinthians have an ear for music, that evening Nero invited their elite to his headquarters where, helped by his suite, he entertained them. Italian wine was served and local delicacies, after which he sang two contrasting arias to the lyre. First as Hercules grown old, then as a Roman playboy singing Rome's latest hit, for which he wore his fair hair trailing to his shoulders. Both arias received compliments and a plea for encores.

At midnight, guests left and Nero went to bed glowing with pleasure at a satisfactory day.

Waking early next morning, he recalled his evening performance but the praise it had won from musical connoisseurs was badly marred. His senior military adviser, Vespasian, seated on one of the couches, had closed his eyes and gone to sleep. Clearly an affront to Caesar's majesty – and in public.

Still undressed, he summoned the offender to his bedroom. Vespasian, strongly built and looking younger than his fifty-nine years, came of modest birth, had fought bravely in Britain and reduced the Isle of Wight. It was Nero who appointed him to the important post of proconsul in Africa. Married with two sons, he led a simple frugal life and was loved by his soldiers.

Asked to explain why he had gone to sleep while listening to a brilliant musical performance, he answered that he had not gone to sleep. He knew nothing about music and could not tell one tune from another. He had indeed shut his eyes because he could not bear the sight of Caesar sporting curly blond hair down to his shoulders, such as youthful libertines do. 'I closed my eyes because I considered you were demeaning your majesty and that your audience would see it like that. Surely not an offence.'

'On the contrary. Because you're tone-deaf, you missed the point of my song, intended for youthful plebeians. It was a mistake to include you on my staff. You will therefore leave Corinth within twenty-four hours and retire to a small town.'

That same afternoon a messenger from Jerusalem raced in with news of the first importance. The Greek-speaking population of Palestine, which Romans call Judaea, had risen against the Jews, who share Palestine with them.

Ever since coming to power, Nero had worked to prevent his procurator and garrison commander from desecrating the Jewish Temple with statues of Roman gods and heroes. Furthermore, he had given them orders to act as a peacekeeping force between Greeks and Jews. And now the fighting in Jerusalem presented him with an agonizing dilemma.

At once he summoned his friend and adviser on Palestine. Flavius Josephus, the same age as himself and highly intelligent, was a moderate Jewish priest of aristocratic descent and a political leader who had visited Rome five years earlier and converted Poppaea to the Jewish religion. He was the author of a long *History of the Jews* and was now writing a history of current events, for which he kept a diary. His theology as a priest centred on the idea that in Palestine, God was currently on the Roman side.

Josephus lived much of the year in Jerusalem and was conversant with the hatred that had erupted in fighting, in effect rebellion against Roman occupation and Nero's peacekeeping orders. He was also conversant with the Senate's hostile attitude to Nero's policy of peace, not war. The most influential senators – retired generals – considered it unworthy of Rome's victorious past. With Nero's gift to Greece, that attitude would have hardened.

Aware that Nero wanted a solution to his dilemma, not a summary of pros and cons, Josephus proferred the following advice, afterwards entering it in his diary. 'You have three legions idle not far from here. Send them at once to Jerusalem with orders to end fighting and remain there until the rebellion ceases. The general in command must have specific orders to protect the Jews' Temple and Holy of Holies, a white stone building with a covering of gold; it cannot be missed.'

Though Josephus did not know it, this was already Nero's preferred solution and he nodded acceptance of it. Josephus had not expected this, knowing that the Senate would blame Nero for taking the army into Palestine, and he felt drawn to express his profound gratitude.

'Since coming to power, you have treated the Jews with respect. First because their religion antedates Rome's by a thousand years and secondly because of their long struggle to find a homeland. Thirdly because of their poetic literature. You have shown that respect by protecting their Temple from sacrilege and now from possible destruction. For all this the Jewish people are grateful. The moderate Jews of Palestine consider you their protector and I happen to know that they would welcome you as their King.'

Nero looked surprised, then pleased. 'Why not? I'm already virtually King of Armenia... Except that I'm *Pontifex Maximus*.'

'A mere advisory post or ritual. That would prove no bar.'

'So be it!... But what of the present? Who is to command in Palestine? Three legions and an exceedingly tricky operation. He must be a proven leader. Otho loves his men and they reciprocate. But he's in Lusitania, and I need someone here and now.'

Josephus offered a suggestion. 'From several intimate talks, Vespasian has impressed me. He's done an excellent job in Africa and can be trusted to carry out your orders to the letter.'

'Can he be trusted? Is he loyal? He scoffs at my acting behind my back. That does not suggest loyalty.'

'I think it's because he's not cultivated. No aristocratic background. Can you blame him for that?'

Nero scowled, then pondered in silence.

'Find the messenger from Jerusalem. Order him to hurry after Vespasian and bring him back to me.'

Nero then began a busy morning. Packing all his personal files and various gifts from prominent Corinthians, sending members of his suite to convey thanks for their hospitality and for holding the Games. Just before midday Vespasian arrived back with not even a hint of pique, and Nero primed him for his role in Jerusalem, emphasizing the importance of protecting the Temple from harm. That afternoon, Nero sailed on the first leg of his return voyage home.

Landing at Ostia earlier than planned, rather than await an official welcome from the people, he drove himself by chariot to the Golden House, decorated inside and now his official residence, and got down to business with his deputies. The mood in the city, they agreed, was excellent; corn from Egypt had been arriving on time and the dole administered. Senators were quiet, still reeling from their infamous plot to kill Nero and from the punishments that followed. In Europe's provinces, a majority appreciated Nero's peacemaking and paid their taxes on time. But there remained a natural urge to be independent which would have to be watched by political governors.

At the end of a month, Nero had time to resume his favourite activities – chariot racing, sports, singing to the lyre, thereby adding to his popularity. Invited as far as Naples, he sang several recitals of classical and popular songs. In the spring of 68, while in Naples, Nero learned of trouble in south-western Gaul. The governor, Caius Julius Vindex, of aristocratic Gallic descent and the son of a senator, was heading a nationalist rising for independence and at the same time hoped to become Caesar.

While the excitable Neapolitans panicked, Nero took the news calmly. Experience had taught him that attempts at nationalist secession soon petered out, while he knew that Vindex had no Roman troops under his command. He showed his calm by going at once to the gymnasium where he watched athletes in competition.

For the next eight days he passed over the affair in silence. Finally, disturbed by abusive pronouncements by Vindex, who called him Ahenobarbus, he sent a letter in his own hand to the Senate, urging them to take vengeance for himself and the State. The Senate, not Caesar, had authority to quell incipient secession.

But now a new rebel had arisen. Servius Galba came of one of the most distinguished and oldest families and observed traditional customs which had fallen into disuse. While still a youth, his freedmen and slaves had to attend him in a group twice a day to offer their greetings in the morning and to bid him goodnight in the evening. Applying himself to the law, he secured magistracies before the official age and, when praetor, arranged power for the goddess Flora with elephants walking on tightropes. After governing the province of Aquitania, he took over the consulship from Lucius Domitius, the father of Nero.

Appointed governor in Upper Gaul, when Caligula was visiting, Galba and his army received greater recognition and rewards than any other province. Galba himself stood out: while deploying his troops in the field, shield in hand, he ran alongside Caligula's chariot for twenty miles.

When his wife Lepida and their two children died, Galba remained single. Nero's mother, Agrippina, left a widow by the death of Domitius, sought with all her powers to attract Galba – even while he was still married to Lepida – with the result that at an assembly of ladies, Lepida's mother rebuked her sharply and even slapped her.

When Caligula was murdered, Galba took no action to fill his place, thus endearing himself to Claudius and was made a member of his circle of friends.

He was specially chosen to be proconsular governor of Africa for two years in order to bring peace to a province troubled by internal dissension and by barbarian revolt. He succeeded by imposing strict discipline and fair justice on the guilty.

Because of his achievements in Africa and earlier, Galba was awarded triumphal ornaments and because he observed religious rites, he was co-opted to be a member of three exclusive priesthoods. Later he was made governor of Nearer Spain, again using severe discipline to punish offenders. But he was now in his seventies and soon went into retirement for fear of giving Nero any grounds for concern, saying 'No one is ever obliged to give an account of his indolence.'

What exactly Galba found unbearable in Nero's years as Caesar, he never revealed. It may have been his extravagance, his pacifism, his boundless admiration of Greece, his cavalier attitude to the State religion, or a mixture of them all. But the moment came early in the year 68 when he decided he had had enough.

He took his judgment-seat in the court as though to conduct a habitual manumission of slaves. But instead of slaves he had placed in front of him portraits of senators who had taken part in the plot to kill Nero and been put to death. The moral was plain: he would free the Romans from slavery. Galba voiced his deep concern at the current state of affairs and declared himself the legate, not of Caesar, but of the Senate and people of Rome.

His next stop was to conscript legions and auxiliary forces to his own small army and he set up a Senate of older men known for their wisdom, which he would consult whenever necessary. He also issued edicts throughout all the provinces, exhorting everyone to join in the common cause. In short, he could not achieve his ambition without help from one or more other governors.

The governor who chose to help him was Julius Vindex, descended from the Kings of Aquitania and son of a Roman senator. As governor of Transalpine Gaul – far from Spain – he had no Roman troops but he received support from many Gauls and the native noblemen in his province. His appeal to other governors for help was ignored; but Galba believed in him and agreed to support him with a mixture of fear and hope.

Nero decided that, for several reasons, Vindex was the more dangerous of the two. He was younger, of higher birth, received support from native noblemen and his rebellion was happening in the Alps, close to Rome. So he immediately wrote a letter in his own hand to the Senate. There it would be read aloud and debated by senators. He called on the Senate to take action at once against Vindex. It was the Senate's job to deal with rebellion, and it would not be difficult since Vindex had no Roman troops.

The Senate did not answer his letter – in itself a disturbing sign. As though they no longer respected the authority granted him by the people of Rome. Or possibly they were paying him back for having cracked down after Piso's attempt to murder him.

The Senate's silence was all the more disturbing since rebellion was spreading to other provinces: Lusitania, Northern Germany and Lower

Germany, where Tiberius's former bum-boy was governor. Nationalist revolt was becoming an epidemic, and with it came calls for the Senate to have more power than Caesar.

Nero had no army at his disposal, whereas Vindex had no Roman troops. So it would be sufficient if he enrolled a non-professional army and marched at its head to Transalpine Gaul.

Nero's first step was to dismiss the consuls before the end of their term and in their place entered upon a sole consulship, explaining that Gaul could be defeated only by consuls. He confided in close friends that when he reached Gaul he would appear to the rebels without weapons, believing that next day they would be brought to recant and he would sing them a victory ode.

As consul, he began by urging the city-voting tribes to join up and obliged masters to provide a certain number of slaves, demanding the very best from each household. He gave orders that men of every census rating were to hand over a proportion of their wealth. He insisted on newly minted coins, refined silver and pure gold, so that many openly refused the entire levy.

As soldiers were enrolled, two of Nero's plans for his amateur army were unique. He had vehicles constructed to transport a water organ of his own invention and making in order to provide music for his soldiers instead of drums and trumpets. He also recruited women as soldiers, just as he allowed women to compete in the Games. Their hair would be shorn and they would carry axes and shields like Amazons. The gutter press ridiculed the water organ and said the women were prostitutes for the soldiers.

A much more serious charge was unfairly levelled against Nero. A ship from Alexandria docked at Ostia carrying, not the expected Egyptian corn, but sand for Nero's wrestlers. As there happened to be fears of a possible food shortage, resentment increased and became public. For instance, a sack was tied to the neck of one of Nero's statues with the tag: 'I did what I could but you deserve the sack' – part of the required punishment for poisoning his stepfather Claudius – a favourite lie of the gutter press.

Resentment too had hardened in the Senate. When Nero attacked

Vindex in a speech, asserting that he would pay the penalty he deserved, this was read out in the House, at which there were shouts: 'It will be you, Emperor, who will pay'. Then, unexpectedly, came good news. Verginius Rufus, governor of Upper Germany and loyal to Nero, defeated Vindex's army to the High Alps, at which Galba abandoned hope for his ambitions and no more was to be heard of Vindex. Nero breathed a sigh of relief. After all he would not have to lead his army into Gaul. Yet the epidemic of revolt plus nationalism was spreading still further.

Otho, to whom Nero had given Lusitania in exchange for Poppaea, announced that he was the obvious choice to replace his youthful friend, the Emperor. In Germany the governor, Fonteius Capito, revolted; in Africa Clodius Macer cut off the corn supply to Rome. Was it his pacifism that made the legions hungry for the loot which would follow a victory? Or was it greed for power by a medley of governors whose authority was strictly limited by Emperor and Senate?

Meanwhile Vespasian's dispatches from Jerusalem showed that revolt in Judaea at least was being kept in check. The three legions were doing their job and Vespasian had saved the Temple but, when Nero urged him to return, he replied that he would need another six months to ensure a lasting peace.

So far, danger had been in the provinces. The people of Rome and Nero's personal bodyguard, the praetorians, had remained loyal. But now a tribune in his bodyguard, Nymphidius Sabinus, the son of a freed slave, to whom Nero had given triumphal awards for his part in suppressing the senators' conspiracy and promoted to joint commander of the praetorians, came forward.

Nymphidius gradually induced the praetorians to desert Nero for Galba by promising them an enormous sum of money which he did not have. But he harboured designs upon the Principate himself, and these were to cause his downfall.

Nero now found himself with no army and no bodyguard. But he knew that the people of Rome would not desert him and he remained calm, continuing the rebuilding of Rome and decoration of his house, which he intended the Romans to inherit.

In the Senate, however, there was little sign of loyalty. The praetorians' desertion allowed members to launch personal attacks on Nero and his style of government, some justified, others illusory. In particular, they targeted his extravagant spending, when he should have been investing his fortune in the Empire's mines – copper in Spain, silver in Britain, gold in Greece and Asia. His heavy spending on shows and Games was already beginning to reduce the value of Rome's coinage. But fully aware of Nero's continuing popularity, the senators dispersed without taking a vote.

Nero meanwhile was facing up to the fact that he no longer had 10,000 praetorians to defend him from revolting armies. Against one, he could have stood his ground, but not against three or four. Unless their leaders fought one another to the death – but that would likely happen only later, as they approached Rome.

For now, he placed his hopes in the people. Their status and power were visible everywhere, embossed in iron or carved in stone throughout the city: SPQR *Senatus Populusque Romanus*. The Senate could do nothing without the people's consent.

By temperament Nero had to keep busy and he gave much of his time to continuing the rebuilding of Rome: street fronts of regular alignment, streets to be broad and houses built around courtyards. Their height to be restricted and their frontages protected by expensive colonnades for which he paid.

He also gave time to enlarging, improving and decorating his already large house. A new façade took the form of a very long portico on two levels, with symmetrical five-sided courts either side of a domed octagonal hall. All this with vaulted concrete construction in an original style.

In the vestibule area, matching the façade's great length, stood a colossal statue of Nero, one hundred and twenty feet tall, a recent gift from the Roman people and paid for by them.

As each wing of Nero's house grew and each of the banqueting halls had more surprising decoration than the last, so the people of Rome gossiped about Nero's purpose in building so extravagant a home. He had no children to share it or inherit it. He had fewer friends to invite now than before the Empire revolted against him. Perhaps he was telling the truth when he said he was building it for the people of Rome, since the house looked on to a park; acres of fields and vineyards, pasture and woodland, filled with domestic and wild animals, as well as a large lake shaped like the Mediterranean – unspoiled countryside within the city walls, where city dwellers could breathe clean air, get exercise and generally keep fit.

As for the interior, like a museum, it was open to all. Visitors could feast their eyes on gold and jewel incrustations, on a dome which revolved continuously day and night, on a coppered ceiling fitted with panels of ivory which scattered flowers and sprayed perfume on a dining table.

Others maintained that Nero had built a house for the gods to feast in. The scale everywhere was superhuman. True, he said he had now begun to live like a human being, but that was only one of his jokes. His real purpose was to seek protection from the gods.

In the Senate, Nero's house caused more serious and worried discussion against the backdrop of five rebellious provinces, with at least one governor approaching Rome. What would Galba or Otho make of this colossal building with its huge statue of Nero inscribed as a gift from the Roman people? They were merely provincial governors, with no following in the capital. Surely they would be tempted to take the safe course: accept Nero as Emperor and be rewarded with consulships?

At an emergency session senators discussed what to do on the assumption that one or more rebel governors would accept Nero. Nero again in power would certainly turn on the Senate for having refused to fight Vindex. They knew from Piso's conspiracy that Nero the pacifist could sometimes be cruel. What action to take? They must order Nero to leave Rome immediately – for his own safety and the good of the Roman people. A vote was taken and the order, signed by a majority of senators, transmitted to Nero's house.

On receiving the Senate's order, Nero went on foot to the Servilian Gardens, headquarters of certain officers and centurions of his treacherous bodyguard who remained loyal to their Emperor. He tried to persuade them to accompany him to the port of Ostia, where he had high-ranking friends in the navy willing to take him to safety. Their reaction was heartless. Some were evasive, others openly refused, one even shouting out: 'Is it really so hard to die?'

He next considered appearing in public on the rostra dressed in black to beseech forgiveness for his past offences, appealing as much as he could to their pity, or, if he could not win them over, to beg them at least to give him the prefecture of Egypt. But that the Senate would never endorse.

Days and nights of inner debate followed and still he had not obeyed the Senate's order to leave Rome. He had no money and wherever he went he would have to make his own way. At last he came not to a decision but to two alternatives and he confided them to a handful of friends, former slaves who owed their freedom to him. 'I shall go to a country where I can earn my living by singing to the lyre or I shall go to Jerusalem where the Jews will hail me as their King.' To which he added Josephus's assurance that the Jews wanted him as King because he had saved their Temple from destruction.

Having put off his departure till the following day, he woke up in the middle of the night and, finding that his guard of soldiers had deserted, he leapt out of bed and sent for his friends. When he heard nothing back from any of these he himself with a handful of attendants went to their bedrooms. The doors were all closed and no one answered. Returning to his own bedroom he found that the domestics too had run away, having even dragged off the bedclothes.

All this could be explained only in one way. The Senate's patience exhausted, they had formally pronounced him an enemy of the State, as such to be hounded to death by any and every Roman, soldier or civilian.

At once he called for Spiculus the gladiator or some other executioner, at whose hands he might obtain death, but could find no one. 'Am I a man without friends or enemies?' he cried, and rushed out as if to throw himself in the Tiber. When he had checked this impulse, he decided to look for some hiding place where he could regain his courage. His freedman Phaon suggested his own villa, about four miles outside the city.

Nero, still without shoes and wearing just a tunic, wrapped himself in a dark coloured cloak, covered his head and held a handkerchief to his face, then mounted his horse with only four attendants. All at once an earth tremor and a flash of lightning filled him with terror and he heard shouts of soldiers from a nearby camp prophesying doom for himself and success for Galba. One of those they met on the road said, 'These men are hunting Nero'. But another who had served in the praetorians recognized him and saluted him.

They turned off the road for a byway leading to Phaon's villa. Leaving their horses, they picked their way through thickets and brambles, eventually reaching the back wall of the villa, where Phaon urged him to hide in a hole where sand had been dug out. But he refused to descend into the earth while still alive. Instead he crawled on all fours through a passage until he was inside the villa.

Emerging into a small room, he lay down on a couch. Despite pangs of hunger and thirst he refused the bread offered to him but sipped some tepid water.

All his attendants urged him to take his own life, whereupon he ordered a trench to be dug, and water and firewood to be brought for the disposal of his corpse-to-be, weeping and repeating, 'What an artist dies with me!'

Meanwhile a runner brought a message to Phaon, saying that Nero had indeed been judged a public enemy and was being hunted down. Nero asked what the punishment would be. Told that his neck would be placed in a fork and his body beaten until he died, Nero was overcome with terror. Snatching up two daggers from his belt, he tried the blade of each, then put them away again, saying that the fatal hour had not yet arrived.

He then berated his procrastination with these words: 'My life is shameful, unbecoming to Nero, unbecoming – in such circumstances one must be decisive, come, rouse yourself!'

At that moment horsemen arrived with orders to bring him back alive, at which he quoted from Homer's *Iliad*: 'The thunder of swift-footed horses echoes around my ears,' then drove a dagger into his throat with the help of one of his attendants.

Half-conscious, when a centurion burst in and, holding a cloak to his wound, pretended he had come to lend assistance, Nero said only, 'Too late,' and, 'This is loyalty.' With these words he died, eyes wide open.

At his request his body was consumed by fire in a simple ceremony. The two nurses who had cared for him as a child had his remains carried to the ancient monument of the Domitii and Ahenobarbi on the Hill of Gardens, where he was placed in a sarcophagus of porphyry beneath an altar of marble, to lie beside the father he had never known.

Nero's death sent shock waves through the provinces. Not one, not two, not three but four different generals claimed the succession. An army from Lusitania – led by Otho – another from Germany, a third from the Tarragon region of Spain and a fourth from Judaea converged on the capital, and the dissension Lucius had spent his life trying to prevent was multiplied many times over in a full-scale civil war of unprecedented savagery. As the legions took charge, senators found themselves marginalized. The situation was made worse because many in Rome believed Nero was not dead but had gone into hiding and would soon return in triumph.

For eleven months Rome has been given over to butchery. Drains are clogged with caked blood and so many have fled that the population has fallen below the million mark of which we were once so proud.

Having largely subdued Judaea by the time of Nero's death, Vespasian decided to return home for his triumph. Days later, however, the prefect of Egypt made his legions commit themselves to Vespasian as emperor, while the army in Judaea swore allegiance to him in person. Vespasian had expected neither honour but he decided to send a detachment of troops to Italy, while he crossed over to Alexandria to take possession of Egypt's gateway and to await events in Rome.

Religious by nature, Vespasian rarely took an important decision without consulting the auspices. Unaccompanied, he entered Alexandria's famous temple dedicated to Serapis, the Greek form of Egypt. He made offerings to the god and when he turned round he saw his freedman Basilides bringing him sacred branches, garlands and cakes. But no one could have let this man in because he was scarcely able to walk, because of a nervous disorder. And on that very day letters arrived that Vitellius had been killed.

In Rome meanwhile, immediately after Vitellius's death, public opinion demanded punishment for those who had caused the bloodiest civil war in history. A majority attributed it to the Senate's hatred of Nero and the excessive power of provincial governors – senators too, though rarely in Rome. Laws were therefore drafted and made, conferring unprecedented powers to the new *Princeps*, whoever he might be, Vespasian still waiting in Egypt for money and ships for his supporters.

The new laws, amounting almost to a new constitution, were draconian. The Senate was declared redundant. It would no longer propose laws or pass them; Caesar alone would do both. Furthermore, Caesar would have authority to act in whatever way he deemed advantageous to the Roman people. His word there would be law. This marked the end of the Republic of Rome, which had got itself into such a mess. Henceforth there would be a new form of government – by one man – to be called the Roman Empire.

A year later, Vespasian arrived in Rome, to be acclaimed as Caesar. After celebrating his success in Judaea, he legalized his unprecedented authority by adding eight consulships to his earlier one. He then convened the Senate and announced that he would continue Nero's rebuilding of Rome. He would also continue Nero's policy of peacemaking and make Pax a principal motif of his coinage. He would double taxation of the provinces in order to meet the nation's debt of forty thousand million sesterces. No vote was taken; Vespasian's word was law.

These were only a few of his constructive plans. Why were all of them to be realized quickly? The answer lies in his character. Vespasian was a good family man and a firm believer in the gods. He was straightforward, honest, loyal: loyal to Nero in his tomb for he saved his colossal statue from the Senate's determination to destroy it. Deference to Vespasian and the wish to imitate him, were more effective than legal penalties, thus making his ten years as Emperor a model for future generations.

When new men fight for power by wading through blood, they seek legitimacy by vilifying their predecessors. Copies of this Memoir, in which I portray Nero, Agrippina and Poppaea fairly, as I knew them, will undoubtedly be seized and burned if published in Rome. For that reason I have decided to entrust the manuscript to my secretary, who will take it to Gades and hand it to Valerius. Valerius has promised to have copies made and circularized, initially in Spain, which has been spared the worst excesses, so that in this age of corruption, conspiracy, plotting, uprising and murder, what Lucius was and what he did may be remembered at least by a few.